KELLY'S PEOPLE

KELLY'S PEOPLE

WALTER WAGER

A Tom Doherty Associates Book

NEW YORK

KELLY'S PEOPLE

Copyright © 2002 by Walter Wager

This book is printed on acid-free paper.

A Forge Book
Published by Tom Doherty Associates, LLC
175 Fifth Avenue
New York, NY 10010

www.tor.com

Forge® is a registered trademark of Tom Doherty Associates, LLC.

Library of Congress Cataloging-in-Publication Data

Wager, Walter H.
    Kelly's people / Walter Wager.—1st ed.
      p. cm.
    "A Forge book"—T.p. verso
    ISBN 0-765-30131-8
    1. Intelligence officers—Fiction. 2. Transplantation of organs, tissues, etc.—Fiction. 3. Terrorism—Prevention—Fiction. 4. Nuclear weapons—Fiction. I. Title.

PS3573.A35 K45 2002
813'.54—dc21

                                   2001054788

First Edition: April 2002

Printed in the United States of America

0 9 8 7 6 5 4 3 2 1

This book is very happily and gratefully dedicated to my splendid cousin, Bruce Herman—
gentleman, mensch, and friend.

w.w.

Author's Note

This entire book is a work of fiction, and that includes characters, names, places, incidents, organizations, bad language, and impure thoughts.

However, if the U.S. government is at this very second actively and extremely secretly exploring military applications of telepathy and other forms of mind warfare, I wouldn't be the least bit surprised. That also applies to the other extraordinary medical program in the pages that follow.

KELLY'S PEOPLE

1

DARK.

Dark and stormy.

It was a dark and stormy night, to quote the first line of a mystery novel written long ago by Edward George Earle Bulwer-Lytton. He subsequently became a baron, and that grabber of a sentence a target for sophisticates who still deride it as a literary cliché.

Different time. Different place.

Now—over a hundred seventy years later—the start of a new millennium.

Across a churning ocean, more than three thousand miles from Lord Lytton's native England.

And hundreds of miles west of the District of Columbia and adjacent headquarters of the main defense and security arms of the federal government of the United States. That distance was important to the rather clever, somewhat paranoid, and anonymously powerful people who'd bought this wooded forty-two-acre estate.

They had their reasons.

What they didn't have was any discernible connection to The St. John Institute, which had been on this property for a quarter of a century. Their names didn't appear in any documents . . . not on the charter of the Institute . . . the deed to the land . . . the plans for the thirty-nine-room stone building filed with the state . . . or the annual application for tax exemption as a non-profit organization.

There was no paper trail.

No faces anyone in the nearby town of Thornton might recognize.

None of them had ever been to The St. John Institute, and none had any interest in Bulwer-Lytton or his 1830 novel. It wasn't that they had forgotten the author or his books. They'd never heard of either. Their education and expertise lay in other areas.

They were far away from The St. John Institute this black and blustery evening as the wind hurled sheets of rain through the trees . . . pounded the building's roof with a mounting drumbeat of water. In a large and soundproof office on the third floor, an attractive woman in her early forties sat behind an executive-sized desk that was quite different from what it seemed to be.

So was she.

Like the desk, she was hiding things. Her simple dress and knee-length white laboratory coat were largely but not totally successful in concealing an arresting female figure, and her proper haircut and gold wire-rimmed glasses suggested that she might be a very prim and correct teacher or an engineer.

She wasn't either.

There was a discreet wooden sign on her door that identified her as Charlotte Willson. That wasn't her real name. None of the dozens of staff here whom she supervised had any idea of what her real name was. They weren't supposed to, and they understood that.

She looked out at the storm through the expensive window with the special glass that blocked all known electronic eaves-dropping gear. After a moment, she glanced at her wristwatch. She saw that the time was six minutes after eight, and nodded.

It was all right.

The package wasn't due for another three or four minutes. She'd allowed for the weather and driving conditions when she calculated the timetable this morning. Calculating and planning were two of the things she did best.

She was always orderly . . . never wasteful. She had a few minutes to recheck—for the tenth time since noon—the security system that embraced this estate. She pressed a button to slide up a very skillfully made panel in the top of her desk. It was a nearly seamless fit, with the wood striations a perfect match—just what a secret panel needed.

Now she eyed one of the things this desk concealed. It was a ten-by-fourteen-inch glass screen framed by a dozen buttons, dials, and switches. None of these was identified by any adjacent nameplate, but she knew what each did. So did the man on duty monitoring the twin brother of this system in the security headquarters on the floor below.

She began her test, working the controls in the checklist sequence.

Exterior infrared television cameras on rotating sweep.

All clear on the screen.

Ground radar readings feeding search data on estate. Outer perimeter—all clear.

Motion and sound detectors closer to the main building—ambiguous in this gusty, blustery storm.

She shook her head. The woman who wasn't Charlotte Willson didn't like ambiguous. She decided it would be prudent to repeat the scans of the grounds with the exterior infrared cameras. She was reaching for that control dial when the telephone on her desk rang.

She didn't hesitate.

She knew exactly what to do, for she had a checklist to cover this, too. First, she turned off the security display system . . . then carefully closed the very fine secret panel that concealed it. Next, she picked up the phone and spoke in a pleasant, cool tone.

"Charlotte Willson," she said.

"I.F.F. report," the security duty officer announced. "We've picked up one of our vans turning off the highway. Reception team ready at the loading dock."

She nodded. Each of the Institute's vans carried a concealed and miniature and up-to-date version of the "Identification: Friend or Foe" transmitter that military aircraft had flown with for many years. With the technology to read such signals, The St. John Institute could know in advance who was coming.

No surprise.

The woman behind the desk with the secret panel hated the very idea of surprises. They could be much worse than ambiguities. They might be fatal.

All this flashed through her highly trained and complex mind in three seconds. Her ability to think fast and make tough, smart decisions was a key reason she was in charge here.

"Thank you," she answered the security controller.

She was breathing just a bit harder than usual when she hung up the telephone. It was happening. After tens of thousands of hours of labor—many millions of dollars—and considerable skepticism from older and narrow-minded men, it was coming to pass. She knew they expected her imaginative plan to fail, but she didn't care.

Thunder boomed overhead.

Jagged bolts of lightning stabbed the black night again and again.

She didn't care about any of that either.

The first "package" would arrive within fifteen minutes.

The others would come tomorrow.

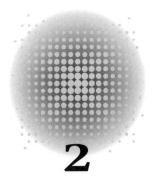

2

WHEN SHE AWOKE AT 7:00 A.M., AS SHE ALWAYS DID, THE DI-rector of The St. John Institute immediately addressed her morning checklist. She didn't hesitate or linger in bed for a second. She rose, put on her eyeglasses, and briefly stared out the window.

Very briefly. About four seconds.

She had (a) no time to waste, (b) to get to her exercise at once. These were nothing casual or ego-driven. These were survival exercises that she'd been doing twice a day ... for six minutes at a time ... for ten months. She'd be delighted if she needed them, but if they were necessary and she wasn't ready, disaster might follow.

A lot of people might end up in unmarked graves.

There was some possibility that she'd be one of them.

So she closed her wide blue eyes, stood absolutely motionless, and did her exercises. Someone looking at her wouldn't have realized how hard the woman who wasn't Charlotte Willson was working. The whole thing was really a no-brainer, of course. She had to protect herself from something she couldn't see or hear or touch ... something that wouldn't draw blood or even bruise ... but could wreak havoc.

She finished the exercise, glanced out the window at the clear morning, and computed. The day was bright and clear, so the sound and motion detectors outside would work as well as the concealed television cameras. With the wind and rain gone and the roads just about dry, her timetable for delivery of the other packages should be met.

Each would come in a separate vehicle.

Each of those bore the name or logo of some fictitious organization, not The St. John Institute. When the packages were delivered—at ninety-minute intervals—those false identifications would disappear when the vehicles were repainted and other license plates installed.

It wasn't just a paper trail she wanted to avoid.

Meticulous and complete deception was basic to this entire enterprise. Her mother might have considered this odd, for the woman who wasn't Charlotte Willson had been an award-winning student and choir leader at a first-class Sunday school. That was history, of course. Her mother was dead, and . . . for practical purposes . . . so was the daughter she'd raised.

The director did her shower and all the other morning things, dressed in attire very much like what she'd worn the night before, and reached her office at a quarter to eight. The St. John Institute day began at eight, but this was her usual time to start. That was why her administrative assistant, a lean, intelligent man with excellent reflexes and the Social Security card and driver's license of somebody who'd never existed, was waiting at his desk.

He was very devoted to her, and could break bricks with his hands. It was an acquired skill, like his ability to speak Russian and Chinese. They exchanged nods of greeting before she entered her office. She had nearly finished checking for e-mail messages and fax communications when her assistant's voice came from the intercom.

Her breakfast tray was here. Eating at her desk was another of her standard operating procedures. It saved time and eliminated potential awkwardnesses that might arise if she dined in the cafeteria. Getting close to staff could lead to misunderstandings that she didn't need, the director thought as she released the electric door lock.

The cafeteria worker with the food wasn't allowed in here. There was no reason for him to know the physical layout of her office, so it was her assistant who brought in the tray—and left at once. As she addressed the orange juice and contemplated the hard-boiled egg, she found herself smiling in anticipation.

The second package would be delivered in less than half an hour. Buoyed by this thought, she picked up the telephone to make certain there was no problem with the first package and that every detail of the preparations for receiving the second had been checked and rechecked.

When she finished breakfast and sipped the last drop of her decaffeinated coffee, she opened the desk panel and went through the whole security routine again . . . slowly . . . carefully. She looked at her watch, and saw that the vehicle with the second package wouldn't arrive for nine minutes. That gave her time to review the first dozen pages in the manual of package procedures.

The phone rang—a minute before she'd planned.

I.F.F. signal.

The truck was less than a mile away. The second package would be in place . . . in good condition . . . in less than a quarter of an hour. All security arrangements and the team were "go."

It went . . . as she'd planned.

So did the delivery of the third package at 10:50 A.M., and there was no problem with the fourth an hour and a half after that. As she'd instructed several times, the packages were taken to different rooms—carefully selected so none were near each other. Each package was accompanied by a security specialist wearing civilian clothes that concealed an automatic pistol.

Now the clouds were gathering again, and the day wasn't bright and clear anymore. She didn't care *much*. Unless there would be another storm that might delay the fifth package, the weather was of no consequence. The fifth package . . . the last one . . . was due at 1:55 P.M.

Twenty minutes before that, she learned that it would be late.

Her strong and dangerous assistant reported that there'd been a message from the city six hundred miles away where the package was to be put on the special plane.

Engine trouble. One jet unit wasn't functioning.

There was no time to provide another special plane suitable for moving the fifth package. Mechanics who'd never heard of The St. John Institute were working conscientiously to fix what was wrong. They were reasonably confident that the aircraft would be ready to fly before six o'clock.

"They mustn't take any chances. They've got to be absolutely sure it's safe," she ordered.

Our own plane.

A crew of our own people. They never risked anything.

Her assistant—a practical professional who carried perfectly forged I.D. that said he was a thirty-four-year-old Caucasian male named Joel LeFave—considered noting these facts to reassure her. He decided that it wouldn't help.

"I'll tell them right away," he answered prudently.

"*Completely* safe," she insisted.

"Completely safe," he repeated, without much hope.

She was going to be tense until the package arrived . . . until all the packages were here, he thought a moment later. She wasn't relaxed under ordinary circumstances, he reflected, and realized there were no ordinary circumstances at The St. John Institute.

Not for a second.

There hadn't been since he was assigned here nineteen months ago.

Today—this special day—he was right in his estimate that she'd be stressed. She checked with him every hour on the status of the aircraft. She ate nothing, sipping cup after cup of the decaf and asking about the other packages . . . again and again.

The signal came at eight minutes to five.

The plane was airborne. Estimated time of touchdown at the field some forty-eight miles from the Institute: twenty after six. The van was already waiting. The package should be delivered before seven-thirty.

It was.

She didn't want to wait, but she knew it was probably the only thing to do. She didn't want any of the packages to be damaged. She'd come too far to make a mistake. With that in mind, she ordered that the packages be rechecked and taken to Room B—carefully—at a quarter after eight.

Room B was in the basement. It was a large chamber, some twenty yards long and a dozen wide, with one wall adorned with a lot of the most expensive state-of-the-art audio and video equipment. Seven comfortable armchairs near the middle of the room formed a semicircle. A bit off to the side and facing that arc at an angle was a desk with a control board. Behind it stood another chair slightly bigger than the rest.

The illumination from overhead spotlights was not bright.

Someone wanted the atmosphere here to be low-key, for this was meant to be a place to listen without argument.

Now two doors leading to the main corridor opened, and through each men in the white garb of medical orderlies pushed wheelchairs. There was a male in one chair, a female in the other. Less than a minute later, another two wheelchairs were carefully guided from the freight elevators by a different pair of men in those hospital uniforms.

A woman in one mobile chair . . . a man in the second.

The orderlies—armed and silent and well-rehearsed—parked their "patients" beside the correct chairs. A door at the far end of Room B opened to admit more light and the director of The St. John Institute. She carefully closed the door behind her, took her seat in the chair behind the desk she'd designed, and squeezed out a minimal smile.

She automatically counted.

Four packages . . . not five.

One was late, probably descending now. She didn't like late. She'd wait a minute before she began. First, she'd clear Room B of everyone but the packages. When she told the orderlies to go they left immediately.

Several seconds ticked by as the packages watched her. One of the men was a dark-haired Caucasian, the other a wary-eyed individual of Asian ancestry. The males had good faces, but the females . . . one black, and the second a striking blonde . . . were even more attractive by conventional standards.

Conventional standards had been a consideration.

They were one reason these people had been picked to be packages.

Charlotte Willson looked at her wristwatch again, and frowned.

"Sorry about the delay," she said, "but I don't want to do this twice. We're waiting for one more."

"I'm here," a voice announced from the shadows behind her.

An orderly pushed forward the wheelchair with the fifth package. As it rolled into the light, she immediately noticed there was something wrong. The patient seemed to be unconscious . . . or worse. Worse would be terrible, a threat to her whole plan.

Now she glanced at the orderly and froze.

She knew this face, and it wasn't that of any employee of The St. John Institute. This man wasn't supposed to be pushing the wheelchair. Her plan called for him to be in it. She was startled for two seconds . . . three. Then her mental computer dealt with this reality.

He was the boldest and most clever of all the packages.

Surprise was his thing. The fact that she hated surprise wouldn't interest him at all. It certainly wouldn't get him to change. He was alive because of his gift for surprise. She had to accept that.

She pointed at the unconscious . . . or dead . . . man in the chair.

"Our orderly?" she tested.

"Your driver. The orderly's in a closet."

This was exactly what she could have—should have—expected from him. Now she pointed at the man in the wheelchair.

"Is he just out, or did you kill him?" she asked.

"Do you really care?"

There was a cold silence. Everyone in Room B knew that she didn't, and for a moment, that annoyed her. She saw her public image as calm and in full control . . . not ruthless.

"Don't sweat it," the fifth package said. He was the toughest and handsomest of the lot, she thought, and it would be a challenge to control him. "I didn't break anything," he continued. "Your driver's just napping."

Cool . . . confident . . . close to insolent . . . totally effective, she thought. Exactly as described in the psychological profile and the whole damn career dossier. He shouldn't have been able to do this, or anything like this, for weeks. The two men he'd overpowered were in much better health . . . in perfect condition. He didn't look like a person who'd had major surgery. Maybe he'd strained himself in the physical confrontations, she worried.

That could ruin her timetable.

"You've had a long trip," she said. "Why don't you sit down and rest before we go forward?"

He pointed at the unconscious driver.

"Why don't you get him out of here?" he countered curtly.

She nodded and began to reach for the call button on the panel. She stopped—hand in midair—when she saw the fifth package reach inside the white jacket he'd stolen from the driver.

"Do you have a gun?" she asked quietly.

"He lent it to me. He wasn't using it."

She took a deep breath before she spoke again.

"Why would you need a gun here?" she tested.

"In case I have to shoot somebody. Keep that in mind when you press that button."

She did. She moved slowly, and spoke in a matter-of-fact voice when the security man came and she ordered him to wheel the driver to the infirmary. When the door closed behind them, the fifth package surveyed the room again before he lowered himself into one of the armchairs.

She saw him wince.

He was trying to hide it, but he was hurting.

The man who'd done the damn near impossible was human after all, she thought as she prepared to start the meeting. She nodded and smiled pleasantly, as she knew she was supposed to. There wasn't the slightest response in any of their faces.

All professionals.

They weren't ready to give her anything.

"I think we can begin now," she said in an almost school-teachery tone. "I hope you all had a good trip. Sorry that we started with this unfortunate misunderstanding. It would have been nicer if—"

The man with the gun stared at the black woman.

"You're right," he said, showing no concern about interrupting the director. "You're absolutely right. *Nice* has nothing to do with this place or this deal."

He was looking directly into the pretty African-American woman's eyes.

It was as if he was reading her thoughts.

The head of The St. John Institute blinked.

She was startled . . . then could barely suppress a smile.

The first meeting had not started out as she'd planned, but that wasn't very important. What had just happened was much more significant. It was perfect.

"We'll address those issues later," she promised benignly. "I'd like to welcome you, and to assure you that you're in a first class facility where we'll do everything possible to speed your complete recovery. We value and respect you, and we'll gladly spend whatever it takes to get you well."

Still no visible emotion on any of their faces.

This probably wasn't the time to mention the half-million dollars already invested in each of them, she decided. She'd save that for later.

"I really should introduce myself," she said. "My name is Charlotte Willson."

Then she went on with other lies.

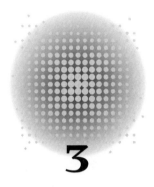

3

SHE DID IT JUST AS SHE'D BEEN TAUGHT.

First, a few things that were true . . . to get credibility.

Then she went on to half-truths . . . quarter-truths . . . total fabrications that weren't obvious falsehoods.

"Welcome to The St. John Institute," she said. "We work in medical and psychological areas. In case you're not aware of it, you all have something in common. Each of you has faced a life-threatening medical problem."

She saw something in the eyes of the Oriental-looking man.

She paused in case he wanted to ask a question. He said nothing. The others remained warily silent, too.

"Not the very same problem," she continued, "but problems that had something in common. Each of you had an important organ that wasn't working and had to be replaced to prevent death."

Still not a word. They were well-trained . . . disciplined.

That had been a factor in choosing them.

One heart, two lungs, one kidney, one liver—harvested five weeks ago. Millions of dollars, including what came next.

"The Institute has an extensive research program," she told them, "and our studies convinced us that it would advance our program if we supported organ transplants as part of our tests to reduce the rejection rate. By saving you, we'd save others in the future."

She paused to smile like a good and generous aunt.

"Tell us the rest of it," the man with the gun urged.

Not nicely. His voice was hard . . . his manner blunt. Not at all nice. She decided to ignore that.

"After considering a lot of people who needed transplants of various organs—needed them very urgently—our scientists concluded that you were the best candidates for the program," she said.

Now the blonde woman with the starlet face glanced at the Oriental-looking man for a few seconds.

Maui, she thought.

She didn't know why, but something told her he was from Maui.

"I'm glad we were chosen," the black woman declared, "and I realize that you did save my life. That leaves me grateful, and curious."

"You want to know why you—all five of you—were chosen," the director reasoned.

Now they all nodded.

"Because you had something *else* in common that interested our scientists," she began.

"Could it be shared skills and life experience?" the fifth package challenged.

He knew the answer. She wondered how.

They'd all had the injections, but why didn't they know?

"That's it," she confirmed. "Our research people wanted to see whether the commonality of skills and work experience would refine our clinical data."

The Oriental male thought and frowned.

"That's double-talk," the fifth package said in reply to the unspoken question. "Or . . . to put it in scientific terms . . . bullshit."

"Wait a minute," the director protested.

"We don't have the time," the difficult man with the gun answered. "And you don't have much sense if you think we'd buy that jargon. You know fucking well who we are. You know we're a lot smarter than that."

She glared at him as she began to phrase her correct response.

"We're an elite group of first-class, cream-of-the-crop, top-of-the-line covert-operations professionals," he said. "We're gangbusters, so spare us the crap!"

The five eyed each other appraisingly . . . and a little proudly. For a few seconds, every one of them flickered a smile.

The fake Charlotte Willson didn't.

"I suppose one might say that," she admitted. "You are exceptional individuals with demonstrated ability in field-intelligence work."

"Gangbusters?" the black woman tested with a grin.

"You bet," the fifth patient confirmed.

"When will she get to the good part?" the blonde asked as she pointed a finger at the director.

"You mean what they want us to do," the man with the gun said. "She's almost there."

"You're not quite ready for that yet," the director told them. "You have more recovering to do to build up your strength . . . and there's training, too. New skills, and of course, new identities. We'll start tomorrow."

"While we're waiting, how about some food?" the fifth package demanded. "I haven't eaten all day."

"Of course," she said and pressed the button to summon the orderlies. This time, there was an additional one with the wheelchair for the man with the gun. Before he sat down, he opened his white uniform jacket and she saw the .38 automatic in his belt.

He's not about to give the weapon up, she thought.

He didn't. He sighed, and the caravan of wheelchairs started out of Room B.

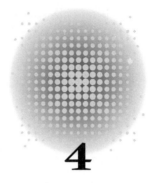

4

THE FOOD WAS GOOD.

It ought to be, considering the care and expense that went into each course at every meal.

Medical rehabilitation experts, specialized dieticians, and exceptional chefs—all of whom were paid a lot of money and were worth it—contributed to what was served to the "packages."

In a separate dining room, of course. The only employee of the Institute who ate with them was the almost too clever woman in gold-rimmed glasses who ran the project. Class distinction wasn't the issue. Security was.

After dinner, the five transplant patients each received an injection and downed an antirejection pill. They knew that the pill was absolutely standard treatment, something they needed daily if the implants were to continue to function. That had been explained before the complex and lengthy surgery.

Daily, for as long as they lived.

That wouldn't be long if they stopped taking them.

Or if The St. John Institute cut off the supply, the patient who still had the gun calculated as he swallowed today's pill.

Even if they could get the pills, the serum might be equally needed to survive. For the moment, the five of them were totally dependent on this St. John Institute, whatever and wherever it might be.

The man who'd broken in on his own spoke four languages, was rated a sharpshooter, an "Expert" with the small arms of six countries, and knew tradecraft backward and forward. Sideways, too, and counterclockwise, as certain Eastern European and Arab covert-action groups—public and free enterprise— could attest.

Ruefully.

He had a reputation, and that was strange, for he'd done his thing . . . his way . . . under a score of different names. None of those people he'd outwitted or outfought had the slightest idea whether he even had a real name. Being realistic, they understood that it wasn't possible for anyone with twenty or more aliases to have a single reputation.

But this man did.

It wasn't just that he had all the moves with instincts to match. He was also endowed with speed and luck and an invaluable ability to judge people. He didn't like most of them, and trusted even fewer. He did sing well and knew the lyrics of hundreds of songs in English, French, and Spanish. That helped pass the time . . . now and then . . . when he had time to pass.

He didn't now.

He had to learn a lot more about the woman who called herself Charlotte and this hard-to-believe St. John Institute. Part of what she'd told them was true, he recognized. All five of them had urgently needed transplants, but how did she know that? People often waited a year or two—or more—to qualify for these various organs, then to locate compatible donors.

She'd moved this group of cloak-and-dagger pros right to the top of five different lists. That was illegal and unjust, and no problem at all for her. She had access to great power, he thought as a black medical technician in hospital whites appeared in the doorway. Each "package" had his or her own room, and the routine was to keep them apart for now.

Why did she think of them as "packages" . . . and how long would that continue?

When would they get names, the man with the pistol wondered.

The technician was carrying a small kit. He entered, closed the door behind him, and took from the metal box a hypodermic and a small vial of something golden. An injection of this was also part of the daily routine . . . had been even before the five had been wheeled into an operating room for their transplants.

What operating room, in which hospital?

Where? Who was the surgeon?

No one had provided this routine information, the man who had the gun and all the moves reflected *again* as the needle pricked him and the golden liquid entered his flank.

What the *hell* was in that hypo?

There had been some rather vague talk about accelerating recovery, but his instincts told him that there was real deception, or omission. That would be the same damn thing, he thought. She—the fake Charlotte—her name had to be false, like so much in this deal, and she figured she was outsmarting all of the five.

Without uttering a word, the white-garbed technician did his best to force out something like an encouraging smile as he packed up the needle and empty vial. He applied alchohol and a Band-Aid to the place where he'd pierced the flesh, tried another imitation of a smile and left silently.

Those were the orders.

That was the security protocol here. None of the staff was to engage in even the smallest conversation with the five. The Institute's employees weren't even to know what the patients' voices sounded like . . . not tone or accent or anything.

She thought she was so damn smart, the patient just injected told himself as he looked at his watch. She thought she knew everything. She undoubtedly had a fat file or computer disk with a lot of information, but she'd made a large mistake—the kind that people with oversized or undernourished egos succumbed to so often.

There was something very important about him she didn't know.

That gave him a significant edge, so he'd do what she would do. He'd keep it secret until he needed it. He wouldn't waste it hostilely or impetuously by tossing it in her face during some difference of opinion or policy. There were going to be such disagreements, he calculated. He couldn't guess what they might be or when, but they'd be coming.

He had to be armed for them.

This secret was a better weapon than any pistol.

With it, he'd be ready to defend himself. Just as he felt re-assured about that, the director of The St. John Institute knocked on his door twice and entered before he could answer.

Her manners could use a little work, judged the man she still thought of as the fifth package. He'd killed more than a dozen people—terrible people, to be sure—but his manners were better than that.

He scanned her instantly like a metal detector. Her watch was on her right wrist, but she held an inch-thick folder in her left hand. Eyes an attractive blue . . . but something shone back in a way he recognized. Contacts. She was hiding the true color of her eyes.

And her hair as well. Yes, that was a first-class and costly wig. Why hadn't he spotted the piece before, he asked himself irritably. He hadn't been looking, and he'd been very tired—exhausted after the massive operation.

No excuse, he judged.

He had to be more careful, and all the time . . . every waking second, and in his dreams, too.

Now she smiled at him confidently. *She* was being completely careful. She'd done her exercise last night and this morning—only nine minutes ago. He looked at the left-handed woman, at her altered eye and hair colors, and he didn't smile at all. She was sure she had the upper hand, and it would be stupid to give the slightest clue that he had his secret weapon to protect him.

It would be prudent to look exhausted.

He knew what face to make . . . what to show in his eyes . . . how to slump his body.

All that worked well.

"I can see you're tired," she announced with barely concealed self-satisfaction.

He nodded as if totally fatigued . . . ruined by the surgery.

"I won't stay long," she promised. "It's time for you and your colleagues to go forward with new names and identities. That's so you can talk to each other comfortably, and it'll make it easier for me and my senior associates to speak with you. With names you're individuals, which of course you always have been."

Not to you, he judged.

We're still packages to you.

"No problem," he said weakly, as if he didn't care.

She sat down in a straightbacked chair and opened the green folder. She studied the top page for several seconds as if she hadn't memorized it twice. She'd never make it in The Actor's Studio, he thought.

Acting: C-minus. Maybe C.

Sincerity: a straight F.

"Max Monroe," she said in her best worst-selling voice. "How about Max Monroe of Albany, New York?" she suggested.

He had to admit that she or they or someone had done the homework. He'd grown up not too far from Albany—in the next state, eighty miles into Massachusetts over the border, where the speech wasn't much different from that in Albany.

Near enough, but far enough so nobody from Albany was likely to recognize him. He'd gone to the state university there for a year and knew the city . . . well, knew it as it had been seventeen or eighteen years ago. He'd looked a lot different then. He'd been a lot different, too.

"Max Monroe," he repeated in a tired tone. "No problem."

She gave him the top six pages from the folder to study. They held a mass of details about the life, family, education, and medical history of one Max Dennis Monroe, who'd been president of his junior class in Lincoln High School. Lincoln High in Chicago. There was such a school, and he knew beyond any doubt that someone had somehow inserted into its computer bank a full record of the imaginary Max Dennis Monroe.

Same thing for his three-year marriage and then divorce in Houston, where he'd worked in cargo sales for an airline. All those records had been cooked, too, along with the tax files of the State of New York that said he'd been an Albany resident and car dealer for nearly four years.

Easy, he thought.

They were very experienced in creating people and life stories. *They* . . . whoever they were . . . did it every day. There were a lot of *theys* in this totally unsportsmanlike game, and he wanted—*needed*—to know which *they* this was. That could be helpful in determining *why* all this had been organized.

It would also assist his efforts to stay alive.

All his experience and instincts—his street smarts and certainty—said this enterprise had to be extremely expensive and hazardous. Nobody collected five top cloak-and-dagger veterans just for some academic research project. Everything he knew told him that he was in grave danger.

All five of them were.

He'd play out the hand carefully.

"Max Dennis Monroe? Okay," he lied. "Yeah, my friends call me Denny."

His fake smile was much better than the one she'd offered.

"May I call you Denny?" she asked.

He was still smiling like that rogue car dealer he was supposed to be as he considered her request. She saw him look at her hands, and she wondered why. It didn't occur to her that this very savvy and slightly paranoid professional was trying to decide whether there'd been surgery to alter her fingerprints.

He wasn't crazy.

He was curious . . . and careful.

This was no time to spoil their budding "romance," he decided.

"Of course," he agreed amiably.

"I'm glad we're going to be friends, Denny," she said.

"You saved my life," he replied. "I won't forget that."

She was in excellent spirits as she left to brief the other four on their new identities. It was going so well, she exulted silently. The extraordinary field agent who was now Max Dennis Monroe was the strongest in terms of leadership. All his highly classified records—aside from the fake death certificate that said he'd perished in an auto accident—convinced her that he had a natural gift for command.

And he'd accepted her as a friend.

She'd lead the leader . . . very subtly . . . leaving his male ego intact. The complex and daring plan she'd shaped was moving from paper to reality . . . to the next step. Every step was tricky, she realized, but it would work.

A first. She'd make history in her fierce dark world.

Three doors down the corridor. She'd fixed it so none of the five was any closer to the others than that. There were armed orderlies outside each room to maintain "privacy" so that each of the five could "rest." She knocked on the third door, punched up her friendly look, and went in to speak with the Oriental man there.

Oriental-American, to be precise.

Chinese-American, to be more precise than that.

Born in Hawaii thirty-six years ago, he spoke Chinese and Japanese as well as he did English, and he was fluent in Urdu and Hindi, too. He could also "converse" in planting and disarming a variety of explosive devices. Like the others, he was showing the impact of the recent and major surgery when she entered.

He was visibly tired when she came in with the folder.

When she departed six minutes later, he was something and someone else. He'd become Harry Chen, night manager of a motel in Denver.

The other male in the group—Room 11 around the corner—seemed less fatigued. This man with the olive complexion and dark, thick hair was powerfully muscled, she recalled, and came from an Hispanic family.

He had down cold the accents and idioms of a dozen countries in South and Central America, and could pass for Cuban or Puerto Rican as well. His mother had been Italian, so he could do that number in the speech of north or south . . . or Sicily, too. He had enough combat skills for an infantry platoon, the nerve of a burglar, and some talent for safes and alarm systems.

Cesar Fuentes, she told him.

He liked the new name. He'd long been a fan of the Roman general. Cesar was also a name that might intrigue females, one of his favorite activities. His notable collection of recordings of Gregorian chants often surprised them, for most of the women he met didn't realize that he was more than a purely physical stereotype. His sophisticated knowledge of this medieval music hardly fit with that image.

Now the director went on to the floor above to settle matters with the two female members of the team . . . *her* team. The cagey head of The St. John Institute had deliberately chosen for them quarters apart from the three males. This whole operation was very delicate. Though she was almost convinced that it would succeed, she admitted to herself that it was an experiment. She wouldn't risk complicating things by letting man-woman relationships add to the stresses.

Keeping contact to a businesslike minimum would be safer, she thought. It was bad enough that the sixth package hadn't arrived . . . never would. She didn't need sexual tensions to distract the five who were going into life-and-death hazards as soon as their strength returned.

And the training was completed.

They had numerous and solid skills, but this was going to be completely different . . . a challenge for all five, and for herself as well. That was what she was thinking when she tapped twice on the door of Room 17.

The black woman was seated in her wheelchair, contentedly studying a chess board on the adjacent table as she considered her next move. She was playing against herself, using her passion for the game, her experience, and the real talent that had made her a state champion some years ago.

At the moment, she was defending her king, and Willson recalled another confrontation only thirty-two months ago when two men with murder on their minds and ten-inch daggers in their hands came at her. The chess player had defended herself very effectively that night as well. She'd thrown one of the attackers out a ninth-floor window and broken both collarbones of the other enemy, who fled before additional body parts were smashed.

She'd acquired Swahili and two more African tongues in the Peace Corps right out of Princeton . . . picked up Arabic, scuba diving and karate later. She'd been wed for a year to Bernardo Amigo, the Spanish chess wizard and Grand Master, before she was recruited into the intelligence community shortly before the Cold War ended.

Allegedly.

Almost all the men and women and hermaphrodites—probably dogs and cats, too—whom the head of this Institute knew didn't think it was really over. For them, it wasn't and it was quite alive and kicking for the African-American woman who'd been test-living someone else's left kidney for the past fortnight.

"Susan Kincaid," proposed the director as she handed the chess player the folder containing an imaginary and not-too-flashy biography.

Not entirely delighted that her game had been interrupted, the black woman scanned the pages covering her new identity and finally nodded her assent. Without a word, she resumed playing.

The thirty-something blonde in Room 22 had something other than chess on her mind. She was an exceptionally pretty woman with a near-perfect face and figure to match. She was looking at herself in the large mirror, studying her midsection. She'd lifted the hospital robe and was eyeing the scar left by the transplant operation.

The director decided that it would be good psychology to say something comforting. After all, all the five needed reassurance, and that would cement her position as the stronger one, the one who cared for the weaker.

She never got to offer comfort.

The half-naked blonde spoke first.

"Sucks, doesn't it?"

It was phrased as a question, but it was a statement.

"The goddam scar," she specified in an oddly matter-of-fact tone. "Doesn't do a thing for me, does it?"

"I'm sure it'll look much less . . . much better when it heals," Willson replied.

The woman with the yellow hair shook her head.

"If it doesn't," she said, "there's plastic surgery, right?"

"Absolutely."

The blonde lowered her robe and grinned.

"I'd probably look worse dead," she admitted. "What's up?"

She agreed to use the name Paula Taylor. Her new biography made no reference to her expertise in the stock market, mastery of things electronic, captaincy of the women's water polo team at college, and talents in opening safes. She could open handbags and pick pockets, too, skills taught her when she was on a joint mission with Colombian antinarcotics specialists.

Paula Taylor was a very different person. According to The St. John Institute, her father had been a Presbyterian minister, and her mother a blood technician in Tennessee. It was reasonable for Paula Taylor to earn her B.A. at Vanderbilt in Nashville, and her move on to a career teaching English as a Second Language was nothing to raise questions. Though this eye-catching woman had appeared in school plays and worked with an amateur theater company, her calling was as an educator.

Some clever nitpicker had inserted an alleged injury when her imaginary school was supposedly wrecked in a gas explosion—a nice touch to explain the surgical scar. Similar fictions bloomed in the fake biographies of the other "packages." The woman who called herself Charlotte Willson made sure of that.

She was obsessive about details.

They had drilled her that even the smallest error—omission or commission—might cost lives, and she remembered that every waking moment.

And in her dreams. She dreamed a lot . . . worried even more. She wasn't worrying now. Everything was on schedule with the five "packages" so she could proceed to the next step.

"We'll all get together for lunch in a few days, Paula," she said in her good-aunt tone as she prepared to go.

"Fine," the blonde responded. "I'm looking forward to that.

You'll introduce us, right? I can't hang out with people who don't have names."

"I can tell you their names right now," the director offered. "Your female colleague is Susan. The obviously Latin man is Cesar; and our Oriental partner is Harry. As for the other gentleman, his proper first name is Max and his middle name is Dennis."

The woman with the shocking scar shook her head.

"I don't mean to be a bad patient," she said, "but he's no gentleman and I doubt that anything about him is proper."

"You don't really know him, Paula."

"And I'm still impressed. How does he have information about us and we don't have a bloody clue about him?"

The director knew exactly what the newly minted Paula Taylor was talking about . . . she had been wondering herself.

"What do you mean?" she asked.

"Who told him that we're cloak-and-dagger professionals?" the blonde challenged. "Was that whole bit of his break-in with the gun staged for our benefit? Is he someone special?"

Everything she knew about him—including the episode last night—convinced the director that her "friend" Denny was special, but she wasn't going to discuss that with anyone else—not now, not yet.

Something wasn't quite right. She hadn't told him that the others were top-quality field operatives. She had to find out who did. How had Denny breached their elaborate and multilevel security? Did he have an ally inside the Institute? Everyone connected with this operation had been checked—deep-checked—four times. Which of them could have leaked this . . . and what else?

"All five of you are special," the director evaded facilely. "I'll spell the whole thing out when we start the training."

She was out the door before Paula Taylor could ask the obvious questions.

What training? What's this all about?

THE WOMAN WHO EXPECTED to be Charlotte Willson for at least another thirteen or fifteen months was halfway down the corridor when Barry Becker heard it again. He'd heard it every day for weeks, and he still didn't understand it.

Becker was a noncommissioned officer in a signal intelligence unit of the U.S. Army. His group was secret, and it served an even more highly secret organization called the National Security Agency. This "ultra-black" and passionately hush-hush federal enterprise listened to all kinds of things in a vast variety of places on behalf of the deep thinkers who guided the defense of the United States of America.

It listened or had listeners, plus sophisticated code breakers, on every continent. Becker's job was to listen on an assigned schedule to certain radio frequencies controlled by the spy outfit that was descended from the K.G.B. in the most powerful of the countries in the confederation spawned by the former Soviet Union.

Russia.

The old center with the most missiles—the biggest nuclear toys—the boldest gangsters, the finest ballet folk and fiddlers, and the brassiest-balled espionage organizations. In flux and quite dangerous . . . absolutely.

Barry Becker didn't know much Russian, but he'd had enough basic education in Moscow's current cryptography to spot the single word that had been broadcast eight times a day for so long.

It had to mean something to someone.

Anna. That was it. Again and again.

His job was to identify the transmitter, record the message, and send the tapes off on their journey to the N.S.A. at Fort Meade.

He did his job today as he did five days a week, and he knew nobody expected him to make sense of this radio traffic.

Anna . . . Anna . . . Anna.

He was tired and bored, but he couldn't help wondering.

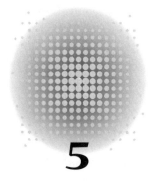

5

THIS WAS GOING TO BE AT LEAST A BIT DELICATE, CHARLOTTE Willson told herself the next morning.

As she'd brooded the night before and halfway to dawn. That was all right, she thought with only the faintest sense of fatigue.

She could do "delicate," and "devious" was no problem either. It wasn't as if she was doing it to screw somebody out of money or a job, the director of the St. John Institute assured herself. She wouldn't speak the word "screw," but she enjoyed some tiny schoolgirl delight in thinking it. The idea was even less of a problem, for she was doing this for a very good cause, and it was her duty.

Definitely her duty, and it should be done well.

The man who was now Denny had done a lot worse . . . many times, she recalled in silent justification. This ability to justify acts that would horrify her mother was one of the director's most practical talents. She knew that she shared it with other effective executives whom she respected, and the fact that it would also piss off her father didn't trouble her at all.

"Piss off"—that was okay to think, too.

Experience in doing "delicate" and "devious" had taught her that these things had to be planned meticulously and executed perfectly. Since she didn't know the secret of the tungsten-tough operative she'd renamed Denny, she was confident that she could pull it off if she carefully followed her time- and slime-tested methods of distraction and deceit. She hadn't invented them, she told herself, but she could execute them as well as anyone else.

She studied her checklist for the tenth time.

She decided to wait another hour. He'd be more tired and less alert then . . . less suspicious . . . after his injection. Some sixty-one minutes later, she clicked on the intercom to ask her assistant to "invite" him to her office.

"Nicely," she specified. "If he isn't too tired. You know the rest of it."

No mistakes, she thought as she waited for Max Dennis Monroe. Denny—yes, that suited him—was dangerous in any identity. She'd known from his dossier that he was the most dangerous—physically and mentally—of the group, and the way he'd arrived had confirmed that beyond any doubt.

He looked tired when he was rolled into her office in his wheelchair nine minutes later. She gestured to the orderly to help him sit on the couch.

"You'll be more comfortable there," she predicted maternally as the white-uniformed escort helped him struggle to the bigger and unmoving piece of furniture.

She waved her hand again, and the orderly left at once. He didn't even look around at her office. That was as forbidden as speaking to these newly arrived and totally isolated patients. He didn't know that they were "packages" or why they were here. He understood that it was safer not to know.

"You could probably use more sleep," she said to Denny after the soundproof door closed behind the orderly, "and I'm sorry to bother you with this when you could be resting."

He nodded silently . . . closed his eyes for several seconds . . . suppressed a yawn before he opened them again.

"Will this take long?" he asked.

"No, just a few minutes. I'm going to introduce you to each other," she replied, "and I thought I'd brief you first."

A hint of wariness flickered in his eyes.

"Why?"

"Because I'm impressed by your record and your initiative," she said. "I think of you as the Number One. First among equals, of course."

"Of course," he ratified mechanically as he waited for her to make her move. He didn't really mind the preliminary small talk, for it gave him a chance to get into position. He'd have only a few seconds to make *his* move . . . probably just one opportunity.

She began to spell out who the other four were.

Not their real identities, but the life stories created for them by individuals who did that sort of thing professionally. The head of The St. John Institute had no idea as to who or where they were, but she wasn't about to criticize their reasonably imaginative and practical work.

She was talking about the black woman who played chess so well and did several fiercer things even better, when one of the lights on the telephone on her desk began to flash. No ring . . . no buzz . . . just the silent flicker of the green bulb on the far right end of the instrument. That wasn't as important as the red light on the other telephone linked to the secure line, but this one was also swept every month and it was significant.

"Excuse me," she said as she reached for the phone.

At the same time, she automatically turned away. It was nothing personal. Whoever was in her office when the green light flashed got the same treatment. This was the democracy of distrust. She didn't want anyone to be able to read her lips during these calls.

As she swung in the swivel chair, he made his move. He was ready, and had been since he first detected the hidden security camera in his room. He'd spotted the other one as soon as he entered this guarded chamber. No surprise—hell, he'd have been astonished if she or *they* weren't videotaping and audiotaping everything in this office twenty-four hours a day, three hundred sixty-five days a year, and that extra one in leap year, too.

He shifted to block the camera with his body as he did what

he'd come to do without it being recorded by the surveillance gear. *Now . . . fast.*

And it had to be *smooth*, nothing that might be noticed.

It was a long shot . . . better than none at all.

Those were the rules of survival he'd learned years ago.

Done. He breathed easier . . . leaned back with no tension or other emotion on his face.

When she finished her telephone conversation and turned to hang up the instrument, she saw nothing to alarm her. There were so many things that did, but none was visible as she put on her sorry-about-that expression and sort of smiled.

Then she resumed her account of the other cloak-and-dagger professionals who'd just come to the Institute. She had rehearsed what she'd say, so it was no problem for her to stretch it out as long as possible.

The First Among Equals recognized what she was doing.

She was buying time.

For a second he wondered why, and then his mind began to probe and compute.

Right. He'd expected this sooner or later. Sooner didn't bother him at all. It was going to trouble her, he thought, and managed not to show any satisfaction. He was as human as the others and he had a bit of malice in him, but this wasn't the time to display it.

Let her sweat . . . if she did, he told himself. She was very cool and controlled, maybe part of a new breed that didn't perspire. It didn't matter, he decided, for he'd done what he had to do to maintain his freedom of action.

Now she eyed the clock on her desk and reasoned that they'd had enough time. She completed her description of the last of the group, told a few more lies, and promised that they'd speak again tomorrow. Less than ninety seconds later, he was being wheeled out the door.

As it closed, a voice came from the intercom on her desk.

"Finished," her assistant reported.

"Well?" she demanded.

"Not really. Zero. Nothing."

"How many men?" she asked.

"Six . . . with handheld metal detectors. They went top to bottom three times. Every inch . . . every corner."

"How can that be?" she challenged. "It's impossible. Maybe the metal detectors malfunctioned. This is not acceptable. It's against our rules."

Her rules. She'd made them. This was intolerable.

"Run the surveillance tapes of his room again . . . and then twice more. Find it!" she ordered.

She wasn't shouting, but the fury was clear in her hard-edged tone.

"We'll find it," her assistant vowed.

He wasn't nearly as sure as he sounded. He knew that this "Denny" was bold and unpredictable. A brief scan of the file— unauthorized because it was Top Secret, like almost everything here—had made it clear that this "Denny" didn't do a lot of things like other people.

And he thought ahead . . . more than one move. She must have seen it in the file, her assistant thought, but it would be unproductive to mention that. It would actually be stupid, he told himself a split second before she ended the conversation.

Click.

She'd turned off the damn intercom, but not her anger.

Where the hell was the gun? She had to know.

And how had Denny managed this? Why was he defying her?

She had to know those things, too, and right away.

If there was a flaw in her system—or someone had made a mistake . . . anyone . . . whatever it might be . . . an accident or omission or a deliberate deed—urgent action to fix the defect was necessary.

For a moment, she almost doubted herself.

Was it . . . could it be . . . something she'd done or hadn't done?

The whole operation was based on a sealed system—total control of everyone, from the Institute staff to the precious "packages." Perfection. The scheme was more than complex, ultrasophisticated, and beyond cutting edge.

It was radical, and she was conservative.

She was also stubborn, the fake Charlotte Willson reflected with a hostile little girl's grin, and that was why this whole operation was going to work. She'd find out where this macho Denny had hidden the gun he'd stolen.

Was it just animal cunning that made him do this, or had he somehow guessed she'd send men to recover it? That was the not very satisfactory but sole explanation that came to her. She was wrong. *Someone* had told him.

That wasn't the worst of it.

It was somebody who knew everything about the operation, and might leak more at any time. This hadn't occurred to her, for all of the Institute's technicians, staff, and scientists were doing their jobs very well.

One had done his job *too* well.

This had already affected the operation seriously . . . life-and-death seriously. That was just the beginning. The impact was going to be much greater—and soon.

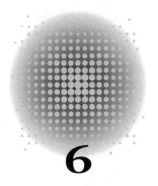

6

"TWENTY-FIVE MILLION," THE HUSKIER MAN SAID.

"Twenty-five million for the five," the other man confirmed.

They were both well-dressed.

Not so well-dressed that they'd attract attention. That was the last thing either of them wanted. The next to the last thing was for anyone on this ferry . . . or elsewhere . . . to connect them with each other.

They weren't even looking at each other. They stood side by side—as if strangers who were there by accident—staring at the old city. This was the afternoon following the unsuccessful search for the gun . . . far away. It was 3:10 P.M. just ahead in Lisbon and on this broad river, the Tagus, that ran beside the Portuguese capital.

The ferry, one of three each hour, moved steadily across the wide mouth of the 620-mile-long Tagus. This was the estuary where it wed the Atlantic. Off to the right was the eye-catching "new" bridge named in honor of fifteenth-century explorer Vasca da Gama. Neither of the men had the slightest interest in history, so they ignored the graceful span.

They were concentrating on more personal matters, such as not being betrayed or killed. It was these concerns that had led each of them to come with armed escorts. A dozen yards to the left of where the vendor's emissary stood were his three body-guards, two of them ruddy-faced and the third with features of his Mongol ancestors. Off to the right loitered an equal number of swarthy security operatives here to protect the other envoy, a slim man of dark complexion.

He might be Greek, Turkish, Egyptian, or something else.

That didn't matter to the burly man who'd asked for the twenty-five million.

The currency did.

"That's U.S. dollars . . . cash," he specified.

"Of course. Any denomination you want," the Mediterranean-looking man beside him agreed.

He glanced around the deck of the slow-moving ferry again. He couldn't afford to make any mistakes. If the slightest thing went wrong, *they*—the people who'd given him this assignment and the suitcase—would kill him.

"The down payment?" the wide-shouldered man asked.

His voice had just the slightest trace of Eastern Europe.

He'd worked long and hard to get rid of the rest of it. His clothes were British, and the guns that his escorts carried were German. All four of his team wore Italian shoes. Details counted.

"When can you deliver?" the buyer tested.

"This has to be done *very* carefully."

"We know that. Now . . . *when?*"

"Eight to ten weeks after the down payment. We'll let you know exactly where and when fifteen or twenty days before."

The ship was slowing.

The dock for this car ferry from Cacilhas to Lisbon's Cais do Sodré was only a hundred and eighty yards ahead.

"Can we have one before that?" the slim Mediterranean man asked.

The representative of the vendor smiled.

They didn't trust his commander.

No surprise. He didn't trust *them* either.

"I think so," he said coolly. "The down payment?"

The buyer's envoy . . . the forged diplomatic passport he carried was as good as the counterfeit papers of the seller's husky representative . . . paused for four or five seconds before he nodded.

The ferry was less than a hundred yards from the Lisbon pier.

Now the buyer pointed to the trunk of his car, a dark green BMW sedan. One of his men opened the trunk, took out the small hard-sided suitcase . . . and looked at him in silent question.

The buyer nodded, and walked away before the case was given to the vendor's representative. By the time the ferry docked, those who'd come to make the purchase were in their car, and the seller and his bodyguards were getting into their black Volvo.

It wasn't until the Volvo was a dozen blocks from the ferry terminal that the man with the very slight Eastern European accent opened the case. He did it carefully. He knew that the people who were buying were both peculiar and ruthless. He couldn't imagine why, but they could have put a bomb in it.

No bomb.

U.S. currency—used and neatly stacked—hundred-dollar bills.

He counted it, twice.

As specified . . . to the penny . . . the down payment . . . $1,300,000.

He glanced into the rearview mirror for several seconds before he closed the small suitcase. As far as he could see, no one was following his car. The down payment was supposed to be a sign of mutual faith, but that was more a hope than a fact. He was thinking about this when he entered Lisbon's airport to catch the Sabena jet to Brussels . . . and then again when he changed there to the connecting flight that would take him home.

Looking down at the Belgian capital, he wondered where the swarthy man who'd represented the buyer was going. No one had said who he was or uttered any clue as to the identity of the purchaser. That wasn't quite the way these things were usually done, the man with the suitcase filled with $1,300,000 thought.

Of course, this whole transaction wasn't exactly usual.

It was just about certain that a lot of people—hundreds of thousands—would be killed.

The man with the down payment hoped that he wouldn't be one of them.

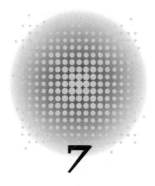

7

ON THE FOLLOWING MONDAY, THE DIRECTOR OF THE ST. JOHN Institute moved to the next step in her plan.

Carefully . . . psychologically . . . with food.

The food was a key part of the psychology. She brought all five of the "packages" together—still in their wheelchairs—to meet at breakfast. It was a very good breakfast . . . hot food . . . nourishing food full of sugar and energy . . . comfort food to make them think of Mom and relax.

Plenty of food and excellent coffee—tea for those who preferred it—opened them to her introductions. Even though they guessed that the names were false since each of them was using the alias and false identity she'd provided, associating with other adults who had names and some kind—any kind—of personalities was a lot better than the days and nights of living alone.

She could see the way that they related to each other . . . and to her . . . as they finished their breakfast. They weren't nearly as guarded. Well, four of them weren't. She couldn't be positive about Denny. He seemed and sounded cheerful enough, but she wasn't sure.

Dammit, you couldn't be sure with him.

She wouldn't be until she had the gun in her possession.

She'd get to that later, she assured herself as she drained her cup of the decaffeinated dark brew. She cleared her throat.

"Ladies and gentlemen," she began as she'd rehearsed. "I'm glad to see us all together, and to share the news that you're all doing well medically. Postsurgery recovery is coming along nicely. Looking and listening this morning, it's clear that we have a positive group that's bonding well."

She paused, smiled, and nodded for emphasis.

"We can work together," she predicted confidently, "and that's good . . . because we've got a *lot* to do."

None of the transplant patients in the wheelchairs disagreed, she noted. They didn't agree either. A little cynical and a lot adult, they were politely but firmly withholding judgment. They were—as grown-ups and cloak-and-dagger professionals—waiting out the rest of her presentation.

"Tomorrow morning, after another good breakfast and good talk together," she continued, "we'll go downstairs to the briefing room, where we first met when you arrived. You're getting stronger by the day, so we should be able to start training before the end of the week."

The man who was now Harry Chen from Denver patted his lips with his napkin—a white cloth of good quality—before he spoke.

"What sort of training?"

"Nothing arduous. Nothing too physical," she replied. "You've got more healing and probably some exercise ahead."

"Mental training?" the blonde woman asked.

"I'd say 'exercises' to develop and strengthen certain skills. I think you'll find this program interesting and rewarding."

It was standard personnel department crap, the man who'd hidden the gun thought. They used the same "cooked" language no matter what they were peddling to presumably gullible field agents. It could be a suicide mission. They'd saved his life with the transplant, but he didn't owe them *that*.

He hadn't asked *them*—whoever they were—for the transplant.

Or for anything else.

There was no way he'd consider a suicide mission, no matter how they tried to describe it, he told himself irritably. *They* were starting to get on his nerves in small ways, too. Putting off a basic explanation was one of them.

"It was good to meet the others, and the breakfast was fine," he said abruptly, "but why don't we cut to the chase now?"

"The chase?" Willson blurted.

"What are we supposed to train for?" he asked bluntly.

"Something new and important. It'll require complete focus, so I think building up your strength for another day would make it easier," she told them. "There can't be any harm in such a brief delay. With the whole group in better health—"

Denny broke in coolly.

"*What* whole group?"

"I don't understand," she responded.

"There were supposed to be others," he answered, and the black woman nodded in agreement.

"The chairs. *Right*," she thought aloud.

Denny agreed with a thumbs-up of affirmation.

"*Right*. Susan is dead on-target," he complimented. "As soon as I got here, I did exactly what I was trained to do, what we were all trained to do. I automatically scanned the situation— instant reconnaissance for physical threats and possible escape routes—the whole bit."

The others in wheelchairs nodded.

"The pro bit," Harry Chen ratified.

"Without any special reason," Denny continued, "I counted the chairs you'd set up for us."

"Seven," the blonde woman recalled.

She'd counted them, too.

"But there are just five of us," Denny said, "and you're not the kind of person to waste things. It's absolutely clear that you're precise and economical, so you must have . . . at some time . . . been expecting two more."

The director was impressed and annoyed.

Impressed with him—this bode well for the potential as Team Leader—and annoyed that she hadn't thought to reduce the number of chairs.

"Where are the other two?" Denny asked evenly.

No urgency . . . no anger . . . no challenge . . . but the question was rock-hard and she realized that she had to address it . . . now.

"There is always some *breakage* in everything," she began carefully.

"Including transplants, right?"

It was almost as if this son of a bitch was reading her mind. She nodded.

"While it's a highly developed branch of modern medicine and we succeeded in getting you optimum care—the finest teams of transplant specialists in North America—" she told them, "the survival rate is not quite one hundred percent."

"Nobody's perfect," Denny said with a trace of irony.

"*Some Like It Hot?* Great flick," the black woman noted as she recalled the last line of dialogue from the Billy Wilder-I.A.L. Diamond script.

The head of The St. John Institute controlled herself.

"I'm sorry to report that, despite the best efforts of one of these outstanding surgical teams, there was a casualty," she admitted.

"On the table?" Harry Chen inquired.

"It doesn't matter, does it?" Denny responded.

Chen shook his head.

"What about the other chair?" the blonde woman asked.

"That person came through the surgical procedure reasonably well," Willson answered slowly. "There were no signs of rejection but something went wrong."

Person? She wouldn't even break security to specify the sex, Denny thought. "Something" went wrong? He looked at her for several seconds before he realized that she didn't know what the "something" was.

He could tell that she was working very hard to mask her thoughts . . . to keep him out. And she was suddenly aware that he wasn't about to accept that.

"You're all in excellent health now," she assured them.

"Would it be goddam rude to ask how long after the operation this second person checked out?" Denny inquired.

She really didn't want to tell him. She hadn't planned to tell him or the others about any aspect of the deaths. She was committed to sticking to *her* script . . . not as witty as the one for the Jack Lemmon, Tony Curtis, Marilyn Monroe movie, but her own creation, crafted just for this single performance.

She told herself that Denny might be difficult to control, but she could do it. She'd control all the packages, the whole operation, and herself. *Herself* was the key, she realized.

"The second unfortunate casualty occurred about three weeks after the transplant," she replied.

Three weeks? She knew to the day, the hour, he guessed accurately. What was equally important—no, *more* important— was what she didn't know about the man she'd named Denny. He hadn't known it himself until he'd arrived at The St. John Institute.

"I'm terribly sorry," she added sincerely.

And more than a bit worried. Well, *uneasy*. While these five showed no symptoms of anything that caused the Institute's on-site doctors concern, the uncertainty of not knowing what had killed the second package was not acceptable.

She hoped that it wasn't the yellow serum.

The injections of that were crucial to her plan. The elite team of pathologists and coroner professionals brought in to redo the autopsy for the third time was almost finished with the full battery of tests. If all went well, they'd said, she'd know then.

Probably.

Almost surely, they'd said with straight faces in sincere tones. She'd wanted to hit them for the polite patronizing—wondered for a split second if there was a course on this in every medical school—and decided that they were being honest with her in their professional look-out-for-malpractice-suits way.

They weren't sure who she was, but they knew she was dangerous.

All their instincts and the whole secret nature of things said the risk could be much worse than any law suit. All this flashed through her mind at computer speed in four seconds.

Suddenly the handsome Hispanic member of the team spoke.

He hadn't said a word since she'd begun her mini-address. Now she didn't like what he told them.

"I appreciate what you've done for us," Cesar Fuentes began smoothly, "but you're leaving out something. Look, we're all field operatives who stayed alive long enough to benefit from these transplants because we had both skills and instincts."

All four of the others nodded in assent.

"My instincts tell me—loud and clear—that we ought to know more. Field agents don't always get the whole story up front," Cesar continued, "and that can get them killed. Can't you share at least some more of this deal with us?"

They were all startled when Denny laughed.

"What's so goddam funny?" Fuentes demanded.

"I don't think any of us have to worry about being killed," Denny announced. He smiled as he pointed at Charlotte Willson.

"She can tell you all about that," he added.

She frowned as she wondered what he meant.

"I'll say it for you," he volunteered cheerfully. "We're not going to get killed, because we're already dead."

The other "packages" stared in shock.

"I'm not speaking about morality, or our future in Hollywood, either," he explained. "This is much more concrete. I'll bet you tomorrow's terrific breakfast, and just about anything else, that each and every one of us is—Scout's honor—legally dead."

Willson flinched.

How could he know?

"Is that a joke?" Fuentes tested.

Denny Monroe pointed silently at the earnest woman who'd brought them there. They could see the answer to the question in her face.

"Holy shit!" Fuentes exclaimed.

"And a half," the blonde woman agreed. "Why?"

"So we couldn't turn back if we wanted to," Chen speculated. "We've got to go ahead with this deal . . . whatever it is."

"Our good friends have all the papers for our new identities,"

Monroe pointed out, "which means they've got all the cards—literally and figuratively. Credit cards, Social Security, the whole bit. We don't even know where we are, let alone what game we're supposed to learn."

The other female "package"—the woman who played chess so well and spoke Swahili—spoke up suddenly.

"There might be a second reason for this legally dead thing," she reasoned. "They don't want our families or friends to think about looking for us. No questions . . . no problems . . . nice and neat."

She turned to confront Charlotte Willson.

"Did we have decent funerals?"

"Of course. Respectful and appropriate funerals, with services that matched the customs of each faith," the director of The St. John Institute said stiffly. "Next of kin were . . . to the extent that we could find them . . . informed and invited."

"Closed-casket services, right?" Denny Monroe prodded.

"Quality caskets. Nothing cheap. Yes, closed caskets," Willson agreed. "We couldn't let anyone see that you weren't there."

"Was anyone in the caskets?" Fuentes asked.

She shrugged noncommittally.

"I'll tell you one thing," she announced defensively. "All your life-insurance policies were paid in full. The beneficiaries you chose have received every penny due to them."

"Get it, Cesar?" Denny Monroe asked with a smile. "These are folks of high principle. They'll kill you but they won't cheat you."

Willson glared in naked anger.

"That's not funny," she said bitterly. "Nothing about this entire matter is the least bit funny. We saved your lives. There were hundreds of people ahead of you on the organ lists. At least two—maybe three—of you would really be dead if we hadn't moved you all to the top."

"She's right," Monroe agreed. "We owe her."

"And now we're prepared to take care of you . . . to provide the finest medical care . . . and to pay very generously for your cooperation."

The yellow-haired woman leaned forward with interest.

"How generous is 'very'?" the new Paula Taylor asked.

"Much more than you've ever made."

"Listen, we've all been underpaid public employees—civil servants and military," Denny countered impatiently. "This is our one big chance for a score, so let's forget the discreet 'much more' talk."

"Please come up with a number," Chen translated.

She hesitated as if trying to remember.

Denny knew she was faking, but that didn't surprise him.

They were all in the fake-and-break trade.

"I think I can get you two thousand dollars a week," she finally said.

"And expenses, of course," the man with the stolen pistol pushed.

"Reasonable expenses."

"They'll be unreasonable," he promised, "but you'll get your money's worth."

Fatigue . . . it was all over him now.

He paused, yawned.

"Nap time," he declared. "Let's talk about payment arrangements tomorrow."

Denny Monroe—the most dangerous, no-holds-barred field agent The St. John Institute could find—yawned again.

"YOU'RE A REAL PISTOL, Denny," the African-American woman judged objectively as they waited to be wheeled from the dining room. "How did you know that we're legally dead?"

"Lucky guess," he replied . . . and yawned once more.

"Bullshit."

"You're absolutely right," he agreed without a trace of embarrassment.

"So you're not going to tell me?"

"Why should I trust you?" he asked pleasantly.

"We're in this together, aren't we?"

"You could be with *her*," he reasoned. "She's the foxy kind who might put somebody inside our little group . . . someone posing as a transplant who'll be her ears."

"If you think I'll show you my scar, forget it."

He grinned.

"Seemed worth trying. Bet it's a beauty," he said and frowned. She knew he hadn't really been trying to look at her scar, and that it was something else bothering him now.

"What is it?" she questioned.

"*Taxes*. Since we're dead, we shouldn't pay any taxes. I'll get that settled tomorrow."

She saw the orderlies approaching to wheel them back to their rooms.

"Be careful with our director lady," she advised. "I wouldn't crowd her."

"Wouldn't think of it," he assured her.

Just before the orderlies reached them, he suddenly said two words . . . softly but clearly.

"Kelly's People."

He immediately wondered why he'd uttered those words. Then he tried to figure out what they meant.

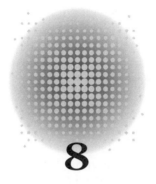

8

SOME THREE AND A HALF HOURS LATER.

Precisely nine time zones east, computing from Greenwich.

Clouds masked most of the stars in the night sky here, and it was chilly.

The weather didn't matter much to General Temkov, and he certainly wasn't bothered by the hour. He preferred the darkness, when others were less alert, or . . . best of all . . . asleep. There weren't too many things that fifty-eight-year-old Alexei Temkov liked, but he did like to comment to colleagues that he was "a night person, like Stalin and Churchill."

It took a certain amount of nerve for a Russian intelligence officer to say anything complimentary about the late Soviet dictator, but the veteran cloak-and-dagger executive with a general's insignia on his shoulders had that much nerve . . . and more. He didn't laud Stalin and the K.G.B. era to today's devious political types in the Kremlin, of course. They couldn't admit to any positive opinions about that man and those decades they wanted to minimize.

Not this year anyway.

Wearing righteous faces and nimbly modifying their politically correct statements to placate the shifting angers of discontented civilians and military alike, they wiggled like belly dancers and took care of their friends. Even for the honest ones, it was a balancing act created to entertain . . . to distract . . . to survive.

The honor of the Russian security organizations and armed forces meant nothing to those self-serving mediocrities, Temkov thought as the light on his desk flickered twice . . . then once . . . finally, three times. As for surviving, he'd forgotten more about that than they'd ever known.

No, that wasn't true.

He hadn't forgotten anything, he told himself as he buzzed in Pankin. Captain Nicolai Pankin—who'd loyally and effectively carried out many assignments, including nine that were fatal to others since he'd become the general's right hand and fist—entered the office on the fifth floor of the Foreign Intelligence Service Tower.

General Temkov was not happy here in the wooded country near Yasnevo, half an hour from Moscow. He was cheered, however, by the sight of the two cases filled with money that Pankin had brought from Portugal. His spirits rose even higher and he almost smiled when Pankin respectfully placed the containers packed with U.S. currency on the edge of the large desk.

Temkov *looked* the question.

He didn't have to ask it aloud.

"It went exactly right, General," Pankin said crisply. "Here is the down payment . . . to the penny . . . and they'll be ready to deliver the rest in six or eight weeks when the shipment reaches them."

Temkov pointed at one case.

His aide opened it immediately. He was pleased when he saw his commanding officer nod in approval at the sight of the neat stacks of hundred-dollar bills. Pankin didn't recognize the dead American whose face adorned the money, but the general did.

Franklin . . . Franklin . . . Franklin . . . yes, *Benjamin* Franklin.

Men who thought globally should know about all the major currencies, the general told himself, and he'd thought globally for years.

And schemed globally—killed globally when it was useful—and now he was preparing for what would almost surely be a global massacre. It would certainly be international in scope, with hundreds of thousands of corpses. That didn't trouble him, for the charred horrors would litter the streets of cities in distant lands.

He wouldn't see or smell the dead.

And he'd have more money than he'd ever dreamt of acquiring.

He couldn't help staring at the cash in front of him for several seconds. He reached into the well of his desk to press the buttons. Not the ones that would summon guards, seal the metal door, or fire the remote-control automatic weapon. He'd put that in when he'd read that a Nazi espionage chief named Schellenberg had such a device in the Hitler era.

The buttons Temkov pressed . . . in proper sequence . . . opened the electronic locks that protected each of the desk drawers. The general reached into one that opened silently, removed a very large manila mailing envelope, and carefully filled it with $40,000.

That was several years of wages for a captain in the Foreign Intelligence Service, Temkov thought as he handed the envelope to his aide. He knew that giving the money in hard currency made it worth a great deal more than it would be in rubles, and he had no doubt that Pankin was aware of that as well.

"There'll be more—a lot more—later," the general pledged as he gave the envelope to his faithful aide.

"This . . . this isn't necessary, General," Pankin blurted.

"Please, your work in this delicate and dangerous operation deserves special recognition. This money isn't from the Russian people," Temkov pointed out firmly. "It's from *them*."

For just a split second, Captain Nicolai Pankin considered asking who were the "them," but he immediately told himself that the general would inform him if and when it was appropriate. It might actually be safer for Pankin if he avoided such information, for even in the New Russia an intelligence officer who knew the wrong things could be in mortal danger.

What was it that the Americans said?

He'd then "be part of the problem instead of the solution." People still disappeared. No, he'd trust General Temkov.

It did not occur to him that Temkov was also impressed by some of the strange but meaningful phrases the Americans used. The idea of looking out for Number One . . . taking care of your own interests first . . . had been popular and widespread since the time of the cavemen, and in the siege atmosphere of twenty-first-century Russia it was hardly challenged.

Temkov was going to take care of his own survival and escape. The captain didn't know that his commanding officer had no intention of giving him any more money or loyalty. Temkov was actually a bit rueful that after so much loyal service all he'd deliver to his conscientious aide later was an unmarked grave. The general had never been seen by the buyers, who knew only Pankin. When the sale was completed and the five items exchanged for $25,000,000, there would be just one other man left alive who could link Temkov to the transaction.

It would probably be necessary to kill him, too.

Temkov hadn't decided on whether it should be a suicide or another disappearance. He'd make up his mind about that later.

"Now don't spend a penny of this cash," he told Pankin, "and don't show it to anyone either. I mean *anyone*. That's not advice. That's an order. Hide this money in a place only you know for at least a year . . . two would be better. The last thing we need is to draw somebody's attention."

He saw the uncertainty in Pankin's eyes.

"I don't know *what* somebody," the general said grimly. "Any damn *somebody*. They might steal the money, or tell someone else. They might cut your throat and dump you in the zoo. They might torture you to find out where you got this money."

"I'd never tell."

"I know you wouldn't," the general said, "but we both know that the safest thing for us and this operation—for our nation— is to put this cash and the rest you'll get in absolute deep freeze until I say it's safe to do otherwise."

Pankin vowed that he would. His promise and gratitude for the money—he'd never received anything like this apparent proof of his commander's respect and appreciation—ought to do it, the calculating general reckoned as the devoted captain saluted. Right after Pankin left, Temkov took $400,000 from the case. He extracted from the desk drawer another large envelope and a worn airlines bag.

This money was an essential investment, he thought as he filled the shoulder bag and big envelope. It was to show his good faith to his secret partner, the man who would provide the very special and valuable merchandise that the buyer wanted. Temkov actually had no good faith at all in this entire affair, but he was counting on the human cupidity that made people confuse cash with honor.

Temkov had lied effortlessly and persuasively from the beginning, describing the purchase price as $10,000,000 and not $25,000,000. That came to $2,000,000 for each of the five items, with Temkov agreeing to give half the money—a total of $5,000,00—to his partner. All expenses would come from Temkov's half, and he'd handle all the arrangements and take all the risks.

Temkov's partner was going to be more than deceived. He would be dead. As a veteran of the Cold War's nastiest "wet" operations—K.G.B. terminology for terminations—Temkov had the savvy, equipment, and expert staff that could take care of this and leave no trail. His people were professionals in the no-trail game.

And they feared Temkov.

Their good work was crucial to his plan. With no trail to him, the general wouldn't have to run. If he didn't flee, *they* would assume he had no reason to do so and wouldn't consider him as a possible conspirator in the theft and sale of the five items. They might even ask him to help investigate, but only if they thought the buyer was abroad, for Temkov's turf was outside Russia, and the bureaucrats who ran internal security were keenly guarding their own nasty little world.

With Temkov's partner and the soon superfluous Pankin gone, and no one aware of the more than $24,000,000 he was hiding, General Alexei Temkov would keep his head down for at least eighteen months. New crises and mysteries would inevitably develop. They always had, always would. The incident—that's what the Big Men in the Kremlin would call it—would be an embarrassment they'd want to minimize, hide, and even forget. Lots of things were being stolen, and it wouldn't be pleasant if the press . . . the grouchy public . . . restless politicians . . . and those damn Americans heard of this "incident."

Incident? In today's unsettled and no-rules world, that would be an appropriate term for such a massive theft and massacre, Temkov thought as he stood up from his desk. There were probably ten more such incidents going on, he told himself and looked at the large wall map.

Incidents on every continent, and nobody cared much, he reflected. What he was doing almost certainly wasn't the worst, he judged as he started out the door. General Temkov, like many others in his profession, realized that he wasn't a great humanitarian. He reassured himself that there were plenty of people in other countries—heads of state and army chiefs of staff and some very righteous tribal and religious leaders—who'd ordered more deaths than he ever would.

As he stepped into the corridor, the armed and uniformed guards who flanked the door of his suite snapped to attention. He nodded in mechanical acknowledgment, aware that his rank required such an expected response. Now he walked down the hall to the communications center.

More guards with semiautomatic weapons.

Probably a good idea, Temkov told himself. One couldn't be too paranoid in this business. Enemies and traitors could strike from anywhere at any moment. Thieves might, too, he thought as he considered the $25,000,000 incident in progress, and he smiled.

He was looking stern again a few seconds later when he faced the Night Duty Officer in the communications center. Multiple computers, banks of shortwave radio gear, decoding and encoding machines, and the small legion of technicians who ran them, were visible through the large glass window beside the balding and bespectacled Night Duty Officer.

The chief of the communications shift tensed and swallowed when he saw the general. All generals made him nervous, especially Temkov, whose temper was as well known as his impatience. Temkov wouldn't come here at this hour unless he was troubled. The suddenly sweaty Night Duty Officer braced himself as he cleared his throat.

"Good evening, General," he said correctly.

Temkov ignored this propriety.

"Anna?" he asked bluntly.

"We've continued the transmissions on schedule and the right frequency," the N.D.O. began.

"Anna? Yes or no? *Anything?*" Temkov broke in harshly.

The shift supervisor shook his head.

"I'm sorry, General. We've been carrying out our orders faithfully and fully for weeks now. I've handled the transmissions at least fifty times myself," he reported. "No response. *Nothing.* We've checked and rechecked . . . tested our equipment over and over. I can't think of anything else to try."

Temkov considered the situation and grunted.

"I can," he said in a hard-edged voice and started back to his office.

There were two things he could do to locate Anna.

He'd begin on the first in the morning.

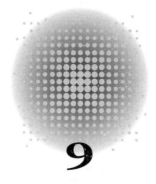

9

THE ST. JOHN INSTITUTE WAS A LIE . . . A VERY WELL-MADE fake.

The bright, clear morning that bloomed there as the five special "packages" ate breakfast was real and—in some odd way—quite encouraging. It was definitely full of promise, or at least it seemed like that to the transplant patients who looked forward to the briefing the director had scheduled.

They wanted to know.

Why had they been saved . . . and abducted?

Exactly who was running this operation . . . and why did they need transplant people instead of fierce, ready-to-roll commandos . . . and precisely what was the dangerous mission ahead?

It had to be extremely hazardous to justify the unusual money already spent and the big wages promised to them yesterday. They would surely be going into mortal danger, so they had a real right to know . . . now.

It was time.

They were glad that the games the cautious director had been playing were about to end, Denny Monroe thought as he finished his coffee. He was a bit surprised and a little amused that they didn't realize that Charlotte Willson had more games . . . and then more.

She wasn't malicious. That was her nature and her training. Her motives weren't evil, but she'd be playing games as her death certificate was being signed.

Maybe after that, he told himself.

The orderlies—including the one he'd disarmed—arrived with the wheelchairs. They didn't say a word as they took charge of moving the five cloak-and-dagger professionals down to the large room where they'd first met Charlotte Willson and each other.

Well, *seen*. They still didn't know each other.

Kelly's People, Monroe thought again suddenly, and he still didn't know why.

Once the five were seated in the big armchairs, the director simply pointed at the rear door of the conference room, and the white-clad orderlies left immediately. The director of The St. John Institute scanned the recovering patients, nodded as if to punctuate an unspoken sentence only she heard, and offered the neo-friendly smile she'd been rehearsing since she awoke.

"Let me start by saying this will be a rewarding learning experience for all of us," she told them.

"Excuse me," Monroe said.

"Yes?"

"Is the meter running?"

She considered the peculiar question for a few seconds before the woman who played chess so well translated.

"I think Denny wants to know when we get on the payroll."

"You've been on it since the minute . . . the second . . . you got here."

Monroe raised his right hand in thumbs-up approval.

That was his gun hand, the director thought automatically. Where the hell was the goddam weapon?

She sighed, then continued purposefully.

"I'll speak with each of you separately after this briefing to make payment arrangements that suit you. We're very flexible," she assured them.

Another five seconds of that motivational-speaker smile. Then back to her scripted litany.

"Your health and rate of recovery will be the primary considerations as we start the training," she said. "We'll continue the daily physicals to make sure that every one of you—we know you're all different medically—is doing well and free of any stress."

They were probably searching his room again for the pistol, he guessed. He was right.

"The first phase of this training will focus on communication and teamwork," she announced. "Personal communication within the group should be strengthened to build trust and confidence."

"How are we going to do that?" the blonde woman asked.

"If we . . . you . . . understand each other and learn to think like each other, it'll be as if we're on the same wave length . . . in a manner of speaking."

"What manner is that?" Harry Chen tested.

"She'll get to it," Monroe predicted, and Charlotte Willson was pleased that he was being helpful.

Pleased for about three seconds.

"First, let's cut to the chase," he urged briskly. "What's the team song?"

Susan Kincaid didn't need her analytical skills as a chess player to judge what he was doing . . . and shake her head.

"He's baad, but he's got a point," she said to the uncertain director of The St. John Institute.

Denny Monroe was behaving like some wise-ass and nearly nasty yuppie, Willson thought, but she couldn't and wouldn't let him bait her. She was going to use him. She couldn't let this turn into a personality conflict—for various reasons. One of them was that he was an expert in violence.

And he had the damn gun.

"I'd be grateful if you'd spell out the point," she lied.

"And I'd be grateful . . . I suspect we all would be . . . if we move on to specifics," he said. "The five of us are alive for just two reasons. First, the transplants . . . for which we thank you.

Second, we are very careful—you could say *obsessive*—about specifics. Field agents who aren't die young."

"Of course. I have no problem with specifics. I was about to share a number of them with you, and every one of you can certainly ask questions at any time."

"*Now* would be a good time," he said. "I don't mean to pry, but I figure it might be a terrific time."

The other "packages" nodded immediately.

"Let's get to it," Willson responded with another of those restaurant-hostess smiles. It didn't bother Denny Monroe. He wasn't used to sincerity anyway.

"Where will the training be given?"

"This building."

"How long?"

"An hour a day the first week . . . two the second . . . three after that."

"How many weeks?" Cesar Fuentes wondered.

She hesitated to phrase her reply.

"Our protocol for this phase of the training is based on an average of eight weeks, but it could be that some people will need double, maybe triple, that."

"To do what? What's the objective?"

"Effective interpersonal communication . . . one on one to start. Later, it should be a group thing," she explained. "It won't be physically or mentally exhausting, but it will be work. It'll be new for all of us."

"This is an experimental program?" yellow-haired Paula Taylor asked.

Monroe answered before the director could.

"Not a program . . . an operation. Right?"

"Both," Willson said.

She saw Harry Chen frown.

"You still haven't said how we're to communicate better after this training," he thought aloud. "Is this some sort of speech-inflection or body-language thing?"

The head of The St. John Institute took a deep breath.

"What I'm about to tell you is more than Top Secret," she

started. "It's that other classification. The one I can't even mention."

Was it ULTRA, or had the Pentagon come up with two or three even higher and more intimidating classifications, the "packages" wondered.

"You cannot . . . under any circumstances . . . say a word about this . . . ever," Willson warned intensely.

"Deal," Monroe responded.

Then the others spoke in unison.

"Deal," they concurred.

"That's fine," the director approved. "Now . . . it's a formality . . . we're asking you to sign this secrecy oath so I can get on to the specifics of how this will progress."

She opened the folder she held to take out a sheaf of papers. First, she handed one of the multiple copies to each of this unique team. Next, she picked up from the table beside her five Plexiglas clipboards and the same number of plastic ballpoint pens. These cheap and ordinary-looking writing tools were inscribed LAS VEGAS HILTON.

Nice joke, Monroe judged.

Usual compulsory deception crap. They weren't in any Hilton, and surely not in Nevada. He didn't know where this "Institute" was, but he knew the rules of the game. If the pen said Las Vegas, the five transplant patients must be a long way from that glitzy desert resort.

Harry Chen was the first to finish reading the agreement. He paused before he began to go over the text again. He suddenly stopped once more, and looked over questioningly to the man who had an implicit, intangible air of leadership. There was *something* that made him trust Monroe's judgment.

"Paragraph three, right?" Monroe said. "You want to know how they'd cancel our employment if there's a security breach?"

Chen nodded.

"Tell him, Cesar," Monroe urged.

"They'd cancel us, friend," Fuentes said. "Nothing to stop them, Harry. We're already dead."

"That's preposterous," the director of The St. John Institute declared.

They all knew that she was lying and that they had no choice. Each of them signed the forms. Willson collected the pages, avoiding eye contact as she put the agreements in her folder and resumed her presentation.

"In addition to the cyclosporine tablets you're getting to fight off rejection of the organs transplanted," she began, "you each receive injections every day. These deliver very special and new medication."

"Figures," Monroe said. "We're new and special, too. What is this stuff?"

"Literally millions of dollars and thousands of hours of work by very imaginative scientists have gone into perfecting this serum," she continued.

"What the *fuck* is it?" Paula Taylor blurted impatiently.

Willson absorbed the impact of the crude word and continued.

"It's a strength serum. Not for your body . . . for your mind. It is a breakthrough."

"This isn't *Stargate*?" Susan Kincaid asked. "Not that long-distance viewing number that the C.I.A. and the Pentagon dumped twenty million dollars into years ago?"

Monroe remembered it.

"Toilet time, wasn't it? Official word was it went down the sewer . . . no significant results, they said."

He paused and shrugged.

"Maybe," he reasoned. "Moscow was supposed to be testing a similar operation . . . plus something else with psychics trying to get into the heads of top American government and military leaders. According to The Tooth Fairy, the Sovs dumped those programs, too."

The head of The St. John Institute looked puzzled.

"What Tooth Fairy?" she asked.

"That's strictly classified," Monroe answered. "It was Cold War time. Wall-to-wall tooth fairies, and the sit coms and game shows were even worse than they are now."

Charlotte Willson glared before she shook her head.

"This is *not* Stargate," she announced, "and it has nothing to do with remote viewing. We're working . . . the object of the serum is to help you communicate with each other. Mentally."

"Telepathy?" Chen tested.

Willson nodded.

"This is better than The Tooth Fairy, Denny," judged the analytical-minded woman who played chess so well and thought even better.

Cesar Fuentes' reaction was more concise.

"Jesus Christ!" he said.

"Buddha, Mohammed, and the Lord of the Israelites, too," Monroe agreed. "Let's not leave out the Hindu deities, and the others. You really think we can communicate telepathically?"

"All our research says it should work . . . under the right conditions," Willson answered stiffly.

"And this magical serum can permit anyone to do this?" Monroe pressed.

It was almost as if the son of a bitch knew, she thought.

"It's a matter of the right conditions," she fenced.

He considered what she'd said and hadn't said, then pulled open his robe to show the operation's scar.

"Would those goddam conditions have anything to do with *this*?" he demanded.

"They would, Denny. The serum is not likely to support telepathic communication between people who don't have certain things in common."

"It has to be more than the fact we've had transplants," he reasoned.

He saw the tension in her eyes.

"There's something unusual about these transplants?" he guessed.

"I was planning to tell you when you were stronger," she assured them.

"What is it? Some kind of computer chip?" Chen asked.

"We've done nothing mechanical or electronic," Willson said. "Each of you got a lifesaving transplant of a regular healthy organ from a very recently deceased human being. The source of the organs is what is somewhat unusual."

"I think we've a right to know the rest," Monroe announced.

He was already speaking for the group. That was all right,

she told herself. She'd expected him to emerge as the leader. The psychological profiles and his record had strongly suggested it.

"Tell us what's special about the donors," he demanded.

"Male . . . highly intelligent . . . thirty-six years old . . . familiar with covert operations."

It took Monroe about three seconds to grasp the significance of what she'd said.

"*One* donor?" he wondered.

"We didn't plan this," she replied, "but we would have if we'd thought it was possible. He died in an accident, and when the specialists tested for matches, it came out perfect."

"One donor for all of us?" Susan Kincaid asked.

"Male and Caucasian. Hope that's no problem. It's better than being dead, you know."

"I'm not an idiot," the African-American woman said in a voice edged with irritation.

"It's better than an urn," Monroe declared, then considered what else they weren't being told.

"I knew you'd be sensible about all this," Charlotte Willson said hopefully.

"All *what*? There's more, isn't there?"

As she hesitated for a moment, he calculated that she'd soon—and compulsively—launch another search for the gun.

"I can't think of anything," she evaded.

"Like which U.S. intelligence organization this unfortunate donor ran with? Was it the Bloods?"

Willson was getting fed up with his provocations.

Then she realized he was probably doing it to trick her into giving them more information than she wanted to at this time.

"That's not funny," she told him. "The Bloods are—if the media are correct—a violent, criminal, and often homicidal street gang, a network of street gangs. This donor . . . who saved all your lives . . . was *not* associated with any street gangs. He had a college education and no criminal record."

She wasn't shouting, but her rising annoyance was visible.

"Denny, why don't we hear Doctor Willson out and ask any questions then?" proposed sensible Harry Chen, who didn't believe this was the time for any differences or disruptions.

Monroe had no problem with the suggestion. He was less comfortable with the fact that the director of The St. John Institute hadn't answered the question about which branch of the American government's cloak-and-dagger community had been home to the donor.

It couldn't be an oversight or accident.

Those things didn't happen in Dr. Willson's intensely efficient Institute.

A second later, the man who was emerging as the team leader found himself wondering whether the donor's death had *really* been an accident after all. If these anything-goes people running this operation *needed* those organs that matched so well, someone might have at least considered accelerating the donor's demise.

It might look exactly like an accident . . . in every detail. Covert-operations units of all the major powers . . . and more than a few minor ones . . . knew how to orchestrate an assortment of not quite fortuitous departures, Monroe thought and shrugged.

There'd be no profit in saying it. He didn't.

Now he "heard" in his head again those puzzling two words. *Kelly's People.*

What did this mean? His instincts told him that the phrase was significant—maybe dangerous—and he lived by his instincts. He decided that Charlotte Willson had the answer, and a reason for keeping it from them.

He'd find out, Monroe promised himself, and he'd get the answer to the other question. How did this phrase get into his mind? This whole nameless operation by some anonymous cloak-and-dagger entity was . . . as far as the five transplant survivors had been told . . . a *mind* thing. The experienced personnel kidnapped for this—all of them veteran field agents—suggested that there'd be something a lot more physical and hazardous down the line.

They'd be in harm's way. At risk.

Did the two words relate to the danger ahead, or to something else?

Charlotte Willson—or whatever her name was—was speaking about how they'd be participating in a "history-making program" that would "advance the frontiers of science." The director of The St. John Institute was shameless, Monroe thought casually. No problem. Shameless was nothing new to him. He was, however, a bit disappointed that she'd try to manipulate veteran field agents with the kind of trash-talk clichés usually featured in presentations of new video games and dandruff remedies . . . and at televised hearings of congressional committees.

She thought she was selling up a storm, the man with the gun judged as he studied her. Maybe she was, in her own way, an innocent, another cynical innocent. She finished her paragraph . . . it sounded almost prerecorded . . . before she gave out sheets of paper listing individual what-where-when training schedules for the next week.

She raised to her lips a slim, tubular walkie-talkie.

Seconds later, the inevitable orderlies arrived to wheel each of them back to their rooms for injections and more rest. Monroe managed to delay so he'd be the last one to leave.

"Doctor Willson?" he asked in a totally nonconfrontational tone.

She eyed him warily.

"Doctor Willson? Are you a medical doctor?"

"I have a doctorate," she evaded stiffly.

"Mind if I ask just one more question?"

"Of course not, Denny," she replied primly.

It wasn't going to work, he thought, but it was worth trying.

"Doctor Willson, I heard something I don't understand," he announced.

"Yes?"

"Doctor Willson . . . Kelly's People."

He watched for her reaction. He saw her freeze.

"Doctor Willson, who are Kelly's People?"

She knew that something had gone wrong.

She also knew that there was no way she'd reply truthfully.

She pretended to consider his question.

"Sorry, Denny," she answered. "I have no idea. Is it some new rock group?"

"I don't know."

His source of the information . . . who'd leaked it . . . was more than important, she realized.

"Why not ask the person who told you about this . . . these . . . Kelly People?" she suggested.

He shook his head.

"I don't know who told me," he confessed.

She didn't believe him . . . and decided that only a complete security review could get the answer. She'd start it immediately.

"Maybe it will come to you. See you later," she said, and walked away so he couldn't continue this dangerous conversation.

She looked grim. Monroe, on the other hand, was smiling as the orderly wheeled him back to his room. He'd found out what he'd suspected. She had the information about Kelly's People. In due course . . . in some way . . . he'd get it from her.

Or from whoever put those words in his head in the first place.

10

THERE WERE EIGHT OF THEM.

Seven men and one woman. Two assault teams.

Between the eight, they carried the passports of five different countries. All these documents were rather good forgeries. The silenced pistols, automatic weapons, and surface-to-air missiles these idealistic imposters also carried were quite authentic and in perfect working condition.

These lethal tools had been supplied . . . free of charge . . . to some other people by the Americans years ago. Those other people had been well trained in the use of these killing instruments by the Americans, and sometime later, those other people shared this knowledge with the holy organization that had sent these two assault units.

It was obvious that mathematics was taught badly in the United States, the pious leader of the holy organization had said before the eight left on this mission. The imperialists in Washington knew so little about elementary geometry that they couldn't project the parabola . . . couldn't predict where the arc might end.

Hassan al Wadi, who'd studied mathematics and comparative literature at Oxford University in England, was right. It had not seemed reasonable to the practical operations types at the Central Intelligence Agency or the policy wonks at the National Security Council . . . very serious and busy people with really hot state-of-the-art computers and outstanding data banks . . . that groups the U.S. trained and armed in sophisticated and expensive covert operations might not *stay* long-term allies.

If there was anything such as a long-term ally anymore.

If there ever had been.

Memories and gratitude are brief . . . ethnic, national, and religious hatreds thrive irrationally and poisonously for many centuries and the Americans are easily distracted by issues such as fluoridation and single-sex matrimony. In such a world, Hassan al Wadi had found it relatively easy to put his assault teams in place here.

HERE: EAST AFRICA in the young nation that now called itself Matamba and was earning a nice flow of cash from stamp collectors around the world who had to own three of everything. Unrecorded bribes from executives of dozens of large foreign companies nearly matched the country's additional income from such traditional Matamban enterprises as cotton growing and diamond smuggling.

Economic and military aid from the U.S.A. was a significant factor in the plans of this well-meaning and adolescent republic. That's why so many prominent people were gathered at this place at this time. The place was the national airport seven miles from the capital. The time was just before sunset on the day that the director of The St. John Institute told the five transplant patients about the telepathy project.

It was actually only nine minutes after Denny Monroe asked about Kelly's People, but the longitude thing with east-west changes by Greenwich time rules made it considerably later in Eastern Africa. That didn't bother either al Wadi's commandos or the dozens of important or would-be important Matamban officials who were waiting for the U.S. Air Force jet transport.

It was bringing in the usual U.S. combination.

An assistant Secretary of State, a two-star Army general from the international security division, and a mission of economic and medical experts who'd negotiate the details of an expanded trade and health program.

With loan guarantees.

Commitments for water-purification gear . . . school books . . . and additional advisers on fighting several widespread fevers, a nasty jump in HIV virus cases, and some leftover and left-wing guerrillas. In terms of dollars, it wasn't a major outlay, but Matamba wasn't a Big League player and nobody else was offering very much to this needy nation.

Now the air-traffic controller in the tower picked up a cell phone . . . Matamba wasn't entirely backward . . . and called down with word that the U.S.A.F. plane would land in three or four minutes. Everyone waiting under the canvas canopy outside the terminal smiled.

The money bird was coming.

Except in the presence of the American Embassy crowd, that's what the down-to-earth Matambans were calling it. There it was—a growing dot on the horizon, accompanied by the shriek and thunder of powerful jet engines. The brightly uniformed members of the thirty-two-piece Matamban military band stood straighter. As soon as the money bird pulled to a halt ninety or a hundred yards from the waiting dignitaries . . . as the first American came down the steps . . . the musicians would launch into "The Star Spangled Banner," which they had been practicing for more than a week.

They had it down cold.

Note for note.

It was really a shame they didn't get to play it.

The big jet looked so shiny . . . so modern . . . so American as it descended smoothly toward the end of the main runway. It was down to thirteen hundred feet when this process stopped abruptly. Instead of coming in gracefully, it fell down in a rain of metal pieces.

Right after the twin explosions.

Direct hits by a pair of obsolete but still effective ground-to-air missiles will cause such noisy devastation. The Stingers from the U.S. infantry arsenal were old but reliable, seven of the commandos thought. The eighth . . . the woman . . . was too busy videotaping the attack to consider such abstractions.

The transport was blown to pieces, as were most of those it carried. A few of the corpses remained intact, but so badly charred by the terrible fires that it was going to take dental records to identify them. This whole area of the airfield was a classic CNN horror show, though that television news organization had nothing to do with this terrorist massacre.

The network wasn't to blame if a lot of people around the world saw its coverage of the flaming wreckage and the body bags three hours later. The public had a right to see, and at least one highly intelligent and homicidal person had an urgent *need* to see. As the head of the Holy Liberation Front, Hassan al Wadi knew it was his duty to see and celebrate what his commandos had accomplished. He was grateful that God and CNN were making this possible.

He kept staring at the carnage on the big television screen.

"Excellent . . . excellent," he judged professionally.

He knew a lot about slaughter, as well as the sacred books of his own and other faiths, . . . he was a twenty-first-century Renaissance Man. Now he looked up for a moment as his most trusted aide, Karim—who'd delivered the cash on the Portuguese ferry—entered this innermost part of the multichamber cave. Heavily guarded and so well-hidden that it would be very difficult for even American smart bombs to pinpoint, the underground complex had been the Front's command center for almost half a year.

Now al Wadi pointed a bony finger at the television set.

"They did a fine job, didn't they?" he exulted as his eyes scanned the dozens of body bags and the ruined airliner.

"First-class," Karim agreed. "And we've just had word that all our people got away clean. They'll be here in two days with video of the attack itself."

The leader of the Holy Liberation Front could afford to smile for only a few seconds. Then al Wadi, a tall and round-shouldered man of fifty-one who had a properly untrimmed graying beard nine inches long and a great deal of hatred for a lot of different people and countries, looked ahead as military commanders and other great men should.

"I'm sure we'll enjoy it," he told Karim, "but we won't have much time for that. I want the rest of the twenty-five million dollars here by the end of next week. We have to be ready to pay as soon as our friend can deliver the merchandise."

"I'll have it all no later than Monday," Karim promised.

"And our arrangements for the three cities?"

"Our people are in place, and they know exactly what to do when they get your order."

"Check *again*," al Wadi pressed. "I want every detail checked now, and again when we have the merchandise. This has to go exactly right . . . and precisely on time."

"It will. You have my word," Karim assured him sincerely.

When the aide left, the head of the Holy Liberation Front concentrated entirely on the twenty-five-inch screen. The camera was slowly panning again, permitting al Wadi to count the corpses once more—26 . . . 27 . . . 28 . . . 29 . . . 30 . . . 31 . . . 32. . . .

Now the unseen American reporter was announcing that another two bodies—parts of two bodies—had been found. That brought the total to thirty-four, he noted soberly.

Not too bad, al Wadi told himself. Yes, thirty-four was a good effort.

Of course it wouldn't compare with the dozens of thousands . . . no, scores of thousands . . . of corpses that would join them soon.

11

ANOTHER CHILLY NIGHT IN MOSCOW.

The operation Temkov had ordered to bring Anna home had begun.

A tough and competent lieutenant named Valchenko—a real hardcase—was waiting with two other security agents in a car a block and a half from the Bolshoi Theater. Three more members of his unit were in an unmarked van parked across the street.

Five minutes past six o'clock. In the Russian capital.

It was noisy . . . drivers sounding horns . . . a steady flow of vehicles contesting for the right and wrong of way.

The streets were crowded with pedestrians hurrying hopefully to shops to make purchases on their way home. The walkers strode purposefully between beggars and peddlers, old women selling soap or candy or pens or cheap lighters to supplement pensions no longer adequate.

Valchenko looked at his bulky steel wristwatch.

Where the hell was the bitch?

It helped to think of her as a bitch though she'd shown no signs of meanness or evil. Valchenko knew that if he were in her situation . . . in her country . . . he'd act as she had. He blinked his tired eyes, trying not to think about the trouble—maybe bloodshed—coming when they grabbed her.

This was a violation of international law. It had been made clear to Valchenko that the general felt this woman was much more important than any law—local, international, or galactic. It wouldn't matter whether the Americans complained . . . denounced . . . or threatened.

Like the old times, Valchenko thought.

Looking ahead through the windshield of his sedan, he asked himself why this was happening *now*. They'd had her under visual and electronic surveillance for fourteen months. Her routine hadn't changed a bit, and the scope of her activities hadn't grown at all.

Why had Temkov ordered them to kidnap her tonight?

Valchenko scanned the sidewalk again, aware that he'd probably never learn why or what the general meant to do to or with her. The bare-bones orders had simply stated that she was to be scooped up here . . . this evening . . . and delivered unharmed to Safe House Five.

With not a mark on her.

Not a scratch . . . not a bruise.

The instructions had been specific on that. It shouldn't be a problem, Valchenko reasoned, for he had the kit and experience in using it. Still, the reality was that these matters couldn't be controlled completely. Something could go wrong, and Valchenko would surely be blamed if it did.

There she was . . . several minutes ahead of schedule. The damn Americans probably taught their field people to do that as we do, the tense lieutenant told himself. He was perspiring.

He picked up his walkie-talkie.

"Stand by. Not a mark on her," he reminded the men in the van.

"Not a mark," the sergeant twenty-five yards away confirmed.

She was neatly dressed in low-heeled shoes and clothes that wouldn't stand out too much, a pleasant-looking woman in her late thirties wearing eyeglasses and modest makeup. As she reached the bookstore, she paused to look into the window as if to study the new volumes being displayed. She was, of course, checking the plate glass to observe who might be behind or near her.

As she usually did when she entered, she first dawdled at the shelves of books on Russian poets, and then the composers and virtuoso musicians . . . and looked around once more. Her visual sweep complete, she made her way to the art volumes. This part of the shop concealed her blind drop.

Tonight it was an illustrated study of Georgian icons that held the microdot from her contact. She took it to the clerk at the cash register, paid for the book and put it in a shabby cloth shopping bag she'd brought in her large purse. She nodded politely and walked from the store.

So far, so good.

That changed a few seconds later when the security agent seated beside Valchenko got out of the car and strode swiftly toward her. His right hand concealed a small plastic squeeze bottle. He "accidentally" bumped into her so hard she nearly dropped her shopping bag.

The man with the squeeze bottle apologized . . . briefly.

Then he squirted the aerosol spray into her face at close range.

"Now," Valchenko said into his small radio.

As arranged, a car screeched to a halt at the far end of the block to avoid hitting an aged man tottering into the street. The sound of the brakes drew every eye to the near accident. Cursing loudly, the badly dressed graybeard who reeked of alchohol held people's attention for some fifteen seconds.

That was all the time Valchenko's grab-and-run required.

The chemical spray dazed the American woman long enough for one security agent to seize her shopping bag and two others to hustle her into the rear of the sedan. The car rolled off as soon as the door slammed behind her.

Another squirt of the powerful spray.

She was helpless now . . . would be for hours. It didn't take that long to deliver her to Safe House Five. Another team was waiting as the sedan moved carefully down the alley to the rear entrance, masked by a fence. When the car stopped, three men immediately emerged from the safe house to carry the unconscious C.I.A. agent inside.

Her diplomatic immunity as a member of the U.S. Embassy staff wouldn't help her here, Valchenko thought. There must be something big in the air, he told himself. Then he pointed the index finger of his right hand straight ahead.

"Let's go," he ordered.

By the time the car reached the end of the alley, two more of General Temkov's operatives were entering the building in which the kidnapped woman lived. They had, of course, keys to the street entrance and to her apartment. Inside, they moved swiftly and purposefully. They filled a suitcase from her hall closet with a few garments from her bedroom.

Two simple dresses . . . three sets of underwear . . . one pair of shoes . . . two of pantyhose.

The security agents collected all the bottles with her various medications from the bathroom. No cosmetics, deodorants, powders, or perfumes—nothing that might reassure her. She was supposed to be isolated totally from her regular support systems.

Now her cat cried.

They had specific orders about the tan Siamese. They poured water from the sink into the pet's saucer . . . did nothing to fill the food bowl.

The agents assumed that there must be a reason or meaning in these orders that didn't seem to make any sense. The two intruders glanced at each other . . . shook their heads . . . and opened two drawers of the bedroom dresser. Temkov's men took five knives from a kitchen drawer . . . put them in the refrigerator before leaving the apartment.

They didn't make the call on the cell phone until they were a dozen blocks away.

"Hello, Mischa. Hello, Mischa. We're on our way to the house."

That meant they'd executed the instructions.

They didn't expect any answer, and there was none.

* * *

BY TEN-THIRTY THE NEXT MORNING, Kathleen Fitzgerald was wondering when Alison Wilk might be coming to work. Ms. Fitzgerald was the keep-your-mouth-shut secretary who assisted Ms. Wilk, who was also in the assisting business in the Russian capital. Ms. Wilk was an assistant cultural attaché (films) at the U.S. Embassy. Being an energetic person, as well as a collector of movie posters, she was able to cover her diplomatic duties in a few hours daily and had plenty of time for her other job. She was one of a classified number of Central Intelligence Agency professionals operating with diplomatic immunity in Moscow in a manner similar to that of the agents of Russia's S.V.R.—successor to the old-hat K.G.B.—working the District of Columbia. They were attached to the Russian Embassy in Washington, providing employment for hundreds of conscientious F.B.I. personnel who watched and listened.

Both sides knew about it.

The game was as old as adultery or tax evasion, and usually not as dangerous under the established rules.

Someone had broken the rules.

Kathleen Fitzgerald didn't realize this at first. In the twenty-three months that Alison Wilk had been in Moscow, she'd made a point of being at her desk by 9:30 A.M., in any kind of weather. On the few occasions when she was ill or had duties that would keep her off that schedule, she'd always called in advance.

Not this morning.

That wasn't like her, judged Kate Fitzgerald, who also served the C.I.A., but she wasn't quite worried.

By eleven o'clock, she was concerned, and began to consider sharing this with the cheerful mustachioed man who was the Agency's able Station Chief. It was probably premature, she decided. Alison Wilk would be phoning or arriving at any minute.

Ms. Fitzgerald waited until 11:55 A.M. to make up her mind to signal the concern to the head of the Moscow station. She was reaching for the phone to do that when it rang. This had to be Alison, she thought and smiled.

She stopped smiling when she heard the man's voice and what he said.

He spoke in Russian-accented English . . . a cold hard tone.

"She's not coming. Feed the cat."

Click.

There was unspoken menace in that voice, even if the words carried no specific threat. Those six words—from a man who'd given no name or explanation—were enough to make Kate Fitzgerald dial the private line of the Station Chief.

She wasn't about to discuss the situation on the phone.

Though the embassy and its interior telephone system were checked for listening devices every sixty days, it was assumed that the S.V.R. might be listening.

The Station Chief picked up his telephone.

"This is Kate Fitzgerald," she said evenly. "Is Stuart McIvor there?"

"Try the Press Office," the chief of station replied as prear-ranged.

The name "Stuart McIvor" meant a possible security problem. That was something to be discussed in the "clean" room . . . the Plexiglas bubble that was (a) swept for electronic bugs every week, (b) itself in a locked room whose door was flanked by armed guards. It was a bit dramatic, but it seemed to work.

Kate Fitzgerald and the chief of station were in the bubble for less than a minute. She told him that Alison Wilk hadn't called or come to work . . . then relayed the six words.

"Feed the cat?" he thought aloud. "Somebody wants us to know she won't be back soon."

Fitzgerald swallowed, nodded.

"I'll take it from here," he said. "We'll have someone in to sweep her office for bugs in about ten minutes, and I guess we ought to feed the cat."

Four embassy people—the Station Chief was taking no chances on some sort of trap—went to the apartment. The head of the Moscow station had provided a key. Thinking ahead, they brought three cans of cat food from the embassy commissary. They fed the hungry feline, and left enough for the next day.

Two of the Americans stayed just in case *she* might return.

When the other two told the chief of station what they'd found, including the knives in the refrigerator, he concluded that the edged cutting things could be a warning . . . a threat. He knew that Alison Wilk wouldn't do anything as strange as putting the knives there. That made no sense, and she was sensible.

It must have been the man who phoned about the cat who left them there.

If *they* had her—and they didn't want the Siamese to starve— it might mean that they didn't plan for Alison Wilk to die either. Of course this was all speculation . . . maybe cloak-and-dagger trade frostbite left over from the still-thawing Cold War, the chief of station calculated.

He couldn't be sure.

One thing was certain, however. The manual was very clear on that. Agency headquarters at Langley had to receive a heads-up alert—carefully phrased as a "preliminary" report—that would keep the staff wizards (a) informed, and (b) off his back for the moment. He didn't need any premature overreaction. The situation might not be as bad as he suspected.

Or it could be worse, he thought bitterly as he reached for a page from the security message pad. He made a draft of his report—rewrote it twice—before he was reasonably satisfied and sent it to the crypto room for encoding. It was en route to Langley in nineteen minutes.

Now the chief of station waited to hear from Langley . . . or from the man who'd called . . . or from Alison Wilk herself. It was possible, he told himself.

The hours slipped away.

Darkness came to Moscow, and there was no message about or from his missing agent. There had to be a logical and pro-fessional . . . a proper intelligence community . . . reason for this, he worried.

A number of possibilities came to mind, but not the right one.

He didn't know about Anna, or what made Anna so special.

12

MONROE WASN'T GOING TO LIKE THIS AT ALL, THE DIRECTOR
of The St. John Institute thought. Since she didn't like him, the
prospect pleased her, and she smiled.

It was the fourth day of the individual telepathy training sessions . . . uneventful thus far . . . just a beginning. The doctors
had said to Charlotte Willson that she should tell them now.
Both the two senior transplant physicians and the psychiatrist
agreed that it was time.

The patients had to know what was coming.

Charlotte Willson didn't mind bringing the news, for it might
well serve her nonmedical purpose. She was still more than
bothered by Monroe's totally unexpected question about Kelly's
People. He had to be deflected from that subject. This medical
briefing could be a useful diversion.

It should certainly seize Monroe's attention.

Life-and-death issues usually did that with almost anyone
who wasn't psychotic, she reasoned. Dennis Monroe's whole
file made it clear that he was as dangerous as any psychotic,
but he wasn't one. That was the "beauty" of the man they'd
named Dennis Monroe, she judged professionally. As much as
he troubled her, she couldn't help admiring him.

He was a very special son of a bitch . . . a valuable one. Possibly invaluable.

He probably knew that, she thought and looked at her wristwatch. Nine-ten. The transplant patients would be finishing their unhurried breakfast. The medical team had insisted on a schedule with minimum stress . . . nothing that might interfere with either physical recovery or growing mental strength and focus.

She'd planned this briefing carefully.

The patients had plenty of time before they went to their training. They'd be strongest in the morning, and the injections of the yellow serum could wait until noon. So far, there'd been no rejection crises, but the doctors said you never could tell.

You couldn't predict what might come to these patients.

Or when.

Of course lots of physicians said that about many other medical "conditions" . . . that was a word they loved. Now Charlotte Willson felt a surge of remembered anger, and immediately pushed it down into that crowded interior place she was so skilled at ignoring. The fact that it was illogical for the director of The St. John Institute—which was so deeply involved in and dependent on medical experts—to resent doctors was something she ignored completely.

For now. She'd get to that later.

The door at the back of the dining room opened, and the three doctors appeared. One of the two surgeons was a trim female. The psychiatrist was a salt-and-pepper-haired male. The transplant patients looked at the three strangers, wondered silently, and waited.

Charlotte Willson took charge.

"Things are going well, and we think you're entitled to know about the next phase of your medical program," she said. "There's going to be some fine-tuning plus a lot of information so you'll understand why. I'll let Doctor Brown explain."

The older man in the white M.D. jacket stepped forward.

Whoever he was, Monroe thought, his name wasn't Brown.

They didn't give away anything at The St. John Institute.

"Let me introduce myself," the senior physician began. "Each of you is alive and here because you had the benefit of an operation by a nationally known transplant surgeon of great experience. I'm told that I can't give you my resume, but I can tell you that I've done over three hundred livers myself."

"You didn't do all our transplants?" Cesar Fuentes tested.

"Impossible," the surgeon replied. "There are literally thousands of transplants each year . . . spread across the country in over two hundred hospitals that have the very expensive equipment and specialized surgeons working with expert teams."

"The governing word is 'specialized,'" volunteered the woman beside him. "This isn't slice-and-dice, friends."

"Doctor Green is a highly respected transplant surgeon who's done hundreds of these organ procedures in the past nine years," the older physician told them.

"Same hospital as you?" Monroe asked.

"Her specialty is another organ. Many of the hospitals have transplant programs that focus on a single organ. I believe that several hospitals were involved in treating your group."

"How many?" Harry Chen questioned.

No answer.

"Four? Five?" Chen tested.

"It doesn't really matter," the liver-transplant specialist fenced as Charlotte Willson nodded.

"What hospital are *you* with?" Monroe asked, with no hope of a serious reply.

The surgeon eyed him warily . . . then remembered the warning.

"You're Monroe, aren't you?" he said.

"About as much as you're Brown."

The psychiatrist shook his head. He'd heard about Monroe, too.

"I'll move on to the fine-tuning now," the transplant surgeon announced abruptly. "You've been getting a daily course of a broad-band antirejection pill named cyclosporine along with . . . let's call it the yellow serum."

"Is there another name for it?" the multilingual black woman probed.

"I won't bore you with the technical stuff," the liver specialist dodged.

"What's in it, Doc?" Monroe pressed.

"It's a secret, Mr. Monroe. Let's say it's good for you and your mental-communication skills. I didn't develop it, and I won't tell you who did."

"You don't know," Monroe guessed. "*They* didn't tell you."

The surgeon evaded the provocation.

"You've all done so nicely that we can proceed to a more comprehensive program of medication that should serve you well in the next phase of your recovery," he declared. "You'll be getting an assortment of pills . . . a very carefully selected set of fourteen for daily ingestion."

He saw that they were surprised and bothered.

"They're to be taken at specific times," he continued. "You will receive written instructions and a special box in which to keep them safe . . . clean . . . in proper order. You must follow the regime precisely."

"And if we don't, we'll die . . . right?" Monroe challenged.

The psychiatrist felt it was time for therapeutic intervention.

"We're trying very hard to help you," he said soothingly.

Monroe studied him for several seconds.

"I'm Doctor White," the man told him.

"Shrink?"

The psychiatrist nodded.

"Yes . . . and I understand why you're frightened. If I'd just come through a life-threatening medical crisis and something as strange as a transplant . . . well, I'd be frightened, too."

"Who said I'm frightened?"

"Anyone might be, but you can handle it. And if you're not frightened, I have another suggestion."

"Yes?"

"Shut up and hear us out."

Charlotte Willson winced, but Monroe smiled.

"I'm listening, Doc," he announced.

Now the female surgeon took over the briefing.

"I'll start with some numbers you might find reassuring," she began. "We're doing about twenty-three thousand transplants of solid organs every year in this country. Heart, lung, liver, kidney, pancreas, and intestine . . . those are the solid organs we can handle so far. The number of transplants is growing all the time. Could be over twenty-five thousand next year."

"Question?" Harry Chen asked.

"Any time."

"What's the survival rate?"

She sat down calmly on the edge of a table.

Not bad legs, Fuentes judged.

Pure reflex.

"Our definition of survival may not match yours," she told them, "and the definition is changing. Now it's up to—don't freak—four years plus. That's sort of an average. Well, we know that you're not average people. You're strong and young—in your peak years. I have no doubt that you'll do significantly better than four years."

"Unless somebody kills us in the field," the patient with the yellow hair reasoned aloud.

The other four nodded.

"Or this building catches fire," the surgeon added archly.

"It's completely fireproof. Sprinklers everywhere . . . modern extinguishers . . . state-of-the-art alarm system," the director of The St. John Institute defended righteously.

Noting that Fuentes was eying her legs, the female surgeon pulled down her skirt about two inches before she resumed the briefing. She didn't mind the looking in general, for she was used to male scans, but at this moment she wanted them all to focus on what she was telling them.

"If somebody's counting," she said, "figures from UNOS show that about eighty-five percent of kidney recipients, and nearly eighty-three percent of people who get a pancreas, exceed that survival term. Those numbers are a few years old. The transplant techniques get better all the time, and patients live longer."

"Hey," said Monroe.

"Hey," she acknowledged.

"Not to pry, but what the hell is UNOS?"

"UNOS is U.N.O.S. The United Network for Organ Sharing,

a life-and-death trade association that works out the rules with the federal government," she explained.

"There are about seventy thousand people on waiting lists for solid organs right now, we hear," the older male surgeon reported. "If you read the papers, you know there's a big debate going on as to what the rules for allocating organs should be. We're not getting enough people to sign donor cards that would give us organs after they die, and sometimes—for religious or emotional reasons—families won't let us retrieve organs from the newly deceased."

Dr. Green nodded emphatically.

"There's a critical shortage of organs," she declared. "You've been very fortunate."

Monroe and the other transplant patients looked at her.

Her open face said it all.

Charlotte Willson hadn't told her who they were or why they were here . . . why they'd been picked to be jumped right to the top of the organ lists. It was even money, Monroe calculated, that the three doctors didn't even know exactly what this St. John Institute was. Odds were they'd been informed that this was an important Defense Department project, maybe for the Army Medical Corps.

The irony was interesting, he thought.

For once, somebody was reversing the pattern and not telling everything to the doctors.

Since saying that aloud might be imprudent, Monroe simply smiled again.

"Very fortunate," he concurred.

"But still, it's a very serious medical situation," the older surgeon warned. "To avoid rejection of the transplanted organ, you are going to take the regime of medication that works to suppress your immune system. That'll make you more vulnerable to a broad range of diseases . . . some of them life-threatening. If you find you have any . . . repeat, *any* . . . illness, even a bad cold, you must get medical care at once. You won't have the defenses of ordinary people, so even a minor thing should get attention quickly."

"From a doctor who's been informed about your transplant,"

the female surgeon added. "It would actually be best if you were seen by us or by somebody from the transplant team at the hospital where you received the organ. You're special people who must be treated by specialists."

"A standard family doctor just won't cut it?" Monroe asked.

"If that was a joke, we don't need any," she replied sharply.

Harry Chen blunted the confrontation by changing the subject.

"Anything else?"

"A whole book's worth," the older transplant surgeon answered. "There'll be a copy for each of you when you go for your next injection."

It happened without warning.

Carefully, careful Charlotte Willson made a mistake.

For just a few seconds, she relaxed the mental defenses she'd worked so hard to build. When she heard the word "injection," she couldn't help thinking of the dead "package" who never made it to the Institute.

Not the one who'd perished on the operating table.

The other one, who died eleven days after the surgery.

To be precise, just over fourteen hours after the first injection.

She was wondering . . . again . . . whether the yellow serum had somehow been fatal, and when the damn autopsy team would deliver a definitive report. She had to know. In a flash, this filled her mind. Monroe found himself "reading" it as if the words were printed large on a blackboard.

A teleprompter would be more accurate, he decided. This wasn't the first time he'd been able to do this. Since Willson hadn't received an organ from the anonymous corpse, what sort of telepathic or other mental link could there be?

"This book's in plain language . . . easy to read," the graying psychiatrist continued. "It's one of the patient-centered guides put out by O'Reilly Publishers in California."

"What does 'patient-centered' mean?" Fuentes asked.

"Written for civilians, right?" the African-American chess expert reasoned.

"Exactly. It's an honest and realistic survey of the basics of the organ transplant scene . . . as of six or eight months ago. It is changing all the time," the older surgeon said. "Improving steadily."

"But it's not perfect yet?" Monroe tested.

All three doctors frowned.

"We've made great progress in the past dozen years," the female surgeon told them, "but there are still major problems. The biggest one is the unfortunate side effects of the medication that patients must take to prevent rejection of the transplanted organ. There are several medications, but all of them lower the patient's immune system."

"In plain language?" Monroe said.

"There is a significantly increased risk of certain types of cancer," she reported bluntly.

"That's pretty damn unfortunate," Monroe judged.

"We know what they are," she said, "and we have a good rate of success in containing them."

"*Most* of the time?" the blonde "package" thought aloud.

"Most transplant patients—the great majority—follow the guidelines and don't get these kinds of cancers," assured the older surgeon.

"Guidelines or rules?" Monroe asked.

"Rules to save your life," replied the man who was Dr. Brown here. "Most of them are in the book, so read it carefully. Eight or ten pages a day. They're important. Read them twice, and if you have any questions—"

"Ask them right away," Monroe broke in to complete the thought.

"Exactly. The book covers almost all the basics, and we're here for anything else. There's always one of us on duty, day or night. Don't hesitate to call," the older surgeon urged.

Then he turned to the psychiatrist.

"You're on," he said.

"What my surgical colleague means is that different people react differently after transplants . . . sometimes sooner and maybe later," the graying mental-health specialist told them in a pleasant and undoubtedly practiced voice. "A variety of emotions is not extraordinary. I'm here to help with that. In the words of that brassy woman comic you've probably seen on television, 'Can we talk?' "

"The Joan Rivers approach to transplants?" Monroe tested.

The psychiatrist smiled.

"If you're hoping to annoy me, Mr. Monroe," he said calmly, "don't bother. It's been tried by people a lot more difficult than you."

"I think that may be enough for this morning," Charlotte Willson announced suddenly, "and I'd say it's a good start for the next phase of our program."

Monroe knew that she feared a divisive personality clash, and guessed that she really couldn't help speaking like this. She probably saw herself as "management," he thought, so the odds were that all this came from some righteous manual.

He didn't say this or anything else until he was in the corridor after the meeting adjourned. Then he didn't speak to the director of The St. John Institute, but to the psychiatrist.

"I've got a question, Doctor," he declared in a casual voice the doctor immediately distrusted.

"What is it?"

Monroe didn't expect an honest reply, but there was no harm in trying.

"It must be the medication . . . or perhaps some postoperative trauma, but I'm a bit unclear about something."

"Yes?"

"Where are we?"

"The St. John Institute."

Monroe nodded . . . pretended to frown.

"*Where* is The St. John Institute, Doctor?"

The psychiatrist froze . . . computed very rapidly.

He looked at his wristwatch before he answered.

"I'm late for a meeting," he lied. "We'll get into that tomorrow."

He hurried away, so he didn't see Dennis Monroe's very small smile. The psychiatrist didn't know where they were either . . . and he had no suspicion that he'd just communicated this to the man whom the Institute considered the most dangerous of the "packages."

This was very interesting, Monroe reflected as he walked to his room to rest before the next injection. He hadn't been aware that he could read the mind of any person other than tricky Charlotte Willson.

He wondered what was happening.

Could he now read *everyone*'s mind?

If he could, why? And would it last?

SOME HOURS LATER and half a world east, the Station Chief of the Central Intelligence Agency in Moscow was holding a glass of champagne and contemplating another question. Standing in a salon at the U.S. Embassy with over a hundred other dignitaries of various nationalities, he scanned this birthday party for the American Ambassador and tried not to perspire.

He'd done a lot of that since they'd snatched his assistant.

On an open street.

In blatant breach of diplomatic protocol and international law.

Days ago . . . and not a word.

It didn't add up.

A well-dressed man who looked vaguely familiar—yes, a cultural-exchange type who was almost surely a Russian intelligence executive—walked up close to him and uttered three words.

They were enough.

"How's the cat?"

Now the Russian strolled away.

He'd delivered the message, and the Station Chief sighed in relief.

They had her, and they were signaling that she was alive.

The next message—in a day or two, no more than three— would present their demands, spell out the price they wanted. The Station Chief had no idea as to what that might be, but he was familiar with the time-tested process in these matters.

Within the hour, he'd send off a coded report on this new development to the Russian section of ops at Langley. Planning and strategies for the coming negotiations would be developed by a working group of experts.

He wasn't aware that the Russians wanted someone named Anna.

All he knew was that the game was on.

13

NOT THE NEXT MORNING.

The one after that.

It arrived at The St. John Institute at 11:35 A.M. in a light drizzle.

"Inbound," the armed guard manning the ground radar said calmly. "Range: three-quarters of a mile. Speed: two-five. I.F.F.: friendly."

The van entered the main building's garage a few minutes later. The man who was delivering *it* was met by two escorts who accompanied him to the director's office. She looked at him for the seconds it took him to walk to her desk.

He was about forty . . . trim and square-shouldered . . . black . . . well-dressed in blazer and gray slacks . . . bright-eyed, with a good haircut. She didn't care about his appearance or his reputation as a forensic specialist. What mattered was the envelope he was supposed to deliver.

Where was it?

She was about to ask when she realized that the exchange of correct sign and countersign phrases had to come first.

"Dr. Knowlton?" she tested.

"He couldn't make it. I'm Dr. Walters," the visitor replied

and reached inside his blazer for the envelope. She took it eagerly, read it silently and carefully—twice.

"You're the head of the autopsy review team?" she asked.

"Yes. All the findings in our report were unanimous," he answered.

Cautious, she thought. These medical types were always so damn cautious.

"I think that our report spells out our conclusions clearly and accurately," he added.

"Let me see if I understand it," she began. "You believe that the patient who expired some days after the transplant may have died because of the yellow serum."

"We considered and tested for several other factors," the forensics specialist said. "We had a problem in regard to the medication you people call the yellow serum."

He wondered exactly who "you people" were.

No one had said.

It was clear that he wasn't to ask.

"What sort of problem?" she probed.

"We were not told what it was . . . or what it was for," he answered and waited for an explanation.

He didn't get any.

"I gather that you did some analysis of this serum," she said, "and you believe it contributed to the patient's death."

"The double injection was the primary factor. Our reviews of the clinical records and interviews with the technician who did the injections indicate that two of these patients received—on the first three days of this therapy—double doses. I don't know why."

He paused again.

"Please go on, Doctor," she urged coolly.

She wasn't going to talk about this either.

"Was this part of the prescribed protocol? I'd hate to think it was an error."

"So would I," Charlotte Willson dodged effortlessly. "As for the protocol, I wasn't there."

The very able and experienced doctor who'd headed the autopsy review didn't appreciate this conversation at all. This entire game—that's what it seemed to be—had bothered him even before he was flown to an airport never named and put in the back of a van so he couldn't see where it was taking him.

"Well, I was there for the whole damn autopsy review," he said angrily, "and there's something I'd like to share with you. In case you didn't notice it in our report, it is entirely possible that the other patient who got the double doses is in considerable danger."

"Of what?" she asked.

"I'm not entirely sure. Nothing good. We've identified two of the ingredients in that serum. If this other patient isn't very strong—a lot stronger than the woman who died—he or she could end up with a cerebral clot, or blindness, or maybe a body bag."

She thought for a few seconds before she responded.

"The patient has shown no signs of any illness or distress . . . no mental or physical weakness. This is a very strong individual, healing at an exceptional pace. Top scores on neurological tests."

"Fatigue . . . blurred vision . . . irritability?"

She thought of the short-tempered son of a bitch who was going to lead her team. "Irritability"—that would be a total understatement.

"Cheerful and cooperative," she lied. "Lots of energy . . . team player . . . a dream patient."

"So far."

"So far," the director of The St. John Institute agreed. "It's been over a month, and our staff is doing thorough physicals twice a week. Zero . . . zip . . . nothing."

"About this serum that killed the woman?"

"Our physicians have seen no side affects or abnormalities," she declared firmly.

Of course, she didn't know—yet.

And if she did, she certainly wouldn't have talked about it to this stranger.

"I would suggest that the biochemists who developed this serum go over their complete research," said the doctor who'd been top man in his class at Columbia's medical school, "and I really believe that the ethical thing to do is to discuss the whole matter with your dream patient."

"I'll do that today," she promised, "and I'll get the research review started immediately."

The black forensic specialist knew a lot of white people who lied better than this one. He wanted to get out of here . . . now . . . to make his way back to honest, open science. He was back in the van six minutes later.

That vehicle was just leaving the property to turn onto the highway when Charlotte Willson made up her mind. While the autopsy review was definitely interesting, she certainly wasn't going to discuss it with the man who'd received the double doses. There was no way of predicting what Monroe might do.

He could do almost anything.

His file showed he often did.

It would be too dangerous to take this up with him.

For a moment, she considered exploring what she'd just learned with the surgeons . . . or perhaps with the psychiatrist. No, she couldn't—wouldn't—risk it. They'd only muddy the waters, and one or all of them might even bring up the issue of ethics and the patient's right to know.

Things were changing in the medical profession.

Only God knew what was the status of *correct* thinking in the fractionalized mental-health community.

No. She'd take care of this herself.

She instructed her assistant to invite Monroe to visit her office.

Right away, please.

Thanks.

She had no way of guessing that he'd been hoping for this.

"SIT DOWN, DENNIS," Charlotte Willson urged, gesturing toward the large armchair facing her.

She didn't suspect anything when he elected to lower himself onto the couch instead. Typical Monroe, she thought smugly. He was one of those compulsively independent and contrary males. She knew how to handle these macho types.

"Just wanted to touch base and find out how things are going," she told him.

Game, he registered.

She was playing her devious game—one of her devious games—he realized.

Which one was it?

"How are the exercises coming along?" she continued.

"I think we're making a little progress," he answered.

"Good. And how are you feeling?"

That was it.

Yes, she was genuinely concerned—covertly, of course . . . about his health. She'd just learned something new that said he was or might be at risk. What was it?

Now she thought about it, and he knew.

Autopsy report. The yellow serum . . . double doses.

Why? Had they been experimenting on him?

Set.

"Feeling fine," he told her.

Now was his chance.

He had to make his move.

"Getting stronger every day," he reported. "I'm even starting to like this place."

He smiled . . . suddenly pointed at the window behind her.

"What's that?" he asked.

In sheer reflex, she turned to look.

That was when he pulled the gun from its hiding place in her couch and concealed it in his bathrobe pocket. He didn't need the wheelchair much anymore, but he'd stayed with the patient's plain robe because it helped him blend in as unthreatening.

"I didn't see anything," she said.

"A big black bird . . . very big. Are they common around here?"

"I don't think so," she responded and asked him if he had any suggestions for the program.

She didn't care about his ideas. She wanted to observe him over another minute or two for any signs of fatigue or eye problems. She was pleased when she saw none. While Monroe spoke of possible benefits from a range of stimulating recorded music, she assured herself that the forensic specialist had been an overcautious alarmist.

Then she wished Monroe well, and he left. When he got back to his room, he estimated that it might be another day before she recognized that the gun couldn't be in his quarters, which had been gone over very carefully six or seven times . . . and that her office had never been searched at all.

The dangerous man who had his gun back was wrong.

His calculation was off by thirty-three hours.

It was almost two and a half days before Charlotte Willson walked out of her office so five men could go over it . . . inch by inch.

Nothing.

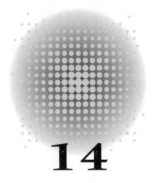

14

About thirty, maybe thirty-five, minutes from Washington, the capital of the United States.

The time depends on how you drive.

There are signs pointing to the headquarters of the Central Intelligence Agency. When a vehicle turns off the highway and moves up to the main building, the person at the wheel had better drive slowly and in a visibly nonaggressive manner. Deviation from that will alarm heavily armed and cautious guards who recall a man from the Middle East who killed several Agency employees in the driveway. There is an ongoing possibility that the security teams would fire their automatic weapons today . . . if alarmed.

Tomorrow, too.

They remember the assassin, and they're still edgy.

In a large office on the fourth floor of the main building—fifty-one minutes after the search of Charlotte Willson's suite at The St. John Institute produced no weapon—Jeffrey Seigenthaler was more than edgy. He was fifty-three years old, very bright, quite fit as the result of regular workouts, fluent in Russian and not bad in Ukrainian after a tour as Station Chief in Moscow . . . and he was annoyed.

The head of the C.I.A. division in ops that dealt with Russia and the ragged comembers of that confederation was often concerned, but rarely annoyed. Of course it wasn't often that a member of his diplomatically protected staff in Moscow was snatched. Even more troubling was the fact that he couldn't buy her back.

Swaps—agent for agent—were routine.

The U.S. and U.K. had exchanged dozens of K.G.B. and G.R.U. spies for American and British operatives in the past four and a half decades. Less than a day after the C.I.A. Station Chief got the "cat" message, the Russians had made their specific demand.

They didn't ask for Anna, since that was an internal code name.

They didn't mention Semyon Deriabin either, because that was the real name of Anna, a fact buried in secret files.

They requested the return of a thirty-seven-year-old person from Warsaw . . . Polish passport . . . male and unmarried . . . Jan Bielski . . . visiting the U.S. to study Web site design.

There were procedures for these exchanges. The first step was to determine which U.S. security organization had the Russian agent, and the next was to determine whether the debriefing was completed. The third question was whether the foreign spy wanted to go back at all, and the fourth involved the price each side would pay.

Humanitarian? Not really. Practical? Definitely.

Seigenthaler, who justifiably saw himself as a practical man after a quarter of a century in the "spook" business, began the four-step process. He never got to the second one. He checked and rechecked the F.B.I. and all the other U.S. counterespionage units . . . and he felt that damn acid in his gut again.

None of them had Jan Bielski.

Not one had ever *heard* of him . . . but they'd look.

Seigenthaler queried each of the agencies again. Now they were starting to get curious. There was just enough of the old rivalry in each of them to make them wonder if the C.I.A. was up to something . . . and what could it be?

Why were they on the outside?

Who was Jan Bielski . . . or whoever he was?

What was going down?

"Situation estimate?" asked no-nonsense Theodore Buckley, Deputy Director for Operations at the Central Intelligence Agency.

Seigenthaler looked at his boss, and frowned.

"Hard to be sure," he replied sensibly. "This has never come up before. It could be some tricky game the Russians are playing . . . or a mistake."

"What kind of game?"

"A new one. Maybe they want to rattle us, and then they'll raise the price by demanding someone or something more valuable," Seigenthaler reasoned.

"Buck" Buckley considered that.

"Who else? What else?" he wondered.

The head of the Russian division shook his head.

"Did you really think there's any chance this might be a mistake?" Buckley asked.

"I suppose it's possible."

"Whose mistake?" Buckley pressed. "Theirs or ours?"

The question had occurred to Seigenthaler, and he hadn't liked it then. He couldn't live with it any better now. He looked directly into the moon-cool eyes of his boss as he replied.

"It has to be theirs, doesn't it?" he asked. "No reason the other U.S. intelligence outfits would lie about this."

Buckley hesitated for just a moment before he answered.

"I can't think of any," he declared carefully. "Listen, please check with them one more time . . . right away. Our clever friends in the F.B.I. must have something more on Bielski beside the fact that he logged in with Immigration at Kennedy five and a half months ago on a Polish passport that was a first-class forgery. What do the Polish security people say about this Bielski? Did they dig up anything?"

Seigenthaler swallowed and sighed.

"Only where we could dig up the real Jan Bielski. Lot two-nine-seven in a cemetery outside Krakow," the head of the Russian division reported. "This is the old K.G.B. routine that Moscow's still using. They grab the identity of some dead guy who left no immediate family, and no criminal record either."

"Okay," Buckley reasoned. "Where the hell did this fake Bielski go when he left Kennedy? There has to be some trace of him."

"We checked all the airlines. No record he ever bought a ticket from New York or anywhere else in this country. Credit cards: negative. He must have come in with or picked up lots of cash . . . and maybe another passport. All the computer scans find no trace of Jan Bielski in the records of any major hotel chain or car-rental outfit . . . no sign he bought traveler's checks at any bank. Same with the phone companies' data banks on long-distance calls," Seigenthaler reported just a bit defensively.

"That means," Buckley thought aloud, "that he's *probably* got a load of cash, and he *probably* isn't Jan Bielski anymore. Who the hell is he . . . and *where?*"

"I'll let you know as soon as I find out," Seigenthaler promised and rose to his feet.

As he walked down the corridor from Buckley's suite, the troubled head of the C.I.A.'s hard-pressed Russian division wondered what was so special . . . so valuable . . . about this Bielski. Then Seigenthaler found himself thinking about something else.

What if some unit or person in the U.S. intelligence community—that very conscientious and sometimes dysfunctional family—was doing the lying about Bielski?

What if the deceiver was in the C.I.A., in this building?

What if it was an individual whom Seigenthaler knew and trusted?

Was this another Ames affair with deadly treason for a huge sum of cash—a million dollars, four or five?

And if it wasn't a sell-out for money, what was it?

It would be extremely difficult to find the answer until they seized Jan Bielski, who almost surely had another identity by now . . . maybe three of them. He might be a mobile operative or perhaps an agent in place. This was a big country . . . he was surely a very experienced professional who knew the other side's tactics.

Search techniques . . . technology . . . patterns.

He was as familiar with all that as Seigenthaler was with how Moscow would hunt down an intruder.

This was going to be cat-and-mouse. Nonstop. And not nice. Not nearly nice.

It might be easier if someone told him what this Bielski was supposed to do in the United States . . . what his mission was. As Seigenthaler reached the door of his own office, he had a hunch. It was mostly visceral, but also based on what he'd heard and seen . . . a hunch that somebody on Our Side knew and wasn't telling.

It could be Buckley himself, the head of the Russian division realized. Buckley knew a lot of things he didn't tell people, and Seigenthaler understood that. Not telling things was part of Buckley's job, his duty. That could be why—if he knew the answer—he hadn't shared it with Seigenthaler.

Or there might be another reason.

A darker reason.

Or maybe . . . it was possible . . . somebody else wasn't sharing this secret with the Deputy Director for Operations.

Who could . . . who would . . . dare to do that?

Someone above Buckley?

How high could this secret go?

Or was Seigenthaler edging into paranoia, a career hazard in this world of shape-shifters . . . conspirators . . . and triple agents?

That had happened to two—no, three—of his colleagues. A pair of them had recovered, but one—intelligent, patriotic, and nearly catatonic with distrust—would be "resting" in a C.I.A. home indefinitely. His dazed-looking wife still visited him once a month.

Not for me, Seigenthaler vowed to himself.

Then he reached for the phone with the secure line to call the F.B.I. for the sixth time.

15

AN HOUR BEFORE THE DEADLINE EXPIRED.

About two miles across Moscow from where the kidnapped C.I.A. woman could herself expire in the not-so-safe "safe house" where she was imprisoned.

Not an "accidental" contact in a diplomatic reception.

An arranged meeting on one of those boats that cruised the Volga with assorted foreign tourists and some guide who kept the sound on his bullhorn and the prose he spoke through it up high.

A bit too assertive . . . a trifle too loud . . . for some of the more refined travelers such as the quartet of earnest choirmasters from Madrid en route to the big music festival in St. Petersburg. Just right for the two generals who'd come to do another life-or-death deal.

The transaction wasn't going to be that unusual in the spiteful romance and intermittent hostility between the self-styled superpowers . . . but it wasn't customary to do these things with each nation represented by a general. Normally, these shabby swaps were handled by mid-level civilian intelligence supervisors.

Today was different.

There was something far from normal involved.

Brigadier General Dallas Johann, the military attaché at the U.S. Embassy, was here to speak for Washington. General Temkov had sent himself because he had to maintain absolutely precise control of this crucial negotiation. He had two important advantages, the Russian intelligence general thought. The other side didn't suspect who or what Anna was, and Temkov's department had the C.I.A. woman as—what was that clever American phrase?

A bargaining chip. Yes, that was it.

And the Americans were sentimental about children and women.

This was a character flaw for a great power, Temkov reflected. It was one that had never afflicted the Soviet Union, and the young Russian Republic certainly couldn't afford anything like that. He had nothing against women or children, or music or pets, but he had to live with today's rock-hard realities.

He had to be smarter and more practical than the Americans now so that he might be rich and free of all this toxic trash later . . . not much later. It should be very soon. His plan would work, he assured himself.

If he got Anna back before the missing agent talked.

If Anna hadn't told them already.

No, they wouldn't get anything out of Anna . . . and Anna didn't know about the big-money private deal with a fanatical terrorist group. There were also things that the Middle Eastern organization didn't know. Those people didn't suspect that their efforts to keep their force's name and headquarters secret hadn't been nearly good enough.

They hadn't noticed Temkov's expert surveillance team following the man who'd delivered the down payment on the Lisbon ferry. As a professional, Temkov's self-respect and survival instinct required that he know with whom he was playing . . . every one of them. It was a delicate job . . . four steps. The experienced Russians ran the operation like a relay race, changing the people following at intervals along the way. It was as if they were passing the runner's baton. The system worked. It wouldn't have if Temkov couldn't provide an agent to take up the last phase inside the Middle Eastern nation where the terrorists had their underground headquarters.

That country lied about it to the U.S.A., and to the United Nations.

Enough other governments did this to qualify it as a team sport . . . maybe an addition to the next Olympics, General Temkov thought cynically. There were so few people or nations to be trusted, he judged as his eyes roved past the approaching U.S. military attaché.

Temkov recognized them.

He wasn't surprised.

"Good afternoon, General," he said to the American as he walked closer stiffly.

The American was in civilian clothes. So were the three men a dozen yards behind him . . . as was the fourth one with the small suitcase . . . off to the left . . . seated on the bench and pretending to watch the birds. He'd have some sort of automatic weapon . . . and maybe a twelve-round combat shotgun in that case, Temkov guessed.

The Americans weren't entirely stupid, Temkov told himself.

After the kidnapping of the woman, they wouldn't count on diplomatic immunity to protect General Johann.

"Glad to see you . . . and your friends," Temkov said.

Remembering how Americans did business, he put out his hand so they might "shake." Johann ignored it, and stepped back to emphasize his point. Though it was merely ceremonial, the American general didn't even want to touch a gangster who kidnapped women who had diplomatic immunity.

"Hello to you . . . and *your* friends," the military attaché responded harshly.

He gestured toward the three teams of Russian security agents trying to be inconspicuous in a semicircle behind Temkov.

"It's a sad world, isn't it?" Temkov thought aloud. "No trust left . . . that's dangerous. Well, I have some good news. The lady is in good health . . . misses her cat . . . and hopes we can complete this exchange as soon as possible."

General Johann braced himself before he answered.

He was a soldier—a no-nonsense infantry veteran—and he didn't like serving as a spokesman for the damn Spooks. The CIA's own Station Chief should have been here, but Langley had vetoed that.

"The news I have for you isn't quite that positive," he said. "Washington has taken your proposal very seriously, and made a major effort to locate this Jan Bielski. Every federal security organization has made and repeated . . . then repeated again . . . a search for Bielski. All we can find is that he entered the U.S. at Kennedy. Nothing after that."

Temkov didn't believe it for a second. It had to be a lie.

Maybe they'd learned how valuable and unique Anna was, the wily Russian general computed.

Perhaps from Anna himself . . . maybe through hypnosis or drugs. Anna had been well trained to resist physical torture. The Americans must have used some other method.

If it was Anna who'd told the secret.

There were so many ifs in this situation. The extraordinary abundance of them had been bothering Temkov for weeks, and he was no closer to the truth now. If such a hard fact existed, he might never know it . . . and that troubled him, too.

It was life-and-death poker again, he told himself.

All he could do was play out the hand.

"You have such a fine network of high-tech systems in your wealthy country," Temkov replied in a nonconfrontational tone, "that I can't help wondering whether some low-level person . . . maybe a clerk . . . accidentally made a computer error. Perhaps your associates in Washington and Langley could recheck."

"We've checked four . . . five . . . six times, but there's no reason we can't do it again," Johann said.

The Americans were being—or trying to look—reasonable, Temkov judged. He wasn't fooled, of course. They must have Anna . . . unless Anna had taken off on his own with all the cash sent ahead for him to pick up on arrival. He'd collected it on schedule from one of Temkov's operatives in a meeting at The Cloisters, a medieval building and museum overlooking the Hudson River in upper Manhattan.

Two hundred eighty thousand dollars in used twenty- and fifty-dollar bills.

To minimize risk of detection, Anna was supposed to report only once a month. There hadn't been a single message from him. Russia's most remarkable agent was gone. So was the money.

Where?

Maybe one of those violent muggers so numerous in U.S. cities had assaulted Anna . . . perhaps even as a random target. If the thief had brutally attacked Anna and grabbed the money, the savagely battered Russian agent could be lost in some hospital, helpless in a coma or with amnesia. Maybe outside . . . crippled . . . in hiding.

It was Anna, not the cash, that mattered.

The $280,000 was unimportant, Temkov thought. Russian foreign intelligence had invested more than $1,390,000 in Anna. What Anna might accomplish couldn't be measured in millions of dollars . . . not even in billions.

It might change history.

Now Temkov focused on the U.S. military attaché facing him.

"I'm confident that if your people look once more . . . make a real effort," the Russian began, "there's a very good chance that you'll locate this individual."

"His mother—his poor old mother with the brain tumor—wants to see her boy before she dies, right?" Johann said cynically.

"Actually, it's his grandmother . . . she's eighty-nine . . . in a wheelchair," Temkov corrected evenly.

General Dallas Johann, a fifth-generation Texan, eyed him with a glance that could chop down oaks.

"As military attaché, I'm supposed to be diplomatic, so I'll speak to you like a diplomat," he said. "I'm certainly not going to repeat those crude comments that even in Stalin's era, U.S. Embassy personnel weren't kidnapped by contemptible street thugs."

His voice was calm. His body was still, his face grim.

"No," he continued, "I'm not paying any attention to remarks about cheap gangsters cynically staining their country's honor."

Temkov knew this wasn't the time to answer.

He didn't. He was a professional with self-control and a steely sense of priorities. Here . . . now . . . Anna was all that mattered.

"To get back to Jan Bielski and the diplomatically protected and unarmed U.S. citizen some of your local roadkill grabbed," the Texan said. "Sorry. You know the expression roadkill?"

Temkov nodded.

"Good," Johann declared. "We'll make another major effort to find this Bielski. We'll check with local and state police—even morgues—in addition to the federal agencies we've already been in touch with several times. I'll be ready to get back to you in seventy-two hours—max."

"Thank you."

"Be ready to get back to me . . . understand?" the American told him. "We want her returned . . . in good health . . . very soon. I'm tired of waiting. We've done everything to meet your price, and my patience is running out."

"You're taking this personally, General," Temkov noted.

"You're damn right I am . . . and I don't forget."

A realistic judge of character and temper, Temkov decided that there wasn't anything he could say now that might be productive. He didn't utter another word. Instead, he gestured to his bodyguard to step out of the way to let the Americans pass.

The tour guide was still rattling on about the history and glories . . . the character and splendors . . . of Moscow, when Temkov saw the landing stage where the trip would end. He watched the five Americans go ashore in the flow of tourists a few minutes later, and wondered how the U.S.A. had become a great power.

I should have found out how the cat is, Temkov thought as he started for the gangplank himself. She was bound to ask, he reasoned for several seconds before his mind turned abruptly to the timetable for the payment of the remaining millions.

And the weapons of mass destruction.

They'd teach this arrogant military attaché and the whole Pentagon a lesson.

GENERAL DALLAS JOHANN DID not keep his promise to "get back" in seventy-two hours. The U.S. brigadier's reply—in a sealed envelope—was delivered to Temkov's suite by an American messenger nine minutes before the deadline.

"I was told to wait in case there would be an answer," the American said in unaccented Russian.

While he sat on a chair—under the eyes of armed guards—in the street-floor lobby, Temkov read Johann's note.

> *Another extremely thorough search on the city, state, and federal levels has produced no information about where Bielski went when he left JFK Airport or where he is or even might be now.*
>
> *We've done everything we could. Now it is time for you to do the same. Please give my messenger a written answer—in a sealed envelope—specifying where you want to meet . . . anytime in the next forty-eight hours to arrange for details of her immediate return to the Embassy.*
>
> *Washington has agreed with my recommendation to hold you personally responsible, and to task-force contingency plans to be implemented if she is not released and out of Russia with U.S. diplomatic and Marine escort by the end of next week.*

It wasn't easy to make out the name scrawled below.

The signature looked as furious as Johann had been on the tour boat.

Yes, the infantry-hardened military attaché had signed the ultimatum. The training Johann had received at the command school in Leavenworth . . . the staff work at the Pentagon . . . and the months of tutoring by State Department teams of "Russian" specialists hadn't really filed off this brigadier general's rough edges.

Temkov's aide watched silently as his commander took a sheet of paper and an envelope from a desk drawer and began to write.

I acknowledge receipt of your message. We remain puzzled and very disappointed by the lack of progress. We hope there may be additional and positive news before expiration of the forty-eight hours mentioned in your note.

He wasn't going to respond to the personal threat.

The veteran Russian intelligence officer was too clever for that.

Temkov signed his reply in a deliberately vague jumble of letters. Then he folded the sheet of paper—which bore no identifying letterhead—and put it in the equally anonymous envelope.

"Give it to the American courier waiting downstairs," he ordered. By the time his aide returned six minutes later, the S.V.R. general had made up his mind about what to do.

"I don't know whether they're telling us the truth," Temkov said soberly, "but I do know that we're running out of time. I've no choice now."

"You're going to give them the Wilk woman?"

Temkov shook his head.

He walked to the wall safe . . . punched in the numbered sequence that only he possessed . . . watched the torch-proof door open. He shuffled several envelopes like a professional card-player before he found the one marked with the first letter of the Cyrillic alphabet.

In English, it would be A . . . for Anna.

He carried it back to his desk . . . studied one sheet of onion-skip paper stamped TOP SECRET in Russian . . . and made notes on a page he tore from a desk pad. It was really old-fashioned to use the instantly inflammable flash paper, but he hadn't changed to the new way yet.

He block-printed two sentences on the flash paper. Then he

signed it and gave the page to his most trusted aide.

"Signal Center—for immediate coding and transmission," Temkov said. "Two messages. First one to our other agents, second one to Anna."

"You want me to stay there while they're doing this and make sure the flash paper is burned as soon as they're sent?"

"Of course," the frowning general ratified.

He shook his head . . . carried the envelope marked A back to the wall safe . . . put it under the other papers, and relocked the door.

Neither the aide nor the people in the Signal Center had any idea as to what the second message meant. The first one, to nine S.V.R. agents spread across the U.S., was a simple instruction to monitor a certain shortwave radio frequency, starting now. The other message was much shorter . . . and had obviously already been encoded. It was a stream of seven numbers and letters. There was no name on it, just the frequency on which it was to be sent at five-minute intervals for the next half hour.

"Now we wait," Temkov said when his aide returned.

The man who'd brought the money from Lisbon considered—for two or three seconds—asking for *what*. He decided against it.

"And we hope," the general continued. "Because Anna is so special, we developed a special plan—a new and unique system for use in extreme emergencies."

"That was the emergency signal to get Anna out?"

"Not exactly," Temkov replied.

There'd be no point in sharing additional details, he thought. It was . . . or might be . . . too dangerous for everyone. If the plan and the system worked, sometime in the next twenty-four hours—thirty-six at most—he'd know where Anna was and whether the extraordinary operative could be, or should be, extracted from the United States.

It was probably going to be a race to Anna, for the Americans had the big staffs and quality radio equipment to monitor just about all frequencies around the clock. They wouldn't know what they were picking up or the time urgency, Temkov computed. With any kind of luck, Temkov's operatives could move Anna across the Mexican border to safety.

Then the menacing confrontation with the furious U.S. Embassy and the C.I.A. could be resolved before it got worse. The usual lies about some unfortunate misunderstanding ought to do. Releasing Alison Wilk—and her well-fed cat—to go home should reduce the bitterness considerably. This entire affair had been one of the ugly games that intelligence services were sometimes obliged to play.

He was a bit disappointed by the American reaction.

After all, he'd never planned to hurt the C.I.A. woman.

Not if he didn't have to.

He looked at his wristwatch . . . calculated what time it was in the Washington, D.C., area where Anna was supposed to be operating. For the thousandth time, Temkov wondered whether his agent was there.

Anna wasn't.

16

IT DIDN'T TAKE VERY LONG.

It wasn't supposed to.

Temkov had planned it that way. The orders to the nine S.V.R. agents were clear and concise . . . totally understandable. They had the equipment to carry out the command, and they had the locations. They were spread out across the U.S. mainland.

Bernard was in Los Angeles . . . Charles in Boston . . . Douglas in Miami . . . Edward in New York. The other Russian operatives in various cities were also code-named in alphabetical sequence. It was a simple arrangement, with all the names so common in American families that they'd create no suspicion.

Some of the S.V.R. deep-cover operatives had been out when Moscow transmitted Temkov's order, but their tape recorders were on just in case a signal came between scheduled "flash" exchanges—ultra high-speed radio messages that took only seconds. Within an hour after Temkov's message left Moscow, all nine of them . . . seven men and two women—had received and decoded it.

They complied at once.

They each set their shortwave receivers to the frequency

specified in Temkov's instruction, and they listened. They didn't know what they were listening for, or why. If he needed to . . . if he wanted to . . . the general would tell them when it suited him.

They expected this process to consume hours, at the least.

Within less than a dozen minutes, three of the S.V.R. listeners heard something. It wasn't static. The regularity of the pattern was man-made. Somebody had created that signal. It pulsed out—faintly but unmistakably—at twenty-five-second intervals.

Two hours and eight minutes later.

Time for the weekly "flash" report to Moscow.

The three Russian "ears" . . . in Chicago . . . in Omaha, where the Strategic Air Command headquarters was . . . and in Houston . . . sent word of the pulse. They noted the direction from where they were. They waited silently and almost patiently while Temkov triangulated to fix the location of the unidentified transmitter.

"Good," he responded minutes later and gave instructions to proceed immediately to an industrial center named Wendell, an hour drive from Kansas City. We told them exactly where and when to meet, and provided recognition signals and passwords for sign and countersign.

They were to bring their radio receivers. He didn't inform them that a special courier was about to board a Moscow-to-New York flight with an uncaptioned photo, and that it would arrive—addressed to the cover name and identity of the agent coming up from Houston—at the General Delivery window of the post office in Wendell by four the next afternoon.

When they got the order to meet in Wendell, each of the spies did what any practical intelligence professional would do. Since they were each on-line, they checked out Wendell . . . saw that it was a community of sixty-one thousand whose only large employers were a soy-bean processing plant and a Veterans Administration hospital . . . and shook their heads.

There was no military air base.

No plant making missiles or sophisticated electronic gear.

No factory producing chemical products or pharmaceuticals

that might also supply germ-warfare weapons or antidotes.

Why were they going to Wendell?

THE AGENT IN HOUSTON—Frank—had just finished packing for the trip north when he received a message for his eyes only . . . destroy on reading. It ordered him to pick up the envelope at the post office . . . and told him what he was to do with it.

Before he left, some instinct told him to tune his receiver once more to the frequency specified in the first of these peculiar messages. The unidentified transmitter . . . from up north, so it might be in Wendell . . . was still pulsing the same way.

Every twenty-five seconds.

The signal wasn't quite as strong as it had been, but still clear. The battery might be running down, Frank speculated as he turned off his compact but powerful receiver.

His damn plane was late, of course. He didn't get to the Kansas City airport until 4:10 P.M. the next day. He immediately rented a car, put his gear in the trunk, and stared at his watch. There wasn't much time.

He was perspiring as he guided the Dodge east.

An hour's drive? That was a bad joke on these roads at this time of day. The fact that the two other S.V.R. spies were also somewhere nearby, struggling to get to the damn rendezvous in time, didn't help much. Frank had to reach the post office before it closed.

Then he saw the sign beside the road.

WENDELL—8 MILES

He had seventeen minutes and an uncontrollable urge to curse.

"Shit! Shit! Shit!" he raged at the top of his lungs.

General Temkov would have been proud of him. The training and language drills had paid off, and the outburst was in English, not Russian. He hadn't risked his cover. Frank swore several more times as he neared the small city, trying to ignore the boring blur of diners, gas stations, food shops, and used-car lots with stupid signs.

WENDELL—2 MILES

He had seven . . . perhaps eight . . . minutes.

Traffic was growing . . . he knew nothing of the streets in this city . . . and he had to find the damn post office.

If he didn't make it in time, what would he do?

And what would those hard people in Moscow do?

It wasn't his fault, Frank thought as he swung around a pickup truck that had a teenage driver . . . and a clearly visible shotgun in a rack. Moscow would blame Frank anyway, he reasoned. Infuriated and frightened, he tried not to consider what Temkov might do if he didn't collect the envelope and carry out the instructions inside it. He felt another surge of anger.

There were always instructions about everything, dammit.

Half the time, field agents didn't know why they were doing things, for the security maniacs gave only part of the story and expected full compliance anyway. Frank pushed this from his consciousness and leaned forward as he approached the turn-off for Wendell.

There it was.

What the hell was it—this nothing place was so important that Moscow would send three of its key U.S. operatives?

He twisted the wheel . . . accelerated a bit . . . took a chance with the traffic and speed laws. He had about three minutes, he estimated . . . and probably not a chance in hell. Now he saw the police car ahead—right where the light was turning red. He had to stop.

That was bad enough. Now things got worse.

A beefy uniformed cop leaned out of the window of the police vehicle. He'd noticed that the rented car's license plates weren't local.

"Visitor?" he asked.

"Yes, Officer."

Every second counted. So did the cop's handgun. Frank couldn't see it, but he knew it would be large-caliber and probably semiautomatic.

"Can I help you?" the policeman offered.

"Looking for the post office."

"Left at the next corner . . . two blocks. Have a nice day, you hear?"

"I hear," Frank replied . . . flashed a very American thumbs-up of thanks and drove on carefully within the speed limit.

He was still breathing hard when he slid the sedan to the curb forty-five feet from the brick post office. Flag flying ... clean federal architecture of the sixties ... who cared? Frank didn't as he leaped from the Hertzmobile. He entered the post office a full thirty-five seconds—by the big wall clock—before six o'clock.

His heart was pounding, his throat nearly choked.

He swallowed ... managed to speak ... and showed the General Delivery clerk the expertly forged I.D. that carried the name on the envelope. The envelope was eight-by-ten inches ... quilted ... containing something flat. When the clerk gave it to him, Frank swallowed again and smiled as he'd learned Americans did so much.

It was a minute after six when he left the one-story building. He heard the door being locked behind him, and he sighed. He was going to live a little ... maybe a lot ... longer. He drove to the far side of town ... stopped at a telephone booth ... found the number and street address of Margaret's Chicken Heaven.

He wasn't breathing as hard now.

Not quite as hard, and his throat wasn't knotted either.

He studied the quilted mailing envelope that must have crossed the Atlantic on a special courier flight. He couldn't guess how they'd gotten it out here to Wendell so fast. They had their ways, he told himself.

And their rules. He'd been ordered to open it only in the presence of the other two—in Margaret's Chicken Heaven—at seven o'clock, and that was what he had to do. He phoned the Chicken Heaven ... got exact driving instructions from some affable woman with a lot of Missouri in her mouth ... and thanked her politely. He spoke in the Houston tones he'd worked so hard to perfect.

He got to the Chicken Heaven eleven minutes early, cruising by twice to check the place out ... compute escape routes if this turned out to be some kind—any kind—of a trap ... look for possibly dangerous cars or vans that might be unmarked police or F.B.I. vehicles. Sometimes they carried those special antennas, a giveaway to professional eyes.

All clear.

Well, it *seemed* clear anyway, Frank told himself cynically as he carefully parked the car in the lot beside the restaurant, edging into a spot that offered immediate unblocked departure. He entered Margaret's Chicken Heaven at five minutes to seven, giving himself a little time to study the interior . . . the exits . . . the patrons and employees.

He was casually scanning a plump lady in a flowered dress near the cash register—wondering whether she might be Poultry Queen Margaret—when he noticed a man at a booth by the big window. Not quite as tall as Frank, who stood six feet one, the tanned stranger wore a zipper jacket, blue-denim shirt, and gray tie.

Not entirely a stranger, Frank thought.

That attire was the recognition ritual Temkov had sent.

"How's it goin', George?" the agent from Houston tested.

The agent from Omaha gave the correct Moscow set response, and they both lifted menus as if they were old friends. Harriet—the S.V.R. operative from Chicago—arrived fifty seconds later. They'd all come early . . . just in case. That was another Moscow rule.

Harriet was an attractive woman in her thirties with good hair and legs . . . and an excellent appetite. As soon as she'd said the words that established her link to Temkov, she flashed a large smile and straightened her blue scarf.

"Let's eat," she urged and waved to a hundred-ninety-pound waitress.

She ordered her food just seconds after the menu was put in her well-manicured fingers. Frank noticed that her hands looked strong . . . like those of a worker or an athlete . . . not like a pampered society matron's.

The three professionals played their roles properly. They talked about baseball and television shows . . . about the lousy weather coming in from the West . . . how to find cheap air fares on the Net . . . the latest scandals about that Southern governor, and the compulsively freaky deeds of the rock star who had so many tattoos and bedmates. This covered the spies nicely right through the establishment's only semidivine chicken right to the adequate coffee.

Then Frank put the mailing envelope on the table.

"Here goes," he said and opened it.

He took out a piece of cardboard put in for stiffening, a small sheet of that rapidly burning flash paper, and a five-by-seven-inch color photograph of the upper torso and head of a brown-haired man who could be forty.

Frank blinked when he saw the picture.

He didn't know the man's name, but he'd seen this person several times—about three years ago—at an S.V.R. course in spoken English. Whoever he was, this man had been the best—perfect in English, using several regional U.S. accents.

The man had been abruptly taken out of the course for a "special" research project that there weren't even rumors about, Frank remembered. He didn't say that now, because he knew that Temkov wouldn't want him to share this information. Instead, he read the terse message on the flash paper.

Code name: Anna.
Recognition phrase: Tell me how you lost the weight.
He may be ill. In whatever condition he may be, it is imperative that Anna come home. This must be done whatever the cost.
When you have found Anna, destroy this page and the photo.

It was signed "Yamchik," the general's own code name and the Russian word for "coachman."

Frank passed the note and picture to the pretty woman with the strong-looking hands. After she'd studied the message and photo intently, she gave them to the agent from Omaha. He read the note twice—eyed the picture for a full thirty seconds to memorize that face, head, and the telltale ears that didn't change—and reread Temkov's order once more.

The man from Omaha—originally from Minsk—returned the flash paper and photo to Frank, who put both back in the envelope.

"I'd say that this person is somewhere near here," Frank reasoned aloud, "and that we can triangulate a precise fix if the signal's still going. You've both got your radio gear and cell phones as Coachman instructed?"

The other S.V.R. agents nodded.

Frank took a small pad from his pocket, tore out three pages and wrote his portable phone number on two. Within thirty seconds, the exchange of numbers was complete. Then it took less than a minute to pay the bill, and they were on their separate ways.

Night was falling, and the unidentified signal was still pulsing at the same interval. It was drawing them out of the city . . . pulling them away from illuminated storefronts and frequent streetlights. The three agents didn't know this area, and they drove warily along unfamiliar roads where every curve might present some hazard.

They didn't like the dark.

They were tense about not knowing where they were going.

And they resented the fact that—once again—headquarters wouldn't tell them what was the point of this whole mission.

What the hell was so important about this Anna?

The S.V.R. operatives drove on, almost feeling their way through increasingly less crowded areas with more small houses framed by trees, and even a few roadside stands with signs reading VEGETABLES.

The signal was louder now.

"I'm almost there," the woman from Chicago reported on her cell phone.

"I think I am, too," the operative based in Omaha said seconds later.

A big sign now.

VETERAN'S HOSPITAL—1 MILE

The federal medical center was also large, but it wasn't *the* place.

The signal was coming from a mile or two down the road. Homing in from different directions, all three cars reached a crossroads. The drivers recognized each others' vehicles and halted. It was Frank who pointed straight ahead, and the others followed him as he stepped on the gas cautiously.

Their destination was a bit beyond a mile ahead.

It was also unexpected and puzzling . . . unsettling.

When they saw the sign, they assumed that the signal was beaming from some other location farther down the road.

NATIONAL MILITARY CEMETERY—WENDELL

There couldn't be any strategic target or intelligence operation in such a place. Knowing that, they wondered what was waiting beyond the cemetery in the place where Anna was working. A secret biochemical laboratory? Some other major installation for weapons of mass destruction?

They'd know in minutes.

Spaced apart some hundred or 50 yards, the three cars cruised past the massive burial ground that was the final resting place for thousands. Suddenly it happened. Each of the S.V.R. agents—now almost a quarter-mile beyond the closed gates of the cemetery—abruptly realized that the signal was weakening. They drove on another half mile before they stopped to confer.

By phone. They didn't want to be seen together, if possible.

"It's back there," Frank said. "Agreed?"

"Probably," the man from Omaha admitted.

"Let's circle the whole place and check it from different sides," proposed the woman Moscow called Harriet.

Making their way by back roads, it took them thirty-five minutes. The burial ground was spread over hundreds of acres, and the S.V.R. agents took wrong turns several times. When they'd checked the signal from five places and completed their journey back to a point a quarter of a mile from the front gate, they made a plan.

Since the signal was coming from the cemetery, they'd enter.

There was no gatehouse visible, but there must be a watchman who could open the portal.

Where?

Probably at some administrative office on the grounds.

"The phone number's bound to be listed. You two stay back here . . . out of sight from the gate. I'll call the office . . . do my sick woman whose car broke down at the entrance . . . ask for help. Ought to work."

It did. The guard drove up six minutes later, saw a female half-draped over the front of her car, and hurried out to assist her. She immediately and expertly hit him in the throat with one of those strong hands. He gagged, and crumpled unconscious. She flicked her vehicle's headlights twice, and the two other spies drove up at once.

Up and into the cemetery. After she followed in her car, they locked the gate so no passersby might notice it open at this unusual hour. They also tied the guard's wrists with his belt and shoved his handkerchief in his mouth to gag him. After locking him in the trunk of her car, they set off down a winding and narrow roadway—the usual thing in big cemeteries—to search for the mysterious transmitter.

After they cruised some six hundred yards, Frank pointed to a light. It shone from the window of a low, square building that could be the office . . . and meant there could be other guards or cemetery staff who had to be neutralized. The foreign agents approached the building as quietly as possible . . . found no one inside. Offices and offices—yards and yards of files, plus three computers—and a wall rack on which hung a score of keys.

Each with a tag.

One read TOOLS, and Frank pointed to it.

"We may need them," he speculated as he took that key from the rack, "so let's grab a few."

As *the* Americans often said, "No problem."

The toolshed was just a few yards behind the office building, next to a garage that housed wheeled vehicles and gear that proper operation of this large burial ground required. After Frank insisted on collecting a couple of shovels, rakes, and some other tools, the intruders turned on their radio locators again and tracked the beam.

It must lead to another building where this Anna was working, the man from Omaha reckoned. It didn't. There was no other structure in sight. Rows and rows of graves.

And more graves . . . still more.

Left turn for more than a hundred yards . . . then right in an arc.

The signal was even louder now.

They continued slowly down this roadway until the signal began to fade, and then they turned and practically inched back some fifty or sixty yards. At the point where the invisible transmitter was the most powerful, Frank stopped his car. The others pulled up behind him.

"Here we are," Frank said and twisted the ignition key to halt the engine of his blue Dodge.

"Where are we?" the S.V.R. man from Omaha challenged.

The woman killed the motor of her sedan and got out to adjust a dial on the tracking receiver she now held. She nodded toward a grave nine or ten yards away.

"That has to be it," she said.

It looked exactly like the thousand other graves that surrounded it, she judged, and then she thought of something else.

"Get the tools," she told the men. "I'll be with you in a second."

It look a little longer than that for her to open the trunk of her car and pull out the guard. He was coming out of it . . . would soon be conscious. He'd also be a threat to her survival.

"He's seen my face," she told her waiting partners. "I don't like that. I like things to be tidy."

Without another word, she reached down with her strong hands and broke the guard's neck. She twisted it twice to make certain he was dead before she untied his wrists and meticulously extracted the handkerchief gag from the corpse's mouth.

"We can leave his body down near the office on the way out," she said calmly as she walked over to join the others at the grave. A meticulous professional, she trod on stones as far as she could to reduce any footprints that might be noticed. When she had to step on the sod surface, she took off her shoes.

"What made you think we'd need tools?" she asked Frank, who'd already taken off his jacket.

"I didn't think. I guessed that maybe we *might*. It's a cemetery, right?"

"You think Anna buried the transmitter here?" the agent from Omaha wondered as he reached for a shovel. "Why here?"

"Maybe we'll find out when we finish digging," Frank replied.

The small metal plate at the grave said that the U.S. Army veteran buried here had been a private named Harry Sontup, age twenty-four. Frank didn't believe that, of course. All his instincts and the goddam transmitter told him it was a lie.

The two men dug for ten minutes while the woman kept watch, looking and listening and scanning what soldiers would call "the perimeter." The two were sweating as they rested for five minutes. They repeated the whole process four times . . . digging . . . sweating . . . resting. They were halfway through the fifth cycle when Frank's shovel hit something.

Not stone or metal. The sound said wood.

The two diggers looked at each other, and for some reason, the woman glanced at the corpse of the dead guard. No wedding ring. There'd be no grieving widow . . . maybe no orphans either. The one other man she'd killed had worn a wedding ring.

She heard the diggers breathing hard. This was quite audible now that the shoveling had stopped for the moment. They resumed the silent digging in a minute. Now it didn't take long to start to uncover a wooden box. It was about three feet wide and some six feet long.

Part of it was still concealed by earth. It took them another four minutes to expose the entire coffin lid. There was a lock on it. This seemed unusual to Frank, but he didn't pause to ponder burial rites in this foreign land.

"All clear?" he asked her.

Her eyes swept around in a full circle twice. She listened hard.

"All clear," she finally reported.

It took eight blows with the spade for Frank to knock the lock off, and he shook his head. Then he used a rake to lever up one end of the lid while the man from Omaha wedged in his own shovel to pry up the other.

It wasn't easy. It took seven efforts to loosen the lid . . . three more to raise it. Then the two S.V.R. agents managed to push it up. As they leaned forward to look in, the woman joined them. The moonlight was bright . . . the contents quite visible.

And shocking. They all stared.

Corpses were no stranger to them, but this was different.

There was no body.

What there was left them speechless.

None of these three cloak-and-dagger professionals had ever seen a skull and a pair of metal-framed eyeglasses in a coffin before.

The flesh was gone. Only bones remained.

It could be anybody.

17

ULTIMATUM TIME.

Pay up or expect something ugly.

Temkov couldn't predict exactly what might be coming, but "ugly" was a sure thing. He knew enough about the Americans to be certain they'd do a lot more than threaten now . . . and now was almost here.

Two hours and five minutes . . . give or take . . . to the U.S. deadline for the return of Alison Wilk. Not much room for give or dodge either, Temkov thought, and wondered when those idiots downstairs in forensics would report.

When and what? The possibilities . . . the whole situation . . . couldn't be defined in any reasonable way. Shaking his head, the general stared at the steel-rimmed eyeglasses on his desk. For a moment, he was proud of these remarkable spectacles with their brilliantly concealed and miniaturized transmitter.

That was the emergency locator beacon Moscow had triggered by a coded shortwave "crash" signal. The transmitter had worked, but something else had gone wrong somewhere . . . sometime. Why?

One thing was beyond question. Just a single model of this device had been made. It was Anna's, but the surgically severed skull could be someone else's. This whole thing with the coffin in the military cemetery might be some elaborate American trick to stop Moscow's search.

Anna could be alive.

The buzz of the intercom broke into his calculations.

A voice from the box announced that the forensics expert was outside. Maybe the news would be good, Temkov told himself. Perhaps Anna wasn't dead, he hoped as he ordered the dental specialist to enter immediately.

The man in the sort of white laboratory coat was gaunt, and uneasy since he'd never been in a general's office before. The box he carried so carefully—wood, lined with metal—was about a foot square.

He swallowed before he spoke.

"I return the skull, General," he said and looked at the desk.

Temkov nodded, gestured to the technician to put the box down.

"Whose is it?" Temkov asked bluntly.

"I don't have a name. All I can tell you is that the person whose dental X-rays you gave me had teeth that are completely identical to those in this skull."

"Male?" the general asked.

"Male. It's the same man."

Temkov nodded . . . pointed at the box for barely a second.

"You can leave it here," he told the nervous dental expert, who welcomed this implicit order to go.

Even before the door closed behind the man in the lab coat, Temkov was staring at the box again. It was as if some tape loop was playing in the senior intelligence executive's brain. Over and over, the same three questions were repeated. Where was the rest of Anna? Why had the damn Americans done this baffling thing? What could—should—Russia's countermove be?

The seconds ticked away without any answers.

Then Temkov's aide entered . . . looked warily at the box.

"It makes no sense," the general complained angrily. "Anna's head was the key to our most important operation in years. Anna was our finest psychic soldier . . . naturally gifted and trained for years to get into the heads of the U.S. President, the top Pentagon generals and admirals, the C.I.A. director. Of the nearly two thousand people we tried and tested and trained, Anna was by far the most promising."

He paused to catch his breath.

"No, the most *effective* of the agents in our special program," he corrected. "A real telepath who could touch minds . . . none of that remote viewing. He could get information . . . influence judgments. His head was worth an army. Why would the Americans chop it off and bury it in that nowhere place?"

"Maybe they didn't know, General."

"And they didn't know about the transmitter in the glasses either," Temkov reasoned. "They wouldn't have left them in the grave if they'd suspected the built-in locator beacon."

That still left the question of why an agent as unique and valuable as Anna had been killed, Temkov thought for the fiftieth—or one hundred and fiftieth—time since the box and coded note from Frank had come. Maybe some U.S intelligence organization went too far in squeezing Anna for information, and was now scattering the parts to hide their deed.

Temkov realized that he couldn't dwell on this now.

He had to think of himself and the message he'd received less than an hour earlier from the man who was buying the stolen weapons for $27,000,000. The price had risen—for a reason.

Things were changing.

The situation was fluid and still very dangerous.

Temkov knew this game. Now he held better cards. He knew more.

"Nicolai," the general said to his aide, "it's time to focus on the next step in our transaction with those people who paid you on the Lisbon ferry. You knew that you were . . . and those people were . . . being covered by several of our units."

"I assumed that, General."

"The man who delivered the cash to you was followed back to his headquarters in the Middle East by changing relays of our surveillance specialists. It isn't that I don't trust our customers," Temkov declared with just a trace of sarcasm in his voice, "but it would be unprofessional not to identify who we're dealing with and where to reach them."

"You've been in touch with them, General?"

"They've been in touch with us. They've offered to pay an additional two million dollars above the agreed-upon price to get one of the nasty little things right away. Why would they do that?"

He answered his own question before his aide could speak.

"They want to test it," the general reasoned. "They don't trust us."

The junior intelligence officer nodded.

In this traumatic trade, no one trusted anyone . . . for good reason. The Arabs were being logical and professional.

"And there's no reason for us to trust them," Temkov continued sensibly. "That first payment you got in Lisbon doesn't mean they're not planning to rip us off or execute some other trick. I want you to be extremely careful."

He saw the puzzlement in his aide's eyes.

"I want you to accompany the technician they insist we send with this sample," Temkov announced. "His job is to teach them how these toys work . . . and your job is to get that money back here. Go with him as my personal representative."

"How far do I go?"

Temkov smiled to reassure him.

"Only to the location in Europe where you collect the cash," the general said. "Not into the Near East. The only one of our people going there is the technician who'll deliver the weapon and show them how it works. They're paying him seven thousand dollars a week . . . for eighteen weeks . . . to instruct them."

"And to keep his mouth shut," the captain added.

That wasn't likely to be a problem, Temkov thought. The odds were better than good . . . excellent . . . that something fatal would happen to the technician when he was no longer needed. The buyers wouldn't—couldn't—trust him to stay silent about them either.

Rules of the game that was no game, Temkov told himself a moment before he wrote off the technician and thought about

Anna again. The general had to take care of himself. His bosses in the S.V.R. must be more than bothered about what had gone wrong. They'd surely savage whoever was responsible for this expensive and terrible failure.

They'd be looking for someone to blame.

Temkov realized there wasn't much time.

It was essential that he stall both the Americans and his own superiors . . . and he knew how.

SOME FIFTY-FIVE MINUTES LATER, the telephone of the C.I.A. Station Chief in Moscow rang. He recognized the caller's voice immediately, and leaned forward in his office swivel chair.

"It's me—Alison. I'm all right," his kidnapped agent said.

They were listening, of course. He'd have to be careful.

"Any medical problems?" he asked.

"Not yet," she replied. "They haven't done anything but grab me and lock me up in a room with no windows. The food's dull and I'm not sleeping well. It could be worse."

"Are you sure they didn't—"

"They haven't hurt me," she assured him, "but I'd like to get the hell out of here."

He heard the touch of controlled fear.

"We're working on it," the station chief said. "Top priority. Take my word on that."

"They say it's going to happen soon," she responded quickly.

Almost too quickly, the Station Chief judged and wondered whether she really believed it. Hope was essential for a captured intelligence officer, he told himself, and she couldn't show any weakness to the armed enemies who'd seized her.

This was a mind game as much as a physical one.

She'd surely learned that in the no-holds-barred training courses and simulations . . . the mock but realistic interrogations and brutal intimidations . . . in the intense field-tactics runs every agent got before going into hostile territory.

All that computing took him three—maybe four—seconds.

That was the time he had before Alison Wilk spoke again.

"Word is that some people upstairs have to sign off on the

arrangement . . . today or maybe tomorrow," she continued. "Tell my mom not to worry. How's Cleo?"

She was still thinking of her beloved cat.

Now the Station Chief assured her that Cleopatra was in good health . . . two meals of her regular diet daily and both company and exercise with an embassy employee who was living in the apartment and liked cats. That was true.

Then Alison Wilk was assured that her message would be relayed promptly to her mother in Arizona. That was a lie. If the mother didn't know that her daughter had been kidnapped, she couldn't leak it . . . not even by accident. This delicate situation was being handled "black" . . . secretly . . . under the table . . . hidden from public opinion . . . indignant politicians . . . hungry media people, and other undisciplined individuals who might rock the boat.

It wasn't that the C.I.A. and the S.V.R. had set this limit.

They didn't have to, for it was a given in this trade.

Everyone at the embassy and Langley was committed to freeing her ASAP—he spelled out the letters twice for emphasis—the Station Chief insisted before he said they'd all be waiting for her next call and release.

TEMKOV—ONE OF FIVE S.V.R. OFFICERS listening to that conversation—nodded and smiled. He'd bought more time with the phone call. It might be enough for what he wanted to do next.

If his agents in the U.S. had covered their tracks at the military cemetery as well as they'd reported, if the Americans wouldn't realize what the S.V.R. operatives had done there—then Temkov could move ahead immediately to collect the additional two million dollars from the terrorists by delivering the first weapon. He was still almost certain that this would be only a sample . . . to be tested before they paid for the other four.

No sane group would do that with a nuclear bomb.

This virtuous and homicidal group didn't care, Temkov thought. Like a lot of other pious pilgrims in the mass death crusades, these people retained the old-fashioned notion that the cause justified large-scale massacres. He shook his head and reached for his "secure" phone link to General Oroshenko. They had to schedule a meeting on the timetable and other details of the theft of the first miniaturized bomb.

HALF A GLOBE AWAY, Charlotte Willson's phone lit up half a minute later. The red bulb flickered on the command line. She tensed. The director of The St. John Institute understood that *they* were the only people with access to this line, and she wasn't expecting to hear from *them* now.

Everything was going according to her plan and schedule.

It must be some administrative matter.

Not exactly. Charlotte Willson didn't fully understand the *what* she was told in the next eighty-five seconds. As usual, they didn't say the *why*, but she didn't ask any questions. The man in Virginia who spoke to her didn't like questions. She listened respectfully to what he said, and she sort of nodded.

"I'll be ready to receive the shipment," she promised.

Delivery: twenty-four hours . . . maybe less.

That night and the next day, Willson tried to focus completely on the transplant patients. After reviewing every detail—again and again, hardly sleeping at all—she visited each of their training sessions, commenting positively to encourage them, of course. Without saying so, she judged that the multilingual chess player teamed with Monroe was doing exceptionally well.

As she expected, Denny Monroe was making the most progress. He could see that something was bothering Willson. She seemed uncomfortable as she continued to check her watch. She was under some kind of time pressure, the man with the gun realized.

She was waiting for someone, or something.

Whoever, whatever—it was important. He must know.

Charlotte Willson wasn't concentrating her mental defenses nearly as well as usual . . . and his "gift" seemed to be getting stronger. Now he found he could hear her thoughts . . . audibly . . . in her voice. What raced through her mind came through in bits and pieces.

A word . . . a phrase . . . a number . . . a name.

Lucky . . . someone or something called "Lucky."

Now the number.

"Twenty-six."

Twenty-six and air-conditioning. Tomorrow.

Guns and danger. Take no chances.

Security alert.

Lucky had been found. No one was safe.

That includes us, Monroe computed. Everything he'd seen told him that the transplant patients were the most secret and important targets in this place . . . wherever it was. He was one of the five patients. The threat was personal.

What threat?

Was it this Lucky who threatened Monroe and the others?

Suddenly Willson's thoughts swung to the telepathy training, and for several seconds, Monroe's focus shifted, too.

It was a reflex thing—years of danger, sudden eruptions of mortal danger—that abruptly pulled Monroe's self-preservation impulses back to twenty-six . . . guns and danger . . . and whoever or whatever was Lucky.

Another wild thought from Monroe's subconscious.

Lucky could be a full assault team or an individual. Lucky might even be one of Kelly's People.

That damn name he couldn't forget had to be important. All his instincts told him that. Now Charlotte Willson's voice broke into Monroe's reasoning.

"See you later, Denny," she announced. As she began to turn, she offered one of those fake flash-card smiles. She wasn't getting any better at it, Monroe noted as she hurried down the corridor.

18

MONROE TURNED HIS ATTENTION BACK TO THE MENTAL-
training exercise that linked him to Susan Kincaid. It was a fifty-
minute hour like those a lot of psychoanalysts favored. Of
course, the Freudian method probably wouldn't get participants
killed, but this setup at the Institute wasn't going to cost any of
the transplant patients two hundred dollars a session.

Four minutes after Willson departed, the exercise ended.

The telepathy specialist who'd been supervising from behind
a one-way mirror voiced his approval over the small loud-
speaker on the wall.

"You're doing fine," said Tommy. His real name wasn't
Tommy, of course, but his judgment was sincere.

"You two seem to work well together," he commended.

The face of the pretty woman who played chess so well lit
up in a quick, splendid grin. She was too clever to share her
true identity with anyone in this smoke-and-mirrors place, but
she wasn't hiding her feelings about her accomplishment.

She was fundamentally an honest person.

Honest and very smart.

That could get her—and agents working with her—into a lot
of trouble.

"We're not a bad team, are we?" she asked Monroe in the corridor a few moments later.

"We're better than that," he replied.

Then—ten yards down the hall—the door to another telepathy laboratory opened. Paula Taylor, the yellow-haired woman with great cheekbones and a gift for cracking safes, stepped out and waved.

She pointed at Monroe.

"Next week it's my turn," she said in a tone that was either funny or flirtatious. The African-American woman standing beside Monroe didn't care which it was. She didn't like either, or that the schedule called for rotation of partners in the training. Susan Kincaid was still annoyed when Monroe announced that he had to talk with the director now.

On his way to Willson's office, he carefully considered the requests he'd make and the questions he'd ask. None of them were what he actually had in mind, of course. He had all the phrasing worked out by the time he finally faced the director. If he did it exactly right, she'd never know that she'd been probed.

She pretended to be concerned . . . even caring . . . as a good administrator should be. She looked earnest as she listened to his requests for more physical therapy to accelerate recovery . . . more telepathy exercises . . . shooting practice in the basement range. She showed interest in his question about next month's schedule, but her mind was much more focused on defenses again and on what the phone call had told her.

Monroe learned just one thing more in his mental scan.

Bestway Heating and Air-conditioning.

It wasn't a lot, but each bit counted.

Her brushoff answers and silent efforts to lock him out didn't bother him. He wasn't troubled by her "we'll see" evasions. He'd already "seen" in his own way, and he was looking forward to Bestway Heating and Air-conditioning *tomorrow*. That was only a few hours away.

NOTHING HAPPENED in the morning.

No Bestway, or anything else unusual.

Then, at 4:10 P.M., the first truck arrived. It was medium-sized . . . dull gray and dusty . . . with three-inch black lettering that read BESTWAY HEATING AND AIR-CONDITIONING.

No address. No phone or fax number.

Just the name of a firm that didn't exist marked on the side of a truck that would be repainted and gone in a few hours. The vehicle backed into the interior loading dock, where four of The St. John Institute's security professionals opened the truck's back door.

A dozen bright-eyed and muscular young men came out quickly. They were clad in dark green coveralls that had no corporate name or logo, no identifying patch or marking of any kind. Eight of them carried big duffel bags that could have held sporting gear but didn't. The other four pushed a wheeled canvas-sided cart of the sort used for laundry.

There were no dirty clothes or household linens under the polyester sheet that covered the top, and none in the second identical cart that two of the strong young men tugged from the truck. Then one of the Institute's security specialists pointed at a door in the wall nine yards away.

"Say it," he ordered.

"General Custer," one of the new arrivals replied.

Procedures had to be maintained. With delivery of the correct identification phrase, the security man who'd demanded it nodded and led the way through that portal into the basement. The entire group in coveralls followed him, muscling the heavily laden carts with them.

The truck rolled out seconds later.

Monroe didn't see or hear any of that.

JUST BEFORE 7:00 P.M., when the transplant telepaths were supposed to be in the dining room, Monroe caught a glimpse of another vehicle. A few minutes late for the meal, he saw a second medium-sized truck moving up the driveway. He couldn't read the name painted on its side.

He guessed that it was BESTWAY.

He knew that Bestway was connected with danger of *some* kind . . . and he sensed that the danger was here, or was coming. He didn't see the additional fourteen men in those un-marked coveralls emerge from this second vehicle, but he felt that he had to protect himself from the threat of whoever or whatever was in it.

He ran this back and forth in his mind all through the meal as pretty blonde Paula Taylor flirted and Cesar Fuentes did his deftly charming macho act that worked so well with most women.

Across the table, Susan Kincaid seemed to be interested. She was more than that, Monroe realized.

She was annoyed. *Negative*. Not Susan Kincaid, but the impact of her attitude . . . the potential for trouble. If she was distracted or offended—if anything pulled any member of this cover-action team from a totally unified effort—the whole group might be in danger.

The Harvard Business School efficiently warned students about the need for practical risk management. Executives who didn't handle such matters correctly might be fired. In the cloak-and-dagger world, field agents who got it wrong could be buried—sometimes alive, Monroe reflected as Cesar Fuentes and Paula Taylor deftly bantered on.

Harry Chen scanned his fellow transplants.

"You aren't listening, are you, Denny?" he noted quietly.

"I'm waiting for the good part," Monroe dodged, and silently wondered why he felt that the truck he'd seen meant imminent violence.

His eyes swung to Dr. Wilson, at the next table. She was doing her cool-administrator act, but he could see she was starting to perspire. She knew why the truck had come and what was in it. She wasn't telling the patients or anyone else here.

The meal ended, Monroe strolled from the dining room with the woman who was his training partner. After all their telepathic exercises together, he felt closer to her than to the others . . . and there was something else besides her intelligence, judg-ment, and honest warmth that he liked. He decided to warn her.

At minimum personal risk. That was his way.

Walking with her down the corridor, he spoke about the food at the Institute and simultaneously sent her a very different message telepathically. Even if this passageway was decorated with concealed eavesdropping gear—a reasonable presumption for any part of the building—his communication would not be noticed.

It was brief and blunt.

"There may be trouble tonight. I don't know exactly what. Stay in your room, and jam the door by putting a chair under the knob inside. Don't open it unless and until I tell you . . . this way. Nothing audible. No questions now. Trust me."

She didn't hesitate.

She realized that she didn't know everything about this man, but she was gut-certain he was the only person in this place—in this operation—she could possibly trust. That had become clear to her . . . without her thinking about it consciously . . . in the joint training.

Without a word or a smile, she nodded, and barely a moment later, he was walking back to his room. He had his moves figured out by the time he got there. There was no space in the plan for an error. With his broad back blocking the view of the surveillance camera, Monroe donned the hospital-patient bathrobe he disliked. It had a large pocket. That was where he concealed the pistol after he slipped it from its hiding place.

He felt oddly cheerful as he left the room. After months of recovery . . . inaction . . . half-truths and evasions, he was going to be doing something. He was tired of being done to . . . manipulated . . . treated like some instrument in a game nobody here would name. By going ahead with what he wanted to do, he risked some unspecified confrontation or collision. It probably wasn't admirable in psychiatric or theological circles, the self-aware field agent told himself as he headed for the stairs, but those were two of the things at which he excelled.

He felt the old tension.

He was totally alert . . . confident . . . and wary.

Now he was the walking weapon Charlotte Willson had read about in the fat, classified file . . . physically and mentally. *Downstairs*, he calculated. Whatever had come in the truck, he'd find it below. Aside from the briefing, no transplant patient had been on the lower floors. That's where he'd look.

There'd be somebody downstairs watching the elevator door, he reckoned. That was why he'd come by the stairs. Ground level. He stepped from the stairwell . . . saw one of the young men in the unmarked coveralls. That didn't matter to Denny Monroe. Seated on a plastic chair beside a metal door, the husky stranger's basic identity was immediately clear.

The assault rifle across his knees took care of that.

The weapon was military . . . U.S. Army.

"I have an appointment with Doctor Willson," Monroe lied and pointed at the door as if he knew what was behind it.

The man with the assault rifle shook his head.

"I don't think so," he replied.

He also had one of those murderous combat knives in a sheath above his right ankle. The blade matched his manner, Monroe thought.

"Please ask her," Monroe urged in a voice that was quiet but very hard. The sentry didn't know what that hard thing was, but he didn't want to confront it.

The guard stood up slowly . . . carefully.

Keeping his eyes on the man in the patient's bathrobe, he rapped on the door three times . . . then twice. Monroe recognized this as a prearranged signal. No surprise here. It was what he'd expect from military personnel on guard duty.

That was who this man with the assault rifle and knife had to be. Next question: Why had he come here *now* . . . and how many more soldiers had come with him?

The steel door opened on well-oiled hinges.

Willson came out, visibly surprised to see Monroe.

"Denny," she began in that crisp professional tone. "Something came up and this isn't a good time—"

"It's good enough," he broke in as a second man in those coveralls—carrying the same model assault rifle—appeared in the doorway behind her. Scanning the scene in a split second and sensing tension, he reacted automatically by raising his rapid-fire gun so it faced Monroe.

Charlotte Willson almost flinched when she saw the look in Monroe's eyes. It wasn't supposed to happen like this.

"I don't like it when somebody points a fucking automatic weapon at me," he announced coldly.

"It's okay," she hurried to tell the guards. "We're on the same team."

As they lowered their guns, she turned back to Monroe.

"Denny, I can't talk to you now—"

"You can talk to all of us—in three minutes," he interrupted ruthlessly. "All five of us. Room B. And don't bring anyone you'd rather not have hear about Lucky."

She swallowed . . . tasted something coppery.

It was fear.

She had never mentioned Lucky in this building. She knew the game and the rules. Lucky could get people killed . . . even medical administrators. Lucky was more than Top Secret. It was bitter and shocking to think that Monroe had learned about Lucky.

It was intimidating. No choice.

Minutes later, the worried, wary director of The St. John Institute faced Monroe and the other four "dead" field agents in Room B. The armed young men in coveralls were outside, barring entry to everyone else. Willson was breathing hard as she pushed down her stress. She tried to frame her opening remarks.

Monroe spoke first.

"Settle down and get comfortable," he urged his fellow transplant patients. "Doctor Willson wants to give us the big picture on the program here . . . and a progress report. She's going to bring us right up to date on the security situation, too."

Willson nodded.

"You're on, Doc," Monroe said as he sat down.

"I'll be briefing you from time to time in the regular course of things," she said, hoping they couldn't see her sweat. "It's the standard procedure in our research projects."

"Tell us all about this project," Monroe pressed.

She inhaled and exhaled deeply . . . twice . . . before she began.

"I'll share with you the basic history of this entire effort," she announced. "It goes back several years—before our Institute was founded."

She didn't mention when it was founded, Monroe noted.

Or by whom.

"We had been working for some time on scientific experiments in telepathy. This was after the Stargate remote-viewing project had closed down several years earlier. From the start, we concentrated on improved mental communication . . . not viewing."

She didn't say who "we" were.

She probably wouldn't, Monroe thought.

"A variety of approaches were explored," she continued. "That's usual in research programs. One effort was chemical. Could there be some chemical or biochemical innovation that might significantly improve telepathic abilities?"

Now they were all leaning forward . . . intently.

"Over three years, our scientists worked to try to find a breakthrough serum. After scores of failures, one of the research teams was making major progress with a serum."

"A yellow serum?" Paula Taylor asked.

Willson nodded.

"It was very promising, but it still had to be tested on people," she said.

Us, Monroe thought. Was the scientist named Kelly?

"Who was the scientist?" Monroe questioned, without much hope he'd get an honest answer.

"I don't know," she replied.

That could be the truth, he realized. No reason they'd tell her. It was all compartmentalized . . . in every country.

"That's not your business, or mine," she confirmed. "While the research chemists were trying to determine the best way to test the serum on people . . . and learn *which* people would be optimum subjects . . . there was a totally unexpected development far from the laboratory."

She paused to frame her words—sentences—carefully.

"Four and a half months ago, a man . . . Caucasian . . . about thirty-five . . . was found unconscious in an alley behind a District of Columbia striptease establishment that featured transvestites. He was taken to a hospital, where an intern who'd left what used to be Leningrad 13 years earlier recognized the man's vague babbling as Russian."

"Far out!" Paula Taylor enthused.

"You could say that," the director of The St. John Institute agreed. "Well, some of the things the man mumbled made the intern mention this to a woman who lived across the hall from the young doctor's parents . . . and worked for a U.S. intelligence organization."

Willson didn't name that either.

"So professionals came into the picture," she continued. "When they saw that all of the patient's I.D. consisted of top-quality fakes, agents naturally proceeded to find and search his apartment."

Very quickly, Monroe reckoned. Very thoroughly . . . at least a dozen counterespionage professionals with all the state-of-the-art gear to go right down to the wiring.

"They found the latest thing in microdot technology," she reported, "and some more top-quality fake I.D.—and over two hundred thousand dollars in cash. Since everything seemed to point to the strong possibility that the man in the hospital was a foreign operative, senior officials concluded that it might be best to move the patient immediately to a secure medical facility for further treatment."

She cleared her throat.

This next part wasn't going to be that comfortable to tell.

"While he was getting very good medical treatment and showing signs of improvement, he also received ultramodern hypnosis, and there were drug-assisted interrogations," Willson said. "I'm told those procedures are standard in counterespionage work."

The five transplant patients nodded.

"The results of these procedures were information about an important Russian operation, and this man's role in it," she told them. "The S.V.R. has been spending a lot of money on a major psy-war effort to train elite operatives in telepathy and mind control. It's very sophisticated, and he was a key player. Everything looked very promising as he continued to recover slowly."

"What went wrong?" Monroe asked suddenly.

"What makes you think something went wrong?" she snapped.

"Just a wild guess," he replied. "What happened?"

"He was very good, you know," Willson fenced. "That's what I hear. Extremely good, and not nearly as weak as he pretended. Somehow he escaped and reached another cache of cash—his backup money. They tell me he had thirty-one thousand dollars on him in Philadelphia the night he was run down by a stoned motorcyclist on a Harley."

Susan Kincaid looked at Monroe.

"Great bike," he said. "Did it kill him?"

"He was seriously injured," Willson replied as she ignored the sarcastic remark about the Harley. "It was remarkable that he survived. So were the accident and the recapture. All this inspired some cynical junior officer to code-name him 'Lucky'."

Good. Lucky had been identified, Monroe thought.

There was still Kelly.

"Though this foreign agent got the best medical care in an even more secure facility, within ten days the doctors saw that he wasn't going to make it. That was when *we* got lucky," Willson said, and nodded in emphasis.

"It all came together. The yellow serum was finally ready, and he was a telepath. *Somebody* in one of our defense units knew that one of you urgently needed a transplant. *Somebody* else had an extraordinary idea. It was a long shot but worth trying. Lucky would be gone in a week or two. Then a massive computer scan of field agents picked up the medical records of the rest of you."

She paused . . . wondering how they'd react when she spelled it out in full. They could get angry, even hysterical.

"Understand that this was a great opportunity to save you and simultaneously help our national defense," she reasoned in her best selling voice. "Some of you might have died if we hadn't done this. It required clearance at the highest level. Everyone knew it was risky."

"I don't mean to pry," Monroe said, "but exactly what are

you trying to tell us. *What* required the clearance?"

She took another deep breath.

"The transplants. It was unusual. As I told you, you all got organs from the same donor."

She hesitated.

"*Lucky?*" Monroe reasoned.

She nodded.

"Was he dead?" Monroe asked.

"Of course. You think we'd kill him?" she replied angrily.

"I think you'd do anything . . . for medical science, of course," he said. "Just like the old baron."

Her face showed she didn't understand.

"Baron Frankenstein," Susan Kincaid explained. "That's not so funny, Denny."

"I'm not laughing," Harry Chen concurred.

"You're saying we've all got parts of the same dead man who was a Russian spy?" the blonde woman tested.

"A Russian *telepath* spy," Monroe specified.

"Holy shit!" Cesar Fuentes reacted.

"My thoughts precisely. Now let Doctor Willson tell us the rest of it," Monroe said. "There's more, right?"

She didn't lose her temper.

"We did everything possible in both phases to protect you," she assured them. "It was a remarkable effort and . . . *overall* . . . a great success."

She paused . . . coughed twice.

"Not a complete success?" Susan Kincaid asked.

"I'm sorry that there were two fatalities. We knew this effort was new and risky, but we didn't expect that. Five of you have come through in good health—better every day," Willson pointed out to emphasize the positive. "Forensic experts are working to determine the causes of those fatalities."

"You mentioned *two* phases," Harry Chen reminded thoughtfully.

"Transplant was the first, and recovery plus the serum to strengthen telepathic skills in the second. Everything has been moving well," the director of the Institute said. "The counter-intelligence people were concerned that Lucky might be missed by his control in Moscow, but there was no sign of any covert activity that might point here."

"Until when?" Monroe said.

"This week. After the seven organs were removed from Lucky's corpse, our security people decided that at least some of what was left should be sent far away—in a regular wooden coffin so it would look like a normal burial. There wasn't a lot left, but it went into a proper box in a large cemetery, along with forged papers and death certificate."

"Nice funeral?"

"I don't know, Denny," Charlotte Willson replied harshly. "What I do know is that within the last three or four days, someone penetrated the cemetery at night, killed the watchman, and looted the coffin. The grave robber . . . or robbers . . . took two items that could specifically identify Lucky."

"They left the hole?" Monroe probed.

"As a matter of fact, somebody did a fairly good job of closing it and replacing the turf. It was almost good enough," Willson reported. "Why do you ask?"

"Because opening and closing a grave isn't usually a one-man job. It had to be a team . . . and I don't think it was the Yankees."

He must have been hell on his mother, Willson thought.

"Whoever it was," she answered, "there was nothing in the coffin or the cemetery records pointing to us here."

Now Susan Kincaid frowned.

"If they could locate the cemetery and pinpoint this one grave," she calculated, "they might be smart enough to find us, too."

"Take it easy," Monroe advised. "No reason to panic, right?"

"Certainly not," Willson agreed. "We're being prudent, though. We're looking into all the possibilities."

Monroe pointed to the exit.

"And that's why you've brought in those fine young fellows in the coveralls," he said sarcastically. "The guys outside with the assault rifles. Or are they here for the bowling contest? I'd guess we've got at least a platoon of paratroopers with us. Airborne . . . mean and lean. Any comment on that possibility?"

"Denny, we brought in additional security for your—"

Showing no respect for her Ph.D., the man she'd named Denny Monroe broke in like a bulldozer.

"I've got another possibility you can try on for size," he said. "I'll bet ten bucks there are some other guys in jumpsuits out in the front yard manning a couple of antitank weapons . . . and crews on the roof with heat-seeking ground-to-air missiles. The chopper should arrive any damn minute."

He sounded angry but very certain.

He couldn't be ignored.

"What chopper?" Paula Taylor blurted.

"The state-of-the-art number that's going to sweep this whole property with thermal tracking beams to pinpoint warm bodies in the dark . . . a real fine night scanner with half a dozen machine guns to keep the neighbors honest," Monroe announced. "Army's been using them for a couple of years."

They all looked at Charlotte Willson.

The helicopter was a sound idea, she thought.

She'd speak to *them*—the people who'd sent the soldiers—about that as soon as this briefing ended.

"All I can say is that we'll do whatever is necessary to protect you," she told them.

"I'm not knocking your intentions, Doctor," Monroe replied, "but you've got five first-class, battle-tested field agents here who could help protect themselves if they had weapons. Check your records. We know all about weapons. We're very good with many kinds of guns . . . knives . . . rockets . . . bombs . . . you name it."

"That won't be necessary," Willson answered cautiously.

"Piano wire," Fuentes said.

"What?"

"We're good with piano wire, too," he explained.

That was true, but Chen shook his head. He could see she wouldn't care about those things.

"Thanks for sharing that," the head of The St. John Institute told them. "We can talk about it tomorrow."

"Tomorrow we'll be down on that firing range you've got in the basement," Monroe contradicted bluntly. "I know it's there, and I'm betting you've got small arms. If you don't have enough shoulder and handguns, pick up the phone. We want a full spread, Doc, right up to silencers and sniper scopes and night-vision toys."

He wasn't asking. He was telling.

"It's getting late," she said to escape the confrontation . . . at least temporarily. Everything she knew about Monroe told her that "temporarily" would not be very long.

The briefing ended ninety seconds later. Fuentes was the first of the transplant agents to leave the room . . . Monroe the last. Avoiding eye contact with him, Charlotte Willson followed him into the corridor. Two of the armed paratroopers stood guard outside the door.

One who'd been on guard duty downstairs recognized Monroe.

He nodded at his back.

"Who is that guy?" the soldier asked Willson softly.

"You don't want to know," she answered in a voice that could cut plate glass.

She walked swiftly to her office. By the time she sat behind the desk with the sophisticated electronic controls and communications equipment, Charlotte Willson knew what she had to do. She used the "secure" line with the scrambler attachment to call for the damn heat-sweeping helicopter scan Monroe had spoken of . . . and for another twenty airborne soldiers.

No, she'd need thirty, to be safe.

She was up making defensive plans until 1:00 A.M. She was tense and tired when she lay down to try to sleep. She didn't feel safe at all.

19

BODY ARMOR.

That was the first thing the director of The St. John Institute thought about when she awoke.

She was no soldier or cloak-and-dagger veteran, but she knew that the man she'd named Denny Monroe would want such protective gear for himself and the others on the team.

Gas masks, too.

If an S.V.R. strike unit tracking Lucky were to attack, gas might be a key weapon, Willson speculated as she rubbed her eyes. That was how Monroe would reason, and she had to take him seriously. She didn't like his blunt, suspicious, difficult manner . . . but she had to respect his survival skills and experience.

For a moment, she wondered whether he respected her . . . her skills . . . her authority. Barely, if at all, she concluded wearily and headed for the shower. She had to be fully alert . . . totally awake and focused . . . when she spoke on the "hot" command line in fifteen minutes.

No problem.

That's what the man at the other end said immediately.

The body armor and masks would arrive with the additional soldiers by eight that night.

The helicopter scan was to start by nine.

None of this seemed to bother him, she realized resentfully. In the mean and no-holds-barred covert-action world where he and Monroe operated, this sort of mortal danger was routine . . . and everyone was battle-ready all the time. She lived at least a galaxy away, Willson told herself. Now she faced the fact that she could deal comfortably with secrecy and deception . . . but the imminent possibility of a violent and potentially fatal assault right here at any minute was a shock.

The St. John Institute was a research-and-training facility.

Nobody was supposed to die here.

It wasn't fair that she should be at risk because of something done wrong at a cemetery many hundreds of miles away. She was an excellent administrator who'd done everything very carefully and absolutely correctly, but that wouldn't matter to the enemy agents who'd dug up Lucky's coffin. They wouldn't care that she hadn't harmed Lucky, or anyone else.

They'd killed the cemetery watchman.

They wouldn't hesitate to kill everyone here . . . unless the paratroopers and the transplant field agents managed to stop them. Reinforcements were on the way, she reassured herself. That helped a little as she started downstairs to check the defenses and begin distribution of the weapons to Monroe and his telepathic group.

She watched as they examined the guns.

Semiautomatic pistols . . . they picked the nine-millimeter models with the fourteen-round clips, illegal for civilians under U.S. law.

Sniper rifles with scopes and night vision.

Carbines, and three kinds of automatic weapons . . . U.S. . . . German . . . Israeli.

Several kinds of ammunition, including the armor-piercing rounds that many indignant law-enforcement people called "cop killers."

She saw them pick up the guns . . . sniff for scent of recent firing . . . heft the weapons. Then the five transplant patients all did the same thing . . . they didn't have to say a word to each other to perform deftly, simultaneously. It was, after all, the logical thing to do.

They fieldstripped the weapons at extraordinary speed, took the guns apart . . . reassembled them . . . inserted clips. Then they repeated the whole procedure. They looked at each other . . . nodded.

They were very fast . . . totally cool.

Utterly professional, the administrator who ran The St. John Institute judged.

"Once more, with music," Monroe said, and they didn't hesitate. They went through the entire process of disassembling and reassembling as if they could do it in their sleep. They could, Charlotte Willson recalled suddenly. According to their files, they were masters of many other weapons—including former Sovblock and Chinese as well.

Primitive things, too. Monroe was extremely efficient with crossbow and throwing spear. That figured, she realized. There was some primitive streak in this complex and oddly sophisticated man . . . a Phi Beta Kappa student at college and now so accurate throwing axes. He wasn't easy to predict or to please, harder to control. The really smart ones were, she reflected a moment before he spoke.

"Not bad, Doc," he said. "What about grenades?"

"Any flavor you want. Incendiary . . . antipersonnel . . . smoke . . . nauseating gas. We'll bring up an assorted crate for the firing tomorrow," she replied.

"You're getting with the program," Monroe complimented.

"Thank you."

"Just remember we *are* the program."

She shook her head.

"You don't have to be a wise guy, Denny," she told him.

He shrugged as he put down the Israeli "Galil" assault rifle.

"I'm afraid I do, Doc," he answered truthfully.

Then the telepaths left. As promised, the additional force of airborne troopers showed up that night in another pair of vans.

These didn't carry any signs linked to the air-conditioning firm. In accord with Company policy . . . following Langley rules . . . these vehicles bore the names of a different set of nonexistent companies.

And the night-searching helicopter arrived on time.

Flying with muffled rotors, it floated overhead in changing patterns until an hour before dawn. It was barely audible, Willson judged as she tried to sleep. Monroe had no difficulty at all in getting his seven hours. He could even doze in the battering din inside an M.R.I. medical scanner . . . though he hated the confinement of the enveloping metal tube still standard in many hospitals.

The tiny sound of a sneakered foot on thick grass would jerk him to immediate alertness, though. So would the whisper of a window being opened twenty yards away. Each of those was a warning.

He knew that from experience.

This night, he slept reasonably well. He was in good spirits at breakfast, rested and fairly sure that if Lucky's friends came, it would be after dark. Only amateurs would attack in broad daylight, when shooters within would have the best targets. The team that dug up the coffin wouldn't have any amateurs, he reasoned as he went off at 9:30 A.M. for the regular two hours of telepathy exercises. This would be his final session with Susan Kincaid.

Eleven-thirty—time to shoot.

Each of the five telepaths methodically took a turn with the full variety of weapons. They fired round after round, getting more accurate every minute after months of physical inactivity and major surgery for life-threatening conditions. It came back to them quickly . . . impressively.

Willson wasn't surprised that they were excellent shots.

She expected that Monroe would be the best, and he was.

Bull's-eye after bull's-eye after bull's-eye.

Left-handed and right . . . then both simultaneously.

He delivered just as his file reported he could. He wasn't really perfect, Willson reminded herself. He was distrustful . . .

sometimes too clever . . . sometimes too aggressive. And he did things how and when he pleased . . . when he thought that was better.

He thought too damn much and was a lot too independent, the intelligent and disciplined head of The St. John Institute told herself . . . for the hundredth time. As the shots echoed in the firing range, she wondered why the others would instinctively accept such a man as leader.

She couldn't see the logic of it.

Maybe it wasn't visible. Perhaps they *sensed* something she didn't, Willson speculated. Whatever it was, the others didn't question it. The gut-cunning of field agents couldn't be debated, and Charlotte Willson wasn't about to try.

The firing continued for several minutes. A paratrooper lieutenant who was watching nodded . . . nodded again. He was clearly impressed by the marksmanship.

"Not bad," he complimented as the shooting ended.

"Beginner's luck," Monroe replied with a straight face.

"Stick with it," the soldier advised in a voice edged with irony.

He didn't say anything else. His whole force was under orders not to talk to or question anyone but the director of this place. No one had spoken of what this place was, or who might attack it. The reinforcements who'd arrived yesterday didn't know either. Realizing that he shouldn't have uttered a word to any of the civilian shooters, the lieutenant turned on his heel and strode away.

Willson saw Monroe leave with smiling Paula Taylor and Susan Kincaid. The head of The St. John Institute didn't hear what he said as he left the range.

"I'M SORRY FOR THE soldier boy," Monroe confided. "They haven't told him."

"Told him what?" Taylor asked.

"That he's going to stay. They're all going to stay here—every one of those paratroopers—for a long time. And no phone calls to significant or insignificant others."

The yellow-haired woman looked puzzled.

"We're *hot*," Susan Kincaid explained. "We're *hot*, so they're in the deep freeze."

"Our savvy chess champ is right," Monroe agreed. "We're top secret and a half, and those poor guys have seen our faces. They don't know exactly who we are or what the hell's going on, but they know the whole deal's Big Time. They could say *something* to *somebody*. That makes them dangerous."

"To us?"

"To us . . . to the Institute . . . to the whole fucking operation, whatever it is. And to the brilliant paranoids who tell Willson what and who to do . . . and what to serve us for dinner. They've got Ph.D. nutritionists planning our breakfast nine weeks from tomorrow."

"Will the paratroopers still be here then?" Paula Taylor asked.

"They leave *after* we do . . . probably three or four months after," Monroe said as they reached the elevator. "If they're lucky . . . if they don't know where this Institute is . . . and a bunch of other ifs. Some ands and buts, too."

He pressed the call button beside the elevator.

"What about us, Denny?" Taylor wondered. "I don't mean to pry, but when do *we* get out of here?"

He was visibly amused.

"First, let's find out where *here* is," he replied wryly. "Maybe after that, they'll tell us where we're going."

"And why?" the black woman asked.

"That'll be the last thing," Monroe predicted. "Of course, they may not know themselves where or why . . . not yet."

"We're a contingency strike force?" Kincaid questioned.

"Maybe. We're in the middle of some kind of very expensive experiment, kid. Actually, we *are* the experiment. If it doesn't work, nobody will be blamed, because it's so fucking secret no one in the Congress or the media will know," Monroe said.

"We'll know," Susan Kincaid thought aloud and frowned. "But we'll be dead, right?"

"*Really* dead. It won't be phoney this time," Monroe predicted. "If we don't die in the operation, or if the mission fails, this crowd won't leave anybody to write a book about it."

The elevator door began to open.

"But if we pull it off, we'll be stars, with good wages and a great dental plan," he added.

"Pension?" Kincaid asked.

"Depends on how long you live," Monroe chuckled.

Paula Taylor smiled at the grim jest. Kincaid didn't. She reminded herself that she might well be dead before this if not for the transplant. That helped . . . a little.

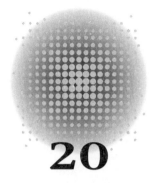

20

JUST OVER AN HOUR AFTER THE ELEVATOR BEGAN TO RISE.

A wide ocean and an entire continent away.

The jet was an eighteen-year-old Boeing 727 that a portly Greek airplane broker who didn't annoy customers with a lot of questions had sold—for cash—to a nonexistent charter outfit.

With a Luxembourg address, but incorporated in Panama.

Using a Bahamas' bank whose staff couldn't even spell "curious."

There were many large and small air services operating in East and Central Africa, some transporting charter groups . . . others moving high-priority machine parts or assorted medical supplies . . . plus a few whose manifests didn't list the boxes of cash, cartons, or who knew what for smugglers, and crates of ammunition for both bank robbers and ambitious guerrilla groups. There were usually a couple of cases of champagne for bribing customs officials.

This 727 had been purchased for Swiss francs and a single purpose.

It wasn't to start any kind of ongoing business.

The goal was to make two flights. This was the first one.

It was a reconnaissance run. The people who bought this jet

wanted to make sure there'd be no problems that might inter-fere with the second flight. That was the real deal. The second would follow in less than seventy-two hours, and people would be killed if it was not a complete success.

The well-dressed vice president of the fictitious charter carrier hadn't explained much to the freelance Romanian pilot and navigator. When he'd hired them in one of the better brothels in the port that used to be called Trieste, he'd given each of them $11,000 and a promise of the same amount when the second flight was completed.

From Cyprus to Khartoum.

After refueling . . . on to the Kenyan city of Mombassa . . . then back to Cairo.

He didn't say what would follow after they were paid off at the field in Egypt. They certainly didn't ask. They'd buy seats on the next flight to Rome, where they knew three very friendly sisters with a lot of experience.

What they didn't know was the cargo destined for Mom-bassa. There were three crates—each about two and a half feet square—a dozen yards behind the cockpit as the 727 bore steadily through the night over the southern Sudan. These boxes were marked MEDICAL SUPPLIES—FRAGILE, but the prag-matic Romanians realized that a recon run wasn't necessary for delivery of such humanitarian cargo.

And nobody paid $22,000 to fly in medicine.

Nobody this pilot or navigator had ever met.

"How much longer?" the pilot asked, and the navigator checked.

"About two hours to Cairo," he replied. They were returning. Now he jerked his right thumb to point over his shoulder.

"What do you think?" he asked. He meant the crates.

"I don't *think*," the pilot answered in a voice that reflected annoyance at the naive question. "I *fly*."

Only a suicidal idiot would want to find out what the cargo was in a deal like this, the pilot thought and silently decided he wouldn't work with this fool again. He scowled half the way to the Egyptian border.

* * *

BACK IN TEXAS, General Temkov's operative code-named Frank was nearly as grim. He had been ever since they sent the skull and eyeglasses to Moscow and got back the order to ascertain where the rest of Anna was . . . and why the dismemberment. It had to be something nasty, Frank sensed, and the idea of searching for the torso or assorted parts was creepy.

He was looking, and a whole army of U.S. intelligence professionals was surely committed to making certain he failed. The odds against finding even one piece of Anna were enormous, assuming the S.V.R.'s most brilliant telepath hadn't been totally incinerated. That wasn't all. The Americans would be watching and waiting, ready to sweep from the board any player who made the slightest progress in solving the puzzle.

It was a very high-stakes game, Frank calculated.

Pieces of him could end up in somebody else's grave, too.

Aware that nobody in Moscow cared much about this possibility because Anna was of paramount importance, Frank began the search cautiously. His survival plan was to do it at arm's length . . . out of sight. He wouldn't search from his residence or with his hardware . . . not at first. He'd stay remote for as long as possible.

After a wary Web scan, he went to Phoenix, where he left his small suitcase in a locker at the main bus station downtown. Then he made his way to a comfortable and busy cybercafé named "Web World," where a dozen young men and several twenty-something women were picking up e-mail, bantering, playing electronic war games, and enjoying a variety of very contemporary things on a score of computers.

They obviously knew what they were doing.

The Russian agent was equally competent. It cost him only a few dollars and less than half an hour to hack into the data bank at the military cemetery where the skull and spectacles had rested. Frank pulled up a map of the place . . . zeroed in on the location of the grave . . . pushed and pulled until he had the exact number.

With that information, he went on to find in a linked list the name of the soldier who had supposedly been buried. Next, the date of death . . . the I.D. number on the man's military dog tag . . . birthplace, Los Angeles . . . age. It was all complete, as routine required.

It was also all a fraud.

First-class. The Americans had grown pretty good at this sort of deception. Frank had to move forward. The sole route was to search the records in Los Angeles to see if the Americans had totally invented the dead man or switched identities with a real person.

Not here. Not now.

The longer he stayed, the greater the risk that somebody might remember him if there was ever an electronic backsweep for who'd been probing the cemetery records. It wasn't likely that the data bank he'd just tapped needed any such protective alarm. He couldn't take the chance.

Time to "bug out."

Some of those American expressions were not bad, Frank thought as he walked back to the large, modern bus terminal on Van Buren Street. After collecting his suitcase, he left the station and circled the block so he might check again for followers. Then he took a taxi to the airport, bought a ticket on the 4:40 P.M. flight to Los Angeles, and purchased a copy of Phoenix's only surviving daily to read while he waited.

There was a great deal of waiting in the supposedly glamorous cloak-and-dagger world, the S.V.R. agent brooded as he scanned the front page of *The Arizona Republic*. He'd done enough so he wasn't usually bothered by it, but now he wanted to get out of town as soon as possible.

He didn't feel safe here.

He shrugged when he faced up to the fact that he didn't really feel safe anywhere. It wasn't just the usual uneasiness. That had significantly diminished when the tactics of both the Eastern bloc—now history—and the West turned less fierce when communism subsided and the U.S.S.R. disappeared. Now he was as tense and worried as before. The very able Anna had been eliminated by some U.S. security group . . . killed and dismembered.

Was the Cold War *really* over, the S.V.R. operative asked himself grimly as he boarded the airliner, to Los Angeles. If the

Americans found him, Frank thought again and felt his heart beating faster, would they chop him into pieces, too? When the singsong voice on the cabin's loudspeakers announced that takeoff was imminent, he hardly heard the words.

He had to move fast.

He had to be in and out on this visit to Los Angeles.

He couldn't offer a stationary target.

He'd check into a decent downtown hotel. All of them had rooms where he could plug in the laptop in his suitcase. He'd spend the night to avoid attracting any attention . . . raid the Los Angeles public data bank for birth information . . . check out by 9:00 A.M. . . . and be in a plane landing at Denver's fine new airport by lunchtime.

There was just one thing wrong with the plan.

The electronic archives of the City of Los Angeles had no record of the one supposedly buried in that military cemetery as having been born in the year specified in the Army data bank . . . not then nor for three years before or after.

That was nothing to celebrate, but at least Frank had gotten out of Los Angeles without incident. He had anticipated the possibility that the information in the cemetery's records was accidentally or deliberately wrong. As an experienced field agent, he'd already planned his next step.

Once again, it would be hit and run. Denver.

He'd be out of Denver by night. The local telephone book had an advertisement for a motel with computer-ready rooms . . . near the airport. Such a motel was used to a blurring flow of nearly anonymous transients in for brief stays . . . for rest between flights . . . for business . . . or perhaps for some carnal connection. It was *extremely unlikely* that he'd be noticed.

He wouldn't be entirely safe, but he never was.

"Extremely unlikely" often had to do in the espionage world. To raise his spirits from that awful reality, he cheered himself with the thought that he already had the electronic address of his next target . . . the central computer for U.S. Army personnel records.

Now he was getting closer, he exulted.

Soon he'd have answers—one way or the other—about

whether the soldier allegedly buried in that grave ever existed. The big data bank had defenses, but these cyber bankers weren't nearly as tough as those of the more strategic Pentagon or C.I.A. computers.

Another S.V.R. agent—a crypto expert—had stolen the passwords to several data banks of American military organizations, including the one crammed with Army personnel records. Within the next two hours, Frank would attack it carefully . . . stealthily . . . swiftly.

Like an expert hunter, he told himself as he strode from the airliner—and the Americans would never know. It was a lot better being the hunter than the hunted, he thought. He'd been in deep cover in the United States for a long time, and he was tired of that. The fact that he couldn't relax or let down his guard for a second was taking its toll.

Suddenly he recalled—very clearly—the open coffin in the military cemetery.

He could "see" the skull and the eyeglasses.

No, he couldn't slow down at all . . . not yet.

Maybe not even after he found the pieces or the fate of Anna.

For a few seconds, he was bitter.

Then he forced himself to straighten up and put on the smile that so many Americans seemed to favor like a fresh shirt. They'd expect it when he reached the registration desk at the motel. He didn't disappoint them.

21

THE SECOND FLIGHT.

The *real* thing, the Romanian pilot thought as he expertly guided the old jet south again in the starry African night. They must have found the earlier recon run satisfactory . . . whoever "they" were.

They had made some operational changes for this trip. The two crates—wrapped in black plastic stenciled MEDICAL SUPPLIES in white block letters—were in the rear of the plane behind a crisscross of heavy-duty straps that denied access.

Neither the pilot nor the navigator could get close enough to examine or touch the boxes. They couldn't figure out just what the cargo might be, but the Romanian told himself that was almost surely a good thing. His mother had repeatedly assured him that "what you don't know can't hurt you." So far in his thirty-eight years, that peasant wisdom had proven sound.

The isolation of the crates wasn't the sole change.

The route had been modified . . . just a bit . . . and the altitude for the flight had been altered as well. They had said it was for safety purposes—to avoid storms ahead, predicted by regional meteorological stations. A practical . . . all right, somewhat cynical . . . man, the Romanian wasn't at all sure.

People lied a lot.

Men moving cargo at night by charter plane in Africa lied more than almost anyone else.

In accord with instructions repeated twice, the pilot had flown the 727 down to Khartoum at four hundred eighty miles an hour . . . at twenty-one thousand feet. After refueling at the main airport of the Sudanese capital, the Romanian obeyed orders to take the jet up to twenty-four thousand feet for the next segment of the journey.

They'd given no reason for the higher altitude for this leg over Ethiopia. Checking with his navigator, the pilot learned that they were on schedule . . . on course by the global positioning gear . . . and within minutes of the Kenyan border. The route he'd been given called for a sharp turn east toward the Eritrean frontier before they went on to Mombassa.

The Romanian didn't know why this turn was necessary.

He was equally ignorant of the jet that had been following the 727 for several hours.

Some twenty miles behind . . . with no wing lights, but effective tracking radar.

The pilot of the 727 turned to the navigator for an estimated time of arrival . . . saw the man seated beside him was grinning.

"Something funny?" the Romanian asked.

"Better than that. I'm thinking of those three sisters waiting for us," the navigator answered with a smirk. "Hey, here's our turn . . . twenty or thirty seconds . . . ten seconds. *Now.*"

The pilot nodded . . . began to swing the 727 to the new course.

He wasn't looking down, for from that altitude, he wasn't likely to see anything much on the surface below. There was a small city—large by the standards of this thinly populated region—down there. It wasn't an important community—thirteen or fourteen thousand according to estimates. No census takers ever got here.

It had no vital mineral or industrial resources.

Half the population was illiterate . . . unfamiliar with shoes . . . hoping that there'd be more rain for the scrubby crops, and that none of the region's unpredictable official or unofficial armed forces would choose to fight here.

With a garrison of ninety-one soldiers who had four trucks and two barely operational armored cars, it had no military significance. The hardworking residents of this city feared a couple of divinities and put up with each other, giving more attention to the need for a new school or two and an effective water-purification system.

No plans for Holy Wars against anyone.

No dreams of aggressive adventures against neighbors who spoke another tongue or lived under a different flag.

Anytown, East Africa . . . and a lot of other places.

Far from areas of conflict and adequate employment.

Intense heat . . . poor communications . . . roads worse than that.

Isolated . . . unimportant . . . just right for the test.

IN THE BLACKED-OUT jet following the 727, a sincere and homicidal man in a business suit bought in London flicked on his small flashlight to recheck the precise location of the chartered plane, now eighteen miles ahead.

"Perfect," he said in his native tongue . . . neither English nor the one his forged passport would indicate.

"Transmit . . . *now*," he ordered a few seconds later.

Three very important things happened immediately after the copilot pressed the switch on the black box in front of him.

This wasn't the kind of black box that experts used to pinpoint the reason for some fatal disaster . . . a devices to prevent future accidents and thereby save aircraft and lives.

This was the other kind.

It killed.

Planes and people. Swiftly . . . efficiently . . . dramatically.

It was a modern and big-time murder machine.

In the 727, the pilot heard—for two or three moments—a whirring sound and saw a gush of what looked like smoke but wasn't. It was an acrid, searing odor. The Romanian and his navigator gasped . . . choked . . . hurt terribly.

Gas . . . some kind of poison gas.

The Romanian fought desperately to breathe—not to inhale this deadly cloud—as he realized his mother had been very wrong.

He was almost surely dying. What you didn't know *could* kill you.

He had an extremely brief opportunity to dwell on this. There was an explosion behind him, and an awful ripping sound followed by a deafening roaring noise as the rear quarter of the jet was blown away.

Blasted . . . amputated as if by a giant scalpel.

The 727 was completely out of control, with severed hydraulic lines . . . no tail . . . a maimed fuselage . . . spinning and rolling. No one in the best of health could have saved it. The two gassed men in the cockpit were choking . . . blinded . . . helpless. They were starting to die.

The severed rear quarter of the plane plunged toward the earth. As the maimed tail section dropped rapidly, every yard of the rolling, twisting descent was measured by top-quality altimeters in the two boxes. One altimeter was a backup . . . rigged to a safety charge in case the other failed. Now the boxes tumbled free into the night sky.

They were dropping faster and faster.

There was a shrieking, howling sound as they accelerated.

Twenty-one thousand feet . . . eighteen thousand . . . fifteen thousand.

"Eyes!" the man in the London business suit shouted and looked away from the black-covered crates.

The pilot and copilot in his jet did the same thing. They knew it was a matter of seconds. A new form of massacre was coming to Africa.

The boxes were dropping at a steadily increasing speed, and the noise kept getting louder. It wasn't the sound level that was going to slaughter all those people.

At twelve thousand feet, the crates stopped falling.

In an ear-smashing blast heard in the next province, they vaporized. They suddenly became a bizarre, blurring ball ringed by an expanding circle of unbearably bright light. The few people on this continent who understood what the thing was knew that it could blind them . . . instantly . . . permanently.

Now the ball was reshaping into a dark cloud that resembled a mushroom. It was a descendent of one born in July 1945 at a New Mexico "site" code-named "Trinity." This one was smaller, more efficient.

It weighed less than a fifth of its lethal ancestor.

It was cheaper, too.

This little one smashed and burned and killed better than the earlier model . . . and for less money per corpse. From a strategic point of view, it was definitely a bargain.

The people in the unimportant city below were unfamiliar with contemporary military strategy or budgets or first-strike concepts developed by great powers. They did know that they'd never heard an explosion a tenth as loud as the staggering blast overhead. They did what human beings—men, women, children—anywhere would.

They reacted automatically.

Without thinking or hesitation, they ran out into the streets . . . mostly earthen here . . . to see what was happening.

Many wondered if this was The End of the World.

For generations, local astrologers and holy men had predicted that the End might come soon, for a variety of reasons.

Now, suddenly—for no apparent reason—it was happening in the middle of the night. With the terrible light in the sky dazzling mercilessly and an incredible heat searing everyone and everything, charred . . . blinded . . . dazed people of all ages began to die. Eyes unseeing . . . hair ablaze . . . skin scorched off as if by a giant blowtorch, they reeled and screamed and rolled and died.

By the dozen . . . by the hundreds . . . humans and other living things. Animals of every kind . . . all kinds of vegetation.

Buildings perished, too—some immediately, others more slowly—as fires attacked like the locusts this region endured.

Flames . . . flames jumped, slashed, and consumed. The fuel tanks of the small power plant and cars and trucks . . . the only two ambulances and the dusty station that sold gasoline and oil . . . all burned beyond recognition.

Now the corpses and the screaming dying numbered over two thousand. The horror would continue, with no help coming from the provincial government, because communications, poor to start with, had been obliterated. The authorities in the capital a hundred and eight miles away didn't know for thirty-nine and a half hours.

GOVERNMENT EMPLOYEES in another capital—across thousands of miles and several borders—were aware a lot sooner. They had much better equipment, and they had a system for watching . . . just about everywhere. It cost a huge amount of money, but the Congress had approved the expense because it seemed necessary.

The first in this other capital—actually, just outside it—to find out about what had happened to the East African city was a man named J. G. Bonomi who "had the duty." In civilian language, he was on duty at the very secret and heavily guarded building that had been classified Wild Dog. This rating meant that the sentries here could shoot to kill.

The fact that the building, equipment, and training of the sophisticated specialists who operated and interpreted here had cost the U.S. taxpayers many billions of dollars wasn't the only reason for the do-whatever's-necessary Wild Dog designation. In nations that relied on space surveillance for survival, nothing was more sensitive than their spy-in-the-sky satellites and their visual product.

It was all about images, and this place was the eyes and the heart of the U.S. imaging network. When the mass destruction weapon Temkov had sold . . . the sample . . . went off some two and a half miles above the African city, it detonated with a flare like nothing natural on this planet. One of the expensive satellites even higher in the sky registered . . . identified . . . and reported that special flash of blinding light.

The news was relayed to this intelligence center . . . then an image followed very swiftly. While Bonomi was triple-checking the identification with his sophisticated computer, information about this extraordinary explosion was being diagnosed by an extremely sensitive device that detected and analyzed shock waves.

It was part of another U.S. network, just as secret and high-tech and strategic. These many sensors—the number no one discussed—were buried in hundreds of places around the world. They reported to a blast-proof cave under a mountain in Colorado. What they signaled were blasts of atomic or hydrogen devices. They were an early warning operation to detect tests that might mean some other power was perfecting a new weapon.

Bonomi's computer completed its identification first.

He rechecked it again before he picked up the phone linked directly to the operations center under the Pentagon.

"This is Blue Bird. This is Blue Bird," he said, and when he was asked, he responded with this month's security phrase.

"This is not a drill," he continued. "Repeat . . . this is not a drill. Magellan Alert. Magellan Alert. We have activity."

Then he spoke the latitude and longitude of the "activity." Not once. Three times. There must be no mistake.

"Level of activity—Class Two. That is correct. *Two.*"

Reminded to communicate any new information immediately, he promised to do so. This was all part of the drill, but the Pentagon masters insisted on this ritual.

Minutes after he hung up, a secure teleprinter line from the subterranean Colorado base to the command center beneath the Pentagon delivered a report of a nuclear blast at the same location where the satellite had detected it. There was an estimate of the approximate power of the device. The "yield"—equivalent to thousands of tons of the latest high explosive—would be significant.

The earth sensors confirmed what the satellite saw.

There was definitely activity.

There was more in the signal from Colorado. Computer analysis of the "footprint" . . . the signature shock wave pattern and related specifics—would follow in four hours. The generals at the meeting would have the precise identity of the weapon.

There was going to be a meeting all right . . . very high-level intelligence experts . . . military and civilian. There was always one of those meetings in such situations. With the weapon type and model identified, they would know whose it was.

They wouldn't have any idea as to why such a sophisticated, mass-destruction device had been used in or over a presumably unimportant little city out in the backcountry of a minor nation that wasn't any kind of player.

They'd work hard to keep this whole thing quiet, of course. There was no reason to discuss it with anyone involved in The St. John Institute. There was no possibility of that. None of the weapons experts had ever heard of the Institute.

They had no need to know.

After the meeting of the intelligence and bomb-warhead experts, more images were taken from both satellite and a flyby at eighty thousand feet by one of the sleek, out-of-sight U-2 spy planes—the kind that had photographed the Russian missile bases in Cuba.

Another hush-hush meeting to review the data—this crowd really excelled at reviewing data. Deciding what to do didn't come easily. Fortunately, the government of Ethiopia helped a lot. The compassionate authorities in Addis Ababa were shocked and baffled by what had killed the small southern city and so many of its people.

Hundreds more dying every day.

No uncontaminated food or water . . . no medical services, and the few health professionals barely extant . . . dazed and desperate survivors staggering or crawling through the devastated streets.

They needed help . . . a lot of it . . . expertise in treating such horrors . . . food . . . plasma . . . even police to cope with the looting that couldn't be more than a day or two away.

They needed a great deal of help . . . right now. The head of the Ethiopian state had no great affection for the African policies of the United States, but he was one of the more realistic leaders on the troubled continent. He was aware that the disorder and armed brutality rending so many nations in the region bothered and confused many in Washington, who weren't sure who to help . . . or whether it was worth getting involved at all.

And there were those stories of C.I.A. deals and deceptions. The U.S. had tolerated . . . even supported . . . some of the most vicious and bloodthirsty tyrants. He wondered what benefit those practical, hard-eyed, national-interest, don't-waste-a-dime men in Washington—the ones his ambassador called "suits"—would see in spending millions of dollars in a country as weak and out-of-it as his.

He couldn't afford wondering now.

He had to ask for help immediately . . . then hope.

THIS WEEK, there was another of those meetings of the suits in Washington to weigh the pros and cons . . . and, governing principle, to do what the Ethiopian ambassador predicted. They had to determine their national interest.

They didn't shirk their duty. After they decided to begin immediately a flow of the biggest cargo planes that the airfield nearest the target city could handle, a lean ramrod of a U.S. Army general . . . two stars, no nonsense . . . chuckled. Several of the others knew that he'd earned top grades in philosophy courses at the Academy at West Point, but they didn't understand what was amusing.

"Here we are, committing thousands of tons of medical supplies . . . water-purification gear . . . four entire teams of doctors with nurses and pharmacists . . . food for a small army for two months. Not a *good* deed . . . a *great* one," he said, and chuckled again.

They nodded.

"What's comical about that?" a senior female executive of the Central Intelligence Agency asked.

"This isn't the first good deed—excuse me, great and generous humanitarian deed—the U.S. has done this year," an alert undersecretary of the Air Force pointed out with pride.

"Humanitarian? Sure," the Army general concurred. "But that's not the main damn reason. The main damn reason is that we're sending in along with those lifesaving folks a dozen nuclear warfare specialists to get us every scrap of information about that bomb. That's the human condition, I guess."

"*What's* the human condition?" the Air Force undersecretary asked.

"We do the right things for the wrong reasons," the former West Point philosophy student replied and laughed again.

No one else in the room even smiled.

They were even more grim when the updated casualty report came in from Ethiopia.

Five thousand and fifty fatalities. Almost eighteen hundred more expected to die within a month.

The weapon had been a Russian-made product, one of the advanced miniaturized Demon class added to Moscow's arsenal only a year and a half ago.

Now they knew what had murdered the Ethiopian city. They still had no idea as to why . . . or what those fused metal scraps of a U.S.-made Boeing 727 were doing around the outer perimeter of the blast area. The last of these machines had come off the assembly line more than twenty years ago, and there was no record in the files of any U.S. or NATO intelligence organizations that even one was in the Russian inventory.

It didn't make any sense.

It wouldn't . . . unless somebody in the meeting was so imaginative or so far-out lucky as to think of al Wadi.

HASSON AL WADI was thinking of them and everyone else in the Washington target area. He was going to send them a Demon as soon as he got the rest of the shipment he'd ordered. Now that his test had been successful, there was no reason to delay.

The Demon would be in Washington soon.

In that crowded metropolitan area, the casualties would be much higher than in the sleepy little city in southern Ethiopia.

The dead could number two hundred thousand. Maybe more, he thought righteously as he began to draft a message to arrange for immediate delivery of the rest of the cash so he could acquire the additional Demons he'd scheduled for the other targets.

He'd picked them carefully, with political and population

density in mind. There'd be plenty of casualties there, too. First, there were a few loose ends to deal with professionally. One was the Greek airplane broker who might identify the man to whom he'd sold the old 727.

The broker should be dead within forty-eight hours, al Wadi ordered.

It actually took only thirty-seven.

22

EVERYONE — EVERYONE IN AFRICA, EUROPE, AND NORTH AMER-
ica—kept the secret. It was in the national interest of various
countries and the private interest of a large number of cunning
individuals to do so. Nobody spoke or wrote publicly about the
horror that had killed over five thousand people in that remote
corner of dusty Ethiopia.

This wasn't like one of those tidal waves or earthquakes in
Asia that fill Western television screens with rows of corpses for
weeks. No television news organization, wire service, radio network, or daily or weekly publication reported on this shocking
massacre.

Nobody knew, so nobody was shocked.

Correction: There were a few people—a couple of hundred
professionals—who knew, but they were used to this sort of
death toll, so they weren't that shaken.

They were, however, very curious about the implications, not
about the corpses. It was difficult to project anything from what
had happened to all those burned, anonymous, and still-
radioactive bodies, because nothing quite like this was recorded
in anybody's computer banks. And if that wasn't troubling

enough, no organization had claimed responsibility for this sensational indecency.

Some group or other . . . either an established paramilitary or fanatical gang of terrorists, or a new band of fiercely righteous head cases united under a bizarre acronym—always took the credit for such an episode. There was traditionally a communique seething with threats, justifications, adolescent slogans, and bad grammar.

Not this time.

Not a note . . . not a manifesto . . . not a defiant tape . . . nothing.

Since the whole thing was messy, it was referred to the garbage collectors. It wasn't a domestic episode within the United States of America, so it didn't go to the conscientious Federal Bureau of Investigation, which had that beat. Brit cops would say "patch," but this wasn't within their jurisdiction. It was dirty and international, so it instantly found its way to an organization whose scope was global and whose expertise was mess.

Ours or theirs . . . anything . . . anywhere . . . anytime.

The Lords of Langley—the earnest war chiefs of the Central Intelligence Agency—sent it to that man named Buckley, who was Deputy Director for Operations. Noting that the weapon's "footprint," identified the weapon as one of Russia's fairly new Demons, Buckley immediately and properly "shared" the crisis with the head of his Russian F.S.U. division. Seigenthaler, who silently mourned being stuck with the totally untidy Former Soviet Union bits, checked it out with his experts.

And his analysts, and weapons specialists, and other arcane civil servants—wizards on African politics and military affairs . . . technicians who could tell which Russian plant produced this awful little bomb . . . authorities on African religions . . . and a clutch of other people who knew a lot and got paid twice what they'd have earned in academia.

They reasoned, computed, extrapolated, and discussed every aspect of the attack as the casualty count neared fifty-nine hundred. They warily touched base with the State Department, NATO intelligence, MI-6, and Israel's foxy Mossad. They collectively attacked from every detail and angle the key questions of why was this attack made . . . who did it . . . and did they have more weapons like the Demon to strike again?

Zero . . . and there might be another devastating attack by the unknowns anywhere at any minute.

Phone taps, Web and radio intercepts by the National Security Agency, and the eavesdropping and crypto legions of close allies added nothing. Satellite sweeps were no more productive.

Lots of heat, but no light. When would the next attack come?

"Let's start at the other end since we're going nowhere," Buckley finally proposed to Seigenthaler. "Let's build on what we *do* know."

"Just about all we know is that the damn thing was a Demon, and one built at Factory Eight east of Moscow within the past nineteen months," Seigenthaler replied, and then he nodded in comprehension.

"How did it get out of Russia?" he thought aloud. "We track that and it could take us to who dropped it in Ethiopia."

"Exactly," Buckley agreed. "I've got an idea. It's just a long shot, but all our experts and big-dollar technology haven't done it. Maybe one agent could do better . . . by himself . . . maybe kill two damn birds with a single stone."

"What agent? What birds?"

"I'd send Nomad."

Seigenthaler blinked.

A lot of people in the Agency did when they heard Nomad's name.

"Where?" the chief of the Russian F.S.U. unit asked.

"Moscow, for the next meet with General Temkov. Temkov has irons in a gang of fires . . . not just the Alison Wilk grab. If there are Demons out of Russia, Temkov might know something. I want Nomad to talk with him."

"Nomad's good, but he's a stone-field agent," Seigenthaler reminded. "What could he get Temkov to say?"

Buckley shook his head.

"Not say . . . *think*," he corrected. "It's Big Secret time. We've been building a very experimental program in mind war . . .

high dollar . . . deep black . . . more than classified. Telepaths, and maybe more. Nomad is the Number One *more*."

Now Seigenthaler was visibly tense.

Eyes, body language, the whole thing.

"Just what does that mean?" he asked warily. "Nomad's an ace field agent and he's damn smart, but what's this 'more'?"

Buckley paused. He wanted to say this just right.

"It looks as if he can read minds. Don't look at me like that. I hear from serious professional people that he knows things . . . secret things . . . nobody's ever told him. Don't ask me how he does it . . . could be something we did to save his life."

"I didn't know he was sick."

"They say he was dying, on the way," Buckley continued in implicit justification. "Don't ask what we did, or even where he is. He *isn't*. He's legally dead. I can't tell you anything more, so no questions—period."

Seigenthaler nodded.

"No questions," he promised. "It's sci-fi time, so let's move on. I've no problem with Nomad reading minds. That's cool with me. He does just about everything else. There's one thing I'm not clear about."

"Yes?"

"This two birds with one stone in Moscow."

Buckley leaned forward as he replied.

"When he meets Temkov there," the deputy director explained, "there's just a chance he might get into the general's head. He might find out where Alison Wilk is. That's One, and Two is that he could pick up what Temkov knows about the Demon situation. Are any circulating out there . . . how many . . . where's *there* . . . and who's playing?"

It was a very long shot, but you don't tell a boss that.

"Hope it works," Seigenthaler evaded loyally.

"You got a better idea?"

Seigenthaler calculated as fast as he could.

"False flag," he speculated several seconds later. "No sign we're the ones looking. Put the word out that some Nigerian or Libyan generals want to buy Demons. Offer fat brokers' fees . . . spread some Swiss francs and gold around Russia and the rest of the former Sov republics. Use Greek and Dutch arms dealers to put out the pitch in the Middle East. Then pray."

The people doing the false-flag ploy might well be lied to, ripped off, or killed in any of nineteen ways, Seigenthaler thought, but he didn't say that. He didn't have to, for Buckley knew it already.

That wouldn't necessarily discourage him.

As a career professional, he expected "breakage" in the game.

The deputy director computed swiftly . . . in a dozen seconds.

"Do the false flag," he ratified, "but Nomad's going to Moscow, too."

Seigenthaler had to ask the question, though he feared the possible answer.

"Moscow station chief going to run him?" he tested.

"Has to be someone *first-class*," the deputy director began in that earnest-awful voice Seigenthaler had learned to dread.

He knew what Buckley was selling. He didn't want to buy.

"Nomad's good, but damn complicated, you know," Buckley continued.

Nobody knew it better, Seigenthaler thought. He'd learned it the hard way during three previous operations.

"You've worked with him," Buckley reminded in that tone of confident Ivy League "con." Then he flashed the boyish, sincere smile. "Most people couldn't handle him, but you know the guy."

Seigenthaler shook his head.

"I'd rather not," he said, without much hope.

Buckley wasn't smiling anymore.

It was the boss look now.

"Sorry," he announced, though he wasn't . . . not a bit. "It's my call and I'm making it. The Demon is Russian. You're head of that unit, and you've more experience with Nomad than anyone else here. Nomad's your deal."

"Tell me what the hell we're dealing," Seigenthaler challenged bitterly. "Wild card . . . ace in the hole . . . or body-bag time?"

Buckley wouldn't be provoked or deflected.

"Let me know when you find out," he said coolly and looked at the gold calendar watch on his right wrist.

Then he glanced at the door.

The meeting was over. Seigenthaler walked out wondering who and how many would die. Nomad was no macho mad-dog type, but by the end of his mission, there was almost always a corpse or two. That was true even for the relatively easy missions. This was a far from easy one.

With Demons involved and the house rules do-what's-necessary, the casualties could be much higher. Two questions came to Seigenthaler's mind as he walked back toward his own office. The first was, why was the usually conservative Buckley rushing into this extremely risky operation and using always dangerous Nomad as the key player?

The second concerned the whole sci-fi matter of Nomad's alleged mind reading and the "deep black" mind-war program. The head of the Russian F.S.U. group had demonstrated his loyalty, sense, and ability to keep thousands of important secrets during more than two decades of frequently decorated service in the Agency.

What the hell was so extraordinary about this mind program?

Why was he being treated like some complete outsider?

Once the Agency stopped trusting you, your career was finished. Driving home that night, Seigethaler kept checking and testing to see whether he was being followed. He detected no sign of it . . . but his tension didn't ease and his heart still beat faster than usual.

He knew *they* were good.

The expert surveillance teams of the Agency's large and shadowy counterintelligence division were skilled in tracking and watching. They'd been on high alert since the terrible shame of the Ames scandal, a disgrace that would take years to live down. They were extremely vigilant . . . close to obsessive . . . and completely smooth in the way they operated.

They could be trailing him right now and he wouldn't notice it.

Now he thought about the Agency's well-established need-to-know policies and the fact that this mental operation—which still sounded very far-fetched—didn't relate to his area of responsibility and belonged to another part of the Agency. The practical, sensible thing was for him to concentrate on what the 274 people in his unit were doing and were supposed to do. There was no reason for the counterintelligence professionals to be on his case, Seigenthaler realized, and his heartbeat lowered.

Nomad would be—always had been—difficult to run, Seigenthaler acknowledged, but he'd deal with that day-to-day, according to the well-tested procedures the Agency had shaped over many decades. He'd overreacted, Seigenthaler realized ruefully. He'd concentrate on the job.

Nothing to worry about.

He still couldn't help checking every few miles for any sign he was being trailed.

Zero.

It wasn't until he parked the vehicle in his driveway and got out that another thought came into his consciousness. Maybe he couldn't observe any surveillance car because they didn't want to risk being spotted by a savvy cloak-and-dagger veteran such as himself. They might have attached a homing beacon under his sedan.

For a moment he considered looking under the car for such a small transmitter. No, he decided. They could be watching his house and driveway with long-lense video cameras from a nearby observation post. It wouldn't look good if they taped him checking out his vehicle for a beacon.

He computed the odds and concluded that it was highly unlikely there was any beacon. He decided not to mention his unrealistic concern about possible surveillance to his wife. There was no point in troubling her with such a remote possibility. He was feeling better know, and he'd feel better than that after a few extra hours of sleep.

He wouldn't say a word about this, Seigenthlater resolved as he put his key in the upper lock of the two on his front door. His wife's nerves hadn't fully recovered from the tragic death of her younger sister in that auto accident seven weeks ago.

And it was possible that *they* had already bugged the house.

23

GENERAL TEMKOV WAS IN MUCH BETTER SPIRITS THAN SEIGEN-thaler.

The operation to sell the Demons was moving ahead.

It was accelerating.

The message from al Wadi that the cash was ready had come in nine and a half hours earlier. Smiling . . . almost smug . . . in his office outside Moscow, Temkov again eyed the first of the four wall clocks, the one displaying local time.

Captain Nicolai Pankin—Temkov's loyal aide and do-anything enforcer—should be getting there just about now.

"There" was some 364 miles miles east of the Russian capital. It was a sparsely populated area . . . a ninety-minute drive from the airfield at Ul' Yanovsk . . . even closer to nowhere. That was why the depot had been located there.

NOW PANKIN, who'd operated under various identities, wasn't a captain in the S.V.R. He wore an Air Force uniform and carried papers that said he was a major and chief pilot of a long-range bomber. As he stepped from the Air Force staff car, he eyed the grubby town and nodded.

They'd done a good job.

It wouldn't be that easy for U.S. satellites to discern what this place really was.

Everything in the tired old industrial town was rundown ... in need of painting, fixing, a big and basic overhaul. That clearly included the sprawling railcar- and locomotive-repair facility on the north side of this wornout community. The dusty buildings—with so many broken windows and several sagging roofs—showed either a lack of funding or a depressing indifference to maintenance.

Like Pankin, this depot wasn't what it seemed to be.

Hidden under the acres of what looked like a half-dead repair facility was a secret base code-named Peter's House. Dug under the sagging repair shops nearly two decades ago, this was where today's take-no-chances Russian nuclear command was carefully and covertly storing 1,286 nuclear and hydrogen weapons never mentioned in any disarmament negotiations.

They saw no reason for adults to trust the Americans.

They didn't.

They didn't trust very many of their colleagues either, so only a small number of key officers, some scientists, and essential enlisted personnel were aware of Peter's House. All of the senior people were convinced that the devious Americans were hiding plenty of these mass-destruction weapons, too. Though the half century of Cold War was supposed to be history, the shrewd and practical Russian defense chiefs were certain that the Americans might still do anything at any moment.

Pankin looked up and down the drab street ... then at the street itself. Those warhead bunkers of reinforced concrete a hundred and ten feet below—perhaps right under where he stood—were in much better condition than what was up here. They were clean ... temperature-controlled ... protected by blast-proof steel doors, and guards just as hard ... patrolled by armored cars rolling through the tunnels on changing schedules that invaders couldn't anticipate ... divided by gas-proof compartments. Motion sensors and surveillance video cameras were numerous and well camouflaged.

Budget and supply problems worsening steadily in the past three years had reduced the staff and morale here, as at other bases . . . but not a lot. This installation and the people who lived underground almost all the time to maintain it at high efficiency were not ordinary so they got special treatment. They were the elite, like the crews of nuclear-attack submarines, Pankin thought as he decided not to light a cigarette. Doing that might cause someone to come close to try to panhandle one. Pankin didn't want any resident or worker in this bipolar community to get near enough to see his face, perhaps identify it later. He wasn't expecting any *later*, but laters did happen.

His eyes roved up and down the broken sidewalks again. It was time for his walk. Pankin told his driver to wait . . . strolled about a hundred forty yards north . . . turned west for two blocks . . . then paused to look around again as if checking the numbers on a house.

All clear.

He hoped he was right.

If he was wrong, there was the semiautomatic pistol in the holster under his left armpit. It was effectively concealed by the well-cut Air Force tunic.

There was a dark brown . . . dusty and several years old . . . nothing luxurious sedan halfway down the alley on his right. Pankin sauntered toward it. Now he saw someone farther down the alley, twenty yards beyond the sedan. Pankin froze . . . watched warily . . . and finally sighed when he saw the man stop and urinate against the south wall.

When the man was finished, he walked away from Pankin, toward the other end of the alley. Temkov's aide advanced slowly toward the car, meticulously stepping around dog droppings and garbage that might soil his Air Force boots. He wanted to return them in good condition.

Now he was at the sedan.

The routine was simple.

As Pankin stopped to take out and ignite the tobacco end of one of Russia's medium-priced cigarettes, the rear window on the passenger side of the vehicle rolled down about three inches. In the lighting process, somehow Pankin's head tilted toward that open window.

He didn't look in. He wasn't supposed to do that.

He'd come all this way simply to utter five words.

"Thursday . . . five minutes to midnight."

He spoke very clearly, for it was important that the man inside the open window heard and understood. That man was important himself . . . and dangerous. He had no experience at this game; that made him dangerous, for beginners made mistakes. The window rolled shut and the brown car cruised slowly to the mouth of the alley, then out of sight.

Pankin hadn't seen the face of the man in the rear part of the vehicle, but he had no doubt as to who sat inside that barely opened window. Though the car bore no military insignia or license plates, it was fifty-seven-year-old General Yuri Oroshenko, who commanded Peter's House.

A strict disciplinarian, respected for the very high level of security at his important facility and his complete loyalty to the Army high command that he'd served for thirty-nine years, Oroshenko was a hard-case professional. What he wasn't was patient. He'd seen the signs of burnout in other career officers worn down by the weakening of the motherland and the unraveling that came with economic anarchy. About two years ago, he'd realized that he was losing his own passion for duty in this hurt land where corrupt politicians, cynical businessmen, and uncontrolled Mafia thugs ran free . . . and almost nothing else ran at all.

It was time to get his. He was Temkov's contact. He was going forward with the invisible theft of the Demons that would bring him millions of dollars. With that cash, he could leave this increasingly difficult job and his even more difficult spouse. Since the grab of the Demons would be done so smoothly that their absence could be camouflaged as an inventory miscount, it would be unseen, unnoticed for a year or more.

Temkov's envoy had just named the time.

That was when the Demons were to be delivered to the place down south they'd previously chosen. Within ten days—no more than two weeks—Oroshenko would receive the additional $4,600,000. It wouldn't be easy to wait another thirty or thirty-five months before he retired "for health reasons," but he'd keep his promise to Temkov to do that.

That Temkov is clever, the nuclear-depot commander thought as he returned to the camouflaged entrance to the underground complex. Of course, those devious spy types usually are, Oroshenko told himself while the elevator took him down to his office. He knew he must be devious, too.

He had to get it exactly right the first time.

There wasn't going to be a second.

He'd mentally rehearsed what he must do and say a dozen times. He'd alerted Major Bastikyan that Moscow would soon be signaling for a covert removal and shipment of five Demons for a special mobility test. The truck and the large metal container had been ready for days.

The personnel had been on standby for nearly a week.

Bastikyan knew the destination . . . how long it would take . . . best-case scenario, and worst . . . reasonable driving speed . . . barring or assuming terrible weather. To give him leeway for a flat tire or trouble with the truck, Oroshenko decided he should tell the major the delivery time now.

Not tell him out loud. The phones or offices here in Peter's House might be covered by eavesdropping devices.

Show . . . not tell.

Bastikyan would assume that the procedure was part of a security drill.

Oroshenko telephoned him to come to his office. When Bastikyan arrived, Oroshenko began to speak about rechecking the roof camouflage of Bunker Four. As he did so, he wrote for a few seconds on a pad, then showed it to Bastikyan.

Thursday—five minutes to midnight.

The major nodded . . . went on speaking about the camouflage inspection. When Bastikyan left the office, General Oroshenko tore up and burned the sheet with the writing and the next three sheets on the pad. Within two hours, the Demons, in their safety cylinders, would be placed with ample packing in a big metal container marked TOXIC WASTE—HAZARDOUS. By nightfall, the large drum would be carefully lashed down on the truck.

It would be on its way—with transit pass and armed escorts—before blackness totally enveloped Peter's House.

$4,600,000. Oroshenko enjoyed that prospect silently for nearly half a minute.

He was lucky that he was dealing with someone trustworthy like Aleksei Temkov.

There were plenty of others in the S.V.R. spy hierarchy who would surely try to double-cross him in such an operation and cheat him out of his money.

He started to consider again where he'd go with his money. It would be warmer than this dreary place.

And the young women there would be warmer, too.

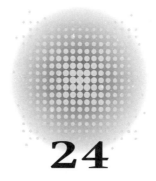

24

THE DEPUTY DIRECTOR FOR OPERATIONS DIDN'T HAVE TO SPEAK a word.

The grim look on his face as Seigenthaler entered the office said it all.

"Bad day?" the head of the Russia and F.S.U. unit asked calmly.

"Terrible," Buckley replied.

He got nothing back from Seigenthaler . . . not a question . . . not a phrase of professional concern or sympathy . . . not even some change of facial expression.

"Don't you care?" Buckley asked. "Don't you want to know?"

"It's going to get worse," Seigenthaler said evenly, "and then you'll tell me."

Buckley frowned.

"You haven't seen Nomad in a couple of years and you're already talking like him," he accused.

Buckley thought again about Seingenthaler's prediction.

"You said it's going to get worse because it always gets worse, right?" he tested.

Seigenthaler nodded.

"I don't need that this morning," Buckley said harshly.

"We're catching a lot of heat from the N.S.C.—big time."

No surprise there, Seigenthaler thought. The sage and powerful members of the National Security Council usually unloaded their concerns and unreasonable edicts on the Agency.

"They want to know about those damn Demons—yesterday," Buckley said, "and I just got a flash signal from our own counterintelligence that there's a Russian agent, or agents, out searching for the place you're going to today."

"Where's that?"

"Where Nomad is. I want you to confirm that he's ready for the trip to Moscow."

"How do the Russians know about this place?" Seigenthaler asked.

Buckley shook his head.

"I have no idea of what they know or suspect, or of how they ever heard of the place," he said. "There is reason to believe they may be looking for one of their agents who's dead."

"Why do they care if he's dead?"

"It's too complicated to go into now," Buckley evaded. "Listen, this place has pretty good security and just got two platoons of paratroopers and a deck of ground-to-air as a bonus."

"You're saying the place is dangerous?"

"Don't worry," Buckley assured him. "I doubt the Russians will find it."

"If they do, they'll attack it?"

"Hard to guess. Anyway, we're not putting you at risk. You're going out with four of our best security people as personal escorts. Round the clock. No problem," Buckley said briskly and smiled.

"That bad, huh?"

"Piece of cake," the deputy director declared in a confident tone that didn't sell Seigenthaler at all. "Odds are a thousand to one the S.V.R. operatives won't get anywhere near the Institute."

"*What* Institute?"

"Where you're going to see Nomad this afternoon. We've got a plane waiting for you. If you leave right now and the traffic's not bad, you can drive home . . . pack a weekend bag . . . and get to the airport by eleven. This is time urgent. If he's in decent shape, we have to deliver him in Moscow in thirty-six hours," the deputy director declared.

It was *definitely* going to get worse, Seigenthaler thought.

"And say hello to Nomad for me," Buckley concluded in that spray-on, good-guy voice.

"I'll do that," Seigenthaler replied as he started for the door.

THE CRISP AND WARY WOMAN in the white medical jacket—the one who said her name was Willson—called Nomad to her office at 4:50 that afternoon.

First, Seigenthaler made himself smile in greeting when Nomad entered. Then he studied the field agent very carefully for a dozen seconds before walking closer for the obligatory twenty-first-century, Western civilization—or what passes for it—handshake.

The Langley executive hesitated for several seconds.

The field agent read his mind. It was easy.

"Denny. Dennis Monroe, but you can call me Denny."

Seigenthaler carefully absorbed this. Dennis Monroe. Under no circumstances could he address the man who didn't make mistakes as Nomad or refer to that name. That would be a big mistake. The woman who ran this place wasn't supposed to know that.

"Good to see you, Denny," Seigenthaler said. "The deputy director told me to give you a big hello from him too."

"I'll file it."

Nomad still had his edge. That wouldn't make this any easier.

"He's been concerned about your health problem, and he's glad you're feeling better now."

"I didn't have any health problem," the new but still fierce Denny answered pleasantly. "I had a little fatal disease. Why me, Lord? The whole bit. Then my government spent a lot of money to cut the bad piece out and slip in a fresh one. Medical miracle. Fade up the music. Dissolve to the fucking credits. Funny thing about the credits. Big-budget picture, but all the names are fake."

"Denny—" Seigenthaler began.

"I'm not complaining. My health problem's history and my new Russian heart is pumping along just fine."

He saw the shock in Seigenthaler's eyes.

They hadn't told him about the transplants from the dead S.V.R. operative.

"I'm almost completely recovered," the man who could read minds said. "The three doctors here . . . this is no penny-pinching operation . . . can tell you that."

"They did about an hour ago. I want to hear it from you. Not charts or tests or X rays . . . you. How do you feel?"

"Stronger every day. Food's good . . . diet's right . . . I'm working out with weights . . . stationary bike . . . a nice selection of handguns and shoulder weapons that Doctor Willson was kind enough to provide us."

Trap.

Seigenthaler took the bait. He blinked at the word "us," and in a flash, the hair-trigger field agent realized that the visitor hadn't been told about the four other transplant patients.

"Now I get one," the hard-edged professional called Dennis Monroe here . . . who knew why? . . . announced. He had a question.

Nonnegotiable. It was a flat statement.

Pure Nomad, Seigenthaler thought.

"Actually *two*," this Dennis Monroe corrected. "You must have seen all the airborne we've got on the grounds. Great for property values. They're patriotic young fellows . . . brave . . . armed to the earlobes. We've also got land mines, sound detectors, ground radar, heat sensors, a chopper up there every night, and alarms that would pick up a gnat. Heavy-duty protection."

Seigenthaler nodded.

"I suppose they told you about this before you left Langley?"

The head of the Russia F.S.U. group nodded again.

"Then why the hell did you come out with those two?" Monroe demanded and pointed to the two security men Buckley had sent with him.

"*Four.* There're another two outside . . . second shift," the

Langley executive said. "It wasn't my idea to come with them. It wasn't even my idea to manage this next step or to fly out here. I was told that this place could be dangerous, and assumed that these four were to protect me from possible kidnapping."

"Makes sense," Monroe agreed, just a bit too nonchalantly.

Seigenthaler wondered why he wasn't being confrontational anymore. Nomad was hiding something. Of course that was automatic with him, the visiting C.I.A. executive remembered. That was Nomad's style. A new name and someone else's heart wouldn't change that.

"They're here to protect you, too," Seigenthaler said. "What's the other question?"

"I figure you came here to see whether I'm ready to do something you want done."

Seigenthaler nodded about half an inch.

"What the hell do you want me to do?"

The director of The St. John Institute interrupted.

The threat to her brilliantly conceived and executed telepathy program left her no choice. The balance . . . the carefully nurtured mental partnerships . . . the whole effort that was going so well . . . might be sundered if the group's leader left suddenly.

"I'm not sure it would be good for Denny and for our whole program if he departed now," she said. "From a medical and psychological point of view, if you consider all factors—"

Now it was Monroe who interrupted.

"You're wasting your time, Doctor," he said. "Your time and *their* time. They're the masterminds who sent him, and they don't give a flying fuck about all your 'factors.' They're in a hurry, and they usually get their way."

She turned to face Seigenthaler squarely.

"It is time urgent," he admitted stiffly.

"If you think you can just come into my Institute," she blazed—

"He can do that," the candid field agent she'd named Monroe said. "Get on the phone. You must have a secure line to whoever you talk to in Washington . . . whoever sends you cash and policy. Let's do it Hollywood style, Doc. Have your people talk to his people. I'll go back to the range for some more shooting while you do that."

She was still visibly angry.

"Don't blame this on me, Doc," Monroe urged. "I like this place, and I like you. You're doing a great job. Saved my life and gave us good contracts. I want to give you something to show my appreciation."

If she bought this she didn't understand him at all, Seigenthaler computed.

"I know you've been pissed about the piece I took from your orderly the night I arrived," Monroe began.

Sounds just like Nomad, Seigenthaler judged.

"You've got much more important things on your plate," the man with Anna's heart said. "I'll give you back the piece before dinner. With all the security here, I really don't need it."

Her face softened.

"Thanks, Denny. I'm glad you see the light," she answered.

It wasn't like Nomad to give up a weapon, or almost anything else, Seigenthaler recalled, but this was no time to tell her that.

She phoned Washington when she was alone with the Langley executive, and Monroe delivered the gun—wrapped in a towel—just before the evening meal. Seigenthaler could see she believed that she'd charmed or tamed or managerially won Nomad over . . . that he had finally responded to her psychology and wisdom. Nomad had always had a surprise up his sleeve . . . or pant leg . . . or both, Seigenthaler remembered.

It wouldn't be that Nomad's brush with death had changed him.

He'd looked at it from up close dozens of times.

There had to be some explanation, the Langley executive thought, and made up his mind to try to find it the next morning when he'd spend three hours with the field agent.

After dinner, Seigenthaler and Willson adjourned to her study, where she began to brief him on the Institute . . . its defenses . . . and why Denny Monroe was important to the morale of the other patients. She was still trying . . . making one more effort . . . to keep Monroe in her program.

"He's doing so well here," she pressed, "and he's a positive example for the others. He seems to be some sort of natural leader."

What would Nomad say at this point, Seigenthaler wondered.

"I gave at the office" . . . or something rude like that?

Nomad couldn't stand emotional good-guy appeals.

No point in telling Willson that, the Langley executive judged.

"I see a lot of progress in this man since he arrived," she continued. "He's not nearly so isolated, so suspicious. Returning that gun proved it. He's learned to share, to trust me."

Trusting was almost a foreign concept to Nomad, Seigenthaler remembered. Staying alive was his priority.

This by-the-book scientist had no experience with people such as the hard-edged field agent. He went by another book. He was self-published. He'd written his own rules—ones he could change without anyone's permission.

Anywhere.

Anytime.

Without notice or explanation.

Minutes passed . . . now it was 10:05 P.M. She didn't give up her effort. She refilled Seigenthaler's demitasse cup again . . . and once more . . . as she tried to persuade him to let the tranplants' leader stay.

WHILE WILLSON WAS PRESSING, Nomad was feeling.

As she went on, he went out. He had to go out there. It wasn't anything he heard or thought. It was something he sensed. The something was danger.

Threat analysis; they taught that in intelligence school.

Enemy. Some kind of enemy. Out there.

He felt the nameless peril like some animal in the woods would . . . wondered if this had something to do with the serum. Maybe he was fantasizing the whole thing . . . could be a bad batch of the serum. What the hell was in that serum, he asked himself silently, and looked at his wristwatch.

Ten-twenty. Too early. Professionals wouldn't attack until the small hours. Now he was pure Nomad. For this moment . . . this time . . . Denny Monroe was just a name in a fat file of lies. He wasn't going to wait.

He'd go out now . . . field position. He'd set up his ambush . . . let his eyes get used to the moonlight. That was the best he could do. The enemy would come wearing night vision, the latest fucking infiltration gear. Nomad could deal with that. He wasn't afraid of it at all.

His heart rate didn't rise one beat.

He knew he was better than any gear. He'd have worn it if it was available here, but he could take care of himself without it, he reflected as he put on the bathrobe. Even though he'd given her the pistol, he didn't feel outgunned.

He grinned for a split second at the bad pun. Then his focus shifted totally . . . instantly. Something like a histamine rush . . . something urgently familiar, though he'd been sick and out of The Game for over a year. It all came back. No, it was as if it had been with him all the time—hiding, resting, ready.

He felt strong, and he knew everything.

Everything he'd need to stay alive if an assassin or hit team was out there in the night . . . or on its way.

Step One—stealth.

Nomad was ready for battle in the darkness. He'd spotted the closed-circuit cameras . . . checked and rechecked and searched again to make sure he hadn't missed any. Now he slipped out of his room and started to make his way downstairs.

Very carefully.

He couldn't afford to be stopped by any of the Institute's security people or those airborne soldiers. He didn't have the time or the desire to explain anything to them. Whoever the enemy was, whenever the surprise attack was to come, Nomad would be waiting to strike first . . . decisively. The weapons of the intruders wouldn't matter, for he—not they—would have the element of surprise on his side. They wouldn't expect anyone to be out there in the dark . . . silent . . . motionless . . . an expert in ambush who knew all the tricks in all the training manuals and a score of his own.

He moved slowly through the Institute . . . pinpointing and avoiding the alarm systems one by one . . . step by step. He wouldn't even think of leaving the building by the front door, where sentries were certain. The prime route in and out always got maximum coverage, Nomad had learned, but there were other portals that somehow seemed less important.

People thought less about those—everywhere—and gave them less protection. He looked for and found the kitchen—empty at this hour of the night. Nobody took the garbage out through the front door. There would be fewer locks . . . alarms . . . on that other door if this building and exotic program so different from anything in the region, maybe the nation, was run by people with the usual attitude toward refuse.

He was right.

The defenses of the rear door were facing out to deal with problems from intruders . . . not from anyone already inside the building. Drawing on his experience as a patriotic burglar for the globe's greatest democracy, he tried . . . and tried . . . then once more . . . before he disabled the protection without triggering flashing lights or loud electronic Klaxons.

He wondered why he hated the sound of those damn Klaxons. They reminded him of his own fallibility and mortality, he realized. He was only *nearly* perfect, and even if he were perfect, he was going to get old . . . eventually die. That stopped him for a few seconds until he could push down those thoughts, one of the things he did best.

Nonstop reality was no help at all, the field agent judged with a grim smile before he cautiously made his way out the service door. He took four steps, stopped to scan the area behind the Institute. It was no small backyard. This was over an acre . . . a cushion for a range of detection devices to pick up intruders.

No trees . . . no bushes near the building . . . no natural screen for over a hundred yards. His eyes roved slowly left to right . . . starting at the distant tree and shrubbery and moving in short sweeps back to the grass scant yards from where he stood. Now he repeated the process.

Good.

His eyes were adjusting to the faint light from the moon. The night was still basically black, but not quite as black. After another ninety seconds, his vision improved a little more. He'd know soon enough if "more" was adequate.

There . . . he saw it. What first seemed like a dark mass slowly emerged as a cluster of low cylinders. Trash cans on a cement platform about fifteen yards from the building. Of course, finicky Dr. Willson would want the garbage set out at least that far from the main building. The collective shadow cast by the can offered the concealment Nomad needed.

Far from perfect.

It would have to do.

His eyes searched the back of the building, then ranged out over the open space to the treeline. He spotted two objects with the standard shape of infrared searchlights—two, no—three projectors at the edges of the grass, pointing inward. Probably heat sensors, Nomad guessed.

It took only seconds for him to recognize the mistakes made by those who installed the temperature-sensitive detectors. Their focus was on the space from eighteen to forty inches above the ground. He'd stay lower that that. He'd crawl.

As any knowledgeable intruder would.

Nomad lowered himself to the grass and slowly inched his way to the large shadow. The cans were of sensible, sanitary black plastic. That could shield him from the search systems probing and protecting this space.

He found an almost comfortable position and settled in to wait. He was good at that. He'd be here for four or five hours . . . maybe six . . . ready to strike. Patience was a basic part of the ambush ritual. He knew every step of it . . . how to shift just barely enough so that a limb wouldn't go numb or prickly with that needle feeling.

All his instincts—or was it something in that serum . . . told him that the intruder or the hit team wasn't far away, but it would come tonight. If that didn't happen, Nomad would be out here again tomorrow night, and the one after that. He knew he could be paranoid at times. He didn't think he was now.

He studied the back of the building again . . . then once more. He was almost sure he saw in one blacked-out window the lens of a night-vision scope. It would be mounted on a free-swivel tripod, and there'd be one of those airborne troopers—in body armor and bad temper—behind it. There could be another he hadn't found, Nomad thought calmly. Two of them working intersecting patterns, or sweeps in sequence, was the standard practice.

The front of the building and the space down to the road would probably have two or three times the defenses. This was out in the country, where access to and escape from the target would be from that road.

It wouldn't bother Nomad if the attack didn't come tonight.

It wouldn't embarrass him a bit if anyone called him crazy for waiting stiff and silent in the chill night for "imaginary" intruders. He had all the time in the world. He wouldn't have any if he rejected his instincts and wasn't ready to engage the attackers when they arrived.

He thought of time, remembered the basic drill, and turned his wristwatch so the face was against his skin. That way, no one could pinpoint him by the phosphorent numbers on the face. He waited and waited. Ten minutes to midnight . . . nothing. Half past one . . . nothing.

He shivered in the chill, and told himself it could be worse if it rained. That would help mask the intruders from the heat and other sensors, and he'd be soaked. That could be serious for a person who had a transplant and was vulnerable to medical problems that would be minor to other people . . . to *normal* people. The doctors with the fake names had emphasized the danger.

Nomad cleared his throat.

He wasn't going to feel sorry for himself. Lucky to be alive, he made himself recall . . . and he was going to stay alive. Now he felt angry with himself for any thought remotely like self-pity. The surge of bitterness made him more alert.

Masking his wristwatch with his other hand, he peered for a few seconds at the phosphorescent numbers on the dial. Six minutes after three. Still no sight or sound of the enemy.

Yet. They'd be coming. Again and again, he scanned the wide-open space and the treeline at the far end. A small cloud . . . then another . . . floated by overhead, reducing the moonlight for a minute and a half in transit. By twenty after three, the clouds were thickening.

Not good, but no crisis.

Things got worse a dozen minutes later.

Son of a bitch, Nomad thought. It was staring to drizzle, and a few whisps of dirty gray mist crept along minutes later. Nomad used the lid of a trash can as a crude roof over a space between the garbage containers. It wasn't complete protection from the drizzle, but it would have to do.

Parts of him were getting wet, but his weapon was dry. That was the immediate priority, Nomad judged as the drizzle slowed just after four o'clock. He was feeling stiff and bone-tired . . . eyes weary, but reflexes still hair-trigger because they must be.

His eyes swept back and forth again and again, staring between the clumps of mist. He was also listening intently . . . feeling and sensing even more strongly. If the enemy was moving in, the hit team would have used the cover of the drizzle and ragged fog to inch forward from the treeline.

He thought he saw something move. He blinked and wasn't sure.

It was probably nothing.

Now it moved again . . . flat on the grass . . . slowly.

Low and slow . . . that was how they'd come.

Nomad inched out from the shadows of the cans. At that moment, there was a noise behind him. A window opened. Another sound. It was happening very fast—too fast, and wrong. Nomad looked over his shoulder to see a paratrooper framed in a window, raising an assault rifle.

The trooper was going to shoot the intruder.

As he leaned forward to take aim, the intruder rose to a crouch in a two-handed firing position . . . and raised his weapon. There were three shots in five seconds.

The first was squeezed off by the intruder.

Nomad's were the second and third shots. As he pulled the

trigger, he yelled to the paratrooper not to fire. The intruder was staggering back—two bullets from Nomad's pistol had broke both his knees. Then the paratrooper began shooting.

One burst . . . seven rounds . . . and then things got nasty.

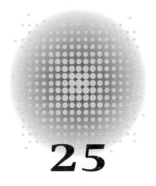

25

RAPID RESPONSE.

Those alert and healthy young airborne soldiers were trained for that, and they showed it.

Within thirty-nine . . . maybe forty-six . . . seconds after the shots sounded, eight of them charged out the back door of The St. John Institute ready to kill somebody. Moments later half a dozen more were at the blacked-out windows, shoulder weapons raised and trigger fingers tensed.

It was a dramatic demonstration of professional readiness that would impress almost anyone.

Nomad was that one.

He was standing over the intruder, covering the man with his pistol . . . just in case. That behavior was automatic. The cursing that poured from Nomad's lips was something else. It, too, was impressive in its own way, and it was loud. It couldn't be ignored.

Charlotte Willson would have preferred to ignore it when she hurried out of the building, but she was intelligent enough to recognize that it would be impossible to do so. Now lights from the Institute illuminated the wide-open space. Seconds after that, Seigenthaler stood in the doorway, right behind one of his bodyguards.

Another of the security quartet from Langley went ahead to determine whether it was safe for the C.I.A. executive to step outside. He watched cautiously as a skirmish line of paratroopers fanned out in a wide pattern . . . advanced slowly like scouts in unfamiliar country infiltrated by cunning and aggressive "hostiles." When they reached the treeline, they stopped to search for snipers or other intruders.

Another eight soldiers spread out, walked forward to establish an inner perimeter hallway from the building. They didn't smile or talk . . . very G.I. in basic Fort Campbell style . . . weapons at the ready, and just a bit edgy.

When they were in position, the lieutenant who'd complimented Denny Monroe's shooting surveyed his force—the outdoor part of it—before his eyes searched the exterior of the building and the soldiers manning the high-tech search gear in the blacked-out windows.

It wasn't until he nodded in silent approval that the senior of the four C.I.A. bodyguards let Seigenthaler leave the shelter of the building. The Langley executive started toward Willson, applied his people skills by not immediately speaking to the visibly shocked woman.

Now she was walking toward the man who might or might not answer to the name Denny Monroe. He might not pause in his swearing to listen, let alone answer, to anyone or anything. Here we go, Seigenthaler thought. Another of those extremely unpleasant Nomad incidents. A scene and a half, Seigenthaler reflected, and the worst of it was that Nomad was almost always a hundred percent right.

At least ninety-five percent, even on a bad day.

From the volume and vituperation, this was definitely one of those. Nomad wouldn't even look at Willson and Seigenthaler as they neared him. He was concentrating his anger on the airborne lieutenant.

"Maybe you can tell me," Nomad raged, "What kind of half-ass outfit are you running? I thought you were pros . . . not a bunch of fucking nervous Girl Scouts? Or is this a mob of Section Eight psychos . . . career idiots?"

"These men are first-class soldiers carrying out orders," the lieutenant answered stiffly. He wasn't going to lose his temper, and he certainly wouldn't be drawn into some hissing and snarling contest with this furious and unreasonable civilian.

"Our orders are to protect the people here and the building from a possible attack by armed infiltrators," he continued coldly. "We were to use such force as might be necessary. We're not city cops, high-school counselors, or social workers."

"Cowboys," Nomad denounced bitterly. "Trigger-happy cowboys."

"These insults are completely unjustified," the officer replied. "The perimeter had been penetrated by at least one armed intruder. Common burglars don't usually carry weapons. Odds are five to one that this man was no burglar—no common criminal—but some kind of agent with penetration and infiltration skills."

"You got that fucking part right, soldier," Nomad scorned.

"Threat level: significant," the lieutenant declared. "I don't know yet whether there was one infiltrator or more—"

"You'll never know, and I won't either," the angry field agent predicted. "He's dead and your men aren't moving out to search the area."

"First priority is the safety of the people here, and we're defending the perimeter to exclude threats," the junior officer said. "That's all we've been told. We don't know where we are . . . what this facility is supposed to do . . . who you are . . . or why anyone would want to penetrate. I have enough people to hold the perimeter, but no one to spare for sweeps outside."

Nomad pointed skyward.

"There's that chopper up there . . . a hot bird with all the big-ticket search hardware. Radios. At least two machine guns," he said. "If you're not too busy, Lieutenant, you might send the chopper out on a search pattern. Now. Anytime in the next twelve seconds."

The paratroop officer didn't continue the argument. He was talking to someone else on his walkie-talkie, short range. He was spelling out to the soldier at the more powerful transmitter what to tell the helicopter pilot.

Willson and Seigenthaler approached Nomad now.

She pointed at the pistol in his right hand.

"I thought you returned the gun you took the night you got here," she said uneasily. "You said you did it because you trusted us."

He nodded noncommittally.

"Where did you get this gun?" she pressed.

"Cracker Jack box," he replied. "Sorry. Of course I trust you."

Seigenthaler suddenly thought of an old joke about a veteran Hollywood film producer.

"Hello," he lied. That was the whole number.

The Langley executive could see that Dr. Willson didn't realize that Nomad was being ironic, that he was as used to untruths as he was to breathing. Seigenthaler shrugged . . . barely.

"It's just that it's hard for me to put my life in the hands of strangers. I don't know these young soldiers, and I've always had to protect myself," Nomad told her.

"But where did you get the weapon?"

"From your arsenal at the range in the basement. I stole it, Doctor. I'm not proud of that."

He might have another gun . . . maybe two, Seigenthaler calculated. Nomad was exceptionally good at stealing as well as lying.

She looked at Monroe for several seconds.

"When did you steal it?" she asked. "After you gave me the other one?"

"Before," he replied. "When I heard that the bad guys were looking for us, I was convinced I needed a weapon. Two days before."

Probably five, Seigenthaler speculated.

"I haven't been feeling well, you know," the field agent said. "I'm not fully recovered."

Seigenthaler looked at the corpse.

Blood stained both trouser legs, just below the knee.

Someone who was an expert marksman had fired two shots to bring down the intruder, not to kill.

"I'm sorry if I lost it, Doctor," Nomad said. "I wanted a prisoner we could question, not a dead man. I doubt that we'll ever be sure who he was or who sent him."

"Maybe the Russians haven't found us," she suggested. "He might be just a common burglar. We can check his clothes, the papers in his wallet."

Nomad pointed at a five-foot-long cape of some black material lying beside the body.

"That's not burglar gear, Doc. It's a heat-resistant plastic designed to defeat detectors and alarms in search choppers. Those birds are looking for intelligence agents, guerrillas, infiltrators, assassins or saboteurs," he told her. "And all the I.D. he might carry will be as phoney as his dental work."

He turned to Seigenthaler.

"Bag him," the man with the Russian heart said crisply. "Don't let the troopers or anyone else mess with the body or his clothes. Get this in a body bag—fast. If you don't have one here, get it and move this to a forensic lab. Dry ice on the way, I'd guess. You might find something in three weeks."

"We've got three days," Seigenthaler said. "Maybe two."

He pointed at the bullet holes in the legs.

"Yours, right?"

Nomad shrugged.

"You're recovered enough for me," Seigenthaler said.

He gestured toward the fifteen-round French semiautomatic Nomad held.

"You need another clip?" the executive asked, "or did you take an extra?"

"Three," the field agent replied casually and walked back to the ring of trash barrels where he'd left the bathrobe. He made no effort to hide the pistol in the garment now. Taking no chances about another armed infiltrator, Nomad was still holding the stolen gun in his right hand as he turned to reenter the building.

THE OTHER TRANSPLANT PATIENTS were waiting just inside the rear door. They'd heard the shooting. Now they wanted to know what happened. Before they could ask their questions, Nomad pointed down the corridor and spoke in preemptive strike.

"Let's see if we can buy a cup of tea in the dining room," he said, "and I'll tell you what's going on."

"Not all of it?" the black woman guessed.

"Of course not."

There was no sign of any kitchen staff when they got to the dining room. That wasn't surprising since it wasn't even half past four in the morning, so they dropped any thought of tea—it could have been one of Monroe's jokes—and sat down to listen.

"To maintain a high quality of service," he began in the familiar litany of so many corporate switchboards, "this conversation is definitely being recorded."

He pointed at one overhead lighting fixture, then another.

His fellow transplant patients understood.

Bugs. Someone was taping every word . . . every sound.

"We had an intruder trying to infiltrate from out back," Monroe reported, "and we're not sure who he was."

"Did he get away?" Chen asked.

"He got *dead*. I suspect that nobody told our soldier friends that we wanted to talk with intruders. That would explain why one of our vigilant troopers cut him half in two with a full burst," Monroe said. "He's past tense, and that could be a future problem."

"Spell it out, Denny," Fuentes urged.

"I think . . . I'm eighty-percent sure, whatever that means . . . he was a Russian, and I'd bet a dollar and a half he was looking for information about the guy who gave us his organs. I think there's a good chance the Russians might be bothered if their agent disappears like the late donor."

"So they'll make another try to get in," Fuentes reasoned.

"Maybe this guy tonight found us because they've already got someone—anyone—inside here," Paula Taylor speculated.

"I thought of that," Monroe declared.

"I was kidding," the blonde-haired woman told him.

"I wasn't," he replied.

She looked uncomfortable and announced she was going back to bed.

Susan Kincaid studied Monroe's eyes for a moment after Taylor left.

"You don't really believe we've been penetrated," she said.

"What do you think?" he fenced.

"I think you're catching a little paranoia."

He nodded.

"My best subject in kindergarten. Any other thoughts?"

"Be careful with Paula," the black woman advised urgently. "Don't know what she's up to, but she's not as fond of you as she seems . . . you or any man."

"You're telling me she's gay?"

"I've said what I have to say. Good night, Denny."

There was a definite hard edge in her voice, but none of the three men said a word until she'd departed. Fuentes smiled. Chen nodded, his face showing nothing. And the man they knew as Dennis Monroe ended the meeting with the remark that he was heading to his room to sleep.

That wasn't where he went.

There were paratroopers with assault rifles on alert in the corridors as he made his way to Charlotte Willson's office . . . and two of Seigenthaler's bodyguards from C.I.A. headquarters flanked the door. The head of the Russia-F.S.U. group was on the telephone as the field agent entered.

Seigenthaler turned to question him.

"You sure you're okay?"

"Tell your uncle I'm fine," Nomad replied.

Now he spoke to Willson.

"And Doc, you can tell your soldiers—tell 'em *twice*—not to kill the next fucking intruder before he's questioned. Concussion grenades ought to do it."

Nomad was right, Seigenthaler thought. There was a good chance—a bad risk, less positive people might say—that another effort to break in would come soon. He wasn't going to say that to Willson. It might panic her.

Seigenthaler refocused on the telephone.

"Sorry. I'll get back to you," he promised and ended his report to Langley on the shoot-out. As he put down the phone served by the secure line, he saw Nomad yawn, turn the face of his wristwatch back to normal so he could scan it, and point toward the door.

He left without saying another word.

"His remarks about soldiers . . . just now and out back earlier," the director of The St. John Institute said. "Does he have some problems with military personnel?"

"Same ones he has with just about everybody else," Seigenthaler answered. "Don't worry about it. He's good at his work."

"I'm not sure I understand."

Her area of responsibility was Nomad's physical health, Seigenthaler thought. Personality was none of her damn business.

"I'm with you, Doctor," he lied. "Let's call it a night."

AFTER SEIGENTHALER WAS GONE, the director's throat felt tight. She swallowed hard and wondered why. It might be the question she'd been about to ask. Then she wasn't thinking . . . she was looking. She found herself reviewing every detail of what had happened in the past hour.

She saw some of it, not the shooting, but the aftermath, in her mind's eye. She heard the gunfire and Monroe's bitter outburst. As the furious words reechoed, her mental screen filled with the bullet-riddled and bloody body of the intruder. Then the screen was blank, the cursing gone. Silence.

Suddenly something else filled her consciousness.

Monroe had mentioned—almost offhandedly, as if any fool would know it already—*another* intruder.

It could be soon, she thought. Maybe very soon.

She wasn't prepared to deal with that. She was a scientist and project manager. Her job description didn't cover an armed intruder chopped into a corpse by gunfire. There was nothing in it about coping with a second or third attack—perhaps multiple intruders—on her Institute, her home.

Violent death had been a stranger to her until tonight.

She wasn't a soldier . . . a city cop . . . or a field agent.

All the war movies and hard-boiled crime dramas on television, with splattered fake blood and crumpled actors who pretended to be dead, couldn't help her deal with tonight's ugly reality. Maybe tomorrow's, too.

She was afraid.

More frightened than at any time before in her orderly, scientific life. It had nothing to do with her gender, she reasoned. Any sane civilian male not totally overcome with testosterone would be equally affected.

She applied her rational problem-solving mind to the fear. It was logical to be afraid in this situation. Still, she was glad that she could deal with it before she had to face Monroe, the man from Langley, and the paratroopers in the morning. She'd have it under control by then.

It wasn't under control now.

Her throat was tightening up . . . she coughed twice in pure reflex. That didn't help. She swallowed twice, and began to shake. This had never happened to Dr. Willson before. It offended her. She clutched the arms of her large swivel chair, held on tightly to avoid being swept away, and tried to breathe deeply to get more oxygen into her bloodstream. A cousin who was a neurologist had once told her this helped some people beat back panic.

She wasn't panicky yet, but not far from it.

The taste of copper seared her mouth.

Fear . . . acute fear. She'd read about this taste.

She could cope. She wasn't that scared little girl alone in the dark anymore. She reminded herself that there were dozens of soldiers from an elite assault unit here . . . trained to a saber's edge. Equipped with first-class weaponry . . . battle ready . . . set to protect everyone at this facility. Reinforcements—thirty more paratroopers—would arrive before sunset.

And there was over a million dollars in electronic defenses.

She quickly opened the panel built into her desk to check every alarm and system carefully . . . twice. The shaking made it difficult to do it normally, but she forced herself, pausing when her fingers resisted her brain. The intense effort made her sweat. Breathing hard, she wouldn't stop until she was sure that it all worked.

The terror began to subside just a bit. It would retreat more rapidly when the horror thing—the bullet-riddled corpse—was gone in an hour or two. That would help a lot.

It was going to be a long night, she told herself.

She was right.

26

IN THE UNDERGROUND GARAGE AT PETER'S HOUSE, THE SECU-
rity guards on the night shift looked right, then left, swinging
their automatic weapons as the rules for training exercises required. It was all in the manual. These drills came up every nine
or ten weeks. That was what Moscow demanded.

The guards watched as a big metal drum filled with toxic
waste—it was clearly marked—was loaded into the back of a
large truck. Half the vehicles in this facility needed some kind of
spare part, but this one was in good repair. They were using the
best truck they had so this exercise would go off smoothly . . . and
look good in the quarterly report.

Now another drum . . . a third . . . fourth . . . five in all. Two
drivers climbed up into the cab. There was a third—a relief man,
with an armed escort—in the back with the cargo. On a real
transfer, there'd be additional guards, but this was only a sim-
ulation to test readiness.

The truck moved slowly down one of the long tunnels for
over half a mile, to emerge from what looked like a graveyard
for dead vehicles to be cannibalized. It rolled through the back
streets to a two-lane hardtop and turned south. The drivers in

the cab took turns at the wheel every hundred and fifty miles, and no chances.

They stayed below the speed limit for good reasons.

They didn't want to attract attention by going too fast.

And they didn't want to push their luck even if this truck really had the quality tires they'd been promised. The drivers assumed that they'd be blamed for any delays—the normal routine in governments and other large organizations since that odd weather back in Noah's time.

The two men in the truck's cab grumbled and told dirty jokes and drove. They shifted . . . complained about the hard seats . . . and kept the vehicle chugging along to a sad-looking petrol station 198 miles southwest of Peter's House. They refilled the truck's tank . . . emptied their bladders . . . grumbled, and stretched their legs.

"Where you from?" the bored attendant at the station asked mechanically in the hope of some/any talk that would ease the nothingness of the night shift and so few vehicles.

"Fuck you," one of the drivers responded with the charm that several of his colleagues admired.

This routine exchange of twenty-first-century roadside pleasantries complete, the men from Peter's House adjusted their underwear, loosened their workpants and shirts, and got back onboard to continue south. There was another stop at a gas station three and a half hours later. This time, there was no profound dialogue at all. The truck with the "toxic waste" was on schedule.

No problems. More driving. Orders.

They were out of dirty jokes . . . hungry, too. Now they saw it . . . where it was supposed to be. There was *nothing* informal or improvisational about this drill. Someone had checked out the route in advance and found the grubby grocery in some easy-to-forget small town. They bought large chunks of second-rate sausage, country bread that could have been worse, and barely flavored soft drinks.

They saw the bottles of rough, homemade vodka and wanted some. What they didn't want was the trouble they'd catch if they dared to buy any, so they shook their heads and returned to the truck. On and on. It was now—literally and figuratively—a pain in the ass.

Not very far to go.

That awareness helped, for they'd exhausted the soft drinks and were thirsty, almost irritable. Even with driving in shifts, they were tired. It was all for Mother Russia, but they looked forward to the end of their run. They were dry-throated . . . red-eyed . . . bone-tired.

And all for some dumb training exercise.

"Hope I never catch another run like this again," grumbled the man behind the wheel. The other driver beside him nodded but didn't audibly agree. Even in the New Russia, anyone connected with Peter's House couldn't give any hint of dissatisfaction.

About a dozen miles from the Ukrainian frontier—just past the old church at the crossroads—a parked civilian car blinked its lights in the proper sequence. The location was correct, and so was the recognition signal. The truck driver tapped his light switch three times . . . then twice . . . and four more times. He drew his vehicle to the side of the road beside the sedan.

Four men in civilian clothes immediately emerged from the car. Nicolai Pankin . . . General Temkov's get-it-done aide . . . and the veteran S.V.R. "wet team," cool and expert specialists in death. They were there to take over the next part of the exercise.

"Right on time. Very good," Pankin approved. "I'll mention this in my report. Now let's switch."

As the weary crew that had slogged down from Peter's House emerged from the truck, Pankin gave each of them a wad of hundred-ruble notes. Used notes, not in consecutive serial numbers, hard to trace even under the best of circumstances.

Or the worst, Pankin thought. Which would be coming soon, he told himself. Then he thanked the men from the truck and suggested they rest for the night at a small hotel—the Dushka. Turn left at the crossroad . . . nine kilometers . . . on the right side.

"You take our car. It's got over half a tank of fuel," he told them briskly. "We'll finish your run in the truck to Base Ninety-one."

They'd never heard of Base 91, but not one of them asked.

It would be "inappropriate."

No, "stupid" would be more accurate.

They were halfway to the hotel when the driver who spoke so rudely to so many people . . . now he was at the wheel of the car . . . said his kidneys insisted that he stop the vehicle "to water the flowers." The others chuckled as he stepped from the sedan. He began to walk. After so many hours in the truck, his legs needed the exercise.

He was about twenty yards from the car when he halted. He surely needed to sleep, he thought as he unzipped his trousers. Maybe there'd be a friendly girl at the hotel, he hoped. He yawned . . . began to urinate.

That was when it happened.

A noise louder than any he'd ever heard stunned him.

There was a tremendous flash of light that almost blinded him, and a shock wave like a head-on collision with a motorcycle threw him a dozen yards.

Away from the car.

That was important, for the sedan was a fireball. It was totally engulfed in flames. There hadn't even been time for the three men inside to scream. The blast had crushed them into pink things that looked nothing like human, and the blowtorch heat of the extraordinary fires that erupted scant seconds later soon reduced them to charred bones.

The heat was awful. Sitting up and staring, the battered driver saw it begin to melt the wrecked car. Almost everything in the vehicle had been reduced to cinders. He was over sixty yards away, hurting from the intense heat. He crawled back another ten yards, then twisted to stare at the corpse of the car as the metal began to glow and sag.

No accident.

Too fast . . . too complete.

High explosives and materials to feed this fire . . . to build it into a remarkable incinerator.

Bomb. First-class. Professional.

Who did it? Why?

Had to be the men who'd given them the car. They were official, part of what had been called a routine training exercise.

Just one reason came to mind. If they killed the team that brought the barrels of toxic waste from Peter's House, no one could describe them or reveal they'd stolen the cargo. This made no sense. That wasn't worth killing for. *Unless—*

Unless the drums didn't contain toxic waste.

Unless they held more important cargo . . . something as valuable as diamonds. People would kill for diamonds or a hundred other things. It didn't matter which. He was in great danger. He'd seen the murders and the murderers. They'd come after him if they had any idea he was still alive.

Maybe they wouldn't be able to tell—the bodies were so fiercely consumed. Phosphorus, he thought as he recalled his three years in the army. Phosphorus would make that kind of white heat. So would certain mixes of aluminum that both West and East used in incendiary bombs.

The bastards weren't going to turn him into ash, he told himself bitterly. Going to the authorities wouldn't help at all. These killers *were* the authorities, or had terrific protection from them. He had to protect himself. He must get beyond their reach and view . . . disappear.

He struggled to his feet. Bruised, panting, and brushing the dirt from his sweaty clothes, he stared at the fireball for thirty seconds more. That was all the time he had. He didn't run. He could hardly walk. He stumbled . . . barely caught himself . . . felt pain that could identify a broken rib. His face hurt, too.

He stood there in semishock for several seconds until a terrible smell reached him. It came from the fireball, and he wondered if this was the odor of incinerated people. That was enough to get him walking again. West . . . out of the country . . . his only hope. If he was lucky, he might make it. If he wasn't, they . . . whoever they were . . . would bury him in a garbage dump.

A FEW MINUTES LATER, the truck with the drums of "toxic waste" reached the border. The usual bribe at this Ukrainian customs post got the vehicle across. Neither Pankin nor the "wet team" spoke as he guided it farther south for nearly three hours. At a rundown airport that survived on fees from individuals who didn't like questions, a turboprop cargo plane with Turkmenistan markings waited with six swarthy men in overalls beside it.

Pankin recognized one as the person from the ferry at Lisbon. That man recognized Pankin, but neither mentioned any previous meeting.

This was here . . . now . . . the main moment.

No time for an extra word or anything but business by the stony rules of the trade. Al Wadi's envoy watched Pankin count the money in the two suitcases, and the hard-eyed "wet team" with Pankin studied the man who'd brought the cash. They also scanned up and down and across the five Turkmeni—or were they Middle Eastern—waiting to load the drums.

Each of the S.V.R. "wet team" wore a light raincoat that covered one of the subcompact Scorpion machine pistols. Nobody commented on that, for this was the standard formal wear for such occasions.

The money count was correct.

Pankin leaned forward to speak softly.

"Do your men know what's in the drums?" he asked.

The Middle Easterner shook his head.

"Good," Pankin approved.

The "wet team" didn't know either. He watched as the drums were loaded into the rear of the old cargo plane . . . waited nine minutes until the turboprops shrieked and the Turkmeni aircraft rose into the night sky. There was one more thing to do, Pankin told himself.

He had fourteen minutes in which to do it.

He completed the task in eleven, and smiled. Having removed the license plate from the truck, he put it in the airline bag slung over his shoulder. It fit right up against the extra clips for his own machine pistol. There'd be no trouble with the truck. Some helpful local would steal it before lunchtime, and by dinner, it would be cannibalized for parts that brought high prices.

He was enjoying that prospect when he heard the sound of

another plane approaching. This was a small jet with no markings. It belonged to the S.V.R.'s private airline. When it landed and taxied up to the four agents from headquarters, Pankin picked up the two suitcases filled with currency. He trusted the three assassins up to a point. Handling millions of U.S. dollars was beyond that point.

PANKIN WAS IN GOOD SPIRITS —a bit tired, but very positive— when he put down the cash-crammed luggage on the floor in Temkov's office some hours later. He knew that the general would be pleased.

"Perfect," he said to Temkov.

"The money?"

"Every penny, and the *other* matter is finished."

He was speaking of the men from Peter's House.

Temkov understood that.

"I checked with some of our colleagues down south, General, and they say that one thing went wrong. Seems there was a car accident. Big fire. No survivors."

"Most unfortunate," Temkov said for the benefit of any hidden microphones S.V.R. internal security might have planted. "I suppose these things happen."

Pankin now opened his airline bag and showed the truck's license plate to his superior. That had been part of the meticulous plan, too. Temkov nodded in approval.

"You know what to do," he reminded.

Acid, to obliterate the numbers totally.

Then into a high-temperature oven to make doubly sure.

"Well done, Nicolai," the general complimented. "I can always rely on you."

Pankin beamed proudly.

"Is there anything else?" he asked,

"There *is* one more thing," Temkov replied and began to tell him what it was. Pankin listened intently.

27

THE REINFORCEMENTS ARRIVED AT THE ST. JOHN INSTITUTE.

So did additional infrared scanners for night sweeps of the open areas in the front, back, and sides of the building.

Inside, life proceeded according to the schedule Willson and her staff of specialists had planned weeks earlier. It was rotation time. Monroe went through a half-hour telepathic drill with each of his four team members. Then roles were switched and other combinations were tested.

Their mental communication was growing stronger.

They were handling the shock of the shoot-out well. They were cloak-and-dagger professionals, so they didn't take extra chances. They avoided speaking about the intruder, and they each carried a pistol now. Monroe had arranged that with Willson and Seigenthaler.

Monroe's ability to do this didn't surprise the other transplant patients.

By unspoken agreement, he was the group leader.

He hadn't asked for that. He didn't have to, for he had the weight, the strength, the expertise that had to be respected. He'd asked for an increase in physical therapy—workouts in the gymnasium to accelerate their bodies' return to battle readiness. No one debated this with Monroe. If he wanted it, he must have a good reason. He probably knew something they didn't, they assumed.

Seigenthaler watched them working out, said nothing.

Not even "Hello," or his name.

Monroe seemed to know who he was and accepted him.

That was enough for the others.

Lunch, as usual. Then to the firing range, where something wasn't quite the same. First, they were polishing skills with a wider range of U.S. weapons . . . and now Russian guns, too. That was new.

Second, they couldn't help recognizing the increased intensity that Monroe brought to the shooting. He was speeding things up for some specific reason. They looked at each other. Susan Kincaid did more than that.

"Things seem to be more urgent now," she said evenly.

Her tone made it a question.

" 'Why should we be in such desperate haste to succeed, and in such desperate enterprises?' " he quoted in reply.

"Thoreau's fine," she acknowledged, "but where's all this going . . . and how soon?"

It pleased him that she recognized the writer's words.

Of course he didn't say so.

"I'm going ahead," he answered, "to get us a room with a view."

"Or a bullet. Do you need to be a goddam hero?" she demanded. "What the hell do you want?"

He considered the question for several seconds.

He also scanned her mind.

She really wanted to know.

"I want a lot of things. What I want most is to find my sister," he told her.

"What's she got to do with all *this*?" the black woman asked uncertainly. "Maybe she'll find you."

He shook his handsome head.

"She can't find me," he replied. "I'm dead, remember?"

Then he excused himself and walked to the language lab to brush up his spoken Russian via hours of tapes. He sensed there wasn't much time. More tape listening after dinner. That night, Susan Kincaid had a peculiar dream. In a very dark room, she heard Denny Monroe say, "I'll be back."

She remembered this clearly when she awoke . . . was thinking about it as she joined the others at breakfast. He wasn't there. She waited. He never arrived. They were walking from the dining room when Charlotte Willson casually remarked that he'd had to get his transplant checked at the hospital.

"Nothing serious," she assured them.

The caring chess player realized two things immediately.

The director of The St. John Institute didn't lie well, and Susan Kincaid hadn't dreamed the three-word message.

Monroe had sent it telepathically to her subconscious.

Would she ever see him again?

28

THERE WERE TWO TAPES.

One consisted of general Russian vocabulary and idioms. The other was special—tailor-made for Monroe—in that same language, but concentrated on military weapons and cloak-and-dagger jargon. Monroe knew almost all this, but he listened to the tapes twice on the flight.

He wanted to be sure.

Actually, to be sure that he was sure. Obsessive? As always.

It didn't occur to him to be anything else . . . except dead.

All the way east, he didn't say a word to Seigenthaler or the four C.I.A. security men. From time to time, they looked at him and shifted in their seats. As they did, he got glimpses of the guns in their belly holsters. They could carry their weapons on this plane. The twin jet, whose registration bore the name of a pharmaceutical firm, actually belonged to another company—*The* Company.

No one in the trade called it that anymore.

The term had been used too often in third-rate movies and fourth-rate feature articles contributed by semi-ignorant writers.

The issue didn't come up when the jet touched down at an Air National Guard field south of Wilmington. It was less likely that anyone here would recognize Nomad or Seigenthaler than at Dulles or Washington's busy Reagan, someone had calculated. Someone had an inconspicuous civilian station wagon and driver waiting.

"How are you feeling?" Seigenthaler asked the telepath.

Nomad shrugged, uttered eight words.

The security men didn't recognize any of them, so they didn't understand why Seigenthaler's eyes lit up as he nodded. He had no problem, for he was fluent in Russian. Travel-weary and a bit uncomfortable about having been kept in ignorance from the minute they took over Mr. Seigenthaler's protection, the guards were glad when the station wagon reached the C.I.A.'s safe house thirty-one miles from Langley and another security detail took "the duty."

Buckley was waiting in a comfortably furnished living room.

He smiled in greeting, shook Nomad's hand, and locked the door.

Just like the good old days, Nomad thought.

"Glad to hear we were able to save your life," Buckley said.

Guilt-trip time, Nomad judged. You owe us. The usual stuff.

"Thank you very much," Nomad replied. "What do you want?"

"You sound like your old self," Buckley said and squeezed out a chuckle. "He is his old self, isn't he?" the deputy director asked Seigenthaler.

"Driving from the airport now, I asked him how he felt and he recited the names of eight consecutive stops on the Moscow subway," the head of the Russian and F.S.U. unit reported. "I'd say he's fine."

"Good. Sit down. Take off your coat," Buckley invited.

"It's not mine. Some doctor at the Institute lent me this," the telepath countered as he removed the garment. Jammed under his belt was the stolen handgun. Buckley stared, and Nomad noticed it.

"I got it at the gift shop at the Institute. Wonder if you could do me a favor," he said, and Seigenthaler recognized the irony in the field agent's tone.

Buckley didn't. He nodded as Seigenthaler waited to hear the provocation.

"I'd like a holster just like the big boys have," Nomad announced. "Belly holster . . . fast draw. And I could use a suit and shirt that fit me. These aren't mine either."

"Shoes, too. Complete outfit," Seigenthaler promised. "The doctors out there had your measurements from the physicals. Our people have been working on this since yesterday. A full wardrobe will be here in a few hours. That includes *two* holsters."

"Appreciate that. Very helpful. Anything I might do to help you?"

Buckley sighed in relief that they'd finally gotten to business.

"We'd like you to go to Moscow . . . ASAP," he began. "It's a top-priority operation."

"Code name?"

"Juno Ninety-two."

"Guess all the good names were used up," Nomad judged. "What is it?"

"One of our Moscow people has been snatched. They want to trade her for something we can't deliver, and we want you to help get her home."

Then Buckley briefed the American with the Russian heart on the kidnapping, the negotiations with a crafty S.V.R. general named Temkov and his meetings with the U.S. military attaché.

"Who's he?"

"A one-star named Dallas Johann, one tough Texan. He's very smart."

"Will he follow the instructions in the package?" Nomad asked.

He could see that Buckley didn't understand.

"Will he do exactly what he's told?" the telepath translated.

"He's a career soldier. You mind spelling this out? Who's going to tell him what . . . and why?"

Nomad crossed his legs, smiled almost pleasantly.

"Let's be democratic about this," he proposed. "We'll both do it. I'll tell you what to tell him, and you'll tell him. I don't much care whether you do it nice or nasty. You know how to manage people. Use your judgment."

Seigenthaler saw the flicker of alarm in his supervisor's eyes. The deputy director would have to handle this on his own.

"What do you think I ought to tell him?" Buckley tested.

"*Think?* That's exactly it," Nomad approved. "First, he's to do precisely what I tell him to do . . . and to think what I tell him to think. That means *not* to think what I tell him not to think."

"I don't get it."

"And don't tell him who I am. Make up a decent cover story . . . none of that computer salesman crap."

"You're going as Foreign Service. State Department, diplomatic immunity," Seigenthaler volunteered.

"No cigar. The woman they snatched had that immunity, didn't she?"

"It's the best we can do on short notice," Buckley defended.

Nomad's face showed his scorn.

"Let's not waste any more time," he began curtly. "Why did you pick me for this?"

The deputy director mentally phrased his reply before he spoke.

"We're told you're the best of the telepaths in that place, and we're hoping you might psych this Temkov out."

"Try that in English."

"Give us some lead on what he's up to . . . a clue . . . anything. Is that possible?"

Nomad decided to be as half-honest as Buckley.

"I'm no fortune-teller," he answered, "but there's a chance I might pick up something. It's a long shot. *He* isn't a telepath, and he won't be trying to send me any messages."

"Will you try?"

Nomad pretended to hesitate.

"I'll try. Now I guess I should spell out why I'm going to . . . have to . . . tell your smart Texan what to think and what not to. It's really simple."

Seigenthaler knew it couldn't be simple.

Simple was a dog-and-pony act.

Nomad was a three-ring circus, with fireworks and multi-media on the side.

"If we're trying to psych out this Russian general," the man from The St. John Institute said, "I've got a hunch they'll be trying the same number on our one-star Texan. You want to know why?"

He paused for three . . . four . . . five seconds.

"I'm going to speak the unspeakable," he warned. "*Lucky.*"

Buckley grunted as if hit.

"Lucky's dead," he said.

Nomad smiled and tapped his chest.

"Not all of him's dead. I'm wearing his heart," he told the C.I.A. executives. "I mentioned the unmentionable Lucky because he was living proof that the peace-loving, kind-to-babies S.V.R. is in the mind game, too. No, the mind *war.*"

"Keep talking," Buckley urged.

"Lucky's proof that they've been training people—more than one, I'm betting. They're not stupid people. If they've got more head cases trained . . . and if this whole deal's as hot as I think it might be . . . they're going to bring in Lucky's cousin to hit on our general."

"Go on."

"That's why you can't tell this Texan anything about me or the Institute. That's why he has to think about *other* things in case the Russians are working his head. *Any* other things . . . West Point's football team this year . . . Dan Quayle's poetry . . . Jennifer Lopez's electric caboose . . . Christmas-turkey dinner at his grandma's. If he wants to go porn, that's cool. The Radio City Rockettes would be fine, too."

"I've got the picture," Buckley said stiffly.

"Blow it up very big and frame it. Make sure your smart Texan's got it and takes it seriously. By the way, when are you going to tell me the rest of it?"

"That's it . . . we'll brief General Johann thoroughly," Buckley assured him.

Nomad shook his head.

"You need help," he said. "You've got to be crazy if you expect me to buy *that*. We all know you're not laying on this big-dollar operation just to save some low-level op in the Moscow station."

"We feel responsible for our people," Buckley defended.

"Try that an octave higher with more strings," Nomad scorned. "Responsible? How about me? I feel goddam responsible for getting me home intact, and I'll have a lot better chance if I have all the facts."

Buckley cleared his throat.

Then he picked up an envelope from the side table and extracted a photograph.

"I was about to get to this," he announced. "Something else has come up. It's quite serious . . . very urgent."

He thrust the picture toward Nomad. The field agent answered before the question could be asked.

"Demon . . . Russian atomic weapon . . . miniature bomb, Type Two . . . estimated yield, fifty-six-plus megatons," he recited automatically as if reading from a cue card.

"Not estimated. Yield confirmed," Seigenthaler said.

Then he reported, concisely and bitterly, that a Demon had recently been dropped on a small city in Ethiopia. Attackers unidentified. Reason unknown. Dead, six thousand and counting . . . a hundred and thirty more every day.

"So it finally happened," Nomad thought aloud. "I guess it had to. It was only a matter of time before some weirdos got their claws on these. Anything strategic there?"

"Nothing that is . . . as far as anyone knows . . . of the slightest interest to Russia or any African country or any of the fourteen revolutionary armies fighting within eighteen hundred miles," Buckley said.

"Media must have gone ballistic," Nomad speculated. "Lots of civilians here . . . U.K. . . . Japan . . . scared out of their skulls, right?"

"Nobody knows yet," Buckley told him. "Letting the story out wouldn't help the Ethiopians. We're flying in tons of aid and medical teams, you know. There's something else I should share with you. Two of the specialists on the inter-agency working group set up for this suspect that the drop could have been a field test."

"So the weirdos may have more, and you want to know how many."

"And how they got them . . . and what comes after the field test," Seigenthaler added.

"And where the Demons are . . . and who the weirdos are . . . if they are just weirdos . . . and whose money is behind them. Can't see this as a Russian operation. They field-tested this weapon four years ago," Nomad reasoned.

He eyed the photo again before he handed it back to Buckley.

"Russian weapons. Who moved them out . . . by what route? You want to seal that up for good," the telepath said.

"We have to—N.S.C. directive. Find them and stop them," the deputy director confirmed.

"At any cost. Do whatever is necessary. Kill them dead . . . twice and nasty," Nomad calculated.

"You said it, I didn't," Buckley noted.

"*New York Times* and the BBC won't like it," Nomad predicted sarcastically. "Maybe we won't tell them."

Now Seigenthaler and Buckley nodded silently.

There was a knock on the door. When Seigenthaler opened it, a security agent announced that a doctor had arrived with "the visitor's medication."

"He'll be out in a minute," Seigenthaler said and locked the door again.

"We've said our piece," Buckley declared. "Anything you want to say or ask?"

Nomad held up two fingers . . . then another to make it three.

"One, I'd like to adjust the deal . . . just a bit. Danger bonus. Temkov and the weirdos won't do much for my life expectancy, so I think some extra insurance would be only fair. I mean real insurance. You pay the cash premiums on an additional two-hundred-fifty-thousand-dollar policy with my sister the beneficiary."

"She thinks you died months ago. It's going to look funny," Buckley fretted.

"Not that funny. Nobody laughs at two hundred fifty grand. Tell her the money was tied up in I.R.S. red tape or some legal screwup. You guys are good at making up stories. This ought to be easy."

Buckley knew he had no choice.

At this minute—in this horror show . . . he had to play Nomad's game.

Time was short, and it was the only game on the damn planet.

"Okay. What's Number Two?"

"Another policy. Same amount. Beneficiary, Susan Kincaid. Right now she's back at your spacey Institute. She's got another piece of Lucky. Susan's my friend, and I don't have a bunch of those."

"Deal. What else?"

"I assume that what General Temkov wanted in exchange for the Wilk woman was Lucky. Is that right?"

Seigenthaler nodded.

"Is that the third thing?" he asked.

"Not really. The third question has to do with . . . well, I'll just ask. *Who are Kelly's People?*"

He could feel the deputy director deliberately *not* think about it.

"What Kelly?" Buckley dodged.

"You tell me," Nomad pressed for a moment before he realized that he wasn't going to get an answer.

"Sorry, I can't help," the C.I.A. executive declared.

MINUTES AFTER NOMAD left the room to meet the doctor, Nicolai Pankin entered Temkov's office with an envelope from the S.V.R.'s communications center.

Messages with the secret call sign of the agent named Frank had been beamed to various parts of the United States a dozen times in the past two and a half days.

On the correct frequency . . . and on schedule.

There had been no response.

As of now, contact with Frank had been broken.

Frank was one of the best S.V.R. agents in the United States.

The general considered the situation, and told himself not to rush to any conclusion yet. There could be a score of reasons, including something as unthreatening as some problem with Frank's radio. If that was the difficulty, it could be fixed.

"Let's give him some more time," Temkov decided. "Two more days. Repeat transmissions on scheduled frequencies and at arranged times."

This wasn't like Frank, the general thought.

Frank knew how to check . . . to repair . . . to replace radio equipment.

That fact shouldn't be avoided.

"And if there's no contact in the next forty-eight hours," the general said, "initiate regular search procedure. Full sweep."

"Full sweep," Pankin confirmed.

As he started toward the door, Pankin thought about the mission Frank was on and wondered whether the people who'd eliminated Lucky might have taken Frank, too.

So did General Temkov.

29

"NOT A CHANCE," NOMAD SAID FIRMLY.

He pointed at the sixteen packages.

Each held a day's supply . . . more than a dozen pills.

"I'm not moving those in any goddam shoulder bag," he told the startled physician. "We're doing the life-and-death number, Doc. I'll body-carry them."

The C.I.A. doctor looked uneasily at the man he was told was Lee Alderdice. That was the name on the stranger's passport, driver's license, American Express card, and State Department employee pass.

"How?" the puzzled doctor wondered.

"Money belt. Two of them. *Three*, to be safe. I wouldn't want some sneak thief to take off with these pills. You're moving the yellow stuff in your attaché case . . . dry ice . . . double locked, right?"

The doctor almost asked about "the yellow stuff."

He decided that if he had a need to know they'd have told him.

"Correct," he confirmed. "I'll carry sixteen vials, and another sixteen left for our Embassy in Moscow last night by diplomatic pouch. I'm told there'll be more of your pills in that shipment."

He was taking all this fairly coolly, Nomad thought. According to Seigenthaler, this physician had never been to Russia and was making his first trip—that was the cover story—as a temporary replacement for the Embassy's resident doctor who was going home on a routine and brief vacation. He could treat staff or dependents if he had the time, but his crucial responsibility was the health of this Lee Alderdice.

The Agency executives who drafted him for this sudden trip had said that Alderdice was just about recovered from a transplant "procedure" . . . but hadn't mentioned why Alderdice merited a personal physician. They did note that no one was to know he was Alderdice's personal medical resource.

Not even the ambassador . . . or the C.I.A.'s Station Chief.

The doctor was wondering how long he'd be away, when a canvas suitcase full of clothes—all of them washed or dry-cleaned a dozen times so they didn't look new—arrived. Even the three pairs of shoes showed some wear.

"Nice job," Nomad complimented and swiftly changed from the borrowed attire he'd brought from the Institute. He dressed quickly, knotted his conservative tie perfectly on the first try, and smiled in satisfaction.

A car and driver waited outside the safe house. The trip was simple. Sedan to Dulles for the shuttle flight up to Kennedy, where they boarded the Delta 767 without incident. The food, like the flight, was uneventful. Nomad enjoyed "uneventful." It might not last very long after the big jet touched down at the Moscow airport where the international carriers landed.

Their diplomatic passports—carefully noted by Russian security people to report to headquarters—moved them through the noisy terminal to a neatly dressed young man holding up a sign bearing Nomad's new name. Lacking total confidence in local taxi service after a rash of robberies hit foreigners en route to the capital, the U.S. and other embassies routinely sent cars and drivers to collect and escort arriving voyagers.

The physician went to the Embassy's medical facility to check in with the doctor he was replacing.

After a required ceremonial exchange with the communications supervisor, Nomad was guided to the special "safe room," built and maintained to defeat electronic eavesdroppers.

Two men stood outside the door.

Another two inside.

The armed security guards who flanked the portal made Nomad's escort sign in, but didn't let him enter.

The other two men waiting inside for Nomad greeted him with wary nods and locked the door. Neither the C.I.A. Chief of Station nor the military attaché put out their hands or smiled. They didn't do that with strangers who came with broad authority and no specific identity.

Being sensible public servants, they wouldn't have believed who he was . . . what he was . . . anyway. Their organizational manuals ignored both telepathy and even the possibility of mind reading. They waited for him to explain what he could contribute to the liberation of Alison Wilk. There had been two coded messages from Washington that said he would.

Both were concise . . . cryptic . . . annoying.

The military attaché made that clear with his first remark.

"We've received priority signals from the chief of G-Two and the deputy director for operations of *his* outfit," he said, jerking his thumb toward the station chief, "and I don't *get* either of them."

"They said you were smart, General Johann," Nomad answered evenly. "I figure you don't get them because there wasn't much in them, right?"

Johann nodded.

"A smart man would recognize that, General. Smart and tough—that's what they told me."

"Who told you? My boss?"

"Your boss is a three-star, and I don't know any three-stars, General."

"Then why the hell did he instruct me to follow your orders to the fucking letter without question . . . without any questions at all?"

"He's smart, too, General," Nomad soothed. "Probably knows a ton of things I don't know, and I don't ask him questions. Maybe he was trying to keep you out of trouble—big trouble."

"You threatening me, mister?" Johann challenged.

"Alderdice. Mr. Lee Alderdice."

"That your real name?"

"I don't remember. I'm not threatening you, General. I'm just speculating. Maybe you'd like a command in Alaska. Great fishing up there, they say."

The station chief decided to break in now.

"Maybe we should move onto the next meet with Temkov," he said.

"We can socialize later over a bottle of Jim Beam," the stranger agreed cheerfully.

General Johann wondered who'd told this man about his favorite bourbon . . . and what else they'd told him. This visitor had to be some kind of a hotshot. They wouldn't share this information with anyone else.

"You speak Russian, Mr. Alderdice?" he tested.

"Yes, and I'm familiar with the structure and tactics of the S.V.R. and the G.R.U., too. It's a hobby of mine. Where do we stand on Alison Wilk? If you don't mind, *all* of it."

The three men sat down on plain wooden chairs—upholstery might be bugged—and the C.I.A. executive started from the beginning. Johann interrupted several times with additional facts and comments. He watched the stranger carefully, noting that this visitor listened to every word, knew when to keep silent and when and what to question.

Cool . . . focused . . . professional, the general judged.

"Now I want to ask something," he said.

"Go."

"Our orders informed us that you were going to tell us what to *think* and what *not* to think. Sounds crazy to me," he announced.

"Shows how smart you are," Nomad flattered smoothly. "It *is* crazy if you don't understand the special situation we may be getting into at the next talk with Temkov. I'm not going to waste your valuable time with a lot of details—"

"You mean it's none of our damn business," Johann interrupted.

"Good thinking," Nomad complimented. "This is a judgment call. My judgment . . . my call."

This guy had to be *some* pistol, the general realized. Three-stars didn't take the judgments of lesser mortals that seriously.

"What I'm about to tell you stays in this room . . . or it's kiss your butt good-bye," Nomad said. "That's no threat. That's a goddam promise, with oak-leaf clusters. Here we go. There is reason to believe that the Russians have made progress in their mind war program."

"You're serious?" Johann asked.

"I am, and they are. They said they'd closed it down ten years ago, but that was a lie."

The military attaché thought . . . remembered.

"We said the same thing about our program," he recalled. "Was that a lie, too?"

"We're the Good Guys," Nomad replied, deadpan. "The U.S. Army would never lie."

Johann eyed him for several seconds.

"You're a wise guy, aren't you?" he accused.

"Not wise enough, but I'm taking night classes. Back to the Russians, the new Russians—today's emancipated hoorah for peace-and-democracy Russians. They've been training people to get into the thoughts . . . the heads . . . of other people. The folks being trained have studied English to A-plus, so a suspicious person might guess that those heads belong to American people."

The station chief frowned.

"They can read minds?" he tested incredulously.

Nomad shrugged.

"I'm not sure. I think that everything I've been told about this Temkov indicates he's a slick operator . . . more than tricky . . . and in a nasty spot because he's learned that the S.V.R. agent he wanted us to send back isn't coming. Can't come. Dead. It's a long story and—"

"None of our damn business," Johann reasoned caustically.

"Give that man another star," Nomad ratified. "If Temkov's

in this jam and scared of his superiors, he'll use everything and do anything. He's got to get *something* from us or he'll look lousy."

"And he doesn't know what we could give him," the chief of station calculated.

"Exactly. I'd say he could be guessing that one of his mind operatives might possibly get into your thoughts . . . like decoding radio messages. Everybody does that big-time . . . we spend billions on the N.S.A. and the A.S.A. Next step might be head-tapping instead of wiretapping. It could be next-step time today."

"You believe this?" Johann asked.

"Yes, but don't ask me to spell it out. That's right, guys. None of your damn business. Hope that doesn't hurt your feelings."

"You don't give a crap about our feelings," the military attaché judged candidly.

"I can see why you were fourth in your class at West Point."

"Son of a bitch!" Johann said without malice.

"Only to my friends. Worse to others. So here's what I want you two patriots to think about. You can't try not to think at all. That's hard to do, and it could be a tip-off to any foxy Russian trying to probe your head."

"*If* there is any such person," Johann added.

Nomad gave him a thumbs-up salute.

"*Dubious* is good," he complimented. "I wouldn't try to crap a smart guy like you, General. This is a definite maybe, but we can't take any chances. What you *can* think about is how pissed Washington is about this Alison Wilk outrage . . . patience running out . . . that sort of thing."

"Anything else?" the bristling Texan asked.

"Random human things that crude Americans might hit on. Women . . . great food . . . how your feet hurt . . . what a pain in the ass the ambassador is . . . are those rumors about Temkov true?"

"What rumors?" General Johann asked.

"You don't have to be specific, just nasty. Any rumor you want," Nomad said.

The C.I.A. official remembered.

"We got a choice of things like that in the message saying you were coming," he reported. "I suppose you made the list." Nomad ignored the implicit question.

He wasn't going to admit to anything.

"Did the cable order that you're not to think about me at all? Nothing. I'm a nobody . . . an extra in this scene . . . just a brief-case carrier," the field agent told them.

"Attaché case," the station chief corrected. "There was one with your name on it in today's pouch."

The black-leather one he took from beside his chair was worn looking, scuffed at two corners, obviously not new. It had been "used" so it wouldn't attract attention. Having chosen the lock combination before he left the safe house, Nomad now accepted the case and opened it.

"When is this next meet with Temkov?" he asked as his eyes catalogued the contents.

"Ten tomorrow morning. Same place—on the boat that does the guided tour around town on the Volga."

"Forget the boat," Nomad ordered. "Tell him the meet's at noon in the Pushkin Museum on Volkhonka Street."

The man with the Russian heart removed from the case and put on a quick-release belly holster.

"Why the switch?" the Texan asked.

"It'll be safer . . . safer for us . . . with all those tourists and the schoolkids in the line of fire if anything goes sour. Temkov's less likely to try anything nasty with children and foreigners around," Nomad replied. "And besides, I like the art."

"You're an art lover, Mr. Alderdice?" the military attaché asked archly.

"Runs in the family."

Nomad reached into the case again to grasp a snub-nosed .32-caliber semiautomatic pistol. He hefted it . . . tried the feel . . . slid it into the holster.

"What kind of 'nasty' do you have in mind?" Johann wondered.

"He snatched one of your people on a public street. Nobody's going to try that on me."

Nomad took three clips of ammunition from the black-leather case and loaded one into the pistol. He held up the other two for the chief of station to study.

"Are those what I think they are?" the head of the C.I.A. unit in Moscow asked.

"I don't know what you're thinking. *I* think these are bad-news bullets that can punch through body armor. Street hoods call them 'cop killers.' "

"You planning to kill any Moscow cops?" Johann queried.

"I love cops," Nomad assured him. "Of course, if some creep of an S.V.R. general makes a move that threatens my health and welfare, I'll have to defend my constitutional rights."

The station chief flinched.

"By shooting the bastard in the face?" the military attaché thought aloud.

He was smiling.

"Twice. At least twice," Nomad declared righteously. "I'm a big supporter of the Constitution. The rule of law is precious to me. You agree, General?"

"I wouldn't knock the rule of law."

The chief of station shook his head. He was *almost* certain that this Alderdice had enough sense and self-control not to shoot a Russian general in front of a hundred tourists at the Pushkin.

"Be careful," he advised hopefully.

"Always."

Nomad opened two buttons on his shirt for a moment to show the Kevlar bullet-proof vest before he left to get his injection. So far, so good, he judged. Then he felt very tired.

IN A LARGE and well-guarded hole in the ground more than a thousand miles south—far away in another sort of country where dissent was an obscene word and the single correct piety prevailed—well-educated, intolerant, and homicidal al Wadi was happily contemplating the three young men who'd just entered his command post.

They were among his boldest and brightest.

Devout, thoroughly trained in memorizing his distorted interpretations of the great Koran, and single-minded enough to destroy strangers of other faiths and dietary persuasions. Infuriated and energized by awareness of the barbaric plots against them organized by Zionists, Americans, Eskimos, corrupt journalists, international bankers, shameless women in Ivy League universities, the United Nations, and the Las Vegas City Council, they were ready to kill the many enemies of decency . . . at a moment's notice.

These three were among al Wadi's most noble and fearless warriors. They'd come to say good-bye to their indefatigable leader. They'd been trained by the Russian technician in what to do with the Demons. They knew their targets . . . the routes, and how to get there. They had funds and allies waiting for them.

After al Wadi delivered a brief but fiery speech, they joined him in chanting several minutes of prayers. "Go and smite the infidels," he told them when the prayers ended. They left to do that with miniature nuclear weapons created by foreign atheists and sold by sinful idolaters whose deities were in Swiss banks.

Al Wadi had accounts in those same banks, and other interests in the international financial world. He was a thoroughly contemporary terrorist . . . as realistic in some ways as he was mentally fixated in others. It took plenty of money to finance these training camps . . . weapons purchases . . . bomb manufacture, and travel to the places where the people . . . airplanes . . . buildings . . . and school buses had to be demolished. He didn't get all of it—under the table, of course—from his secret supporters, respectable governments that denied any link to him.

To keep track of his investments, he turned on his computer seconds after the three departed. His stocks weren't doing too well, and that didn't cheer him. He felt better, however, when he looked ahead to the atomic blasts his heroes would detonate.

Those devastating explosions would encourage his covert allies to provide additional funds . . . as well they should.

After all, his cause was blessed, and they knew it.

30

AT 9:00 A.M., TEMKOV GOT THE NEWS.

He'd been waiting for it eagerly.

He needed it if he was to maintain control—and in his world, control was everything. You couldn't protect your back without it . . . your front or sides either. Lethal danger could also come from above or below . . . from your own players, or from one of the other sides.

The number of them kept growing every month.

The corpses were multiplying, sometimes for no apparent reason. These weren't the Good Old Days . . . not by a long shot.

As Pankin entered the general's office, his glowing face signaled that the news was positive.

"We're picking up three transmissions, General," he reported. "Loud and clear. They're moving."

"You're tracking?"

"Of course. We detected the first one just after midnight . . . the second one forty minutes later . . . the third half an hour after that. Our monitors wanted to make sure about speed and direction before they alerted you."

"Speed?"

"Variable . . . from truck to jet aircraft. You'll find the directions interesting, General."

"I will when you tell me," Temkov nudged.

"North and east. We can't guess how far."

"Keep tracking."

TEMKOV WAS IN HIS CAR en route to the museum at 11: 28 A.M. when the radio telephone rang. He listened to the update with the latest position reports, and repeated what he'd said earlier.

"Keep tracking."

He was hanging up the phone when his aide asked the question.

"General, there's something I don't understand. If we've told the Americans we must have Anna in any exchange for the Wilk woman . . . and if we know Anna's dead . . . what are they going to exchange?"

"Now or later?"

"Any time," Pankin replied.

"Today we'll both do the usual," Temkov said. "What we'll exchange are lies—the bread and butter of international relations. We'll start with creative fictions and try to build on that. We've got to find something we can show for all our high-risk kidnapping."

He paused for a moment.

"Any new word on Frank?" he inquired.

"I checked just before we left, General. There's nothing."

Temkov frowned . . . was still frowning when he led his five men into the large lobby of the handsome old Pushkin Museum so rich in both ancient and twentieth-century art.

"Anybody new?" Nomad asked Johann softly.

"The thin guy . . . far right."

Nomad noticed that the S.V.R. general was eyeing him . . . guessed he might be wondering who this addition to the U.S. team might be. That took three seconds—just until Nomad began his mental scan. He didn't rush it. He knew he couldn't.

Nothing . . . nothing . . . nothing.

Maybe he was wrong.

Paranoia was sensible in this trade, but was he overdoing it?

Nothing . . . nothing . . . *something.*

"The thin guy's working," Nomad whispered to the Texan. "I'm calling a new play. You better concentrate completely on the thinking number. I'll do the talking."

Then he read the question in Johann's mind.

"Yes, I know what the fuck I'm doing," the field agent assured. "Here we go. Wish me luck."

Ignoring the shock in the U.S. military attaché's wide eyes, Nomad turned to Temkov. It was time to do the diplomatic number.

"General Johann has a very bad throat," Nomad lied as smoothly as any career ambassador, "so I'll have to speak for him. My name's Alderdice. I'm just in from Washington."

Temkov, whose trade had taught him to believe almost nothing he heard or read, wondered who this man really was and which of the seven thousand primary games he might be playing . . . or not playing.

"I'm fully authorized to speak. I represent the Deputy Secretary of State," Nomad continued effortlessly.

The "thin guy" was trying hard.

One by one, he worked on each American, but it was going poorly. He'd keep trying, of course. He'd get through.

"How are things in Washington?" Temkov fenced to buy time for his mind spy.

Nomad shrugged eloquently, then deceived just as well.

"Congress is complaining . . . investigating . . . pontificating . . . compromising . . . and doing its best. The media are hungry, hysterical, and often ungrammatical. That big strike out West and the latest round of Hindu-Moslem violence in Asia are bothering a lot of people, and I suppose you've heard that some maniac set off a nuclear weapon in eastern Africa."

The last "casual" remark was designed to provoke.

Long shot . . . but why not?

It succeeded.

Though his face showed nothing, Temkov's mind lit up like a Christmas tree. *Five* . . . Nomad picked up the number "five." And "Arabs."

There were tens of millions of hardworking and don't-kill-anybody Arabs . . . and some others. Which Arabs were these? Where? Probably just as important, five *what*?

"I hadn't heard," Temkov answered.

Almost smooth enough, Nomad judged.

"That's good," he complimented, "because some half-wit is hustling a rumor that the *footprint* of that bomb was Russian."

Al Wadi. The name filled the S.V.R. general's consciousness in a flash like a strobe light. The mental picture of that name was in big type—Cyrillic—blindingly clear. Then the image changed abruptly.

Aerial bombs. Demons. *Five* of them.

Jackpot.

Instant computation. How did Temkov know it was five?

He must be part of the deal.

Defense time, Nomad realized. The thin guy could be targeting him at this moment. To purge his own thoughts of Demons and Temkov, Nomad focused on an overweight and celebrated belly dancer he'd known two . . . or was it three? . . . years ago. Her erotic undulations should distract most heterosexual mind-sweepers.

All this blitzed by in seconds.

"That footprint couldn't be ours," Temkov declared and scowled. "Someone must have read it wrong."

"That's what I said," Nomad ratified. "Could be the Chinese trying to stir up trouble . . . or those creative types in Baghdad. A lot of players these days."

"Too many," the Russian general agreed.

"You and I don't have time for rumors anyway," Nomad told him. "My instructions are to move ahead positively in the talks about Alison Wilk and that Bielski fellow who's missing . . . or was. I'm sorry to report that he's dead."

Temkov wondered why the Americans were admitting this.

"It was a stupid accident, believe it or not," the man who said his name was Alderdice said. "We're sorry. Okay, now what can my government . . . and yours . . . do?"

This blunt talk didn't sound like the U.S. State Department at all, Temko judged. In a moment, his attention shifted. He couldn't help thinking about how well the ultra-small transmitters they'd hidden in the Demons were working. Twins of the one concealed in Anna's eyeglass frames, they were the key to the tracking. Temkov had planned on these beacons from the start. He certainly wasn't going to go forward unless he knew what the buyers had in mind—the targets. Even before he'd identified the group purchasing the Demons, the S.V.R. general didn't trust any people—anonymous or not—trying to acquire weapons of mass destruction in private transactions.

There were a lot of lunatics out there this year.

A bumper crop . . . with access to very large sums of cash.

Plenty of people in a score of countries would cheerfully peddle a freight car of automatic weapons . . . three truckloads of antitank rockets . . . two thousand land mines . . . or other conventional hardware. The stuff the Americans called C.B.R.— chemical, biological, radiological—was much more dangerous.

C.B.R. could unbalance things and grab attention.

Slaughters like the thousands killed by the Demon in Ethiopia were more than violent attention-getters.

They were clear signs that al Wadi was a fanatic capable of anything—a man who must be monitored extremely carefully. He might have the cash, but Temkov wasn't about to give him total control.

That's what Temkov thought.

That's what Nomad "read."

"We still want Alison Wilk," he said, "and we want her right away. We regret the death of Bielski, but that's history. General, it's going to get ugly if she isn't free soon. Tomorrow would be good."

No tact at all, Temkov decided. This Alderdice showed no polish or patience. He obviously had no respect for the usual diplomatic amenities.

While Temkov silently condemned the C.I.A. field agent, Nomad was scanning Johann. The U.S. military attaché was doggedly following Nomad's instructions. He was thinking what he'd been told to think. Battle scenes. Now Nomad recognized them . . . the costumes helped. Right, footage from the big film of Tolstoi's *War and Peace*. The novel was better, Nomad recalled, but this would do.

The chief of station was remembering another motion picture. It was an energetic sexual extravaganza with three busty young females of diverse races and one muscular male who grinned—a pornographic production that still thrived in North American and European video stores.

Not great, but good enough to deceive the thin Russian mind operative, Nomad reasoned as he turned his focus back to Temkov. The S.V.R. general was worried about his own future. The spy whose heart Nomad had *was* history all right, and Alison Wilk had shifted from asset to problem.

Temkov knew he'd be in trouble if he didn't make a good deal.

For who or what . . . that bothered him.

"I don't know about tomorrow," Temkov responded to the blunt "Alderdice" threat, "but we should explore possible arrangements for Miss Wilk to leave Russia . . . on an equitable basis, of course."

Temkov realized that he had to move quickly. It would be best to trade her for someone or something right away. The process would occupy the attention of the Americans while he kept track of the Demons. For a moment, the question of Anna's missing body broke in, but it was rapidly overwhelmed by the much more urgent issue of where the three bombs were going. The radio beacon on one of them indicated it was over the North Sea, moving in the direction of Scotland.

Another seemed to be off the coast of Lebanon.

A third was traveling at jet speed over Spain toward Portugal.

The voice of the American named Alderdice interrupted.

"We can live with 'equitable,' " he said. " 'Prompt' is important, too. It's in both our interests to set the terms within the next forty-eight hours so Alison Wilk can be across the border by the end of the week."

Temkov nodded.

"What's your idea of equitable, Mr. Alderdice?" he asked cautiously.

"There's a man you may know in our Leavenworth prison," Nomad answered. "Fellow who calls himself Arthur Landau.

He's got six more years to serve on an espionage conviction. I think he'd like to go home."

"I'll get back to you . . . before forty-eight hours," Temkov promised.

WHEN NOMAD, THE STATION CHIEF, Johann, and their body-guards returned to the U.S. Embassy, they went straight to the "safe room," where no one else could listen.

"That was a sound idea you had for swapping Landau," the Texan complimented. "We made some real headway, and you didn't shoot anybody in the face."

"It went well," the chief of station concurred. "I think we're finally making some progress."

It was time to tell them.

"Progress on Alison Wilk . . . and that's fine," Nomad said.

"But that's not all," the military attaché guessed.

"I was going to surprise you."

"Nothing you could say or do would surprise me, Mr. Al-derdice. Why, I wouldn't be surprised if your name wasn't Al-derdice."

"It's good to be appreciated," Nomad replied. "The other reason I was sent here has to do with the recent massacre of over six thousand Ethiopians by a Russian-made Demon. Since the weapon came from here, I'm told you've already been alerted to find out whatever you can."

"Emergency Flash . . . top classification. We heard and we're looking and we haven't found a damn thing," the station chief reported.

Johann studied the field agent with the Russian heart.

"You know more than we do, don't you, Mr. Alderdice?" he speculated.

"I'll share it with you. I believe the slaughter in Ethiopia was a field test. I *know* that the bastards who did it got five Demons, so there are four left."

"Where?" the C.I.A. executive asked.

"Let's start with *who*. It's al Wadi. As for where, three of the four are on the move right now. I'm not sure about the targets yet, but you don't have to be a rocket scientist to figure they'll be at the top of al Wadi's enemies' list."

"How did he get the Demons?" Johann asked.

"General Temkov didn't say. Yes, he has the information we want . . . and I don't know how he collected it. By the way, that thin Russian who showed for the first time today *was* trying to play head games with you. Watch out for him. He'll try it again."

"With this big Demon deal going down, I can see why Temkov wants to wrap up the Alison Wilk confrontation," the Station Chief analyzed. "He doesn't need it."

"Let's concentrate on what *we* need," Nomad said. "We need to stop those three bombs. That's our absolute priority if we don't want a million or two dead."

"Any ideas, Mr. Alderdice?"

Nomad looked at the military attaché . . . thought for half a dozen seconds . . . nodded.

"One or two," he answered evenly, then glanced at his wristwatch. "Injection time. Be back in fifteen minutes and tell you just what I've got in mind."

"Anybody going to get shot in the face?" Johann tested.

"A lot of people," Nomad answered, and left for the medical center where the yellow serum waited.

31

NOMAD RETURNED IN TWELVE MINUTES.

Walking swiftly . . . visibly in a hurry.

He began speaking the moment the inner door of the "safe room" clicked shut behind him.

"My ideas . . . here we go," he started. "Three targets. Three Demons going somewhere. Very little time to stop them or take out al Wadi's demolition teams that are almost goddam surely already in place."

The military attaché and C.I.A. official nodded.

"Where are the teams? What are the targets? It's roll-the-dice time. On the basis of al Wadi's previous oratory and threats . . . and considering the enemies he's already denounced a hundred times . . . factoring in his other targets in actual strikes over the past couple of years . . . *and* . . . this is a big one . . . a good look at the routes and directions two of the Demons are taking right now."

"Two? What about the third one?" Johann broke in.

"I'll get to that. On the basis of all these factors I mentioned, I say there's a fucking-fine chance one bomb's going to Israel and another to England," Nomad announced.

"In this deal, fucking-fine's not bad," Johann said. "I've played with worse odds."

"You ready to talk about the third Demon?" the chief of station asked.

"You're not going to like it," Nomad predicted. "Figuring in everything we know—and adding a lot of gut instinct—I'd bet they'll hit Washington."

"I don't like it, and it figures," the general said grimly.

"That's one hell of a bet," the head of the C.I.A.'s group in Moscow pointed out. "You could be betting half a million lives . . . maybe more. Are you sure?"

Nomad shook his head.

"Absolutely? Not nearly. I considered New York because it has a bigger Jewish population," Nomad told them, "but what I know about al Wadi . . . his thinking about prime targets to shock . . . and with my world-famous gut . . . it added up to Washington."

Eight . . . nine . . . ten seconds of silence.

"You got any more ideas, Mr. Alderdice?" Johann asked.

"You can call me Lee. Yes, there are a couple, and you can help. Who's the Mossad boss in town?"

"Avram Gur," reported the Station Chief. "Why do you ask?"

Nomad answered the question with two of his own.

"The one-eyed ballet lover? Is the Bolshoi on tonight?"

"Yeah. You know him?"

Johann was amused when Nomad didn't reply to that question either.

"Get the damn tickets," the American with the Russian heart ordered.

AT THE HANDSOME and historic Bolshoi Theater that evening, General Johann and Nomad moved through the crowd minutes before the curtain was to rise. The man who directed Israel's foreign intelligence programs in the Russian capital was well-dressed in a dark wool-silk suit whose color didn't clash with that of the artificial left eye he'd worn after that incident in Istambul. The trim and pretty woman in an effectively fitted "little black dress" with whom he was chatting was a former Israeli Defense Force lieutenant he'd wed after his first wife died.

They were being watched, and knew it.

They were used to round-the-clock surveillance by Russian security agents attached to a large special unit that dogged the diplomats of a score of foreign countries which might be hostile. Gur's official cover was assistant cultural attaché at his nation's embassy.

Nomad assumed that they were being covered tonight.

Every night, every day. Standard procedure.

His plan had that as a basic premise.

Nomad began to stroll toward the Israeli couple, leading Johann and pretending not to notice them. Now Gur recognized Nomad . . . nodded about an eighth of an inch while his face showed no acknowledgment of the American. In an instant—a computer's nanosecond—Gur went operational.

Still speaking with his attractive wife, he immediately assumed that Nomad's ignoring him meant that the American was working. "On the job," as New York City undercover cops said when stopped by uniformed colleagues. Something was "going down," Gur judged, using the jargon of his favorite U.S. crime shows on television.

Something was always going down when he met Nomad.

What the devil was he doing at the Bolshoi with the U.S. military attaché?

Gur and his wife turned toward the doors into the grand old theater. Striding more rapidly between the clusters of ballet enthusiasts, Nomad passed the Israelis. The C.I.A. field agent was smiling and talking with Johann as he went by. He barely brushed against the Mossad executive in the surging, bustling throng.

Gur was impressed but not surprised.

Nomad still had the tradecraft down cold. The brush-pass was letter-perfect, executed so expertly that the Russian agents watching the Israeli noticed nothing. Gur seated his wife, excused himself effortlessly, and hurried to a booth in the men's lavatory.

He didn't have much time, but he didn't dare wait. If Nomad had done this, something urgent must be involved. Gur barely had the twenty seconds it took him to read the folded slip of paper Nomad had inserted into his inside jacket pocket. He flushed the toilet in case one of the watchers had followed him into the lavatory, and he made his way back to rejoin his wife a minute before the orchestra began.

He'd made his plan before he took his seat.

Gur had a talent for improvisation . . . a gift of cunning.

Aware that the innocent-looking "civilians" beside him might be surveillance agents, he merely whispered half a dozen words to his wife, apparently a husbandly intimacy. Nothing suspicious here . . . nothing during the whole first act. At the intermission, the Russian watchers saw that Mrs. Gur seemed dizzy and had to lean on her husband when she rose to join the pilgrimage to the bar. Like most foreign diplomats and hard-currency-carrying tourists, the Gurs usually found refreshment and leg-stretching there.

Not tonight.

She seemed ill as her husband guided her out, then helped her into their car. That didn't bother the watchers on duty tonight as they trailed the vehicle with diplomatic license plates back to the Israeli Embassy. These two surveillance agents preferred the circus to ballet any time.

Less than fifty minutes after the Gurs entered the embassy, the excellent decoding machines in Mossad headquarters back home in the Promised Land stuttered out a message addressed to Dr. David. Upon receipt of the message, a captain who was neither a physician nor named David picked up the "action phone" on his desk.

"Task Force Alert," he said in accented Hebrew that reflected his youth in Morocco. "We need a *minion* by ten o'clock. Boy Scouts and the swimming team. We'll meet in the gym."

A *minion* was the Hebrew term for at least ten adult males, their presence required under religious law for formal prayer. The Boy Scouts weren't adolescents who excelled in pitching tents or helping elderly women cross the streets. They were a crack and very secret unit of heavily armed soldiers. The swimming team was an equally elite and combat-ready unit, and the gym wasn't anything like its name.

Seconds after that first call, the captain made another.

"Shalom . . . Shalom," he said. "I wonder if you'd do me a favor, Moshe. Yes, this is Itzak, your cousin. Our damn air conditioner's broken down and we need someone to fix it. Could you come by soon or send an electrician?"

The response was an immediate affirmation.

The man he'd called Moshe knew that the word of the dead cooling machine meant that things could be getting very hot . . . very soon. Moshe and two other technical experts were on their way in ten minutes. They didn't go by staff car. They came in the special truck.

32

GO WITH THE FLOW.

Do nothing to attract attention.

It was standard procedure for Nomad, who stayed at the Bolshoi with Johann through the end of the performance so they would leave in . . . and with . . . the crowd. The two Americans blended in nicely with appropriate small talk about the ballet just concluded.

"Did you like it?" Nomad asked in generic question.

"I've always been a fan of *Romeo and Juliet* . . . and who wouldn't like that Prokofiev score?" the military attaché replied.

"I didn't know you were a ballet fan, General."

"I suppose you think I'm some kind of dumb soldier," Johann answered. "Tomorrow night they do *Eugene Onegin*, with all that hot Tchaikovsky. I could get you a ticket."

"If I'm in town," Nomad said.

The Russian surveillance team covering the U.S. military attaché trailed them back to the embassy and watched the lights go on in Johann's office. The special glass that cost the American taxpayers so much was a real problem. The wire filaments embedded in the windowpanes blocked listening. Even with the most powerful night-vision binoculars, the watchers couldn't see Johann take the message form from the station chief, who'd been waiting for him.

The Texan scanned it twice.

"It's for you, Mr. Alderdice," he announced and gave it to the field agent.

The signature was the code name of the deputy director of operations at Langley.

The message was short and communicated little.

Just enough.

"Your saintly family will meet you as requested."

Johann and the station chief wondered whether Nomad would translate it.

He didn't.

"None of our damn business?" the military attaché guessed.

The chief of station concentrated on the freshly decrypted message itself. Where would the saintly family meet Alderdice? Not here, he reasoned.

"You're leaving?" he tested.

"Sorry to eat and run," Nomad answered. "I've got a hunch I'll be back soon."

"For the ballet?" Johann said.

"Among other things. I've got to pack."

He left before dawn with the doctor who'd come with him. They caught a 7:00 A.M. flight on the British Embassy's weekly shuttle to London—the safe flight for couriers and things that Her Majesty's government didn't want the S.V.R. to sample. With the time change, it was 11:55 A.M. when Nomad dropped off the physician at the busy, comfortable and conveniently sited Thistle Victoria Hotel, at one end of the legendary rail station.

"Get some sleep," he told the red-eyed doctor.

AT 12:40 A.M., Nomad entered the museum.

Not the massive British Museum, or the serene Victoria and Albert, or the right-now-with-it Tate Modern, on the bank of the Thames and known for its good restaurant on the top floor.

He walked into the no-nonsense Imperial War Museum that was quite different from the others. He stared appreciatively at the World War I tank, and the magically quaint French taxi—part of the fleet of vehicles that had rushed reinforcements into battle so they could save Paris from the Kaiser's advancing Huns.

That's what they called their foes then.

It had grown more difficult to name the enemy . . . no, enemies . . . since then, Nomad reflected as he turned right to enter the gift shop. First, he scanned the reproductions of old posters warning that the foe might be listening, an admonition to watch what one said because there were spies about.

Even then, he thought.

And long before that . . . back to biblical times.

Now he saw a trim woman who might be thirty-seven or forty-three eyeing an exotic sales item at the counter near the cashier—a large pair of men's boxer shorts patterned with World War II fighter planes. The Spitfires were remarkably real and hard to ignore.

"How wicked of you, Gillian," Nomad said softly. "For yourself or your roommate?"

"I haven't quite decided," she replied.

The exchange wasn't exactly the usual sign and countersign, but it would do. Gillian worked very quietly but well for MI-5, the counterintelligence cousin of Britain's MI-6, which handled secret foreign espionage for the United Kingdom. She'd known Nomad for years . . . under one of his other names, of course.

"I'm glad to see you, and you're looking well," he began.

"Amenities accepted. You can finish the sentence. Well and *what*?" she said cheerfully.

"Company's coming, and you won't like it," he predicted.

She sighed.

"*Again*? What bloody nightmare are you unloading on us this time?"

"Your choice of words remains unerring, Gillian," he said. "NATO designation: Demon. Nasty Russian miniature nuclear weapon. It's a nightmare all right. I think it may arrive in Scotland or England in a day or two."

"Who's bringing it?"

"Your favorite Middle Eastern terrorist. Al Wadi's moving it," Nomad reported, "and that prick means to detonate it within the next week."

"That prick would," she thought aloud in her crisp BBC tones. "Target?"

"I'm almost sure it's London. He's the splashy sort, so his logical target should be the national capital. This Demon's one of three he's put his hands on."

"Not to be small-minded, *this* Demon is the one that bothers me most. I appreciate your heads-up, but I hope you've brought something else as well," the MI-5 officer said.

"*Me.* I think I can help you find it and the team al Wadi's shipped to blow it."

"What else do you think?" she asked.

"I think his people will be well-armed and hair-triggered. I'd say you'll have to take them down *fast.* Stun grenades . . . lots of automatic weapon fire . . . one of those ferocious smash-and-grab rips that your high-powered S.A.S. commandos do so noisily. Al Wadi's crew won't be easy to flatten."

"What does that mean?"

"You might not take any prisoners," Nomad told her.

"Do you care?"

Nomad shrugged.

"You're getting cynical, Gillian," he reproved.

"And curious. How are you planning to locate this Demon?"

"With a lot of help from your efficient signals intelligence people and their antennas," he answered, then spoke of the small radio beacon sending from the bomb.

"That little transmitter," she began and prepared to inquire how it got on the weapon.

"A marvel of modern science," Nomad interrupted in a tone that made it clear she'd be wasting her time.

It wasn't *that* easy dealing with these Americans, the MI-5 woman reflected and decided not to press the issue . . . now. Her government's electronic establishment and radio-monitoring operation was big enough and sophisticated enough to find the beacon . . . with a bit of luck. It wasn't as huge or massively funded as the Yanks' global National Security Agency, she thought.

What the hell was? N.S.A. had billions to spend.

This was no time for envy, she calculated, and this wasn't the moment to ask him how al Wadi got the Demon or how the C.I.A. found out about it. If this American field agent hadn't told her by now, he probably wasn't going to in the near future.

"Why don't we continue this over lunch at my club?" she suggested in a bright voice that didn't affect him at all. His hunger did, so he thanked her and accepted her invitation to eat at a famous London club that had begun accepting women members only nineteen months ago.

She turned toward the door from the gift shop . . . remembered . . . smiled . . . and bought the boxer undershorts with the Spitfires rampant before she led him out to the lobby. Nomad was in good spirits as they walked from the building, and so was she. They had high regard for the battle skills of the S.A.S., and she was looking forward to something in addition.

MI-5's leaders and the heads of Britain's nuclear weapons establishment would be grateful when she delivered the Demon. It would be a major intelligence coup that wouldn't hurt her career. Hell, it might be even better if the whole operation remained hush-hush and the bodies were buried in secret, she reflected. If the gunfire drew public and press attention, the whole thing might be called an aborted attack by some I.R.A. splinter group, she speculated.

Nomad's face and voice gave no sign that he was reading her thoughts. He had a plan of his own, a bipolar job that could benefit the defense of the U.S. and might not be bad for his retirement fund. The deep thinkers who ran the C.I.A. and the Pentagon had deep pockets, and there was an excellent chance they'd give somebody a meaningful bonus and a medal for bringing them a Demon.

Nomad didn't need a medal.

He still had . . . somewhere . . . the one he'd received for being the best in Latin at high school.

He'd enjoy the praise and the bonus, he reflected as she

pointed at a nearby taxi. And there'd be all that self-satisfaction when his plan for the next phase of this operation—far from London—succeeded. If somehow it didn't, he'd have to go to Plan B. A good and professional field agent always had a dynamite Plan B.

There was one small problem, Nomad realized.

He didn't have a dynamite Plan B.

He didn't have any Plan B at all.

And that son of a bitch al Wadi had the bombs.

33

"HOW ARE YOU, DENNY?" SUSAN KINCAID ASKED.

The chess player was trying to sound casual, but the man with the Russian heart knew better. He could "hear" the words she was suppressing.

"Thank God you're all right!"

It was five minutes past two on the afternoon after he'd visited the Imperial War Museum.

The place was Building R at Fort Meade near Baltimore—one of the top-secret installations at this heavily guarded U.S. intelligence center for eavesdropping on and decoding the communications of other nations. Gentlemen didn't do this, as an American secretary of state declared righteously before World War II. He was correct. It was governments that ran these sorts of larcenous programs . . . big time.

Susan Kincaid managed to smile. Paula Taylor beamed beside her.

"We missed you, Denny," Paula assured him warmly. She was openly radiating concern and an interesting new perfume.

"I'm doing fine," he answered archly. "I've just received a very expensive pain in the ass . . . cost the taxpayers a ton. To put it simply, my tail's a wreck from flying a long way as the backseat guy in one of your Uncle's supersonic fighter bomb-ers."

Chen and Fuentes nodded sympathetically.

"We refueled in midair twice," the fellow transplant they knew as Denny Monroe continued and rubbed his red eyes. "I'm really tired, and I don't have time to be. If I read it right, *we* don't have time to be."

They didn't doubt him for a second.

Exhausted on not, he was the team leader.

They trusted his judgment, and they were glad he was back. They didn't ask where he'd been. If he thought they ought to know—for the common good—he'd have told them.

"Problem?" Harry Chen asked.

"King-sized. I'm a little bit scared . . . hell, more than a little bit . . . because some world-class psycho who's already killed thousands of people has acquired a few A bombs."

"Shit," Fuentes said softly.

"That's the good part, friends. The lousy part is that I believe this idealistic head case means to gut three cities on Wednes-day."

The muscular Latino frowned.

"*This* Wednesday?" he asked.

"Yes. You can say 'shit' now if you want to, Harry. I wouldn't mind."

Chen shook his head.

"Pass," he announced.

"Moving right along," the leader continued and yawned, "I figure our country's scenic and historic capital is Number One on his list. It's Big Bang time in Washington."

Then he spelled out succinctly why he believed this.

"That's where," Susan Kincaid said. "How about when? Are you dead cert about Wednesday?"

"Can't absolutely guarantee either," he admitted, "but in our trade, we live and die on experience and instinct. Mine say Washington is very probable . . . a best bet. Hell, nothing's really sure but bad weather, crappy sitcoms and heavy traffic."

None of the other four laughed.

"As to when," he told them, "I'm convinced that Wednesday

is especially likely to be the date here in D.C. because that's when al Wadi might get the biggest payoff. The President's going to address Congress . . . both houses. Lots of wonderful media folks, plus the entire cabinet—minus one. The rule is that one has to stay elsewhere just in case."

"And this could be just in case," Paula Taylor said.

"It's a perfect setup for al Wadi," he reasoned. "The Supreme Court will be there . . . foreign ambassadors . . . half a dozen of our top admirals and generals. We've got to make sure the President's dear mama is sick."

"That's *good,*" the black woman approved.

She was the only one who understood.

Maybe it was all that devious chess scheming.

"We want to make sure our President isn't there," the field agent she knew as Denny Monroe explained. "That might push the attack date back. If he's not there, the rest won't be. My estimate is that the Demon will be hidden within ten or fifteen blocks of the rostrum. The bang comes a few minutes into his speech."

"How do you keep the President away?" Fuentes worried.

"I do my famous humanitarian number. I've advised the deputy director-ops at Langley to brief the President on this acute threat, and ask him to cancel because he has to visit his sick mother down in Texas. Our guy's on his way to the White House right now."

"We're buying time," Chen diagnosed.

"Not a lot of it," the team leader warned. "That son of a bitch al Wadi will hit Washington with his Demon within the next month in any case."

"No case if there's no bomb," Susan Kincaid said.

"Exactly. We've got to find this bomb and take it in the name of the American people."

"Al Wadi will try something else in a couple of months," Fuentes predicted sourly.

"I was thinking about that on the long flight," the spy with the Russian heart announced. "I've a nice idea on the future of Mr. al Wadi and his hateful associates."

"Body bags?" Fuentes proposed.

"I'm thinking of ashtrays. Okay, friends, in or out? If you're in, we've got a ton and five ammo clips of work. The fine patriots at the N.S.A. have to help—starting yesterday. We need them to spot the mini-beacon sending from the bomb."

"You've got the frequency?" Paula Taylor asked hopefully.

He shook his head slowly.

"That's just one of the things I don't have," he confessed. "If you don't like the odds, join the club. I don't like them either. This whole damn thing is a long shot."

It was his kind of deal, the chess player thought.

In some utterly irrational way she found it admirable.

"I'm in," she said.

The others nodded assent.

"You're all professionals and crazy. It's a pleasure to work with you," Denny Monroe-Lee Alderdice-Nomad told them.

He didn't seem especially worried.

If he was frightened, it wasn't showing.

This man is going into battle, Kincaid thought, and he *likes* it.

IT WAS TIME for their injections and antirejection pills. After that, Nomad excused himself to catch up on his sleep. At ten minutes to six, Seigenthaler arrived to awaken him with the news. His face showed that it wasn't good.

All three updates were negative.

Mossad reported that it didn't know where the Demon that al Wadi had destined for an Israeli target was at this time. Spotted by radio location last night some forty-one miles north of the Lebanese border, it appeared to be on the move today . . . west . . . as if in a truck.

An air strike . . . if and when the probable truck was pinpointed . . . had been ruled out by the prime minister because of the possibility of "substantial" civilian casualties.

MI-5 was still trying to locate the second Demon. Major electrical storms had been making radio location unusually difficult. Two of the best S.A.S. assault units were ready to attack at a moment's notice. Search for the bomb was continuing . . . so was the storm.

"I suppose you're saving the worst for last," Nomad speculated.

"Are you some kind of damn psychic, too?" the head of the Russian F.S.R. group replied defensively.

"Let's have it."

"The President said no. He doesn't believe that there's probably a Demon in his neighborhood . . . or in his immediate future," Seigenthaler said. "Says he's tired of being spooked by the Spooks. That's a quote."

"Has a nice ring to it. I wonder who wrote it for him," Nomad thought aloud.

"He remembers we gave him some bum information three or four months ago, and he was embarrassed."

"If he plays his cards right, he could be dead this time."

"He likes the speech he's going to give. Told Buckley it's important . . . and suggested the Agency clean up its act. Then he pointed to the door. It wasn't nice."

" 'Nice' isn't the issue."

"Okay, it's scary. Why don't you look scared?"

Nomad paused to remember one of his favorite slogans.

Right.

"Charlie Parker," he said. "Great jazz man. He once said, 'Don't be scared. Just play the music.' That's what I'm going to do."

Seigenthaler eyed him warily. He'd read Nomad's personnel file many times. There was no mention in it of Charlie Parker.

34

UNIT ONE WAS READY TO ATTACK.

Al Wadi had honored it with that designation because it was composed of his best fighters. It had moved closer to the border as darkness fell. Now just nineteen miles north of the Israeli frontier, the force was dividing into two groups.

That was the plan.

Al Wadi had told them you couldn't just hit the Zionists head-on. A diversion was necessary. It had to be cunningly devised and skillfully executed. This diversion was to stretch over twenty-eight hours. The smaller part of Unit One—four heavily armed young men—was to advance to the border under cover of darkness and attack a sentry with automatic weapons, a rocket launcher, and several grenades.

It was to look like a botched effort to infiltrate a sabotage team. There was to be a firefight . . . lots of shots exchanged . . . and a scream or two after several minutes of combat. Afterward, the Israeli patrols would find three backpacks loaded with explosives. One pack would be wet . . . red stains . . . real blood.

This theatric was to grab the attention of the Israeli troops . . . suggest that some Arab group thought defenses here were not solid. If they bought the deception, the Israelis might expect another attack in this sector in the near future.

Some twenty-seven hours later, the same quartet of Unit One warriors would fake another probing attack about a mile down the border from the first one. This time, the Israelis would be ready with light tanks and helicopter gunships.

Several hours before the second raid, the larger part of Unit One—ten fighters, including two trained by the rented and well-paid Russian technician—would load the bomb onto a small fishing boat in a little port a dozen miles on the Lebanese side of the frontier.

A *wooden* vessel.

Less likely to be picked up on Israeli radar.

With no lights showing, and moving at half speed south to cut down engine noise, it would cruise furtively to a point some twenty-six miles south of the border. It would idle to a stop one mile off the coast.

The bomb would be lashed into a cradle of floats.

Undercover agents of al Wadi on the shore would be waiting with a truck, and watching for the fishing boat. Listening, too . . . with walkie-talkies. A light flashing from the fishing skiff was more likely to be noticed than three words—repeated twice—on a radio whose range was barely a mile.

The bomb would come ashore seventy minutes after the second ground strike pulled the Israel Defense Force's attention in that direction . . . away from the landing point on the coast. The truck carrying the Demon would roll down back roads for half an hour to clear the immediate area. The vehicle would be hidden in a garage until morning since Arabs driving at night were more likely to be checked by police or military road patrols.

It was nearly midnight . . . time for the first diversion.

The four dedicated enemies of Israel and at least half a dozen other shameless countries picked up their weapons and got into their comfortable Japanese minivan. It had been bought with funds smuggled to al Wadi via several camouflaged Swiss accounts created by countries that wouldn't admit it.

The financial arrangements hadn't been discussed with these

foot soldiers. They wouldn't have understood or ap_____ed the fine points even if they were interested. They weren't. What they cared about—what filled them with pride—was that they were carrying out another brilliant plan of al Wadi's.

They were on their way to deceive and hit the Israelis.

The attack—the biggest and deadliest al Wadi had ever devised—was beginning.

They were making history.

35

BREAKFAST AT FORT MEADE WAS NO MONTH IN THE COUNTRY.

Not even a week . . . but it was ample and edible.

The five recent and special patients from The St. John Institute ate in a private dining room. This was a logical sequel to their being isolated in separate quarters apart from the small legion of N.S.A. interception and cryptographic experts.

The half-dozen visitors from the Institute—the sixth was a physician—finished their toast and decaf. After that, it was time for the first batch of each day's antirejection pills. Each of the five then received the regular daily physical, blood pressure, visual scan, thumping, and a dozen questions. After each examination, the doctor uttered the same words.

"See you after lunch for the injection."

With this ritual complete, the impatient leader of the "transplants"—that's what the doctors called them—said that right now was time for a meeting. They assembled in a small conference room.

"It's going to be soon . . . damn soon," he predicted, "so we'd better get some backup."

"How soon?" the African-American woman asked.

"Maybe tomorrow . . . next day at the latest."

"Backup like those paratroopers from the Eighty-first?" Fuentes said.

"Those were good guys," the man with the Russian heart replied, "but I want shooters. Ace shooters . . . specialists. I want the best with us when we move in on the creeps who have the bomb."

They all thought the same thing.

Susan Kincaid spoke first.

"You want The Band."

There was no question in her voice, just a statement of fact.

The Band wasn't a musical group. Some years ago, somebody in the C.I.A. had put that tag on a then new team of crack shots, champion marksmen with many weapons and cool in action with all of them. They were now recognized as the most efficient and effective assault unit in the U.S. intelligence community.

Four Army sharpshooters.

Two Marine snipers.

A pair of quick and deadly Air Police, extraordinary "long guns" who had medals to prove it.

"They're the best," Fuentes agreed.

"That's why I've asked Seigenthaler to get them to D.C. before tonight. I told him that on my way to breakfast."

Paula Taylor pursed her lips.

"Did he tell you anything, Denny?" she asked.

She'd probably done something to those lips, Susan Kincaid decided.

"The President won't cancel his speech, and the beloved Director of Central Intelligence thinks there could be panic in the streets and on the highways—not to mention rail and air terminals—if word got out that there could be a genuine nuclear massacre in the immediate future. He might have a point there," the man she knew as Denny Monroe admitted.

"Where does that leave us?" pragmatic Cesar Fuentes pressed.

"*Not* where you think, friend. *Not* . . . to quote some great American infantryman of World War Two . . . shit out of luck.

No, we're going to make our own luck. You meet a better class of people that way."

He seemed quite confident. They had no idea why.

"I'm calling for *another* backup team—an electronic one. A small electronic one . . . practically handheld. I'm sure N.S.A. is a great and huge outfit, but it can't hurt to add our own modest effort—a relatively low-budget supplement."

"Just what are you saying?" Chen wondered.

"It's simple. One . . . two . . . three. One, if the Demon's going to blow during the President's speech, the creeps will try for maximum kill by detonating within ten or fifteen blocks of where he'll be talking."

"Figures," Fuentes agreed.

"Two, we can let the N.S.A. continue its massive scans of a big area, and we zero in on that small piece of real estate I've just described. The noble folk at the Federal Communications Commission have radio-detection trucks to pinpoint unlicensed radio broadcasters . . . pirates. The F.C.C. gear is perfect for us."

"Army has some radio-location trucks, too," Fuentes said.

Nomad shook his head.

"We can't let the guys with the bomb know we're looking for them," he warned. "If they see a military vehicle cruising the neighborhood, who knows what they'll do? There's the same damn risk in an F.C.C. van with that direction-finder loop on top. Al Wadi's gang will spot the antenna . . . realize there's a search in progress."

"I know you've got a better idea," the analytical-minded chess player declared. "Can we cut to the chase?"

"We're chasing in a pair of those vans you see around a lot, the ones TV news crews use to relay their footage directly to their station. We take the location gear out of a pair of F.C.C. trucks, install it in the TV vans, and lose the search antennas in all the gear on top of the news vehicles anyway. Our vans work in concentric sweeps on opposite sides of the capitol."

"So no one will see two vans and think something funny's going on," Chen reasoned.

"Not even amusing," the leader concurred. "Our shooters are

due here this afternoon, and I want our two vans on the streets by four o'clock at the latest. The vans will carry the names of a couple of local stations, and both will have a regular camera—under a rainproof hood—where they'd normally carry one."

"Cool," Fuentes judged.

"We're leaving here for D.C. at two. Injections from 1:30 to 1:45. See you in this room at five to two. If you need weapons, tell me now."

They did.

Susan Kincaid was the first to get the injection of yellow serum, so she was back at the rendezvous point before the others. She was in good spirits. She saw that the team leader she cared about was not.

"Bad news?" she questioned.

"Bad math," he replied. "Just got the latest numbers on the place al Wadi dumped a Demon about two weeks ago. Death toll's up to seven thousand . . . still climbing."

"Oh, my God!"

"After we take care of his crews and their three other damn bombs," he continued grimly, "I have to do something about Mr. al Wadi himself."

"Wait a second," she appealed. "You said *I* . . . not *we*. Is this going to turn into something *personal*?"

"It already has," he answered.

Then the others came in, and he nodded toward the door. It was time to board the cars that would take them all to the killing zone in the District of Columbia.

36

LATE.

Everything was behind schedule . . . and time really counted.

The Band didn't arrive until nearly 6:00 P.M. That was when they drove down in an RV into the basement garage of a drab building owned by a C.I.A. dummy corporation. Nomad, Susan Kincaid, and Fuentes were waiting for them in a small blue panel truck registered under the name of that firm.

A boyish-looking young man with short blond hair and an instrument case in his left hand stepped from the RV and waved at Nomad.

"Hey," he said.

"Hey, Junior," Nomad acknowledged.

"Real damn sorry we're not on time," the young man apologized as he walked closer. "Our plane had air-traffic trouble . . . a bunch."

No one who knew The Band would consider asking where they'd flown in from. Nomad didn't.

"It's okay," he said to end the exchange.

"Hell, I guess this just ain't our split-second day," Junior added.

"That's tomorrow . . . around two in the afternoon if we're lucky," Nomad predicted.

"Pardon my French, but what the fuck happens then?"

"That's when we take out some very bad people who've got a mean little atom bomb and plan to use it."

Junior looked surprised. He was.

"Here in the District?" he asked.

"That's it."

"Well, pardon my French again," Junior began in a substantial Louisiana accent.

"Screw the French and do us both a big favor," Nomad told him. "We can do the language lessons tomorrow night. I'm buying. I've got a lot to tell you and your buddies right now."

The leader of the transplant team saw that Susan Kincaid was studying the blond man and his instrument case intently.

"Junior plays automatic shotgun in The Band. Junior, this is my friend Susan . . . and my other chum, Cesar."

"It's an honor, Ma'am. I'd like you to meet my friends now."

He gestured toward the RV . . . twice. Five people—each carrying a musical instrument case that concealed a weapon—emerged. Nomad and his partners scanned the strangers. One of them caught his eye and held it for several seconds.

She had the face and figure that would do that.

"You know everybody except Grace, right?" Junior asked.

He didn't wait for a reply.

"Grace is our new player. Took over for Harry, who some drunk driver put in a full body cast fifteen or sixteen weeks ago."

Nomad understood that Junior couldn't say what actually happened to Harry. At this point, it didn't matter.

"Pleased to meet you, Grace," Nomad told her. "Any friend of Junior's—"

"—is a damn good shot," Junior broke in with a grin. "Did I mention that Grace is a real ace with a long gun? Class A sniper-rated on seven different rifles."

Grace smiled modestly, showing a pair of girlish dimples.

Why not a young woman sniper? Nomad thought.

Female executioners might be next . . . if they weren't at work already. There was no way to hold back progress and workplace equality. If "they" had picked her for The Band, this curly haired Grace was probably more than equal, Nomad told himself.

Then he told her how glad he was to be on this job with her, and they shook hands in a highly professional way. She held up the case with her sniper rifle as she answered.

"Do my best," she answered in a strong, clear voice that suggested New England . . . maybe Maine. "Who're we playing, sir?"

Military . . . cool . . . businesslike . . . with service courtesy.

Probably loaded her own rifle shells just right with the exact amount of the correct powder for maximum accuracy and kill power.

"A gang that wiped out thousands of civilians last month just for practice. They're going for half a million here . . . I'd say within the next eighteen hours."

"Black-hat, bad-ass terrorists," Junior translated for the rest of the shooters. They all responded alike. Same gesture . . . same slogan. They raised their gun cases in promise.

"All the way! All the way!" they chanted.

It sounded like some Marine or Airborne thing, one of those motivational exercises. Now they lowered the weapon sheaths.

"Where do we take on these black hats?" Junior asked.

"Downtown. I don't know *exactly* where downtown," Nomad answered, "but I'm pretty sure about the neighborhood."

Junior looked uneasy.

"You joking me?" he tested.

"I think we'll have a precise address in a couple of hours," Nomad said firmly. "That'll give us time to check out the whole neighborhood . . . study the building they're in . . . set up our command post . . . and pick out the best firing positions for you."

"I like that part," Junior said. "Tell us again. How much time have we got from the moment you expect to find the place where these bad guys are holed up to when we've got to burn them?"

"Hard to say. Could be twelve hours . . . or maybe four."

"That part I don't dig at all . . . but we'll make do. Hey," Junior remembered. "Who's gonna take care of that A bomb?"

The rest of The Band was visibly startled.

"Yeah, these black hats have a friggin' A bomb," Junior acknowledged. "Who did you say they were? Terrorists?"

"They're visiting from the Middle East," Nomad reported. "About ninety-two percent of the people out there don't go around killing for a living. We're blessed with the furious minority."

Grace cleared her throat.

"About how many do you think we'll run into?" she asked.

Hostile force estimate . . . according to the manual.

"No more than a dozen . . . maybe less. They'll need one or two who've had special training on the weapon. I'd guess two. This al Wadi's no dummy. He'd want a backup man in case the prime bomb guy's sick or hurt."

The shooters recognized the terrorist's name.

The woman with the long gun instantly recalled newspaper and television pictures of his bloody deeds. Seconds later, she visualized him through the scope of her sniper rifle. The image lasted for only a flash. That was enough.

"He kills women and kids," she thought aloud.

"Anywhere . . . anytime," Nomad agreed. "You folks got cell phones?"

Junior, Grace, and another of the shooters nodded. Nomad tore two sheets from a pad he took from his pocket. He gave one leaf to them to inscribe their numbers . . . wrote his on the other. They exchanged the rectangles of paper.

"I suppose you're tired," he began.

"We know the drill, friend. There'll always be two of us awake with a phone within reach," Junior promised. He told Nomad the name of the middle-range chain hotel where the Agency was quartering them.

Then the shooters got back in their vehicle and rolled into the humid Washington night. Nomad's phone jangled scant seconds later. He raised it to his ear.

"Doctor Monroe's office," he said.

"Glad I caught you, Doc," the voice replied. "Sorry to tell you there was a little paperwork problem about putting the new air conditioner in your wife's van."

Seigenthaler's aide wasn't about to say on a nonsecure radio call that the F.C.C. had a mass of very bright employees *and* one moron in the motor pool who wanted the order to release the two radio-location vehicles to be "properly" countersigned by the head of that department.

Who was out at the dentist's for a root canal job.

Or maybe he was seeing his girlfriend for a matinee.

"We've got it straightened out now, Doc," the irate C.I.A. administrator continued, "and the new unit's working fine. Your son's VW is ready, too. He's here with a buddy. They'll drive both vehicles out in a couple of minutes. Sorry about the delay."

Nomad pretended not to be angry.

He said something generic and meaningless before he ended the call.

Every minute counted, and the vans were more than two hours behind schedule in initiating their search.

It's going to be close, he thought.

Just as bad, there was nothing he could do about it . . . and he hated that. Well, it wouldn't help to discourage the others.

"Both vans are moving out in a few minutes," he said in an upbeat voice.

Susan Kincaid and Cesar Fuentes looked at each other.

He didn't fool them at all.

37

SEVEN HOURS.

As many professionals in the intelligence community could tell you, the time difference between Washington and Tel Aviv is seven hours. The day starts that much earlier in the Israeli city. It might be metaphysically connected to the fact that Israel had a head start of about twenty-two or twenty-three hundred years, or there could be a more mundane reason.

Whatever your thinking . . . faith . . . or dietary preference, shortly after The Band left the underground garage, it was 1:30 A.M. on the Israeli coast of the Eastern Mediterranean. So the link to the previous night's border raid wouldn't be too clear, the commander of al Wadi's fearless Unit One had decided that tonight's land-and-sea incursions would happen later.

Now it was "later," and the low-hulled fishing boat was slowly moving into position at the designated rendezvous. The men aboard could just make out the shore a mile to the east. With their craft's muffled motor barely idling, it circled as the team head listened to his radio.

He was waiting for two transmissions.

The first came at 1:34 A.M. It was the agreed-upon strike signal. The other part of Unit One left back in southern Lebanon had begun its noisy assault at the border. A separate group of al Wadi's guerrillas—poised in the darkness some hundred and ten yards from the water's edge—heard the strike signal, too.

Seconds after that, the captain of the small vessel spoke hopefully into his limited-range walkie-talkie radio.

"Shalom . . . Shalom . . . Shalom."

Only three words to minimize the possibility of being overheard or located by some direction finder.

In the language of the Israelis, so they wouldn't be alarmed if they did hear it.

From the shore, a light blinked.

Twice . . . then three times.

Exactly as al Wadi had planned it.

The party that was to get the bomb ashore was ready. The Demon was securely lashed in a ring of floats, and in a waterproof bag on top of the nuclear warhead were four loaded M-10s, U.S.-made submachine guns from the arsenal of a nearby and supposedly neutral nation.

Six swimmers were to guide the Demon to the waiting shore party. They were strong young men, each with an antipersonnel grenade in a sealed plastic pouch tied under his arm like a shoulder holster. If it was needed, there'd be covering fire from the shore party crouching beside the truck they'd brought.

It wasn't going to be needed. They could see that.

No Israelis were on the scene. Al Wadi's detachment and the crew of the fishing boat had watched and listened carefully—and repeatedly—during the previous hour for any hint of Israeli coastal patrol craft.

Nothing. They'd outwitted the enemy's navy, and in a very short time would have the devastating-burning-killing thing ashore. In a few hours, it would be in position near the center of Israel's largest city. They'd set the timer and leave it to gut Tel Aviv . . . wiping out a hundred fifty thousand or more of the Zionist devils.

They'd detonate the murder machine at ten minutes after eight in the morning.

Just about the same time that their comrades would set off another atomic weapon in London . . . and a third in Washington.

It would be a great day . . . one that would be remembered.

Yes, they thought proudly, they were making history.

They were only eighty or ninety yards from the shore.

Nothing could stop them now.

38

NOMAD COULDN'T HELP IT.

He checked with each of the mobile location units every fifteen minutes by scrambler-mounted cell phone.

They were crisscrossing their assigned areas slowly, taking pains so they wouldn't pass any location more than once in twenty minutes.

Zero. No sign of any transmitter sending a steady beacon signal. They asked Nomad what frequency to focus on—or even which area of frequencies was most likely. He wanted to tell them, but he couldn't. Neither Nomad nor any communications specialist of the C.I.A. or N.S.A. had ever had an opportunity to examine Anna's eyeglasses.

The minutes were fleeing as if they were in as much danger as Washington itself. Seigenthaler had booked a three-bedroom suite in a hotel just two blocks from where The Band was. The head of the Agency's Russia F.S.R. group was feeling the pressure, too. He telephoned four times between 6:55 P.M. and eleven o'clock.

Just checking.

Anything?

Not yet.

He apologized for so many calls. "It's okay," Nomad told him. "Listen, I'll let you know the minute there's news."

"I won't call anymore," he promised.

But he did. Seigenthaler had a son, daughter-in-law, and grandchildren of six and eight living within a mile of where the President was to speak in less than fourteen hours.

If Nomad was right.

And a lot of other ifs.

The threat to his blood kin had him by the throat, and he could barely talk. Everything in him wanted to tell them to run, but he might critically injure the already risky effort to find and seize the bomb. His own career could be wrecked if he warned them, and one of the family—perhaps the guileless eight-year-old—somehow let the word get out and the terrorists slipped away with the Demon.

Mass destruction . . . personal destruction . . . and the numbing fear of an adult with many years of command experience twisted by uncertainty. Seigenthaler tried to push it all aside so he could concentrate on performing as a professional. Just before midnight, he saw he was losing so he drove to the hotel where Nomad's team was waiting.

"Anything?" he asked hopefully.

Nomad recognized the stress and hurt in his voice . . . his eyes.

He'd never seen him like this before . . . a span that covered more than a dozen years.

"Not yet. Why are you here in the middle of the night . . . and looking like death warmed over?"

Visibly drained, Seigenthaler lowered himself into an armchair and described his conflict over whether to tell his son about the Demon. "I know I can't," he concluded, "and I can't let them die either."

"That's a tough one," Nomad replied sympathetically, "but I have a much easier one for you. You're not going to mention any bomb. What you're going to say is 'Wow! Great news. I just got one of those random phone calls from a radio talk show. They asked me four questions about roses. Guess they had no idea I've raised fine roses for twenty-four years.' "

"What the hell are you talking about?" Seigenthaler blurted.

"Saving your good-citizen and swell-grandpa ass. Don't interrupt, will you? Well, you just aced those questions and you won this week's prize. It was a motorbike last week, but you hit it for an all-expense, five-day, airfare-included visit to the swinging Disney Park in Orlando. The whole thing . . . including balloons and unlimited rides for four people."

"And they've got to leave for Orlando tomorrow morning?" Seigenthaler guessed.

"You're one foxy grandpa," Nomad complimented. "Don't forget to mention the free T-shirts and a disposable camera for each of the four winners. Got your credit card with you?"

The older man took out his wallet and extracted two plastic rectangles that were replacing alcohol as America's painkiller.

The field agent pointed at the mauve telephone that matched the dumb framed prints on the walls in bad taste.

"Go, Grandpa, go."

Three calls. Five and a half minutes. It was done. The airline was pleased . . . the hotel was happy . . . and Seigenthaler's kin were so delighted by this wonderful surprise that it never occurred to them that they were off to whoop with Mickey and Minnie—the entire Mike Eisner clan, including tax lawyers and acrobats—thanks to a homicidal gang of foreign terrorists who thought big and low.

Seigenthaler sighed in relief.

He was sitting up straighter now.

"Thanks," he said to the American with the Russian heart. "I'm so used to thinking of you as the very rough and very ready field agent that I forget how damn smart you are."

"I don't," Nomad confided.

"I don't either," announced Susan Kincaid.

Harry Chen, Paula Taylor, and Cesar Fuentes simply nodded in accord.

Not entirely comfortable with the admiration, the transplant leader chose to change the subject.

"We're still nowhere on locating the Demons, or even whether my time estimate's right," he reminded them and turned to the older man. "Any word from London or Tel Aviv?"

"MI-Five just signaled that the damn electrical storms are fading fast."

"But they haven't pinpointed the beacon on the bomb, I'm sure . . . *almost* sure . . . al Wadi sent them. That means they don't know the frequency. Any better news from the Mossad?"

Seigenthaler ran his hand through his hair to straighten it.

"No news at all. Any suggestions?"

"Yeah, let's not waste any time, because I'm betting we don't have any to spare," Nomad urged. "There are a couple of things we ought to do now, while we have a little free time. You got any black-bag units here in D.C.?"

Those were the federal government's unmentionables . . . very secret, because what they regularly did for the U.S. was highly irregular, totally criminal. On the payrolls of both the F.B.I. and the C.I.A. under deceptive job descriptions, they were first-class burglars. When a U.S. intelligence or counterintelligence organization urgently wanted information locked in a safe at a foreign embassy in the U.S. or at some military headquarters abroad, the expert burglars mounted a clandestine raid. These illegal break-ins were known in the trade as "black-bag jobs" because for decades, the thieves usually carried their tools in black leather or plastic luggage.

For over half a century . . . in a lot of countries.

Nations of diverse philosophies and religious convictions.

The burglars broke in late at night . . . disabled alarms . . . opened safes . . . took out and photographed important documents . . . put them back very neatly . . . closed the safes and reconnected the alarms . . . and slipped out extremely quietly without leaving any trace they'd violated local laws and at least one of the Ten Commandments. For behaving so immorally, they were well paid and enjoyed comprehensive health insurance and retirement programs.

"One or two teams," Seigenthaler grudgingly acknowledged.

"Put them on standby," Nomad said. "I think I'll need them."

The C.I.A. executive didn't understand.

It was most unlikely that the Demon would be in an embassy.

"For research," Nomad said. "If this goes down as it might, I'll need research right away. Maybe sooner. One more thing . . . an Army chopper ready for takeoff wouldn't hurt my feelings either."

Seigenthaler eyed him uncertainly.

"I'm not crazy," Nomad assured him. "Trust me on this."

"You've got a plan?"

Nomad's cell phone vibrated. He'd turned off the ringer.

"I'll tell you all about it," he promised as he turned on the telephone. He listened for twenty-five seconds.

"Get back to me fast," he ordered and clicked off the call.

"One of the radio-detection trucks thinks it may have picked up something."

"Something? What the hell is that?" the C.I.A. executive erupted angrily.

"That's better than fucking nothing," Nomad replied.

"If you'll pardon his French," Susan Kincaid added.

"Two points for that," the leader of the transplant team complimented. "I've got a good feeling about this. It could be our first break. Anyway, the other van is moving closer to try to triangulate. We should hear more in eight or ten minutes."

Seigenthaler shook his head.

"What do we do in the meantime?" he grumbled.

"Excellent thinking. Plan ahead . . . that's the American way," Nomad said. "There are two significant problems I'm counting on you to handle . . . you or the D.C.I."

What the hell did the Director of Central Intelligence have to do with this, Seigenthaler puzzled.

"We're violating a couple of laws . . . if we do it my way," the man with the Russian heart began.

Nobody in the room doubted that it would be done his way. They waited for him to explain what that way was.

"You see," he said cheerfully, "I have in mind a burglary by armed civilians who might feel free to use significant violence."

"How significant? Like shooting?" asked Seigenthaler.

"Hope not. I think it would be best to let ace shooters like The Band do the shooting. More professional. Look, we're not going to put down anyone we don't have to put down."

Seigenthaler stared at him.

"Put down? That's a term you use for animals. These are people . . . in Washington, D.C.," he reminded.

" 'Land of the free and home of the brave,' " Fuentes added archly.

Nobody smiled.

"And respect your parents," Nomad ratified. "If I'm correct, these people are very close to animal and they intend to murder many tens of thousands of U.S. taxpayers with an atomic weapon. We may not have time to read them their rights and get them a lawyer who believes in Santa Claus."

"You believe in Santa?" Susan Kincaid wondered.

"Of course, but not in his right to bear nuclear arms without a license. Let's get back to my plan. An armed break-in in Washington, so you'll have to fix it with the D.C. cops. I wouldn't want them to get hurt if they ride into the line of fire."

"I'm not crazy about this," Seigenthaler declared slowly.

"If you've got a better idea, drop it in the fucking suggestion box. We'll limit the shooting to try to keep the noise down. Hey, we'll use silencers."

"I hate this," the C.I.A. executive said. "This isn't supposed to happen in Washington."

"You're absolutely correct, but nobody's told that to Mr. al Wadi and a gang of other terrorists . . . lots of gangs of other terrorists. Now, please listen to what I'm telling you. The Agency must have some liaison with the local lawmen . . . and women. Some lines of communication."

"Yes?"

"About ninety minutes before we make our move, I want our contact with the D.C. cops to be at their headquarters for a meet with the police chief. Urgent . . . call ahead three hours earlier to set it up."

"And what do we say at this emergency meeting?" the head of the Russian F.S.R. group asked.

"How about this? A crew of neo-Nazi terrorists—*racist* neo-Nazi terrorists—are here to kidnap the President and bomb five schools in the District. We've tracked them from Europe, and we've got to grab them right away."

"Before they murder all those little African–American kids?" Paula Taylor volunteered. "That's not bad, Denny."

"Thought you'd like it," he answered. "So we respectfully ask the D.C. cops to help save the kids by sealing off the area near the terrorists' hideout when we give the signal. The story could be a report of a large and dangerous gas leak. Those happen anywhere."

"And what do the cops say when the truth comes out?" Seigenthaler worried.

"Truth? What is truth? This is a national security matter. We repeat that a lot to the cops, and if that doesn't play, I'd bet they'd rather not have the devils of the media—and those folks in Congress who vote on the District's budget—hear how they were deceived. That's for the best interests of the country, of course," Nomad answered with a straight face.

Seigenthaler frowned.

"Any way you slice it, they're going to be mad," he predicted.

"Send candy. Try Guylian—the Belgian chocolate. Can't miss. Now, pay attention. There's more."

"There always is with you. Share it with me."

"Maybe you'll have to speak with the police chief more than ninety minutes before our strike force hits. That's going to be the second break-in. The first one's essential to the success of the second. I want to send a black-bag team into the head office of the Buildings Department."

"It's a government building. Can't we just ask for whatever you want?"

"No time. There's no one in the place at this hour of the night who could authorize it," Nomad pointed out. "And if we did find such an official, how could we be sure that person wouldn't find the whole number so exotic that he or she had to mention it to a loved one or a bartender before the second operation goes down?"

Seigenthaler thought of lighting a cigarette . . . decided not to. Planning an armed break-in with sharpshooters as backup was one thing, but he'd rather not offend anyone in this hotel suite now.

"So that's it?" he asked hopefully.

"Two more small things. I know you can handle them," Nomad cajoled smoothly. "It isn't just the D.C. cops who might get sore about what we're really going to do . . . for the country . . . saving lives. The whole thing . . . the F.B.I. is going to be totally pissed, and rightfully so."

"You going to send them candy too?" Seigenthaler asked.

"Be serious, will you? By statute, we're not allowed to operate domestically. This is their turf. If that's not enough, we've had an agreement with them for years that domestic counterintelligence and antiterrorism are their domain. I'd say there's a good chance they'll go ballistic by dinnertime tomorrow."

"Unless a Demon demolishes their headquarters and burns up one hundred or two hundred of their senior people," the C.I.A. executive said. "If you screw up and their top officials are dead, there'll be no point in complaining. That was a bad joke. What the hell would you like us to do?"

Nomad pointed his finger at the executive . . . nodded in emphasis.

"Major apology. Show respect. Federal cops appreciate that, too. Point out that the operation began abroad and that's *our* turf. You didn't suspect these Bad Guys were coming here. Say that somebody at the Agency was supposed to work with the Bureau on this, but the guy screwed up. Blame it on him. If you think sexist would play better, blame it on her."

"*Her*? I don't believe that's necessary."

"Blame it on me," Nomad proposed. "I don't mind. I'm legally dead, so they're not going to dig me up, right? Tell the F.B.I. that I had a heart attack and—here's the beauty part—give them all the credit for brilliantly and bravely thwarting these ruthless foreign terrorists."

He turned quickly to Harry Chen.

"Think that'll fly, Harry?" he asked.

"I can't comment, and I can't think either. I'm dead, too."

Now Nomad held up a single finger.

"One last thing," he said to Seigenthaler. "I'll need a command truck with two transmitters. Maybe something that looks like a U-Haul. Put on a U. of Maryland football sticker, 'Go,

Terrapins.' Throw in another with a dumb slogan. 'I brake for cheerleaders.' That kind of thing."

Seigenthaler seemed a lot less irritated.

"I'll get the dumb stickers," he promised.

"What about my command truck?"

The head of the Russian F.S.R. group eyed his wristwatch.

"Should have arrived downstairs about ten minutes ago," he said coolly. "I figured you'd want one. There's an assortment of silencers and plenty of ammo in the back. Grenades, too—both stun models and antipersonnel."

"Spike microphone and amplifier?"

"Two. The gear's no problem. Now, where the hell do we use it?"

"Take it easy," Nomad tried to placate. "I'll check with our radio-location units now."

"What happens if we don't find anything?" Seigenthaler asked tensely.

"You get a full refund," Nomad promised and took out his cell phone. As he reached to flip it open, the instrument—set for silence—vibrated in his hand.

"Go," he said and listened.

He picked up a pad provided by the hotel . . . raised the pen with the chain's eye-catching logo . . . wrote for ten seconds.

"Good work. We're rolling," he said.

"Found it. Just thirteen blocks from the Capitol," he reported moments later.

He paused to scribble the street address on another sheet of the pad.

"Identify and tap every phone line at that address," he told Seigenthaler. "And have the N.S.A. locate and cover any cell phones operating out of there. There's no big rush. Half an hour ago will do."

Then he explained what he wanted "the black-bag boys" to do.

"Let's move it, medical marvels," he told the other telepaths.

Seigenthaler stood up as they neared the door.

"I'll give this address to The Band too," he pledged. "Just

because we found the beacon doesn't make this any less dangerous. If these hoods realize you're moving in, they may not wait for the President's speech to detonate."

"You're right," Nomad agreed. "We'll be *very* careful, Dad."

"Tell me . . . I worry . . . what will you do first when you get there?"

Nomad loosened the fifteen-round P-15 Highpower in his holster. He'd left the smaller .32 in Moscow.

"I already told you," he answered briskly. "The Charlie Parker thing."

"Don't be afraid and just play the music?"

"It's always worked so far," Nomad replied and led the others out the door.

Seigenthaler stood there, hoping that the music would help this extraordinary field agent survive. He'd come to like and admire this sometimes difficult and often rule-breaking man who'd always been different . . . and was even more so since he went to that Institute.

He'd make it all right, Seigenthaler told himself.

Of course if he didn't, there'd be still another problem.

He'd had so many names—the one he was born with . . . at least three others at the Agency before they designated him Nomad . . . then Denny Monroe after he was officially deceased. In Russia last week, he'd been Lee Alderdice. There were probably other names even the man with the Russian heart barely remembered.

All this left Seigenthaler facing two questions.

If something went wrong, under which name should the veteran field agent be buried?

The second question was more challenging.

Putting aside the cloak-and-dagger rituals . . . in basic human terms, who was he?

The C.I.A. executive pondered this for more than half a minute before he went to telephone The Band.

39

THE COMMAND TRUCK—ACTUALLY A LARGE AND DARK GREEN van—was pulling up as Nomad led the telepaths from the hotel. The passenger seated beside the driver looked at them . . . saw the mix he'd been told to expect.

Black woman . . . blonde woman . . . three men, one an Asian and two others.

Check.

The passenger gestured toward the back of the van. A rear door opened. The well-lit interior had a row of six bucket seats along one wall, three covered metal bins, and two radio sending-and-receiving setups. A swivel chair was bolted to the floor in from of each. Seated on one of those was a well-fed female with curly brown hair, wearing a University of Southern California T-shirt and a semiautomatic pistol in a shoulder holster.

She was starting to draw the weapon.

"I don't mind," Nomad told her.

She realized that this was part of the strike force, slid the gun back into the holster.

"Get in. Get in," she urged.

They complied swiftly . . . closed the door behind them.

They sat down . . . listened to the faint hum of the air conditioner.

"My name's Elaine," she said and pointed at the machinery in front of her. "This is what I do—radio."

"You go to U.S.C.?" Nomad asked.

No way, she thought. She wasn't going to let this get personal. She pointed at the metal bins.

"That's ammo and grenades . . . next one's handguns and silencers . . . last one has jackets and the dog thing. You dig?"

"I dig," he acknowledged.

"Now let's hear where we're going . . . and who the hell's waiting for us there."

She clicked on a microphone in front of her so the driver and passenger beside him could hear it all.

Nomad announced the address. Then he added that a unit of Near Eastern terrorists was there setting up a very big bomb.

"How big?" she questioned.

"Bigger than that," he replied automatically. He estimated that if he mentioned a nuclear warhead, she might get extremely nervous. There were people like that, Nomad reminded himself.

"Got the frequencies of the two radio-detection vans, *Elaine*?" he asked politely.

"You bet."

"Call them on scrambler, *please,* and tell them to meet us in twenty minutes at the corner of Thirteenth Street . . . two blocks from *the place*. They'll know where that is."

"I'll do it as we roll," she answered, and she did. While the command vehicle started toward *the place* from where the minibeacon was sending, she relayed his instructions to the two mobile units that had located it.

"Roger," she concluded and turned to the transplants' leader.

"What do I call you?" she asked.

"Roger's fine."

Something in his voice told her that this man—clearly some kind of leader—wasn't named Roger at all, and that it wouldn't be productive to pursue this. Whatever his name was—whoever he might be—it would be risky to confront him about anything.

She was silent for a dozen seconds.

Then, "Message coming in," she reported. "Van A cruising past Zero."

That would be Ground Zero when the warhead exploded.

"What else?" Nomad pressed.

"Four stories . . . looks like a town house . . . could be some doctors or dentists . . . there's a brass plate just right of the door. Alleys on either side. All the lights are out. Cars parked in the street aren't cheap."

"Tell the other van to circle the block behind this Zero to see if there's a backyard . . . some kind of fence . . . anything," the hard-voiced operative who'd named himself Roger ordered.

Two and a half minutes of crackle.

"Fence. About five feet high. Got a glimpse of what could be a backyard. Lights. There are lights on . . . large window on the top floor. Our people are working night glasses. Nothing. Shades are down," the second van reported.

"Message to both vans. Are you absolutely sure this is the Zero? Have you rechecked?" Nomad dictated.

"Positive. Positive. Positive. Rechecked four times. Now moving toward Eleventh."

"Turn the corner and wait until the musicians arrive," the telepaths' leader said to the radio operator. About ninety seconds after that—when the van with The Band reported it was "on station"—Nomad reached for the microphone. Since he was clearly running this assault, Elaine handed it to him and flicked on the overhead speaker.

"Take up inconspicuous blocking positions . . . at least a hundred yards from Zero . . . all exit routes. I'll have more information about the party from High Five in about sixty or seventy minutes," he said.

"This is Junior. Gonna be a big party? More guests coming?"

Coming and listening, Nomad thought.

The wiretap and cell-phone eavesdrops should be operational at any minute.

"I've invited a few college friends," Nomad said. "It's going to be an all-nighter, so hang loose."

"We're good at that, old buddy."

The radio operator considered what the strike leader had said. It didn't matter that he'd played games about his name. That was standard in this profession, and he came across as coolly and highly professional. In more personal terms, she didn't think he was likely to get them all killed in some screwup.

She pointed at the four thermos bottles in the rack.

"Long-night department," she identified. "There's the john," she added and gestured toward what looked like a closet.

She wondered about how long the stakeout might be.

This was a command truck, and they'd told her a raid was coming. They didn't say when.

"Thanks, Elaine," he replied politely. "That's coffee?"

She nodded.

"Come in handy," he predicted. "This may not go down for hours."

She was glad that he had answered the question she hadn't asked. She had no idea of why he'd done it.

He was on the scrambler-equipped microphone again.

He instructed somebody to pick up the drawings . . . top to bottom . . . next door, both sides . . . out back. . . . across the street. Phone and gas lines, too. Urgent and a half. Express service. By 4:00 A.M. . . . my house . . . you know where.

Seigenthaler agreed.

He also promised to attend to the bird right away. He didn't use the word "helicopter" or the model number of the recon chopper with ultramodern, infrared cameras. He didn't have to think about those precautions. They were part of him after all these years.

"If you need anything else—" he began to offer.

"You'll hear."

"I'm not going anywhere. One more thing. About Orlando . . . thanks."

"Buy me a Delamain tonight," Nomad answered.

Seigenthaler knew the deluxe brandy well. He was less certain about whether Nomad would be alive that evening to drink it. There were too many things that could go wrong. If Nomad perished, the other four telepaths—a $30,000,000 investment— might well die with him. It would probably be the head of the

Russia-F.S.R. staff who'd get the heat from the bigger carnivores higher up the C.I.A. food chain.

Seigenthaler wasn't sure what to say now.

"I wish I had a better idea," he finally declared.

"So do I."

Click. Each man went his own way seconds later.

There was no time for reflection. They both appreciated that.

Seigenthaler began making the calls he'd promised.

Nomad looked at his watch.

There was nothing he could do in or from the command truck for the next half hour. He wouldn't waste a moment of it.

"Going to take a walk," he announced and stood.

"Recon time?" Susan Kincaid guessed.

"You got it."

"Can I come?"

"I'll try it solo," he replied and set off to walk around the battlefield. He'd stroll slowly past Zero, wander on to the corner and continue until he'd scouted all four sides of the block . . . and the buildings and alleys across the street. He'd study the terrain at eye level, observing the things maps didn't show. He'd look for firing positions. . . . exit routes . . . ambush possibilities.

There was going to be an infantry assault.

"Commando raid" would be more accurate, he thought.

Either way he put it, he had to execute the attack with minimum losses among his force and maximum penetration of the enemy position. It would help if he knew how many fighters—with what weapons and defenses—al Wadi had in that building.

Five or twenty-five . . . it made a difference, Nomad calculated as he neared Zero. He modified his stride to signal consumption of several strong drinks . . . gave the front of the enemy position a carefully casual scan as he reached it.

There was the brass plate on the wall beside the front door.

Jeezus, Nomad reacted.

No, it wasn't a religious edifice. The building housed the trade mission of a notoriously corrupt Central American regime. That dictatorship had a history of being soft on rich-major narcotics traffickers. Al Wadi had probably given somebody high in that government a substantial bribe to use the top floor for in-transit storage of a large suitcase.

There'd been a hint that it contained cocaine, Nomad guessed.

No mention of any Demon, he reasoned.

The suitcase would be in and out fast . . . three or four days at most. That piece of luggage had probably come in without any search . . . diplomatic immunity.

The whole building had diplomatic immunity.

That was why Nomad had gasped the name "Jeezus." He meant no disrespect. It was sheer shock that made him do it.

Walking on without breaking stride, the leader of the strike force continued the independent thinking that often bothered senior officials in the ritualized intelligence community. This building housing the Demon might be diplomatically immune to the let's-not-offend legion of the politically correct, but not to Nomad.

Not tonight.

Not with a massacre possible in a scant twelve hours.

The odds were long enough against pulling this off without the additional obstacle of diplomatic immunity. None of the proper and virtuous would be talking about diplomatic immunity when he showed them the little city killer. They'd be too shocked.

And probably scared to do more than speak in tongues for a few minutes, the veteran field agent speculated bitterly. They'd look like idiots if they tried that international-law number, he told himself. The Demon made it all simple. It was an equal-opportunity devastator. Race, creed, education, or social status wouldn't save anyone.

He mustn't let his anger interfere with his reconnaissance, Nomad reminded himself as he turned the corner. He was still playing it just a bit tipsy. That wouldn't be unusual in a man wandering the streets in the small hours of the morning. He wouldn't seem dangerous to anyone.

He didn't to the burly man in the checked sport shirt and dirty jeans who stepped out of the dark alley. Pig-eyed and reeking of cigarette smoke, he had a very unfriendly look. It matched the seven-inch-long switchblade knife in his right hand.

"Nice and quiet . . . and you won't get hurt," he promised.

Nomad didn't try to scan his thoughts. It happened.

This acrid-smelling mugger was (1) arrogant, (2) lying.

The combination was close to intolerable.

He felt equally negative about the boozy stranger. He resented Nomad's good looks . . . upscale wool-and-linen sports jacket that covered the holstered nine millimeter . . . well-made and quietly stylish shoes. The field agent's cool blue button-down shirt and deftly tailored gray slacks added to the thief's hostility.

This sort of expensive "uniform" was a class thing and some sort of putdown to street people, the amphetamine- and envy-fueled thief felt. This helped him decide that when he got the wallet, he'd slice this tipsy guy up—especially his face. Teach the bastard a bloody lessen, he exulted.

"Give up the wallet and roll on home," he assured cynically as he decided where he'd put the scars. "If you try something stupid with me, Jack—"

He gestured menacingly with the blade.

Nomad didn't like being called Jack . . . and he had a physical aversion to loudmouths who tried to intimidate him with knives. He also had no more time for this cheap melodrama. It had already gone on too long.

He'd rather not get involved with this petty thug.

Nomad would give him a chance . . . just one . . . right now . . . to leave in good health. A shot would alarm the terrorists nearby, but there were quieter ways to end this.

"No thanks," the field agent said evenly and began to turn.

The mugger stepped forward, raising the knife.

Nomad saw this in shadow, spun and simultaneously drew his nine-millimeter handgun in a smooth movement that seemed almost choreographed. The street thief was astonished at the sight of the weapon . . . startled at how professionally the supposedly tipsy stranger handled it.

Shaken and furious that he was no longer the powerful aggressor, the mugger reacted in out-of-control reflex. He started to swing the knife forward, and he began a desperate shout. That was what it would have been if Nomad hadn't crashed the semiautomatic against his head . . . then barely a second later, clubbed it against the thief's throat.

The hoodlum dropped the switchblade as he crumpled to his knees. Semiconscious and fully overcome by hurting, he made almost inaudible noises . . . choking sounds . . . gasping and gagging as if he were about to vomit. It wasn't only the pain and trauma that overwhelmed him. He was wondering whether he'd ever speak again.

Nomad saw a flat cellar door flush with the surface of the alley. He took a metal pick from the slim packet of burglar tools in his jacket, opened the lock on that door, and then raised it as quietly as he could. When he pushed the ruined robber into the opening, he heard a satisfying thump. There was a lot less noise when he carefully closed the lock again and wiped off his fingerprints.

They could be on file somewhere as those of a deceased civil servant, Nomad calculated, but why give any police organization anything to consider? He resheathed the gun, glanced up and down the alley, and resumed his reconnaissance patrol of the four sides of the block. He surveyed both sides of the street, checking for clear lanes of fire for the shooters, and for ways to approach the building that housed the bomb.

Approach and depart.

The Band's guns would have to control both.

Now up a passage between two private homes, he saw the rear of the target trade mission. His eyes ranged up to the top. The roof was flat . . . two chimneys some seven or eight yards tall . . . and that large window dominating the floor just below.

It was lit . . . after two in the morning.

On the north side of the target there was an alley wide enough to park a car. The south side was flush against another building that looked very similar—a sister structure put up at the same time by some dollar-wise real estate entrepreneur at least three decades ago.

He'd break in from the south side.

It was a no-brainer.

Crossing the eight-foot-wide alley or trying to enter by the front door—which might well have alarms, or even an armed night watchman—had to be much more difficult and dangerous.

He realized that even now the parked command truck might be in some kind—any kind—of hazard. Random break-in by cruising crooks was one risk . . . a curious foot patrolman was another. He'd better touch base now. Those weeks at the Institute would help.

Radio cross-talk might be overheard.

His thoughts were inaudible to even the most sophisticated and expensive gear of the global N.S.A. networks.

He reached out telepathically to the woman who played chess so well.

"Queen . . . Queen . . . Queen," he sent—using the chesspiece name they'd worked with in training sessions.

"Bishop . . . Bishop . . . Bishop," she answered immediately.

"I've completed half of recon circuit. Have you any update for me?"

"Three land lines and two cell phones have been located by N.S.A., which starts monitoring any minute. Satellite link to our board in vehicle going on right after that."

That would help, Nomad judged. She was fluent in Arabic—probable lingua franca of al Wadi's operatives—and other telepaths in the truck spoke several additional tongues.

He mentally quizzed her about the status of the black-bag break-in. She reported "they" would be inside by 3:00 A.M.

Real estate report, he asked. Going in from south side. Will that play? Her answer made him smile. The building on the south side of Zero was scheduled for demolition next month, so it was empty. There'd be no occupants who might be a problem.

"We'll need details on the building facing Zero . . . floor plans . . . front and rear access. Any alarms?"

"I'll communicate that immediately. Need anything else?" she sent.

"Climbing gear. Ropes. Clamps. Two sets. Okay, I'm on my way."

A dozen minutes later, he rapped the security signal on the command-truck door and entered. He felt them all light up in silent welcome. This odd team of legally dead had spirit, he thought, and shrugged at the unintended jest. There was nothing amusing about the barbaric duo of Demon and al Wadi.

There was also no time for sociological insights or anything else, he realized as he reached for the microphone to talk to The Band. The conversation was curt and hard-edged . . . stone-professional. He reported that the command vehicle's extensive communications gear included a state-of-the-art fax machine that would soon spit out first-class floor plans, photographs, and maps sent by "the Sat guys."

He didn't mention they ran one of N.S.A.'s satellites that was so secret its launch had never been made public. He did say that he'd found "some nice views you'll enjoy," and invited Junior to stand by for a detailed briefing within the next hour.

In that time, Nomad extensively briefed the telepaths and the command-unit crew—who had no idea the strangers had any extraordinary mental powers—on what he'd seen during his reconnaissance of the area. He pointed out that they needed a lot more information before they could seriously attempt to break in—overpower or destroy a defending force of unknown strength and weapons—and seize The Thing.

"Maximum intelligence is our minimum need," he said bluntly, "and it should get here soon, because a daylight raid would be even crazier."

They nodded. Harry Chen asked a practical question.

"If we manage to pull this off . . . and I'm thinking positive, Denny . . . what the hell do we do with The Thing?"

"I had a one-week course on this general family of weapons," Fuentes said, "and I don't know enough to touch one."

"Mass-destruction toys aren't my game," the blonde woman told Nomad. "This is for specialists."

Susan Kincaid seemed the calmest.

"I know you've got a plan, Denny," she said evenly. "Let's hear it."

"Brownie points and hot cocoa for everybody," he announced. "All of you are right on target. Harry's wise to look ahead at a very real problem, and Cesar's absolutely realistic about not touching this complex and insanely lethal machine. As for Paula's view, I agree nine hundred percent that removal—no, disarming and removal—has to be left to specialists."

"How is this horror fired?" the chess player asked.

Nomad shrugged.

"Could be by timer . . . could be by radio signal. I don't think they'd use a contact fuse, because the damn thing is less than forty feet off the ground. My guess is that they'll set it off where it is," he reasoned aloud.

"So they'd all get out of that building at least twenty-five or thirty minutes before, allowing for local traffic jams," Chen speculated.

The black woman shook her elegant head.

"That's what sane people would do," she began, "but this is the al Wadi mob of anything-goes terrorists. They might leave behind one or two people—martyr types ready to fry for the great cause . . . to protect it and make sure it goes on schedule."

"She's right," Nomad agreed. "Every week we hear about intense former dental students around and about the Near East . . . recently in other warm areas, too . . . strapping to their bodies large portions of explosives they can detonate when near their enemies. Then it's straight to heaven for the suicide bombers, and hell on earth for anyone else hammered by the blast."

"So there could be armed guards," Fuentes accepted. "What else?"

"Booby traps, attack dogs, motion detectors, and who knows fucking what. Expect everything, and don't forget your body armor, gas mask, throwing knife, or protective goggles."

Nomad gestured toward the radio operator.

"Headsets. We'll need five, and another five for The Band. Range at least two hundred yards. Same frequency. Backup battery units. Okay?" he asked.

She pointed at a wall unit, announced the frequency.

"We're hoping for surprise," Nomad went on. "That's why I intend to attack at oh-five-hundred . . . quietly. That means a sneak assault . . . silencers," he instructed. "If we can break in and remain undetected for ninety seconds, we're halfway there. Once we're discovered, noise won't matter. Just take the bastards out as fast as you can . . . any way you can."

"All of them?" Chen tested.

"Rules of engagement," the team leader said. "There's just one in this action. We do whatever we have to do. You could make that *whoever* we have to do to grab The Thing. When we've got it, we have to hold it . . . and make sure it isn't about to go bang. I wouldn't look good in an urn."

Then a small red bulb began flashing on the console.

Nomad leaned forward as the communications controller who'd said her name was Elaine reached for the switch beneath it.

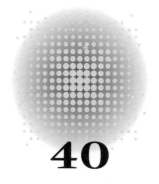

40

THE TEMPO WAS ACCELERATING.

Progress report from N.S.A.: Expect document feed in sixty or seventy minutes. Phone cover now fully operational.

Progress report from Army G-2: Helicopter with intelligence photo and electronic search gear will be over target by 0320. Expect to transmit to your command-truck printer by 0345.

Update from Seigenthaler: We're baby-sitting the five phone circuits N.S.A. is monitoring. Please confirm that you are, too.

Nomad nodded, and the woman at the console confirmed.

"Do you need additional personnel . . . gear . . . anything?" the careful C.I.A. executive asked.

Nomad took the microphone to reply.

"We have weapons and eavesdropping equipment for listening from next door," he said, "but we'll need a team of nuclear-warhead specialists with full gadgets and one of those fancy removal trucks. No, *two* teams and two trucks. Not here . . . not close, but not that far. Park them out of sight in a garage eight or ten blocks from Zero, with radios tuned to my command frequency."

Seigenthaler warned it could take over an hour to bring those units in from an Army base outside the capital. Nomad said that he must be notified as soon as the special trucks and crews were in position.

"No sirens or escort armored cars or flashing lights," he stipulated. "Nothing to wake up anybody before we go in at oh-five-hundred."

"Anything else?"

"You might tell the D.C. cops to pick up a mugger locked in a cellar . . . third alley west of Zero. He could be waking up soon. As soon as we select the firing positions of our shooters, you can share that with the cops, too. If they know it in advance," Nomad said, "they won't get hurt in the cross fire . . . or bother the shooters. I'll get back to you."

As the exchange ended, Susan Kincaid stared at him.

"What mugger?" she asked telepathically.

"I never got his name," he replied in the same way and took the microphone to update The Band on the timetable.

The target intelligence began to arrive thirty-eight minutes later.

Over some twenty-one minutes, infrared aerial photos—street maps showing the neighborhood building by building . . . floor plans of Zero, houses on either side and the building across the street . . . phone and gas lines—came down from the satellite. While Nomad and Fuentes—who'd break in with him—studied these graphics intently, Susan Kincaid did that and something else.

She had her language skill and a headset.

She was listening to guttural voices.

Nameless, faceless people speaking in N.S.A.-captured phone calls.

Speaking in Arabic, as the assault team leader predicted.

One voice bore an accent she identified as Tunisian. A second male sounded Pakistani. She reported this to Nomad, who silently filed it in his mental computer.

At least two inside now. Probably more.

They'd guard the damn Thing with more than that.

Where were they in the building?

What defenses? What fire power?

Whatever their numbers, al Wadi's operatives would be ready

to die to carry out this massacre. Their dedication didn't impress the man with the Russian heart at all. The telepaths and The Band wouldn't hesitate to help them achieve their martyrdom.

Now Nomad decided it was time to brief The Band.

There was something else he must do first.

Routine precaution.

If the strike force was studying the target and adjacent streets, al Wadi's people might be looking out at them.

"Scan for infrared," he ordered and pointed toward Zero.

He had to assume that an amply funded terrorist apparatus would have bought the latest technologies. The men with that Demon might well be sweeping with invisible infrared beams.

The seen-it-all radio operator turned a dial on her console— studied the guage for a dozen seconds—then yawned and eyed it again.

"Negative . . . negative," she reported.

"Thank you, Elaine," he said.

Good manners, she thought. Strike-unit leaders weren't usually that courteous. This leader seemed different somehow, she judged. The way the rest of his team regarded him said the same thing. She couldn't define it, but she didn't doubt it.

For a few moments, she wondered what made a leader.

Then he was talking again . . . on the microphone to someone named Junior.

"It's warming up," he said. "Got a fax in your van? . . . I've written it down," he announced as he scrawled the number on a message pad. "I'm sending you what we just received. I'll call back in five to discuss firing positions."

He did.

It was a short conversation.

They agreed on where each shooter would be . . . within ten minutes . . . and Nomad promised to alert this Junior before leaving the command truck to take up a close-in reconnaissance post.

"Let's try that coffee," the man with the Russian heart proposed as soon as he ended the conversation. No one disagreed. They needed the caffeine rush to prepare for the assault. As they sipped the hot, strong brew, Nomad spelled out the plan.

"How soon?" the yellow-haired woman asked.

"Now would be nice," he answered and drained his mug.

They put on the bulletproof vests . . . donned zipper jackets to cover them . . . took weapons and silencers from the bin. As they screwed on the sound-muffling tubes, Nomad reached into the next bin for two grenades . . . then two more.

"What do they say in those shitty movies?" he asked.

"It's show time!" Fuentes answered.

"That's it. Let's—"

The red bulb was blinking again.

"Depending on your point of view—" Seigenthaler began.

"Can't this wait?" Nomad asked impatiently.

"You should know it now. The F.B.I. is not happy about somebody violating their turf. They're really steamed. They're making threats."

"I'm sitting about thirty yards from a gang of terrorists with a fucking A bomb. That's the only threat that scares me right now," Nomad answered.

"It's not all bad news," Seigenthaler assured him hastily. "They're going to play nice. We've made a deal. They'll move in units to seal off your area when you're ready to hit . . . not before."

"And they'll get credit for saving Washington, right?"

"Does it matter who gets credit?" Seigenthaler pressed.

"Not to me, friend. I'm dead, so I don't care," Nomad replied bitterly.

The radio operator puzzled over what that meant.

He didn't explain it.

He said "son of a bitch" instead and took two more ammunition clips.

"Headsets," he reminded.

They each took one of the lightweight, clear-plastic, talk-and-listen devices that were almost invisible. The range was only a hundred and eighty yards . . . enough for close-in assaults. As Nomad put his on, he saw the concern in the radio operator's eyes.

"Not to worry," he said. "I'm not mad at the F.B.I., or at

anyone else who doesn't plan to blow up D.C. in the next day or so."

He turned to the other telepaths.

"Paula, you go out first. When you're up on the roof across the street," he ordered as he handed her the night-vision binoculars, "check whatever you can see and let us know if the coast is clear."

She left.

"Susan and Cesar and I will then break into the empty building next door to the trade mission," he continued. "After we sneak and peek . . . and listen . . . for fifteen or twenty minutes, I'll give Harry the go to cover the front door. I figure we should smash into the room where they've got the Demon at oh-five-hundred."

"Inshallah," the black woman added.

"Absolutely," Nomad agreed. "If Allah's willing."

Some eleven minutes after that, Paula Taylor reported that she had a clear view from her observation post. There was no threat in sight.

"How about another infrared scan?" Chen proposed.

"That's prudent, Harry," the team leader complimented. "I respect 'prudent.' "

Once more, the woman named Elaine—too wary to offer any additional identification to a transient assault unit—probed electronically for invisible search beams from the trade mission.

"Sorry," she said and pointed at the guage on her console. "It just came on ten seconds ago. Could be a periodic check they do."

Three minutes . . . maybe four.

"It's gone," she reported.

"I don't like it," Nomad said. "Smart terrorists bother me. Okay, we stay positive. We'll wait another minute and hope your timing's right."

They picked up their weapons and other gear . . . tensed.

Nomad counted the final seconds aloud.

"Nine . . . eight . . . seven . . . six . . . five . . . four . . . three . . . two . . . one . . . *go!*"

They went.

41

THEY MOVED OUT QUICKLY. THEY DIDN'T RUN, FOR THAT MIGHT attract attention. They walked at a normal pace, pretending to chat like ordinary civilians returning from a late party. They didn't go to the trade mission. Instead, they strolled up a nearby alley . . . turned left to the back of the empty building scheduled for demolition.

They scanned the rear door and windows . . . up and down . . . twice.

Fuentes looked for an alarm . . . found it.

"It's a piece of crap," he judged. "A nine-year-old could take it out."

"Pretend you're ten," the team leader advised.

He did.

Inside—walking warily in the unlit rooms—pausing to make sure the physical layout matched the floor plans supplied by the U.S. Government's burglars—they looked left and right, high and low, for any other alarms. There weren't likely to be many in an empty building that had nothing for anyone to steal. There wasn't a single piece of furniture, only light switches and wall sockets.

"We're inside," Nomad reported to the radio controller in the command truck. "Ready to go up. Everything still chilly with the red beam?"

"Negative. They came on a few seconds ago. Guess the neighbors changed the timing."

"Lucky, huh?" Fuentes said.

Nomad didn't bother to reply.

He pointed to the doorway to the corridor. Down at the end—up near the front door—a staircase led to the second floor. They paused there to study the rooms . . . a musty smell . . . some scraps of worn carpet that had been abandoned. Then they went on to the third floor.

In the trade mission next door, the rear room whose lights were on ran the width of the fourth floor. Nomad led the way to the same one in this adjacent building. With no furniture, they sat on an old wooden floor, and the chess player went to work. She took from her shopping bag the eavesdropping equipment they needed.

She tuned it to the frequency of her headset.

Then she tested it again. Fresh batteries were delivering.

With a chisel, she slowly and quietly carved a small hole in the wall, pushed it deeper bit by bit with a drill. When it was more than an inch into the outer wall of the trade mission, she put on a rubber glove and cleaned out the bits.

She was ready now.

She connected the spike microphone.

It ought to work. Developed by London's S.A.S. commandos and improved just a bit by compulsive people at Langley, it had a solid track record. Now she patted it as if it were a puppy and turned it on, low power.

She listened . . . and smiled.

"Two men . . . Arabs . . . same voices we heard on the phone cover," she announced.

"I want it all," Nomad told her.

In bits and pieces . . . a phrase here . . . a remark there . . . a bad joke . . . a proud boast . . . she managed to put together some of the basics he needed. It didn't flow in any neat sequence. It zigzagged . . . rambled . . . repeated. Like life in any culture, it was erratic . . . surprising . . . a bit of a mess.

After nearly twenty minutes, she paused in the spasmodic translations when one of the two terrorists left the room. She sighed and seized the opportunity to summarize.

There were seven operatives in this al Wadi unit . . . all of them male.

In addition to the pair she'd overheard, there were five more downstairs. Their job was security—to protect the building and The Thing. One of the two upstairs with the weapon seemed to be in command. The other was in that room because he'd been taught how to use The Thing.

"Seven?" Nomad thought aloud. "I don't like that."

There was no one else in the building today. This was a national holiday of the country whose diplomatic immunity cloaked the whole structure. That would make it easier to carry out the plan without interruption. Each of the seven was healthy and ready to do exactly what he'd been assigned to do.

On schedule, as they'd rehearsed.

Precisely on time . . . just like the other two groups.

London and Tel Aviv, Nomad guessed.

What was happening there . . . maybe at this moment?

She'd heard a radio in the background. One remark suggested that the seven were waiting for updated news on when *he* would start to speak. There was no reason to suspect *he*'d be late. *He* made a point of being on time.

It would still be necessary to check repeatedly.

The all-news station made that easy.

Withdrawing the security force before The Thing was activated would be done in stages so that nobody would notice. One would leave the building at 10:35 P.M. . . . a second at 1:10 A.M., and the third at half past one. The fourth would depart just before 2:00 P.M.

That would give them time to get at least two miles away before *he* spoke, Nomad calculated. He wondered what about the other three. He asked her.

"No mention of them leaving," she reported. "Maybe they stay for the whole show."

"Save a lot of money on burial expenses," Fuentes reckoned.

The thought of the Demon vaporizing the trio didn't move

Nomad. His focus wasn't on the men but on the number. Attacking seven terrorists was much more risky than fighting three.

"If the four security guards split by two o'clock, that's when we can hammer the other three. We'll have both surprise and more guns," the team leader judged. "I like those odds."

He pointed at Kincaid.

"So you were probably . . . well, possibly . . . right about a couple of suicidal martyrs hanging in to detonation," he said.

Now it was her turn to point . . . at the wall beside her.

"I wish I could be right about something else I'm picking up," she said. "I hear these irregular sounds . . . no fixed interval . . . definitely not mechanical. They don't make sense."

"Could they be human? Humans don't make sense half the time," Nomad answered.

"Not funny . . . and not human," she judged. "It moves around."

"Don't worry. It'll come to you. While you're thinking about it, I'd better touch base with Junior."

He told Junior what Susan Kincaid had overheard . . . repeating the timetable for the four terrorists to leave the trade mission.

"I don't want to lose these hoods when they come out," Nomad said emphatically. "I'm calling in a dozen surveillance units to cover all exits from the block . . . to tail them to wherever they're going and grab them. Our Near East experts will want to shine lights in their eyes and tell them very complicated lies. If they're extremely polite, half-truths."

"Be easier to let Grace take them down. She's got a great new scope on her long gun," Junior replied.

"After two, it's a free-fire zone for Grace . . . when I give the order."

"Not to be disrespectful, Chief, but you're cuttin' it kinda close, aren't you? If you're right about these terrible people burning up the whole damn neighborhood at a quarter to three, that doesn't give us much of a window of opportunity to grab the bomb before they try it."

"Or to get the hell out of range . . . at least two miles. Three would be better. Yes, you're absolutely correct," Nomad said.

Six . . . seven . . . eight seconds of silence.

"These foreign devils could blow the damn thing *before* a quarter to three," Junior warned, "and we'd just be some bits of radioactive dental work."

"Or they might detonate if we don't wreck them in the first goddam ninety seconds of our assault. We get one shot. Winner take all," the leader of the telepaths said.

Four . . . five . . . six more seconds of dead air.

"You figure we got a good chance to win?" Junior asked slowly.

"Bet you ten bucks," Nomad replied ironically.

He heard Junior breathing heavily.

"Would you like to explain something to me?" the shooter appealed.

"I don't think I'm up to it," Nomad answered candidly. "I'll try before I leave town tonight. I can't get killed before then. I've got something very important to do in Russia."

He didn't sound quite crazy, Junior realized, but he had to be.

"We'll be watching for those four hoods as they come out," he promised, trying not to think about nuclear mushroom clouds as the conversation ended.

Nomad summoned the surveillance specialists. They were in circulating patrol three blocks from the trade mission by five o'clock . . . half an hour before the F.B.I. containment teams approached the neighborhood. While all this movement built outside, Susan Kincaid sat on the floor inside the room on the fourth floor and listened intently for any additional scrap of information about the homicidal zealots only yards away.

Time slid by silently . . . inexorably. There was no dramatic sound of ticking clocks. All the watches on the wrists of the up-to-date terrorists and the equally contemporary men and women assembled . . . by the dozens . . . in scores . . . to stop them were modern digital devices that made no noise. This lack made the waiting seem longer . . . more eerie.

Still the watchers and shooters Nomad had assembled weren't exhausted. Tense, yes. Red-eyed, sure. Weary, not really. Their bloodstreams flooding with histamines . . . their necks stiff . . . legs sore . . . mouths dry with anticipation, they looked at each other to see if the man or woman beside them was alert or bored or sipping from another container of coffee.

Now and then—without any schedule—reports reached Nomad.

The woman at the communications console in the truck was the "switchboard."

4:55 A.M. The Band had the compatible headsets tuned to the control frequency.

5:20 A.M. The screen of F.B.I. surveillance units was in position with—of course—a communications van of its own.

6:31 A.M. The Army nuclear-weapons teams—with the skills and special tools to disarm and move tactical "devices"—had found garage hideouts for the two groups of trucks . . . one a half mile north of the target, the second some twelve blocks west. The scrambler-equipped radios on each truck were "working" with both Nomad's command vehicle and, of course, a mobile Army control group.

And there was a just-in-case message, too.

It didn't surprise Nomad one damn bit.

Just in case they might be needed, a special assault unit designated Force Five—a secret outfit that could protect or storm the White House or the Senate building or other "very hot" spots—was now on full alert, with light armored vehicles and antitank rockets.

It could hammer its way to the trade mission in twenty minutes, preceded by motorcycles whose sidecars mounted heavy machine guns. Two platoons rolling in Humvees were a fire team, flamethrower specialists.

The Army liked to prepare for all contingencies, Nomad told Kincaid and Fuentes. It was entirely logical and commendable, he said, and shook his head. He didn't need a sledgehammer. This operation had to be done with an ice pick. That was obvious and he was trying not to be impatient, so he didn't say anything bitter.

He'd save the bitterness for later.

It might fuel him during the nasty hours ahead of waiting.

Now Fuentes spoke. One word.

"Can," he said, and went looking for a toilet. He returned a few minutes later.

"It's still working," he reported. "They haven't turned off the water yet."

Nomad smiled at the thought that they were concerned about a "can" while they were less than fifteen . . . maybe twenty . . . yards from a bomb that could massacre hundreds of thousands of people still deep in sleep. Human frailty—unchanged back to biblical times. He wouldn't include this in his report to Seigenthaler . . . if he lived to make one. It would make the very decent and earnest head of the Russia and F.S.R. group uncomfortable . . . uneasy . . . uncertain as to what he could or should comment.

7:53 A.M. Something was happening outside.

The sounds from the quiet street were growing louder.

Minute by minute . . . more automobile noises . . . after 8:00 A.M., a horn or two. The workday was slowly beginning . . . more traffic. More people dressed for their offices in this office town were on the move.

8:20 A.M. Two men not dressed for offices—workmen in white overalls, wearing white caps to protect their hair from paint. Clearly painters, carrying a ladder and two boards some eight inches wide and five feet long. They approached the street door of the building being readied for demolition.

While the nondescript truck that had brought them here moved off, one of them dragged a heavy plastic sack that had to hold brushes, cans of paint, and the miscellaneous gear of their trade. The other paused to scratch his rear—masterful in his role—and take a key from his pocket. He yawned and unlocked the door.

"No smoking," he told his partner.

"Yeah . . . yeah," the other workman answered as they began to haul the ladder, boards, and sack inside. As soon as the man with the key closed the door behind them, he removed from the plastic bag two headsets of the same type Nomad and the others upstairs were wearing. He gave one set to the man in white beside him. Then each of the duo did something that wasn't in the membership rules of the D.C. painters' union.

They reached under their shirts and took out semiautomatic pistols. From the way they did this, it was obvious that they'd had experience with these weapons. They scanned the ground floor very carefully before the man who'd opened and locked the front door spoke into his headset.

"Hello, leader. Hello, leader. The painters are here."

"Front door locked?"

"Affirmative. Okay to bring up your stuff?"

"Okay for one," Nomad replied. "The other stays downstairs to cover the door. Move it."

The C.I.A. agent who'd opened the front door managed to maneuver the boards and the black-plastic bag up to the fourth floor. He was panting as he entered the room where the three telepaths sat on the floor. He froze in the doorway when he saw that the two men were pointing big-caliber handguns at his face.

"Nothing personal," Nomad assured him and gestured to the spot where he should put down his cargo. When the agent took out the white painter outfits he'd brought for the two men, they donned that garb immediately.

"Good," Nomad told him.

"You're the leader."

It was a statement . . . not a question. He could tell.

"Sure . . . and *she* plays chess," Nomad said. "*He* plays everything else."

Now the false painter reached into the big bag again.

He took out three containers of coffee, one of tea, two quarts of club soda with several paper cups, a sack of sandwiches, and a large box of paper tissues.

"Can you tell me what's going on here?" he asked warily.

Nomad pointed at the outer wall where Susan Kincaid was still eavesdropping.

"There are seven shallow thinkers just next door with a genuinely significant bomb," he reported at he reached for a container of coffee.

"Really big?"

"Huge and dirty. You wouldn't like it."

The "painter" considered this for four full seconds.

"Then I guess my partner and I can collect our ladder downstairs and split," he said.

"That *I* wouldn't like. Thanks for coming by. Now you stay and cover that front door. Nobody comes in . . . and no shooting. It's National Keep It Fucking Quiet Day."

Visibly troubled, the "painter" left. The telepaths were munching on sandwiches at noon when the call came from the command truck. Nomad recognized the relayed voice immediately.

"The D.C. police chief is raising hell," Seigenthaler reported, "and the director of the F.B.I. agrees with him. The proper tactical drill in such a high-danger situation is to evacuate all the civilians for a block or two in all directions."

"That's the title song from the new rock opera *Bullshit*," the man with the Russian heart replied bluntly. "Don't you think the Bad Guys next door might notice something if we start to move out six or seven hundred people? I suppose they want us to stop all vehicles from entering the kill zone, right?"

"That's the way they do it."

"Here's how I do it. If we execute perfectly, we can save about a hundred fifty thousand people, including the six or seven hundred in the neighborhood. If the Bad Guys spot the evacuation and go for glory at once, a big bunch of taxpayers die, people who didn't have to," Nomad said irately. "For God's sake, do the numbers."

He heard the C.I.A. executive sigh.

A highly intelligent bureaucrat, Seigenthaler had long followed Agency practice and done the numbers for years.

Forward and backward and sideways—old math and new.

None of it helped in dealing with operators . . . no, life forces . . . such as Nomad.

"Listen," Nomad continued. "We'll stop the cars from moving into the kill zone when we hit the building. I'll give you ninety seconds' warning. Do us all a favor and keep the F.B.I. and cops off my back, will you?"

He heard Seigenthaler sigh again.

"You think I'm losing it, don't you?" Nomad challenged.

"I never said—"

"You're *wrong*," the strike-force commander interrupted harshly. "I'm the team leader, and I've already lost it. Now we've got a war to fight, so get the hell out of our way."

He ended the exchange . . . looked at the black woman.

"You've got great people skills," she said wryly.

Fuentes bit into a sandwich before he spoke.

"I'm cool," he announced and chewed for a few seconds. "You are the leader, and this is our war. If we pull it off, we're heroes and get all those frequent-flier miles and medals. If we blow it, we're really dead and nobody can do anything to us."

He chewed again for another several seconds.

"The hero thing would be better," he added matter-of-factly and handed Nomad a sandwich.

They ate silently for several minutes.

Then the voice of the woman at the console in the command truck sounded in their headsets.

"Stand by. Stand by. According to the timetable you gave us, somebody should be taking a walk in twenty-seven . . . twenty-eight . . . seconds."

"Bet on it," Nomad answered.

Al Wadi's fighters were well-trained and disciplined.

They followed plans and schedules meticulously.

"Nobody touches him or follows too close," Nomad reminded. "Don't bag him until he's at least three blocks away."

"Affirmative. Okay, twelve seconds."

"Take him *quietly* . . . repeat, *quietly*."

"Affirmative. Five . . . four . . . three . . . two . . . one. Hey, he's late."

But only by ten seconds.

"Door's opening," Elaine reported enthusiastically. "Here he comes. Sport jacket . . . dark pants . . . sliding right into the crowd. Walking left . . . carrying small canvas suitcase . . . dark green. Turning the corner now."

Another voice . . . male.

"We've got him covered. This is Adam One. We've got him covered."

Nomad eyed his wristwatch.

12:38.

It had started, and he had about two hours in which to stop it. Maybe less.

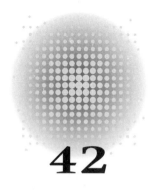

42

AT 1:10 A.M., ANOTHER MAN—ABOUT TWENTY-SIX OR THIRTY years old—swarthy . . . wearing jeans and a Georgetown University zipper jacket . . . came out of the trade mission.

On schedule. Number Two.

He carried the shopping bag of Washington's biggest department store. "The bastard probably has some nasty little submachine gun in there," Paula Taylor speculated from her observation post across the street.

"Just the facts, ma'am," the team leader instructed.

"Right. He's turned right."

"On your toes, musical friends," Nomad said.

"We've got him covered," Junior assured. "He's about to turn at the corner. Left. He's heading left."

"Ready for handoff," an anonymous F.B.I. surveillance supervisor reported in the jargon of air-traffic control centers who "acquired"—by handoff from an adjacent center—a plane entering the acquirer's sector.

"Handoff complete," the F.B.I. supervisor confirmed seventy seconds later.

Number Three emerged a minute early.

1:29 P.M. Nomad was on the phone to Seigenthaler.

The President had again refused to call off the speech.

He knew better than the C.I.A. or anybody else. He was The Chosen One—head of The Free World. He'd been elected by the American people . . . big majority. His six writers had crafted a great speech for him, and dammit, he was going to deliver it.

"Number Three . . . baseball cap . . . gray sweatshirt . . . chinos . . . sneakers," the observer with the gold hair reported. "Carrying blue gym bag . . . something on it."

She squinted through her binoculars.

"Reebok. That's what it says. He's looking around."

"They taught him to," Nomad thought aloud.

"He's walking slowly. On your toes, fellas. Lot of people in the street. Don't lose him."

They didn't.

The surveillance screen tracked him for five blocks before making its move.

"Off the board. He's off the board. That's three for our team," an F.B.I. special agent announced.

That was when Susan Kincaid began to hear those puzzling sounds once more. She shook her head, muttered something.

"That's Arabic?" Nomad tested.

She nodded, concentrating on her listening.

"You swore in Arabic?"

She nodded again.

"I'm impressed," he told her and eyed his watch.

"Don't sweat it," he said a few seconds later as he got to his feet. "You'll figure it out."

She hadn't been communicating telepathically, but it was as if he'd picked up her thoughts. That was impossible, of course.

She was still straining to identify the noises when the men she knew as Denny Monroe and Cesar Fuentes collected and inspected their weapons . . . again.

"Time to check the roof," the team leader declared.

They picked up the boards and climbing gear . . . tested their headsets once more.

"Time check," Nomad requested.

"Six minutes . . . six minutes to two," Elaine's voice said from the command truck.

"Street clear?" he asked.

"Clear," Paula Taylor answered.

By the time Fuentes and Nomad reached the exit to the roof of the empty building, it was four minutes to two. The roof wasn't exactly flat. Neither was the one at the trade mission next door. Both had been built at a slight pitch so rainwater would flow down.

A human being carrying the extra weight of weapons and climbing gear could fall down, too, Nomad judged. He pointed at the hazardous roof, nodded to Fuentes.

"I know. I know," the battle-wise Latin telepath said. "Watch your ass."

"And everything else," the team leader added.

They put down the boards to the next roof . . . looked up and down the street.

All clear.

They crossed to the trade mission very carefully . . . paused . . . and swung their climbing ropes in wide loops to encircle one of the chimneys. They studied the roof, and didn't like what they saw.

"We've got the wrong shoes," Fuentes said calmly.

"And almost no time," Nomad added.

They looked down into the street again. On schedule, the next member of the terrorist group emerged from the building onto the now busy street. He glanced left. Then he put down the Delta shoulder bag . . . took a handkerchief from his pocket . . . blew his nose. He did something else at the same time.

He looked right carefully . . . professionally.

Nomad noticed that.

This one—Number Four—seemed smarter than the previous three.

"Stand by, crash car," Nomad said into his headset.

Down the street, a middle-aged woman in a lady-executive suit turned the key to start the motor of a small station wagon. She opened the top button of her jacket to provide quicker access to her pistol.

"Why the crash car? What's happening?" Junior asked.

"I'll let you know," Nomad answered.

It was just a hunch—no, an intelligent guess, based on his experience and his gut instinct. No harm if he was wrong.

Number Four walked another thirty yards. Stopped again to light a cigarette.

And look up. He was checking the roofs. The others hadn't been that careful. His gaze was moving back toward the building he'd just left.

"Crash car . . . crash car. Prepare to commit. Stand by meat wagon," Nomad ordered.

A block away, an African-American man with excellent teeth and a bright future in the public sector started the engine of a second vehicle.

If this had to be done, Nomad told himself, it would be quieter than a shoot-out and less likely to get the neighbors or the media crazy. Now the team leader saw the terrorist stare right at the two men on the roof. He probably wondered what these males in white painter outfits were doing up there.

For about six seconds.

Then he reached into his pocket.

What he took out wasn't a gun, but just as dangerous.

Small, black-leather case. He removed the compact cell phone. He was going to warn the three remaining terrorists who were protecting the bomb.

"Go, crash car. Go. Go. Go!"

The station wagon picked up speed.

"She's rolling, meat wagon. Give her thirty seconds. You're on!"

The man with the cell phone was looking down at his compact device when the woman in the station wagon did something unusual. She deliberately swung her vehicle—nice wooden sides—in a tight arc and smashed him bloody. Though he sprawled unconscious on the sidewalk, she didn't slow down at all. Ignoring him, she drove on at full speed.

A score of people who'd seen this were horrified.

They gaped in shock at the hit-and-run outrage.

Then a minor miracle happened. A D.C. police car suddenly appeared and halted beside the battered body. The two uniformed patrolmen who jumped out . . . one black and the other white . . . were quick and efficient. They sized up the situation at once.

"He's still alive," one policeman said. "If we get him to the emergency room immediately, he'll make it."

The civilians watching were impressed. Though normal procedures called for an ambulance to come and collect the unconscious victim, the time saved by the police taking him off right now might save a life. The D.C. cops weren't that bad after all was the consensus as the man . . . he seemed Middle Eastern . . . was loaded gently into the police car.

Nobody thought to take down the license plate or car number of that vehicle as it moved away. Of course nobody had noted the plate number of the station wagon either. Such caring wouldn't have helped much, for they were all false.

The fifth terrorist—guarding the entrance and ground floor of the trade mission—didn't understand what had happened. It took place at the edge of his view, so all he saw was a group of people come together for a few minutes and a piece of a radio car that stopped for two or three minutes. Then everyone dispersed.

It wasn't worth reporting to the men upstairs, he decided.

On the roof, Nomad was making a decision of his own. There were too damn many things that could go wrong if he waited any longer. He and Fuentes hooked up to the main lines . . . began to inch toward the back of the roof. They had to stop again and again. They began to slip . . . again and again. Their progress was very slow.

Drenched with sweat, they cursed . . . paused . . . inched forward again for another three minutes that felt like an hour. They were panting by the time they finally reached the rear of the roof.

"We're about to go down," Nomad said into his headset. "Is everyone ready?"

The chess player's voice broke in . . . not about readiness.

"I've got it! I've figured it out! It's a dog! That damn noise is a big dog! Probably an attack animal."

"I love animals," Nomad answered. "Don't worry. We'll be careful."

Now the command truck ... The Band ... the F.B.I. surveillance force ... the local cops ... and even the Army's hush-hush Force Five ... reported they were ready. Seigenthaler added that the convoy was just leaving for the Capitol.

The presidential convoy.

"Whatever you're going to do—" Seigenthaler warned.

"Do it now. Right. Here we go."

Five yards apart, Nomad and Fuentes began their descent on the climbing ropes. The leather gloves they wore helped to control their speed ... firm their grasp. We should have sacrificed a chicken or given more to charity, Nomad told himself. If their luck held ... if the Goddess was with them, as a former girlfriend used to say ... the terrorists wouldn't be watching the damn window.

If they were, the raiders could be shot down before they broke in—and the devastating Demon fired.

Nomad drew his pistol from the weapons sack hung around his neck. He held out three fingers.

Fuentes understood. They'd attack on the count of three.

As he drew his nine-millimeter, he saw Nomad lower one finger. Both men tensed and sucked in their breath as the team leader folded down a second digit. The third followed almost at once.

They pushed themselves out from the building as hard as they could ... using all the strength in their powerful legs. The momentum and their body weight joined to shatter the window. The glass wasn't bulletproof. It was ordinary windowpane.

The men who broke through weren't ordinary.

Battle-tested ... in exceptional physical condition after the Institute's special diets and body-rebuilding programs ... hard-muscled and hard-minded professionals, unwilling to lose ... intensely, almost chemically, aware they might die ... they had no hesitation.

They were focused ... fierce.

And there was just one of al Wadi's fighters in the room.

That was the good news, Nomad judged as he covered his eyes to protect them from a storm of shards and icicles of glass.

The bad news was that the terrorist stood barely five feet

from a metal cylinder cradled on a table. The Thing—some six inches in diameter and about three feet long—had something at one end that resembled the tail assembly of a practice bomb. This wasn't for practice at all. For a few urgent seconds, Nomad and Fuentes couldn't take their eyes off it.

It didn't look like a weapon of mass destruction.

They knew it was.

Demon. The code name fit.

The brave and half-mad terrorist who stood five feet from it decided it was time to go to heaven. He lunged for the bomb. Cesar Fuentes made a split-second decision of his own. It was really a reflex reaction to the problem. He knew he must stop al Wadi's martyr from firing the terrible weapon . . . or even from shouting an alarm.

Solution: simple.

Fuentes shot him through the throat with the silenced pistol.

Determined not to die in vain, the mortally wounded man summoned his last bit of strength to hurl his sagging body toward the Demon. Even more determined to keep him from the crowd-killer, Nomad threw himself through the jagged ruins of the window to knock him away.

They fell to the glass-littered floor. The man with the Russian heart was bleeding from half a dozen cuts. Eight inches from him—five inches from the bomb—the other man, so full of hate and virtue, was more than halfway to eternity. Knowing that he had little time, he tried to say something heroic as dying legends did. What he accomplished was more visual than audible: Red bubbles erupted through the bullet hole in his throat.

Another threat sounded from the far end of the room.

Over twenty-nine inches high . . . four legs . . . many more large teeth.

It was the big dog Susan Kincaid had warned about . . . growling and snarling in raw menace. This was a promise, not a mere threat. Trained as an attack dog, it prepared to do its duty.

Nomad was prepared, too. As the furious animal advanced, he pulled from his weapons sack the odd-shaped plastic tube casually called the "dog thing." It was a gun. It wasn't the sort that fired bullets or numbing darts. What it fired was invisible and inaudible.

To people. To men, women, and children of all sexes, ages, races, and prejudices. Not to dogs. Dogs were the target of this exotic thing—a weapon designed by an animal lover to save lives.

Dog lives. People would have to look out for themselves.

The weapon was set for one-third power.

Nomad flicked on the switch. The dog jumped into the air as if shocked by an electric cattle prod. What hit him was a focused sound beam . . . one that human ears couldn't pick up, but striking at a high frequency that canines couldn't stand.

Or sit. Or do anything but flee.

This dog fled. It wasn't just that his ears hurt. The fact that he couldn't see what hit him frightened this usually nothing-stops-me animal. He raced from the room just as another terrorist charged in—gun in hand—alarmed by the noise of the window shattering.

The dog was halfway down the stairs.

The terrorist sprinting to protect the bomb was only eleven feet from Nomad, who still held the dog device. He had no time to change weapons. Instead, he pushed the lever to full power . . . three times what had stopped the dog . . . and fired the inaudible sound blackjack at al Wadi's warrior.

No one had ever tested this weapon at full power on humans.

It hadn't seemed necessary to the designer, who was going to be stunned when the report on today's "incident"—no names or location, of course—reached him.

The sincere terrorist preparing to gun down the two intruders was stunned right now . . . disoriented . . . half nauseous . . . vision blurred . . . balance battered. He remembered that it was his solemn duty to kill in defense of the bomb, but he couldn't do it.

He couldn't see whom to shoot.

He couldn't even stand up straight. He reeled back out of the room . . . stumbled into a wall . . . tried to lurch back to protect the bomb . . . tottered, and fell down the stairs.

Six steps . . . no, seven.

Right on top of the dog, who was starting up again. Like the others here for al Wadi, the man who collided with the animal was ready to give his life if he could save the extraordinary weapon—and take some of the infidel enemies with him. Dedicated to his important cause, he'd planned carefully. He wore a special vest that contained several packets—a total of two and a half pounds of Czech-made Semtex plastic explosive, with contact fuses.

The guard inside the front door jumped from his chair and turned when he heard the blast. He stared at the bizarre carnage. The martyr who had accidentally blown himself up was in three pieces . . . four, including one leg. The attack dog had been cruelly ripped into even more sections, and the wall beside them was crimson splatter of their mingled blood.

A second-rate art critic might have called it a third-rate rip-off of the late Jackson Pollock. The guard gaping up wasn't into any kind of modern art. As of this instant, he was into surviving, and he ran for the door.

He holstered his gun as he reached for the knob. He jerked the door open and stepped outside. He had no idea of how fortunate he was. As he crossed the threshold, he stopped to catch his breath. Harry Chen persuaded him to linger longer by jamming a handgun with a fat silencer against his ear.

"*Shi-it*," Nomad heard The Band's female sniper complain into the microphone of her headset.

"I had a clean shot," she complained. "One more damn step and I'd have dropped him."

"What's happening?" Nomad asked.

"I've got the last visitor," Harry Chen reported. "Well, I hope he's the last one."

"So do I," the team leader said. "Is the block sealed off at both ends?"

"No walkers . . . no drivers. We pulled the plug when you said you were going in."

"If nobody minds, I'd like to say a few more words," Nomad announced. "Move those two Army nuclear crews and their trucks in five minutes ago. Cover story is that some crazy janitor . . . how about the well-known disgruntled ex-employee . . . set a half-ass bomb to blow up the boiler."

"Disgruntled ex-employee is good, Denny," Susan Kincaid approved. "Are you all okay?"

"Just fine, if you don't mind a dog in seven or eight pieces and some head case who tried . . . damn near successfully . . . to do something lousy with a Demon."

"You didn't do the poor dog, did you?" the highly ethical chess player blurted.

"I don't do any kind of dogs, rich or poor. We're the Good Guys, remember? We don't do kittens or music teachers either," Nomad told her. "Where the fuck are those trucks? There could be a timer on this Russian toy."

The two Army vehicles arrived as the F.B.I. net around the immediate area began to tighten. Watching the nuclear specialists get out of their trucks, Nomad heard Seigenthaler report that the President was starting his speech.

"That dog didn't have to die, dammit," Nomad thought aloud.

"What dog?"

"Later," the team leader answered and greeted the soldiers.

"Captain McIvor," one of them said.

He waited for Nomad to offer his name, show some I.D.

It didn't happen.

"There's a Russian nuclear bomb—NATO designation Demon—up on the fourth floor. It may have a timer on it, so I wouldn't dawdle."

"Timer?"

"Probably set for about fifteen minutes . . . twenty max. There's a stiff about a yard away. Oh, be careful on the way up . . . the steps are slippery. Chunks of some antisocial foreigner and an unfortunate dog all over the place."

"You're not joking?" the captain asked.

"Not this year."

The Army officer signaled his men to carry their gear inside.

"You don't sound like an F.B.I. man to me," he judged.

Nomad silently pointed at the door. Now a D.C. police lieutenant approached. So did a crowd of curious civilians.

"You in charge?" The lieutenant asked.

"God's in charge. Listen, win a medal and get these people out of here. A couple of blocks out of here. A mile would be better. Big bomb inside. Army's trying to disarm it now."

Nomad studied the insignia on the cop's uniform.

"Protect the public, Lieutenant," he continued sincerely.

The lieutenant strode off to do that as Fuentes emerged from the building.

"Harry wants to unload that guy he grabbed," Fuentes said, "so I called for one of our vans to haul him out of here. Can we go, too?"

The police were beginning to move the crowd back. People were hurrying away. Word of a bomb can do that.

"Just a minute," Nomad told Fuentes . . . and thought again about that timer.

"Susan, grab your stuff and get the hell down here right away," the team leader instructed. "Junior, the party's over. Please apologize to Grace for me. Next time, she'll get a shot . . . promise."

"Takeoff time?" the head of The Band questioned hopefully.

"Go . . . go . . . go."

Nomad studied his wristwatch.

The Army specialists had been upstairs for five or six minutes.

They must know something by now, he thought and waved to Paula Taylor on the roof across the street. As he gestured to her to come down, five F.B.I. men drove up in two cars to collect the terrorist Chen had captured.

"You might get a hearse, too," Nomad suggested. "There's a pair of his late friends inside . . . and a dead dog . . . in pieces."

"Anything else?" the senior federal agent asked evenly in a firm voice that said nothing could surprise him anymore.

"I'm sure you've heard about it," Nomad answered. "There's that Russian atomic bomb on the fourth floor. If I were you—hey, it's your call—I'd leave that to the Army guys up there disarming it. Correction: trying to disarm it."

The federal agent thanked him and guided his men inside.

They'd be coming outside shortly, Nomad guessed.

Being sensible adults, they'd want to get away from here as soon as possible. Considering the threat to the people of Washington, the man who could read minds concluded that "sensible" wasn't always the most important thing.

"I'm going in to find out what's happening," he told the woman at the communications console in the truck.

And somebody else.

"Not a chance," he heard the head of the Russia and F.S.R. group declare suddenly. "You're going to get in the truck and report back to the hotel immediately."

"So you've been listening?"

"You know the game," Seigenthaler said bluntly. "We're playing boys' rules. We're always listening every damn chance we get, and we do worse . . . because we have to. What the hell do you think you can do about a Demon?"

"I'd like to find out."

"You are not responsible for all those people, dammit. You never used to be this kind of a romantic. What the hell is happening to you?" Seigenthaler demanded.

"I'm going in."

"What for? You've already done the damn near impossible. You've captured a Demon. We've been trying to get one for nearly two years. You're a hero. Okay, all five of you are heroes. Can't you settle for being live heroes?"

The other telepaths heard this on their headsets.

"He's got a point," Paula Taylor judged.

"Never trust men who've got a point," the team leader said grimly.

"Or women either," the chess player added.

"I'm not asking for a vote," Nomad said, "but do you think he's right?"

"No, you're right," the black woman declared, "and we ought to go."

That didn't make a lot of sense, but the other three telepaths nodded in agreement.

"Heads up. Heads up," an unfamiliar voice announced over their headsets. "Somebody must have phoned the media. Three TV news trucks are trying to get past our checkpoints, and there are five cars of print people flashing press cards. We can't hold them much longer."

"You've got to leave immediately," Seigenthaler pleaded. "We can't afford . . . *you* can't afford . . . to have your faces show in papers or on the tube. You'll be risking your lives . . . and one of our most important operations."

"What about the Demon?" Nomad pressed.

"You've made the damn thing your personal demon," the C.I.A. executive declared. "Fine. Now get the hell into the truck."

After a few seconds, Nomad shrugged. He led the others to the truck, and they entered less than a minute later. Unlike the Army bomb-disposal vehicle, there was nothing about it to catch the eye. Two animated crews in television news trucks paid no attention to it as it passed them.

The telepaths left all their weapons and body armor in the truck when it stopped twenty yards from the hotel.

"Keep in touch, Elaine," Nomad said to the communications woman he'd probably never see again.

"I'll send a Christmas card," she lied.

As the command truck moved away, Nomad nodded toward the hotel entrance.

They all knew the drill.

He didn't have to remind them that they shouldn't enter together.

Less chance of being identified as connected.

"I'll go in first with Harry," he told them. "Then Susan and Paula. Cesar, three minutes later. Pack your stuff—fast. We're checking out."

He paused.

"Seigenthaler was right," he said. "You're heroes. Did the impossible. Now we've got to do it again."

They looked at him. He hadn't said what they were supposed to do next . . . or where. They didn't ask. They trusted him. There had to be a strong reason why they were leaving in such a hurry. He'd explain it all when it was safe to do so.

In staggered sequence, they made their way to their rooms. Each of them began to pack their small overnight bags. Wondering about that timer, all of them turned on the room radios and tuned to the all-news station.

The President was still speaking.

That didn't mean a damn thing.

The Demon could still go off at any second, and they couldn't be sure how wide the kill zone might be. Maybe it would encompass the hotel. They packed faster.

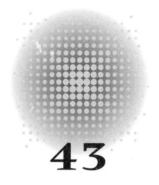

43

NOMAD HEARD THE KNOCK ON HIS DOOR.

For a minute, he regretted giving up the weapons in the truck. Then he decided it was unlikely that any of al Wadi's men had followed them, so he stepped forward to open it.

Seigenthaler entered with four men who had to be security specialists. That meant somebody had to be protected from someone else . . . maybe several of them. Nomad thought of probing the C.I.A. executive's mind, but guessed it probably wasn't worth the effort.

"Good news," Seigenthaler reported brightly.

Perhaps a touch too brightly. He wanted something.

"Just got word *you* were right," he announced. "There was a timer on the Demon. It was pretty close. In the movies, they'd stop it nine seconds before it was set to blow. Today our Army pros turned this bomb off a full three minutes and eight seconds before."

"Mother," Nomad said.

"What does that mean?"

"It's a very popular idiom. No reference to your family," Nomad told him and thought again about the goddam three minutes and eight seconds.

Horror show.

"Any more good news?" he asked.

"Signal for you . . . you *personally* . . . from the Mossad."

ON THAT DARK NIGHT, al Wadi's team was floating another Demon toward the Israeli coast. Six swimmers . . . four more men waiting just behind the beach in a lorry.

The Israelis still used British words like that.

Force of habit. The Demon was less than fifty yards from the shore when it happened. Maybe *they* would be more accurate. "They" were a dozen young frogmen, members of an elite unit of top-drawer commandos that had no name . . . just a number.

They came out of the water like sharks. They fired low-noise spearguns and they didn't miss. Then they pulled from water-proof cases advanced model Uzis . . . silenced Uzis—and they didn't miss with them either. In twenty-five seconds . . . maybe thirty . . . al Wadi's half-dozen swimmers and his clever plan to infiltrate the Demon into Israel were dead.

The men waiting in the lorry were astounded.

It happened so fast. They decided to escape at full speed. That didn't happen. Some other people had been waiting in the darkness nearby . . . silently . . . professionally. Eighteen more of the commandos—experts who'd blasted terrorist groups be-fore—were ready to take out the men in the lorry.

In a second.

At the least sign of resistance. There wasn't any. The men in the lorry raised their hands when they saw the gun muzzles and gleaming commando knives inches from their heads and throats. While the frogmen were dumping al Wadi's dead swimmers and moving the Demon to the beach, the shore party that ambushed the lorry was tying up and blindfolding the men waiting to receive the bomb.

"They didn't say what happened to the Demon," Seigen-thaler concluded.

"That's not their style."

"One more thing. They thanked you by name," Seigenthaler said. "See, we're not the only folks who appreciate you."

The four security men looked at the door.

Nomad put the last of his toilet articles in the shoulder bag . . . waited for Seigenthaler to finish what he'd come to say. It wouldn't have anything to do with any timer, or the Mossad either.

"Glad you're packed," Seigenthaler announced. "We've got two cars waiting downstairs, and a jet standing by to take all of you back to the Institute to complete your recovery."

"Nice try. No cigar," Nomad said.

"What does that mean?"

"*All* of us are not returning to the Institute this week . . . maybe not this month. Tonight I'm on a plane to Moscow, and they're flying to Helsinki."

"Why Helsinki?" Seigenthaler asked.

"My plan. Helsinki's part of my plan. They can bring that Russian agent we're trading for Alison Wilk with them."

Nomad asked Seigenthaler to tell the security quartet to wait outside. When they left, he explained the plan, and the head of the Russian F.S.R. unit didn't like it.

"You've done your job . . . very well. The rest of the deal isn't really your business," he insisted.

"I don't share that view."

Bad, Seigenthaler thought. When Nomad started speaking in the correct language of a high-school English teacher, he was very angry.

And that almost surely led to trouble.

"I respect your intentions," Seigenthaler dodged carefully, "but I'm afraid your plan might be too complicated."

"I'm a complicated guy. I was even before I died," Nomad answered in a voice edged with irony. "And there's no reason for *you* to be afraid of this deal."

"You're saying someone else should be afraid?"

"I'm saying I know what I'm doing, and I think it has to be done," Nomad replied. "Please get the airline tickets . . . the toys . . . the van . . . the satellite . . . and the station chiefs in Moscow and Helsinki up to speed."

Seigenthaler studied him intently for several seconds.

"It can't be just the Wilk woman," he judged slowly.

"It isn't," Nomad answered honestly.

He closed his bag, then led Seigenthaler and the four security men to the elevator. When Nomad saw the other telepaths in the lobby, he nodded toward the street. A few minutes later, the two large sedans were rolling toward the airport. Nomad was telling his team about the timer and the Mossad message.

Seigenthaler was on the scrambler-equipped cell phone. He was organizing the details and the gear Nomad had specified, and he was worried.

The same thoughts raced through his mind again and again.

This wasn't correct.

He had a right to know.

If it wasn't just Alison Wilk, what the hell was it?

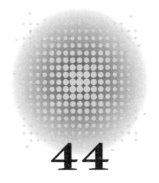

44

TWO DAYS LATER. FOUR O'CLOCK IN THE AFTERNOON.

Moscow time . . . but this place wasn't in the Russian capital.

It was far north . . . a non-place on the Finnish frontier.

A nowhere in the woods . . . not important enough to be on any map . . . a curve in a two-lane back road that drew little traffic since the bigger and better highway was completed thirty-one kilometers east.

It wasn't raining. In the past—well, in the days of Colder War and even worse television series—these things were done in the small hours of the morning and it generally rained. Maybe God didn't like the timing either, Nomad thought as he got out of the C.I.A. van that carried Finnish license plates. Even a Supreme Being who created and controlled eternity and all the galaxies had a right to some peace and quiet.

The border was forty yards away. Nomad looked across into the peace-loving New Russia and saw two dark sedans parked about fifty yards beyond the frontier. Nomad held a walkie-talkie. He had no intention of using it, for Temkov's nearby people were sure to be scanning all frequencies.

Temkov would have other precautions going, more tricks

ready. Rules of the dumb game, Nomad told himself as he walked toward the border.

"This is Bishop," he sent telepathically. "Everyone in position? Please confirm."

Susan Kincaid, at the communications control in the larger van—the brown one—answered first. Then each of the other three telepaths replied from concealed positions in the nearby woods. After that, the black woman reported that the "music" was ready.

The Band was out there, too . . . had been, in sniper concealment, for two hours. Nomad had ordered radio silence. When they had sighted in their weapons, each had spoken one number . . . in the random sequence he'd selected . . . into their headsets.

Not a sound since.

They were professionals. To steal from G. B. Shaw, Nomad thought, ambush was like mother's milk to them. Seigenthaler hadn't argued in the car from the hotel in Washington when Nomad asked for The Band to cover this operation. That was considerate, and good business, of course.

There was the possibility of a double-cross at the border.

There was *always* the possibility of a double-cross at the border, or anywhere else. Maybe a triple-cross if anyone could figure out how to do it.

Now the American with the Russian heart saw a pair of men in civilian clothes emerge from one of the sedans across the frontier. They carried regulation Russian military submachine guns. One of them opened the rear door of the vehicle for the important passenger.

General Temkov stepped out, sniffed the country air, saw Nomad, and waved. His gesture was almost friendly. That irritated Nomad, but he kept cool and focused. He had his own plan . . . his own agenda . . . for the next five minutes and the next five days.

He began walking to the border.

"Sat frequency clear?" he asked the black woman telepathically.

"Clear and ready," she replied. "Detection network on full alert."

Two more of Temkov's men stepped from the other car. They carried automatic weapons, too, and their body bulk suggested bulletproof vests.

There were neither Finnish nor Russian guards at the border. It had been arranged that they should leave their huts and proceed at least a mile back into their own territory. They weren't supposed to see what was to happen here. That way they couldn't gossip about it, and the conscientious, ravenous media were less likely to hear of it.

If they did, both sides would deny it ever happened.

Easily . . . expertly . . . patriotically. No problem.

As Nomad crossed onto Russian territory, the general advanced a dozen steps toward him. It was a vague gesture of good will—sort of. Temkov wanted this thing over with so he could return to his headquarters. He had other matters—now more important and more dangerous matters . . . to settle.

Convincing his superiors that snatching the Wilk woman had been worthwhile . . . key to this exchange for their agent . . . was the first. Getting rid of the commander at Peter's House who'd stolen the atomic weapons—and could be a problem for Temkov at any time—was the second. This swap at the border would be a much less risky affair, the general judged confidently. As a cloak-and-dagger veteran, he'd taken the appropriate precautions.

Temkov and the American met some thirty yards inside Russia.

"Glad to see you again, Mr. Alderdice. I didn't know you'd gone to Finland. Lovely country, isn't it?" he asked and pointed at the lush green forest across the border.

"The trees are beautiful," Nomad agreed, "and they save lives. They purify the air, and they're great cover for snipers."

Temkov shook his head reprovingly.

"Why would you ruin a pleasant occasion like this peaceful exchange with talk of snipers? Why would anyone ever need to put snipers in that fine forest?"

"To take care of the shooters you've got hidden there . . . and there . . . and over there. There's a sniper covering every damn one of them," Nomad told him evenly.

"You're serious?"

"Serious and democratic. There's one who's got you in his crosshairs, too, General. Wouldn't want you to feel left out. By the way," Nomad added, "my friends are firing armor-piercing, so those vests your fellows are wearing don't mean anything."

Temkov nodded.

"State Department people don't play the game like that," he declared. "You're not State Department, are you?"

"I'm with the Environmental Protection Agency," Nomad replied. "I'm here to help clean up the mess. Is Miss Wilk in the car?"

"She *might* be if our man is in one of your vans," Temkov tested.

"Let me see her."

The general gestured, and two men took Alison Wilk out into the chill afternoon. She was blindfolded, and they each held an arm. She seemed less than steady on her feet.

"Lose the damn blindfold," Nomad said impatiently.

Temkov pointed to his own eyes . . . then to the woman. They took off the double thickness of black cloth that had kept her in darkness from the time they came to take her to the car. She stood there blinking . . . wary . . . trying to take in the whole scene.

Nomad stared at her left ear—the one with the scar.

"I'd like to talk to her . . . up close, please."

Temkov signaled to the men holding her, and they began to walk her slowly toward their general.

"No tricks," Temkov warned.

"You're a very suspicious man," Nomad replied, and considered what tricks the Russian might have in mind. He probed mentally.

He learned that the Russian mind warrior—the thin man he'd seen in the Pushkin Museum—was in the second car, and he was searching.

Nomad had expected this might happen.

He'd advised the other U.S. telepaths what to do if it did. Now he silently told them to attack.

It wasn't visible or audible, but the concerted barrage of images—some of auto or train wrecks, others of explicit sexual activities—jumbled together in a troubling and apparently incoherent torrent. While the Russian mind prober tried to resist disorientation, Alison Wilk reached Temkov and Nomad.

Nomad spoke first . . . a series of questions.

Your grandmother's name? Your brother's college?

Your sister's birthday? Your father's favorite football team?

He listened to her answers carefully before he waved to the van across the frontier. Two of the three men who got out held M-11 silenced nine-millimeter submachine guns . . . and the arms of the third male. He was the Russian agent being traded for Alison Wilk.

As they crossed into Russia, Nomad spoke to her.

"Time to go home," he said. "See that van just across the border?"

She peered . . . nodded.

Then . . . somehow . . . he answered her questions before she could ask them.

"Your cat's in the van, and there's a Sat phone to call your mom."

She swallowed, and he knew she was trying not to cry.

"Who are you?" she wondered.

"Good, keep talking," he evaded. "Phone your mom. She's waiting for your call."

The exchange proceeded. As she entered the van and the Russians helped their tired agent into one of the sedans, Nomad spoke to Temkov again.

"See, it went off nicely, with no tricks. By the way, our tech people asked me to thank you for that fine little suitcase bomb."

"I don't know what you're talking about," Temkov answered.

He was scared . . . mind and body. Nomad read it easily.

"One of those you dealt to that lunatic al Wadi," Nomad explained in a voice free of rancor. "Some of his people were trying to use it to deep-fry Washington three days ago. They're past tense now."

"I have no connection with al Wadi," Temkov insisted, "and nuclear weapons are outside my jurisdiction."

Nomad ignored the denial.

"Our tech experts are giving this thing an A-to-Z, top-to-bottom. They've found some real nice stuff," he confided. "Lots of bang for the ruble . . . and that miniaturized locator beacon's a neat piece of work."

"I think you must be misinformed," the general stonewalled.

"They were impressed by the little radio-controlled detonator, too . . . the backup for the timer. That kind of gee-whiz hardware must have cost al Wadi a lot of hard currency, right?"

Temkov couldn't help it.

For a second, he thought of the exact sum. Nomad "read" it.

"Mr. Alderdice, we've completed the exchange and I'm sure both governments are willing to leave it at that. Baseless speculation and fairy tales about imaginary weapons deals won't contribute anything to maintaining good relations," Temkov reasoned, "so let's shake hands and terminate this discussion."

"How about terminating al Wadi? How about contributing to *that*, General? We'll both contribute. You put in the frequency of the damn radio-control . . . and I'll contribute the rest of your life."

"Are you threatening me?"

"Shit, no, General. State Department employees don't threaten anybody. They're gentlemen . . . and ladies. They wouldn't think of leaking to some foreign government that a senior intelligence officer sold stolen nuclear weapons to a notorious terrorist and pocketed a ton of dollars. No way. That could put somebody in mortal danger."

"You're making this up," Temkov said.

"I want the frequency. Correction: I want the fucking frequency *right now*."

The general couldn't help it.

For two seconds—maybe three—he thought of the frequency.

That was long enough.

"Bishop to Queen," Nomad began, and sent Susan Kincaid the frequency. "Transmit to Sat control."

"What about radio silence?"

"Transmit immediately. Transmit."

Temkov was furious. There was no way he could admit he knew the frequency, and he took Nomad's threat seriously. There was something . . . no, there were several things . . . about this Alderdice that had to be taken seriously.

For a few seconds, Temkov's left hand began to rise as if to rub his jaw. That was the signal to one of his snipers hidden in the trees. The marksman recognized it . . . zeroed in on Nomad's forehead. The sniper's trigger finger began to tighten.

Temkov suddenly lowered his hand. He hadn't been thinking . . . just hating. No, it wouldn't help to deal with this damn American violently. It could unleash all sorts of very bad consequences.

IN HIS UNDERGROUND bastion in the Near East, al Wadi was also considering consequences, as any sensible twenty-first-century terrorist commander should. It was three hours since the reports of the failures in Washington and Israel had reached him. He wasn't going to wait for another infidel blow.

He'd planned for such a situation.

The enemy might know where his headquarters were.

Now he was moving himself, his staff, and the remaining bomb to another fortified bunker . . . 270 miles away.

TEMKOV WASN'T MOVING at all. He stood still . . . rigid . . . calculating urgently to find some way, any way, to deflect the American from the frequency . . . from the bomb altogether.

"I can understand your concern, Mr. Alderdice," he said in a decent imitation of a conciliatory voice, "and I'm sorry I don't have the information you want. It wouldn't solve the long-range problem of al Wadi anyway."

Nomad nodded.

"You mean the people and governments backing him," he said. "You mean that creepy prince whose daddy claims to be one of my country's most devoted allies. I have a feeling somebody's going to send that nasty young fellow a major message. Auto accidents are popular this year, I hear."

"The American government would do that?"

Nomad shook his head.

"Absolutely not," he insisted. "Of course, the Mossad might. If they did, I can guarantee we'd send at least five hundred dollars' worth of flowers to the funeral. We pretend, and the Israelis make lists. I wouldn't want to be on one of their lists, General."

Another threat.

This Alderdice definitely wasn't a regular State Department type. Maybe he would tell the Israelis. Yes, Temkov thought, it might be time for General Oroshenko to have his accident . . . somewhere near his secret warhead depot. That way, he couldn't dispute "evidence" he'd done the deal with al Wadi alone . . . a rogue operation.

Time to go, the S.V.R. general decided as he scanned the woods once more. He'd made the exchange, and he'd succeeded in denying the Americans any information about the bomb. If he put out the story that Oroshenko had sold the bombs in a private deal—there were certainly plenty of private deals every month—then he might not draw Mossad's wrath upon himself.

He'd won . . . and he had all the money. No one knew that.

He held out his hand in proper farewell.

The American shook it, but then he said something Temkov didn't like.

"I wonder if you'd like to join me in a generous gesture of charity. I know that military officers in any country don't get big salaries, but there's one cause you might want to help out with a modest donation."

"What cause?"

"International Red Cross. Some son of a bitch dropped a little atom bomb . . . same footprint as yours . . . in Ethiopia. Killed over seven thousand civilians. You could send the check to the Red Cross in Geneva. Hey, they take cash, too."

First, death threats. Now, money blackmail.

Not at all like the disciplined diplomats of the U.S. Embassy.

"How modest a donation?" Temkov tested.

"Nothing huge. A million U.S. would do it."

A million was a lot of money, but Temkov would still have more than twenty million and some peace of mind.

For how long?

"I'll look into it," he forced himself to say.

Then he couldn't hold back the question.

"Just who are you, Mr. Alderdice?" he demanded tensely.

The almost-handsome American smiled for a moment.

It wasn't that pleasant.

"*What* I am is more important," he replied. "I'm *bad*. Some people say I'm one of the worst. I hold grudges. It's a character flaw, General. I don't forgive or forget . . . ever."

Suddenly, Temkov wasn't at all sure he'd won, and he didn't know what to do about it. This uncertainty filled his consciousness as he watched the American walking toward the border. Nomad strode on into Finland. He was near the command van when he saw the long gun of The Band . . . Grace . . . step from the trees with her weapon.

They spoke for some twenty-five seconds . . . shook hands . . . separated.

As he entered the van, the multilingual chess player's face lit up in welcome. At that moment, the satellite phone began to buzz. Nomad pointed to the front section where Chen was ready . . . ready for anything . . . in the driver's seat.

"*Right now*. North. All our people and wheels . . . away from the border. Let's roll," the team leader said curtly.

While she relayed this message, he scooped up the phone.

"You did it! Congratulations!" Seigenthaler celebrated. "You got her out. The deputy director sends his *personal* congratulations, too."

"Team effort," Nomad replied.

"You have another personal message," Seigenthaler continued with a chuckle. "A courier delivered it to our London station chief. He took the liberty of opening it."

"Yes?"

"Short note. Quote: 'Thanks. The Scandinavians took care of it. It got a little untidy, but that's life. Here's your Christmas present, chum. Hope I got the size right.' "

"And it's signed with the letter G," Nomad said.

"How did you know?"

"She does things like that."

The van was moving . . . away from S.V.R. snipers across the border.

"I'll translate," Nomad volunteered. "By Scandinavians, she meant S.A.S.—not the airline—Special Air Service commandos. G is for Gillian . . . very charming . . . very MI-Five . . . very with it. She sent in an S.A.S. assault unit to grab the Demon that al Wadi greased into London."

"What about 'untidy'?"

"Probably that British understatement," Nomad thought aloud. "It's much nicer than 'corpses.' I suspect that the S.A.S. lads ripped al Wadi's crew to pieces."

"Want to guess about the 'present'?" Seigenthaler tested.

"Long shot. No, not so long. Boxer shorts adorned with Spitfires. It's a private joke. Any more thrills?"

Seigenthaler paused to pick his words.

"There's been an incident. You broke radio silence to transmit the frequency of the remote control on the Demon."

"I believe in sharing," Nomad answered. "Is that a problem?"

"No. We're not criticizing. Actually, getting that information from Temkov was very fine work."

"Are we getting near the good part?"

Seigenthaler controlled his temper.

"A minute and a half after you did that, our global detection network picked up a nuclear explosion in a certain Near Eastern country . . . in an area there where we believe al Wadi has his main headquarters."

"I hope nobody was hurt," Nomad said coolly.

"Our Sat pictures show two trucks and about fifty people right near a large cave entrance. Next photo, they're gone and there's a white-hot nuclear image. We're checking the footprint to see if there's a Demon match."

"Sounds good to me. You're doing a thorough job. I like that," Nomad complimented. "And if one of those possibly fifty people who may or may not have been toasted was Mr. al Wadi, that would sound even better."

"There's no one left alive for almost a mile."

"Sounds like that town in Ethiopia where someone—not yet officially identified—dumped another goddam Demon and massacred more than seven thousand people. Well, you know what they say."

"Share it with me."

"What goes around comes around. It's a folk expression . . . North American . . . late twentieth and early twenty-first centuries."

Seigenthaler considered how to proceed.

"You wouldn't know anything about this incident?" he probed.

"If you say so, I'm sure you're right. I've complete faith in the Agency, you know."

"I'm told it looks as if the whole mountain collapsed on the cave entrance. There could be another eighty or one hundred people buried in there. We're expecting the local government and six or seven other members of the United Nations to protest. They'll probably blame us," the head of the Russia-F.S.R. unit predicted.

"That could give the President a headache," Nomad noted.

"My boss—deputy director ops—already has one. What do I tell him?"

"Tell him to take two bullets and call me next week," Nomad suggested. "I wish I could be more helpful. I'm not exactly at my best right now. Someone almost killed me about nine minutes ago."

That seized Seigenthaler's attention . . . Susan Kincaid's, too.

Grace—The Band's long-gun expert—had emerged from her ambush position a few minutes earlier with something she wanted to tell the team leader. She'd spotted one of Temkov's snipers in the woods, taking careful aim at Nomad. To a professional, it was obvious that his intention was terminal.

"I had a clear shot and I took it," she'd reported to the team leader. "My rifle has a flash suppressor and a silencer. They'll find him out there sooner or later, and they'll be mad. Are you mad?"

"What did you say to her?" Seigenthaler asked.

"I said 'Cool,' and that was it. I figure I was six seconds from

'Hello, Forever.' That leaves anyone shook. I think I need a couple of weeks off duty."

"What else do you need?" the C.I.A. executive invited.

"Answers to two questions. I really miss my sister. When can I see her?"

"The question is *how*," Seigenthaler pointed out soberly. "Is there a way that doesn't threaten the national security of our country? You're not just intelligence operators anymore. You've become unique and important weapons . . . secret weapons. We have to protect every one of you, and the Institute."

"Can you do this?"

"I'll ask. What's the second question?"

None of the other transplants was aware that this question even existed, so it wasn't an obsession with them. It was with the team leader.

"Something's been bothering me for weeks," he said frankly. "I can't let go of it. I'm convinced that these two words relate to me . . . probably to us . . . in a secret and basic way. I'm also sure that we have a right to know."

Seigenthaler braced, grateful that Nomad probably couldn't read his mind from over four thousand miles away.

No way to be sure how great Nomad's powers were.

"To know what?" the C.I.A. executive asked cautiously.

"Kelly's People."

Silence.

"Who are Kelly's People? What does that name mean? Are we five transplants Kelly's People? Who is . . . or was . . . Kelly?" Nomad challenged.

Silence.

"What do those words say about us? Are they a threat to us? Are we some kind of unmentionable threat to someone who is very frightened or powerful? Why won't anyone tell us?"

"I don't have the authority to—" Seigenthaler began.

"Find someone who does," Nomad broke in irately. "I don't think I believe you. You're cleared to classifications so high that people won't even name them. You're stalling. We risk our lives juggling A bombs and suicidal fanatics and devious Russian generals I wouldn't trust my piranha to . . . and you won't trust us with two words."

"It's not a matter of—"

"Yes or no?"

Silence again . . . but for a shorter period.

"I'll get your answer," Seigenthaler promised.

"When?"

"Soon."

There was nothing more to say. It was hope-and-wonder time now. How long is "soon," Nomad asked himself as he put down the telephone. He closed his tired eyes to rest them. It was not to be.

"Now it's my turn, Denny," the chess player said gently. "Grace had something she needed to tell you . . . so do I."

He opened his eyes . . . leaned forward . . . and listened intently.

"I haven't told you the truth," she announced. "I'm going to correct that now."

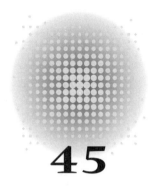

45

"NOBODY TELLS ME THE TRUTH," NOMAD SAID AND MANAGED to stifle a yawn.

"Save the wisecracks," Susan Kincaid advised. "I don't know what's ahead for us . . . for you and me . . . for the whole team . . . so I want to tell you now. I was lying when I told you not to waste your time thinking about pretty blonde Paula because she wasn't interested in men. I hinted she might be gay, re-member?"

"That's not true?"

"Totally false. I'm ashamed of myself."

She watched him consider this revelation soberly.

"I appreciate your honesty in telling me," the man she knew as Denny Monroe said. "That took courage. Why would you do such a thing?"

"Because I had my own plans for you," she confessed.

Then it came to her, and she pointed her index finger at him.

"You knew it all the time, didn't you?" she accused indig-nantly. "You son of a bitch . . . you let me make a damn fool of myself. You could scan her head . . . mine, too. I feel like an idiot."

"No harm done."

"Don't you dare patronize me, mister."

"Hey, I respect you. I respect everybody except al Wadi and a select group of politicians, talk-show hosts, racist jerks, columnists, and car thieves. Tell me, what kind of plans did you have?"

"What do you care?" she replied defensively.

"I care because I've got my own plans for you, and I hope they'd mesh with yours."

For a second, she wondered whether he was teasing her.

Then she decided he wasn't, and her face softened into a warm little smile. It got bigger seconds later.

"May I ask you a personal question?" he asked as the van began to navigate a curve.

"I'd probably like that."

Now he was smiling, too.

"Would you mind if I kissed you?"

"Not really."

It was a wide turn in the road . . . then straight ahead for miles. Sometime later—they didn't look at their watches—they reached downtown Helsinki. The room service at the modern Intercontinental Hotel was even better than the view of the harbor . . . for three days. They found that their plans meshed perfectly.

They didn't read any newspapers, so they had no way of knowing that a Russian general named Oroshenko had perished in an auto accident . . . and couldn't sell any more weapons of mass destruction. It wouldn't have mattered if they'd interrupted their mutual appreciation to scan even the headlines. The demise of General Oroshenko wasn't in the papers . . . anywhere.

The day after his demise, a playboy prince from an oil-rich nation was enjoying Chrystal champagne and two of the most expensive call girls in Monte Carlo when the house exploded. Half of the mansion caved in, and the prince was seriously burned.

Local authorities reported that there'd been a gas leak.

It was in many newspapers.

A short article . . . three inches.

That was all it was worth.